MR CAMPION'S VISIT

MR CAMPION'S VISIT

Mike Ripley

This first world edition published 2019
in Great Britain and the USA by
SEVERN HOUSE PUBLISHERS LTD of
Eardley House, 4 Uxbridge Street, London W8 7SY.
Trade paperback edition first published
in Great Britain and the USA 2020 by
SEVERN HOUSE PUBLISHERS LTD.

British Library Cataloguing in Publication Data
A CIP catalogue record for this title is available from the British Library.

ISBN-13: 978-0-7278-8897-6 (cased)
ISBN-13: 978-1-78029-618-0 (trade paper)
ISBN-13: 978-1-4483-0240-6 (e-book)

All Severn House titles are printed on acid-free paper.

Severn House Publishers support the Forest Stewardship Council™ [FSC™],
the leading international forest certification organisation.
All our titles that are printed on FSC certified paper carry the FSC logo.

Typeset by Palimpsest Book Production Ltd.,
Falkirk, Stirlingshire, Scotland.
Printed and bound in Great Britain by
TJ International, Padstow, Cornwall.

For Tim Coles, once more my technical expert

Author's Note

Albert Campion made his first appearance in *The Crime at Black Dudley* by Margery Allingham in 1929 (*The Black Dudley Murder* in the USA), though the house was always referred to as 'Black Dudley' and never 'The Black Dudley'. I have tried to imagine both Mr Campion and that 'great tomb of a house' some forty years on. I have also followed Margery Allingham's noble example and taken yet more liberties with the geography of Suffolk including the spelling of Monewdon. In 1970 Suffolk was one of the few counties in England without a university and Monty Python caused outrage by suggesting there was 'a lecturer in idiocy at the University of East Anglia', something hotly denied by the university where the Monty Python team appeared live in 1971. I was there.

Contents

The Campus of the
UNIVERSITY of SUFFOLK COASTAL

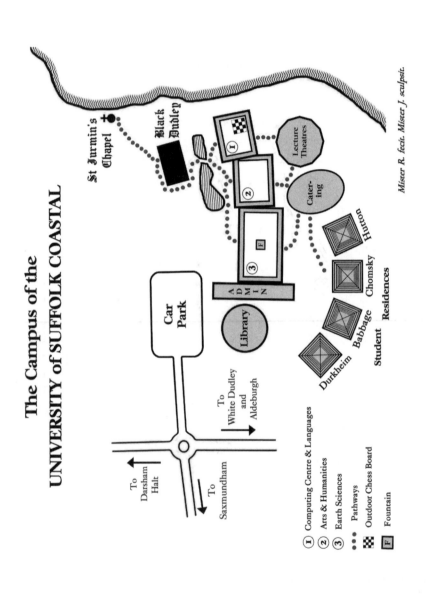

Mister R. fecit. Mister J. sculpsit.

Ten Years Previously . . .

'They have a university in Norwich?' spluttered the aggrieved bishop. 'Last time I was there they didn't have running water!'

'It's highly thought of by modern educationalists, so I'm told,' said the deputy lord lieutenant. 'The ideas behind it are quite exhilarating and innovative, according to reports in the press.'

The bishop did not look impressed and the snorting sound he made emphasized this.

'And of course they have a new university in Essex now, though they chose not to put it in the county town where the cathedral is,' offered the town clerk.

The bishop expanded his range of undignified nasal expressions and shook his head in despair, but at least appeared interested.

'Well, if Norfolk and Essex have one, I suppose Suffolk should keep up with the times; though it must be a decent, God-fearing place of learning and not a holiday camp for long-haired coffee-bar tearaways – and it will teach theology, not sociology, for the latter can lead only to ruin and damnation. That means, gentlemen' – he scanned the two rows of anxious faces reflected in the highly polished surface of the long oak table, as if to reassure himself that none were female – 'that the campus must be as close as possible to the religious and spiritual centre here in St Edmondsbury.'

The county education officer cleared his throat, signalling an intervention, but the bishop, an old committee hand, pounced to forestall him.

'I do believe that St Edmond's would be the perfect name for a new university,' he said in a tone which suggested the conclusion of a sermon rather than the opening of a debate. 'The Scots have St Andrew's, we should have St Edmond's.'

'It would be an excellent name if the campus was within the city limits,' said the county education officer, finding his courage, 'but the remit for this committee, and the instructions of the University Grants Committee, emphasize the need for *county* involvement to spread the cultural and economic benefits of a new university beyond St Edmondsbury.'

'But it is the county town!'

'My Lord Bishop is correct, of course,' smoothed the MP, whose constituency boundary began in the sugar-beet fields beyond the city limits and the bishop's immediate remit, 'but he cannot deny that there has always been a feeling in the county that St Edmondsbury is perhaps too much the centre of attention and that other towns and institutions tend to be over-shadowed. We have, for instance, the Monewdon Hunt in the east of the county, one of the best hunts this side of Leicestershire; and then there's Ipswich Town, which is doing wonderfully well under their manager, Alf Ramsey.' The bishop looked askance but the MP pressed on. 'Mark my words, Bishop, Mr Ramsey is destined for greatness beyond winning the Second Division title.'

Even though he bore the scars of numerous bruising encounters in the House, the politician faltered under the glassy stare of the churchman.

'Perhaps so, but not in the fields of academe. I repeat, we are the county town. We have the cathedral, the best schools, a fine repertory theatre, an excellent library, a flourishing Rotary Club, a half-decent golf course and, for those so inclined, a cinema.' The bishop paused to allow his case to sink into the irritatingly blank faces staring back at him. 'We even have a railway station which can connect us to Cambridge, should anyone wish to go there. What better place could there be for a university?'

The bishop glared down the table at each face in turn as if mentally transmitting the words 'rhetorical question' to his congregation; something he had done many times in the cathedral.

'In principle, no one could disagree with the bishop,' said the town clerk, his tone suggesting that no one would dare to, 'and it would only be a question of how much church land he would be willing to make available.'

A silence descended like a shroud on the meeting.

'Excuse me?'

The town clerk allowed himself a casual shrug of the shoulders.

'The church, specifically St Edmond's Cathedral, is the largest landowner in the city. Any campus university built here would require a substantial amount of church land, perhaps compulsorily purchased, plus inevitably the clearing of certain sites and possibly a complete overhaul of the transportation infrastructure.'

The bishop may have found himself in 'check', but it was not yet 'mate'.

'The church would naturally not wish to disrupt the infrastructure of the city,' he said smoothly. 'It is an historic city and has suffered quite enough from the town planners since the war. Perhaps a rural site just outside the city could be found.'

The chairman of the county council, a brewer of some girth and a landowner of considerable worth, had remained silent up to now but felt compelled to enter the fray.

'Can't upset the farmers, Bishop. This is an agricultural county and the land around St Edmondsbury is the most productive and most valuable in the county.'

'I agree entirely,' said the MP, thinking of votes and party donations rather than crops. 'The cheaper, less fertile land is over to the east.'

He did not add that it was also beyond his constituency, but the majority of those present assumed that.

To the surprise of the committee, the bishop's face brightened.

'We could call it the University of the Eastern Marches,' he said with a self-satisfied, rather unctuous smile.

Although he hated admitting to any failing in the education services he might be responsible for, the education officer said: 'With respect, I doubt if anyone actually knows what a March is, these days, and would that not be too close to the University of East Anglia for comfort? UEA and UEM could be easily confused by young minds when applying and we would, alphabetically, always come second.'

'Then how about the University of the Suffolk Hundreds? Surely, that's distinctive enough not to be confused with anywhere else?' The bishop's naturally pink face crimsoned as it always did when he scowled.

'A similar problem, I'm afraid,' said the education officer, who was now admitting to more searing ignorance in the county. 'Suffolk may have been divided into twenty-one hundreds in 1831, but few people recognize the term these days; not the post office, or for collecting the rates or for planning purposes. Is that not so, Mr Planning Officer?'

The county planning officer, who had remained silent and hopefully invisible up until now, smoothly laid his trump card on the table, even as the bishop was digesting the latest setback.

'Actually, there is a potential site near the coast which may be suitable – and could be acquired relatively cheaply.' This last qualification ensured that the planning officer had the committee's full attention. 'There's a big house much in need of repair and it comes with a thousand acres of land which has been sorely underused for the past twenty years. In fact, I think the house has been uninhabited since 1945. The army had it during the war and knocked it about a bit, but the Ministry of Defence has no interest in it these days.'

'You're not thinking of the Black Dudley estate, are you?' asked the chairman of the county council. 'It's dilapidated, miles from anywhere, and totally exposed to the winds off the sea. You can't grow anything worth growing on that land, so you might as well plant students there. At least they'd be out of the way.'

The majority of the committee thought *sounds perfect*, but did so silently, as such thoughts should not be minuted.

'The house at Black Dudley has a bad reputation, doesn't it?' ventured the MP.

'And why is that?'

'There was a murder and some rum goings-on there, back before the war, involving gangsters, would you believe.'

'Gangsters?' exploded the bishop. 'Gangsters? This is Suffolk, not Essex!'

'It was all a long time ago, Bishop. I'm sure people have forgotten all about it.'

The bishop was not mollified, but he could be, eventually, pragmatic.

'In my experience, Suffolk folk forget very little. Still, Black Dudley sounds a possibility. And if it's on the coast, we could call it the University of Suffolk Coastal. USC has a certain ring to it, wouldn't you say?'

'I think those initials have already been taken,' said the education officer dryly.

'Really?'

'The University of Southern California. In America.'

A pair of bushy ecclesiastical eyebrows rose in surprise. 'They have universities in America?'

ONE

Freshers

Michaelmas Term, 1970

'Could you possibly point me towards the geological centre?'

'Of what? The earth, Suffolk, or this particular building? I am afraid you'll have to humour an old man and be more specific.'

'I'm awfully sorry, but I meant the Geology Centre. I'm late, you see.'

'Sadly, I have no idea where that is, but from my own miserable scratchings at an education, I believe geology is quite a patient mistress and will wait for you.'

'I think it must be in Earth Sciences.'

'I am afraid I am no wiser. I am not a member of staff here.'

'Just visiting, are you?'

'Actually, I am *the* Visitor,' said Mr Albert Campion, 'though hopefully the title comes with as few responsibilities as it does privileges. I suspect we are both freshers at this shiny new institution, are we not?'

The freckle-faced and slightly chubby bespectacled girl shook a mass of long red hair and examined the thin bespectacled white-haired gentleman she had waylaid as if he had only just come into focus.

'Well, I'm a fresher, but aren't you rather old to be one?'

Mr Campion was amused; not so much by the girl's forthrightness and powers of observation, but by the way her voice rose to a higher pitch at the end of each sentence. It was as if she spoke only in questions, albeit non-aggressive ones, but it was not an affectation, it was an accent, and for a moment Campion could not place it.

'One is never too old to learn,' said Campion gently, 'but it could be argued that I have left it a little late. Still, that is my problem. I suspect yours is more pressing.'

'Yes, it is. I'm late already and I want to sign up for the Geology Society before I meet my tutor at eleven o'clock to make a good impression and it's already ten past.'

'Am I to deduce that the Geology Society is recruiting as part of Freshers' Week?' Mr Campion probed, and the jolly redhead nodded enthusiastically. 'And that they're doing this in the Geology Centre which is in the School of Earth Sciences?'

'You're catching on,' said the girl, with the modern teenager's grasp of quiet sarcasm.

'That's exactly what my tutors at university used to say, although never often enough, nor quite so sincerely. Still, I think I may be able to point you in the right direction.'

The girl's eyes widened behind the lenses of her red plastic 'cat's-eye' frame glasses, which even Mr Campion thought were rather on the fuddy-duddy side for one so young. He suspected that his wife, who had a liberal attitude to modern fashion – to most things, in fact – would describe the girl's dress sense as 'cheerfully accidental', but he felt in no position to offer an opinion on the combination of lime-green ski pants tucked into knee-high leather boots with a bright red turtleneck top under a rather shabby sheepskin waistcoat.

'We are presently in the Administration block on the third floor, I believe.'

'I know *that*,' said the girl, her eyebrows rising in exasperation. 'I've spent the last two hours negotiating my rent with the Accommodation Office. That was hard *yakka*, I can tell you.'

'New Zealand!' exclaimed Mr Campion, with more force than he intended, and immediately felt guilty at the way the girl rocked back on her heels. 'I've just placed your accent. You're a Kiwi, aren't you?'

'Kiwi and proud, and thank you for not calling me an Aussie.'

'My dear, I am old and often confused, but never that reckless. Now, as I was saying, we are in what is colloquially known as "Admin" – a building which is, for reasons best known to the architect and he alone, shaped like a bridge. Somewhere, three floors below us, an unceasing flow of students run like a river from the schools of study to the university library in their quest for knowledge. Now one curiosity of this building – as you may gather, I've been exploring – is that all the windows in it are in the offices which line these interminable corridors, and those windows remain the very private property of the occupants of those offices. From inside the building, crawling along its intestines, so to speak, there is absolutely no view out on to the real world, otherwise I could get my bearings and instantly point you towards your destination.'

Now the girl tilted her head on one side and studied the old man with intense curiosity.

'You're a bit of a *dag*, aren't you?' she said with sincerity. 'Or you think you are.'

Mr Campion smiled and raised a finger to make his point.

'Now there are two meanings to "dag": one refers to the rather unpleasant bits of wool dangling from a sheep's rear end; the other is an affectionate Antipodean term for a wag who does not take himself too seriously. I'd like to think you were employing the second interpretation.'

'You got that right,' said the girl with a quiver of a smile.

'Good. I'm delighted to have made an impression on a real live student. You're the first one I've met, as it happens, and so I really should introduce myself. My name is Albert Campion.'

He offered a hand and the girl hitched up the rucksack on her back before shaking it.

'I'm Beverley Gunn-Lewis and that's Gunn with two *n*s.'

'My, that's an impressive moniker. I suspect you have a nickname or two.'

'Mostly people call me "Bev",' said the girl without a trace of irony, 'and though I'd love to stay and chat, I really am running late.'

'Ah, yes, the Geology Society,' said Campion. 'You mustn't keep them waiting, so what I suggest is that we follow the fire drill.'

'But there isn't a fire.'

'Thankfully not, and I do not intend to start one; but I have noticed these very helpful signs saying "Fire Exit", with an arrow pointing the way dotted along this corridor at strategic points. They will, I very much hope, lead us to a stairwell and certainly not a lift shaft, as the lifts should not be working during my imaginary inferno. In that stairwell we should find a notice, prominently displayed, informing us of the location of our nearest Fire Assembly Point, which, if my sense of direction has not deserted me, will be located on the ground floor in Piazza 3, as it is called. It is there that numerous student bodies, political organizations, revolutionary and otherwise, societies and glee clubs have erected a market of stalls from which to dispense their wares and recruit members. I saw them setting up earlier. It's a positive Moroccan *souk* down there, and I am sure the Geology Society must have staked a claim and pitched their tent.'

Beverley Gunn-Lewis studied the old man with the mixture of curiosity and sympathy which only the young and still innocent can manage without causing offence.

'You surely do make hard *yakka* of the simplest things,' she said, 'but I think you're a kind soul who means well.'

She gave Campion a curt nod, tugged on the shoulder straps of her rucksack and broke into a slow trot along the corridor following the Fire Exit signs.

As he watched her go, Mr Campion reflected that it was a good thing this new university specialized in languages and linguistics. With luck he might find someone who could tell him what 'yakka' meant.

Having met his first real, live student and performed for them a good deed, Mr Campion felt inordinately satisfied with himself. The rest of the day was, he felt, now his own, and he could concentrate on his prime objective, which was to find his way around the new campus, hopefully with as much self-confidence as Beverley Gunn-Lewis was doing, although the girl had a clear sense of purpose which Mr Campion felt he lacked.

His remit for being on campus was tantalizingly vague, something which in his younger years would have appealed to his curiosity, not to say devilment, as it was an opportunity to observe a goodly cross-section of the country's youth – perhaps the world's – embarking on a university education in a purpose-built playground with most modern comforts, minimal financial responsibility, an equal ratio between the sexes (and few rules about their mixing) and safe in the knowledge that their parents were scores – if not hundreds – of miles away.

As he saw it, it was his duty to discover the way a modern university worked, for his own experiences as an undergraduate at St Ignatius College Cambridge were so far in the past as to be not so much history as archaeology. Clearly, major changes in student life had taken place in the previous half-century. In Campion's day, students had not been allowed cars, although the university statutes were conveniently vague about the status of chauffeurs who garaged their cars out of sight of the colleges. The University of Suffolk Coastal, according to its prospectus, not only allowed students to own cars but actively encouraged them by the generous provision of free parking. This could, Campion mused, be a cynical ploy by the university to attract a better class of student or, alternatively, a recognition that the campus was geographically isolated, three miles from the nearest village, six miles from the nearest railway station (technically a 'halt' rather than a station) and nine or ten miles as the country lanes snaked from Saxmundham, which was hardly a humming metropolis.

Clearly the students were expected to venture further afield, to the fleshpots of Yarmouth or even Ipswich, for entertainment, should they require it, although from what Campion had read about the new generation of universities springing up as fast as concrete could be poured all over the country, the intention was very much to cater for all a student's earthly needs on campus. There was to be a pub, a restaurant, a coffee bar and lecture theatres which could double as concert venues or cinemas when the lectures got too dry and boring, and a medical centre to cure all their ills. Certain sections of the popular press had even suggested that study-bedrooms in the university residences would be equipped with, of all things, televisions. The same popular press also claimed that readily available alcohol and illegal, but accessible, drugs would rot the minds of young undergraduates but Mr Campion, being an optimist, dismissed this alarmist view on the grounds that if there were televisions in bedrooms, their minds would already have rotted beyond repair.

Yet the physical needs of the student intake, although part

of his remit, he assumed, were not his priority. Rather it was the spiritual needs of the student flock and, to be truthful, it was the priority of the Bishop of St Edmondsbury, one of the guiding lights behind the creation of the University of Suffolk Coastal.

Mr Campion was no more than the bishop's unofficial agent in the matter, and it was not a role he relished, for it made him feel uncomfortably like a Jesuit spy at the court of the first Queen Elizabeth, which explained a certain amount of foot-dragging on his part.

It was why he was wandering rather aimlessly in the Administration block, inhaling the mingled perfumes of fresh plaster and new paintwork, seeking the office of the university chaplain who was, Campion felt, far better suited to be the bishop's special agent.

After two more angular turns in the windowless corridor – why did a rectangular building have to have internal twists and turns? – and peering at the name plates on more than two dozen identical doors, he identified the lair of his prey.

The name stencilled on the plywood door in a fashionably bold font said simply: George Tinkler, Chaplain. There was no 'Reverend' or 'Rev.' in front of the name and, unlike the row of labelled doors he had passed to get there, no university degree signified behind it, which struck Campion as odd. George Tinkler, he surmised, did not seem keen to advertise his presence on campus but, given that his immediate superior was the Bishop of St Edmondsbury, that was probably a shrewd tactical move.

His polite knock was answered by a muffled squeak, which Campion took to be an invitation to enter. The man who had squeaked was sitting at a flat-topped desk aligned against the right-hand wall of the office, to which had been attached a metal frame holding four long shelves which ran the length of the room. Apart from five books, clearly Bibles, and a pair of bronze elephants acting as bookends, the shelves were completely empty. The desk, however, was covered in paper, sheet upon sheet of loose lined paper and several open spiral notepads which High Street stationers called Reporters' Notebooks, all covered or in the process of being covered with spidery handwriting.

The spider scribbling away with a vintage Pelikan tortoiseshell gold-nibbed fountain pen did not look up from whatever manuscript he was working on, which might have been a sermon, a shopping list or an angry letter to *The Times*. It was impossible to tell from Campion's restricted view over the spider's hunched shoulder and to lean over and peer would be simply rude. Therefore he coughed discreetly, which at least caused the spider to stop scratching and say, 'Yes, my dear, how can I help?' although his eyes remained fixed on the hieroglyphs marching across the page he had pinned to the desk by his left forearm.

'I do hope I am not interrupting your creative flow,' said Campion, 'but I thought I had better introduce myself as I think we are sharing a platform tomorrow.'

The interrupted scribe slowly and with some ritual screwed the top on his fountain pen and laid it perfectly parallel to the top of the sheet of paper in front of him before raising his head to observe his visitor for the first time through a pair of gold-rimmed *pince-nez*.

'You must be Campion,' he said in a sing-song falsetto. 'The bishop warned me you would be coming.'

Mr Campion, being of the generation who valued good manners, bit his tongue to counter the immediate thought that, with a name like Tinkler, that high-pitched voice and the *pince-nez*, the chaplain was best suited to a post in an ivory tower, albeit one made of concrete, as he would not last a week as the incumbent of one of the rougher parishes of, say, Felixstowe or Ipswich, and probably not five minutes as a teacher of religious education in a boys' prep school.

Mr Tinkler, who struggled to his feet with laboured reluctance and offered Campion a handshake so limp his wrist positively drooped earthwards, like a divining rod casually indicating water, was blessed with little in the way of charm or charisma. The only reason, Campion supposed, that students – if they were his congregation – would be tempted to visit his office was because its floor-to-ceiling window offered a spectacular view over the piazza below where, as he had advised Miss Gunn-Lewis, tables, colourful banners and even balloons indicated that the Freshers' Fair was under way and drawing a healthy crowd.

'I hope it wasn't a storm warning,' Campion quipped. 'I'm really not worth more than a prediction of a light morning dew.'

Behind his *pince-nez*, Mr Tinkler's face remained defiantly impassive, while behind his oversized tortoiseshell frames, Mr Campion's assumed a deceptive vagueness.

'I don't get many visitors,' said the chaplain, as if answering an unasked question.

'Well, term hasn't technically started yet,' offered his visitor.

'Even when term is in full flow, I am rarely consulted and usually never on spiritual matters. It's normally the girls asking if I think they should go on the pill.'

Mr Campion hid his surprise that any young female should seek counsel from Mr Tinkler on any subject, let alone one so sensitive.

'And what advice do you give them, if I may ask?'

Tinkler put his head on one side, made a great play of removing his *pince-nez*, and wafted the air with them before replacing them firmly into the indentations they had already made on either side of his rather fleshy nose.

'I tell them to go and see the university doctor. She's a woman and far better equipped than I to advise on such matters, though from what I hear she dishes them out like Smarties. Still, it's not my place to lecture them on the sin of carnal lust.'

'Forgive me, Chaplain, but I thought that would have been *exactly* your remit.'

Mr Tinkler sighed as he sat down again, waving a limp hand to indicate that Campion should avail himself of the plastic chair against the wall, the only other seat in the office. As if on cue, from down in the piazza below came the sound of a trumpet and a clarinet giving a fair impression of traditional New Orleans jazz.

'If I had a church and a parish and a pulpit, I would naturally be preaching most vociferously against the loose morals of today's youth, but I have none of those things. I compose sermon after sermon' – he waved a hand over the explosion of paper on his desk – 'but never get to deliver them. I am confined to this concrete box by the liberal ideals of a modern university which does not accept that it is *in loco parentis*, especially now most students have the vote. I am the victim of liberal attitudes, Mr Campion. Liberal attitudes!'

Campion crossed one long thin leg over the other and felt an unexpected pang of regret that he had given up smoking.

'My dear chap, are you suggesting that your activities on campus are being restricted by the university administration?' he asked calmly.

'Restricted?' There was distinct colour in the chaplain's cheeks now which Campion noted thankfully as a sign of life in this otherwise cold fish. 'I would go further than that, sir, I would say I was being muzzled. Muzzled by the radicals and liberals in authority. From the vice chancellor downwards, they proudly profess atheism and agnosticism in equal proportions.'

'Surely the bishop, who was so instrumental in the founding of the university, must take a dim view of that.'

On even the briefest of acquaintance, Campion was pretty sure the bishop took a dim view of most things in the twentieth century.

'Oh, he does,' said Tinkler, 'if you are referring to the Bishop of St Edmondsbury, that is. Unfortunately, by some bizarre ecclesiastical oversight or quirk of history, this particular corner of north-east Suffolk is not actually within the See of St Edmondsbury, which has sometimes been called . . .'

'The Cruel See,' said Campion cheerfully, pleased that he could complete the punchline.

'Quite,' said Mr Tinkler, clearly familiar with the role of straight man. 'We are in fact in the See of Norwich, and the bishop there is as progressive and as liberal as Edmondsbury is . . . is . . .'

'Not?' Campion offered with a straight face.

'I was going to say "traditional". He has a seat on the university council and certainly has influence, but no direct power. I understand that he is keen to make sure the university, which has started from scratch, establishes its own traditions as quickly as possible, though I fear his ideas have so far been roundly rebuffed by the academic and administrative staff.'

'My own *alma mater* had lots of traditions, none of which enhanced my education, such as it was,' said Campion. 'Many were incomprehensible to me, then and now, and appeared to be only there to limit my enjoyment.'

'Bulldogs and scouts, that sort of thing?'

'Good gracious, no. You're thinking of Oxford. I was a Cambridge man, not being clever enough to be considered for Oxford but wise enough to realize that a light blue goes with my complexion much better than a dark. But that was back in the mists of time and we did indeed have some strange rituals, such as wearing academic gowns when sitting examinations, although silk pyjamas would have been far more comfortable. Come to think of it, there was a chap who sat his finals in silk pyjamas *and* a gown, though it didn't help with that sticky question on the Enlightenment . . .'

'The bishop certainly suggested that students should wear academic dress at all times,' said Tinkler, 'but that idea was quickly rebuffed, except for the day when they collect their degrees. When most of the lecturers here do not possess a tie, let alone a gown, one cannot expect students to wear them, not these days. Anything goes, it seems, and the student uniform of choice seems to be jeans and a T-shirt advertising a dubious political message. The bishop's other ideas – an official university grace in Latin, a requirement to eat a set number of dinners in hall, even though we have no halls, only a self-service restaurant where the quality of the food is abysmal—'

'Well, that is certainly traditional,' interjected Campion.

'And then there was the question of segregation,' continued Tinkler, flexing the fingers of his right hand as if counting off a list. 'Edmondsbury was quite insistent that the sexes should be completely segregated, not just in residential accommodation but in lectures and seminars as well. That was clearly seen as a backward step too far in this day and age. "This is a modern university, not a monastery!" was the vice chancellor's response.'

'That was brave of him,' mooted Campion.

'Perhaps so, but it might have queered his chances of a knighthood if the bishop has anything to do with it. If the VC has a failing, it is his determination to be *progressive* at every opportunity. I take it you know him?'

'Only by his academic reputation, which is outstanding,' said Campion. 'I will be meeting Dr Downes for the first time over lunch today. I was something of a last-minute replacement for the original Visitor, I fear.'

'Ah, yes, of course.' For the first time Campion detected an emotion flitting across the chaplain's face, something akin to a smug salaciousness. 'The disgraced MP – Labour, of course. Isn't he suspected of spying for the Russians?'

'No, he wasn't a Cambridge man,' said Campion patiently, 'and I think he had rather dubious connections to the Czechs rather than the Russians, though that is pure speculation and the trial is still pending. For some reason the position of Visitor was thought too important to be left vacant and the bishop recommended little old me.'

'So, you are the bishop's man?'

Campion bridled. 'My wife would claim I am her man exclusively, and I would happily agree to that, but otherwise my allegiances are fluid when it comes to football teams and non-existent if politics are involved.'

'Then how was it you were offered the position?'

'I'm not exactly sure. I did once have an uncle who was the Bishop of Devizes, which may have counted as a sort of reference, but otherwise I consider myself totally unqualified. I do, however, have family connections with Suffolk and, having long since abandoned the hope of any sort of gainful employment, I now have time on my hands, so I could hardly refuse.'

Mr Tinkler, suddenly confident, probed further. 'So you do not report back to the bishop?'

'Not if I can help it,' said Campion reasonably. 'Unless you think there is something which should be reported . . .'

'No, no, not at all. I was merely trying to establish why you should have called on me this morning.'

'Time spent in reconnaissance is never wasted, which I believe is the motto of the Girl Guides,' said Campion. 'I thought I would make contact informally with the key figures at the university as soon as I could, before the more formal proceedings tomorrow.'

Mr Tinkler adjusted his *pince-nez* and his face melted with satisfaction at the implied compliment.

'The Freshers' Welcome, of course.' Mr Tinkler spoke as if the concept had only just occurred to him, but without any trace of enthusiasm. 'Yes, we'll all be there giving our two-minute party pieces.'

Campion flashed a glance at the reams of paper covering the chaplain's desk and wondered how all those scribblings could be pushed through a two-minute eye of a needle.

'The vice chancellor gives his all-inclusive speech of welcome,' continued Tinkler, 'stressing how modern and liberal and progressive we are here. Then the dean of students, who is supposed to be responsible for discipline, though his workload cannot be heavy if you ask me, will lay down the rules and regulations such as they are. The medical officer, that's Dr Heather Woodford, who looks young enough to be a student herself, but thankfully doesn't dress like one, will talk about sex, which is always the most popular part of the proceedings if the giggling is anything to go by. To prove we are an egalitarian institution, the head porter, a local man employed for his bulk rather than his intellect, will treat us to his usual folksy homilies about Suffolk and how to mix with the indigenous population, not that the students get to meet many of them as we're rather isolated out here. Then, and only then, will the university chaplain' – Tinkler gave a slow bow as if acknowledging imaginary applause – 'be allowed to say a few words.'

Campion stretched his long legs and made to take his leave.

'Well, that all sounds rather jolly; I look forward to it. I always appreciate a young, fresh-faced audience, they are so innocent and often remarkably gullible, which is something I will have to rely on when it comes to my turn to spout. I don't suppose you know what I'm expected to talk about, do you?'

'I don't know about the first-year intake,' said Tinkler, his ridiculous eye-glasses aimed squarely at Campion's face, 'but the academic staff, all the staff in fact, will be dying to hear of your experiences at Black Dudley before the war. You are *that* Albert Campion, aren't you?'

Nine Years Previously . . .

'Do we have to use the word "radical" quite so much?' asked the bishop.

It is difficult, nigh impossible, to stop an architect dead in his tracks when he is presenting his latest 'vision', but the bishop had come close. The rest of the enlarged steering committee no doubt felt the architect's embarrassment, but none came to his aid.

'But our mission is to lay down roots and to be radical is to grasp things by the root,' said the architect nervously.

'Are you quoting Karl Marx at me, sir?'

An unidentified voice down the table, from a bowed head with a hand across the mouth, quietly observed: 'Should have gone with Groucho.'

The architect, as architects are wont to do when criticized (even by bishops), stuck to his guns.

'But this new university is a radical experiment in higher education and it deserves a radical approach to its architecture. What is being created here is not an ersatz Oxbridge nor an upgraded redbrick university, but something new and exciting which is to be celebrated. I do not use the term "radical" pejoratively.'

'I do,' muttered the bishop under his breath.

The chairman of the county council, and *pro tem* chairman of the meeting, who had to work alongside the bishop more than most of those present, was seated at the far end of the long table on which was displayed a balsa-wood model of the architect's vision of the University of Suffolk Coastal. It meant that the chairman was half-hidden by a series of khaki-coloured pointed structures.

'I believe the building materials you propose are equally' – he searched for a suitably conservative adjective – 'innovative, are they not?'

The architect sensed an ally who might share his enthusiasms. 'Concrete, Mr Chairman, will provide our building blocks; concrete poured and shaped as never before.'

'Except by the Romans, who invented the stuff,' growled the bishop, 'and by the Nazis with their Atlantic Wall.'

Perhaps the architect needed more than one ally.

'It is the fashionable means of construction,' volunteered the chief planning officer, 'and makes the statement that the university will be modern and forward thinking, representing all that is progressive about the decade.'

'Exactly,' the architect said gratefully.

'And of course,' said the planning officer, playing his trump card, 'it provides a quick and cost-effective means of construction, well within the budget allocated by the government.'

From one side of the table, peering over the top of a balsa model resembling a large cylinder, came another supportive voice.

'I estimate the basic university buildings could be open and functioning by late 1965, which would be an academic year earlier than those of the University of East Anglia.'

'Really? That is interesting,' said the bishop. 'Who might you be?'

The chairman, thinking he was on safe ground, performed the introductions.

'This, bishop, is Mr Gregor Marshall, who has recently been appointed estates officer for the campus.'

'And what,' asked the bishop, with an intonation worthy of Lady Bracknell, 'is an estates officer?'

'I am responsible for the safe and efficient running of the buildings and grounds of the new campus,' said Mr Marshall from behind the cylindrical-shaped model, which reminded many at the meeting of the tube inside a toilet roll.

'Are you saying you have power over this empire?' The bishop waved a hand at the six-by-two-foot model laid out on the table before them like a bizarre ritual feast.

'Responsibility perhaps, but hardly power,' said Mr Marshall, glancing quickly at the architect. 'I merely oversee the safe and efficient operation of the site once the plan is implemented and constructed.'

'So we cannot call this a Marshall Plan?'

As the bishop was not known for making jokes, witticisms or pleasantries of any kind, not a single smile flickered across any of the faces around the table, although under the table feet shuffled and toes curled.

'This is the architect's plan, his vision,' said Marshall. 'It is my job to ensure that the lights stay on, the roofs don't leak, the plumbing works, and the students have enough hot water for at least one bath a week once that vision becomes a solid reality.'

'How interesting,' said the bishop, 'especially that latter point about bathing regularly. And you think this "vision" could be made flesh, or at least concrete, by 1965?'

'Not all of it,' said the architect, daring to stand and point to the model with what looked like a black fibreglass conductor's baton, 'but the main academic schools around the three piazzas and the Administration block should be ready and a good start made on the library and the lecture theatres.'

As he tapped a large hexagonal piece of balsa wood, the bishop leaned forward.

'Is that the thing shaped like a threepenny bit?'

'Yes, it is, and the students will probably nickname it so, which is no bad thing.'

'And those pyramids? They look like a range of hills in the distance.'

'Those will be the student residences and yes, they are pyramidal, with a flat for a member of staff or a trusted postgraduate at the peak and then each descending floor alternatively male and then female undergraduates, each floor complete with self-catering facilities. Naturally, they are of lower priority than the academic buildings, but should follow quickly as student numbers grow.'

The architect, who felt he was getting in to his stride, had a sudden crisis of confidence as the bishop got to his feet and bent forward until he loomed over the model, casting a good proportion of it into shadow. He silently reached out a hand and the architect, without question, handed over his pointing baton, which the bishop began to use like a rapier.

'This is the library and that is the lecture-theatre complex?'

The architect murmured his agreement.

'And these are the schools of study, based in these very Italianate piazza squares?'

'Correct.'

'And those pyramids in their own little Valley of the Kings towards the south of the site will be the halls of residence?'

'In due course, yes.'

The bishop straightened up and weighed the baton in his hand before turning to face the architect.

'So where, sir, is the chaplaincy?'

The silence round the table was deafening and it was the bishop himself who ended it.

'Not only radical, but godless!'

TWO

The Visitor

t had been more than forty years, but Black Dudley was still as cold and unwelcoming as Mr Campion remembered it. It was, as it had always been, a great grey building, as ugly as a fortress without a twig of ivy or wisteria to soften its face. Several of the long, narrow windows and its guttering had been replaced but otherwise there were few signs of modernization, although the lower stonework showed the scars of modern life in a patina of chips and scrapes where, Campion suspected, bicycles and motorbikes had been propped up during its occupation by the military. It was one of the few signs that the site had experienced human habitation in a history which had included use as a monastery, a farmstead, a country house, the headquarters of a tank regiment during wartime and finally the nucleus of a modern university. In essence, Black Dudley remained, as someone had famously described it: 'a great tomb of a house'.

Mr Campion could put it off no longer. He had seen the west end of the house from the huge car park where he left his Jaguar earlier that morning, having arrived at the university ridiculously early for his lunchtime appointment with an unsettling sense of foreboding, but had chosen to stroll in entirely the opposite direction.

He could not explain his feelings of unease, though he did try to quantify them. They fell well short of the 'someone's just walked over my grave' tremor, but were more concerning than the increasingly familiar 'where did I leave my glasses?' niggle.

Whatever the level of his discomfort, the source of it was, he was sure, Black Dudley itself, though he was not sure why. His previous visit – his first and only – had been a frantic mixture of danger and farcical drama involving ruthless gangsters intimidating an ill-matched gaggle of house-party guests, who survived the ordeal intact more by luck than judgement. Amidst the confusion there had been the bizarre 'ritual of the dagger', which had made Black Dudley famous in certain circles, and then a murder, which had made it infamous in much wider circles. Campion had played little part in the solution to the murder of the then-owner Colonel Gordon Coombe, and only through his private intelligence network had he learned that no one had hanged for it, though there had been several worthy candidates.

Perhaps it was the suspicion that he had not done as much as he could to see justice done which clawed at his memory, but it had been a long time ago in a society far, far away. Today was a different world and Black Dudley was no longer an isolated fortress guarding the rights and privacy of an elite few, but the nerve centre of opportunity for a new generation to enjoy a higher education that their parents had never even aspired to. On Campion's pre-war visit to Black Dudley, it had been to a weekend house party – a fashionable and respectable pursuit for a certain stratum of society in the 1920s – but this one had always had the air of what he later termed 'a Miss Havisham production'. Rather like Dickens' gothic jilted bride who lured children to Satis House to play for her amusement, so the proprietor of Black Dudley, a wheelchair-bound invalid, had invited the gay young things of society down to darkest Suffolk to amuse themselves and, by extension, himself.

Still wary of approaching the house directly, Campion chose to wander once he had found a ground-floor exit from the Admin building. It was a way of finding his bearings, getting orientated; or so he told himself.

Emerging from the archway of the bridge-like building, the tubular library, raised on thick concrete pillars, was behind him. Before him was Piazza 3 which led into Piazzas 2 and 1, each of the latter built at a slight angle and a lower level to the other to disrupt a clear line of sight and introduce corners and steps to break up the blank slabs of concrete.

In Piazza 3 the university had gone to the extravagance of a central fountain, albeit of rectangular shape and concrete construction; or perhaps it was a goldfish pond, for there was no spurting jet of water and only on closer inspection did

Campion discover that the reservoir of standing water in it was
no more than four inches deep. As a conversation piece, it might
have some point, but as a fountain it offered no competition to
Rome's Trevi and it was unlikely anyone would throw a single
coin into it, let alone three.

The task of disrupting the stark outlines of the piazza and
softening the bare concrete walls and plain uniform glass
windows had clearly been left to the student body and Campion
felt they had made a fair fist of it. Tables and chairs lined the
four sides of the piazza, each draped with banners and posters
announcing their provenance or intention, ranging from artisanal
efforts advertising Pottery Club to suitably theatrical backdrops
promoting the Drama Society. More strident, and mostly in red
print, were the agitprop declarations of the Socialist Workers'
Society. Most stalls were manned by students with fashionably
long hair and a kaleidoscope of sartorial designs: wide, bell-
bottomed trousers for both males and females and colourful
tie-dyed T-shirts being the nearest thing to a dress code. All the
students looked slim and tall and Campion mused that his mother
would have pronounced them 'undernourished' and their height
as 'unnatural' because of the high platform heels which made
their footwear somewhat precarious.

Although he had likened it to a North African street market,
the Freshers' Fair was an innocently uncommercial affair, though
Campion's nostrils did detect a peculiar scent of something
botanical burning. It originated, he discovered, from the array
of joss sticks and scented candles which adorned the table of
something called the Transcendental Meditation Society, and
Campion was so relieved he thought it churlish to question the
spelling of the club's recruiting banner.

Recruitment seemed to be the order of the day. Incredibly
young, fresh-faced first-years, some wearing fragments of
school uniform (but as casually as possible) and a few, even
more embarrassingly, accompanied by a parent or two, shuffled from stall to stall to see if anything caught their interest
and was worth signing away their social life for a term or
two. Most of them, Campion felt, were actually looking for
friends to share the experience of being away from home for
the first time, so the actual activity on offer was probably

immaterial. The Choral and Drama societies might well offer a group friendship; the sporty clubs – Rugby, Hockey and Football – would succour those of a competitive nature; the Chess and the Computing societies attracted the quieter, more cerebral among the new intake; and the Gliding Club, presumably utilizing one of the county's many former airstrips, sought out the more adventurous. At least six political clubs and two student newspapers demanded the commitment of likely volunteers with the offer of physical exercise, friendships forged or even excitement.

Most baffling of all was the obvious, judging by the queue waiting to sign up, popularity of the Mountaineering Society, and Campion was duty-bound to ask one of the officials behind the stall, 'Where are the mountains in Suffolk?' only to receive the instant, non-ironic reply: 'Scandinavia. We take the Students' Union transit van on the ferry for a long weekend of climbing.' When he said 'climbing', the official made the universal drinking sign by a tipping motion of his wrist near the mouth. Campion smiled at that, his faith in the ingenuity of young people confirmed.

The young were also, he was pleased to see, still capable of being embarrassed by their elders. At the Geology Society stand – a table covered in maps and rock samples – he spotted Beverley Gunn-Lewis deep in conversation with a short-haired young woman wearing a khaki military shirt, whom Campion presumed to be a member of staff rather than a student judging by the way 'Bev' was hanging on her every word. When she caught Campion's eye, she automatically raised a hand in a childlike wave and, blushing, almost immediately dropped it back to her side. Campion raised his fedora with a flourish, nodded his head and moved on with a smile.

He was further amused while passing a table groaning under the weight of long-playing records disporting the musical stylings of virtually every American jazz legend and a smaller selection of British jazz royalty under a home-made banner stretched between two broom handles bearing the slightly redundant explanation: Jazz Club.

At first attracted by an LP featuring Fats Waller, recorded on a visit to Britain before the war, which had Scotsman George

Chisholm, now better known as a television comedian, playing trombone, his eye had been caught by a small, crudely printed flyer showing a line drawing of a mountain peak from which issued a trill of musical notation. The message of the flyer was equally enigmatic: *Every midnight – the Phantom Trumpeter.* Was it an invitation or an advertisement? Campion could not decide, but both options appealed to his sense of fun, for surely there was mischief afoot here, and with sublime dexterity he palmed a flyer from the table and had it folded and tucked in a pocket before any of the students crowding around him realized that a thin, bespectacled old man, fifty years their senior, could move so smoothly and so quickly.

Before the steps leading down into Piazza 2 (and then the steps down to Piazza 1), Campion followed an opening in the solid wall of the classrooms and laboratories akin to a short tunnel leading out of the temporary marketplace and on to a vista of green grass rather than concrete.

Once out of the concrete rectangle of the piazza, Campion found himself on a curving shingle path. Behind him was modern concrete and glass, ahead of him a man-made lake bearded by tall reeds and grasses and clearly the home to a variety of waterfowl. Two-thirds of the way down the length of the kidney-shaped man-made lake, the path converged with two others and pointed the way to a wooden bridge which would not have looked out of place on a willow pattern plate.

It was from the middle of that arched bridge that Mr Campion got a full view of the front aspect of Black Dudley and the grey North Sea beyond. Each was as cold as the other.

In the distance, beyond the house and close to the shoreline was a small building which might have been the remains of a Roman watchtower or a World War II pillbox. Campion could not tell, and it niggled that he had no memory of seeing the structure before until he remembered that on his previous visit to Black Dudley there had been neither time nor opportunity to explore the land or the pebble beach which lay to the rear, seaward side of the house. The distant structure or building or whatever it was would also have been hidden by the trees lining the two-mile-long drive to the house from the main road. Those trees and indeed that impressive driveway were long gone either at the hand, or tank tracks, of the military, or as part of the transformation of the estate into a campus university.

There was one twinge of familiarity: the shapeless pitch-black timber and brick structure to the left of the main house, so close it seemed to be leaning on it. It had been refurbished and strengthened, but Campion remembered it as a rather ramshackle garage where house-party guests were expected to deposit their cars for the weekend and once out of sight, out of mind. They would not need them as there would be no escape for those invited to Black Dudley, especially those partaking of the ritual of the dagger (whether they wanted to or not).

That idiotic, puerile game, played with the lights off, of course, with the sole purpose of eliciting squeals of mock outrage from young ladies and embarrassed huffing and red faces from the young men who had pursued the wrong female into the darkness. It was a choreographed piece of social frippery in which one had to partake or face the shame of the stigma of being the one who sucked the life and soul out of the party. Campion knew that the young people arriving at the new campus would go through their own embarrassing rituals of youthful interaction, and he was confident that by dint of the fact that they came from a wide variety of places and backgrounds, their only common denominator being their intelligence, they would survive the process and probably better than his generation had.

He was, however, resigned to the fact that he would have to talk about the ritual of the Black Dudley dagger, foolery though it was, so he adjusted his fedora to its regulation jaunty angle, strode across the remainder of the bridge and marched up to the house.

'Campion? You are early – or am I running late?'

'I am unforgivably early for lunch, Vice Chancellor,' said Mr Campion, 'and usually only late on the uptake, as my wife would say. I got here early to have a snoop round the campus, get my bearings so to speak. If it's inconvenient, you could put me in a cupboard somewhere with a torch and an improving book.'

'Nonsense, my dear fellow, you are more than welcome. I

am sure we can rustle up some coffee, or perhaps you might like to look around the house. There have been a few improvements since you were here last, I think.'

'Electricity being one innovation, I see,' observed Campion.

Dr Roger Downes was terribly young for a vice chancellor, though Campion really had no notion of what the optimum age should be. Perhaps it was a sign of his own age that vice chancellors, like policemen, seemed to be getting younger.

Having done his homework as a good student should, Campion knew that Downes was more than twenty years his junior and – when the same age as most of those innocent and slightly confused faces swarming around the Freshers' Fair in Piazza 3 – had been a teenage pilot flying a Boulton Paul Defiant, the Royal Air Force's make-do-and-mend night fighter during the Battle of Britain. He could imagine Downes as a dashing young pilot, his immaculate uniform kept immaculate in order to attract the girls, which it undoubtedly did, for he still retained boyish good looks, especially when he smiled. The hair would have had fewer flecks of grey, but the eyes would have been just as blue and would have twinkled just as much. Campion wondered if Downes had ever allowed those females who fluttered moth-like around his uniform to assume he was a Spitfire pilot, the Spitfire being the pin-up aircraft of the battle rather than the ungainly Defiant or the Hurricane, which actually did much of the hard work, but he dismissed the thought as ungenerous.

Downes would still be attractive to the ladies, the uniform now replaced by a fashionable Italian-cut two-piece suit and a healthy tan which Campion guessed had been acquired in his academic career, which may have been budded in rainy Oxford but had bloomed into flower under Spanish suns both in Europe and South America. For Dr Downes was that relatively rare breed: he was a Hispanist. It was a field of academic study which had been fruitful for him, having brought him a fabulously beautiful Spanish wife (or so Campion had been briefed by *his* wife via the glossier fashion magazines); regular appearances on radio and television news bulletins as an interpreter of South American politics and, given the year, football; a useful sideline as a book reviewer and authority on Spanish and Catalan literature; a reputation as an outspoken political campaigner for students of all ages to speak a foreign language; and now the vice chancellorship of one of Britain's newest, and Suffolk's first, university.

'Yes, Black Dudley has all mod cons now,' said Downes, shaking Campion's hand warmly. 'I think the electricity was put in by the army during the war but the whole place has been rewired courtesy of the Ministry of Education. Both the plumbing and heating now work without shaking the plaster off the wall, we have telephones, telex and the latest facsimile machine, which can transmit a letter to the recipient in six minutes!'

'That could make the second post redundant,' Campion said with a smile, 'assuming that the addressee of your letter also has a fax machine.'

'And we have a computer,' Dr Downes continued enthusiastically, proving his credentials as the very model of a modern vice chancellor. 'Well, actually we have a terminal here in the Dudley – we tend to call it that, by the way. The main Computing Centre is in Piazza 1 and, on a fine day, you can play it at chess.'

'Really?'

'Yes. Outdoor chess. The piazza is marked out with chessboard squares and we have large wooden black and white pieces.'

'I think I saw them in the distance,' said Campion airily. 'At first I thought it was a gathering of penguins. Something to do with the Zoology department, perhaps?'

Dr Downes, having experienced student rags and pranks on more than one continent and several languages, knew when his leg was being pulled.

'It would not surprise me in the least if the Students' Union had started a Rescue-A-Penguin Society, as they are something of an endangered species in Suffolk, but the university does not run to a Zoology department, at least not yet. We are very young and taking our first steps here and I am determined that we should only offer subjects where we can deliver top-quality teaching and the best facilities for research. We do not, for example, offer courses in theology.'

The vice chancellor's choice of example was clearly a testing of the water.

'I got the impression that that was a source of disappointment to the Bishop of St Edmondsbury who chaired your Foundation Committee,' said Campion. 'Though I believe I am also something of a disappointment to the bishop, being a last-minute substitute, as it were.'

'Ah, yes,' sighed Dr Downes, 'our original Visitor . . . shocking business, really. Who would have suspected an MP of sleeping with the enemy, as it were?'

'Probably quite a lot of people. I hope his apprehension by our security services has not had an adverse impact on the university.'

'Not at all. If anything it has boosted applications from the more left-wing student fraternity, but then anything slightly left is always popular among the young.'

'And is that not healthy?' quizzed Campion lightly. 'Let them march, riot and blow off steam calling for the revolution. Just as long as they don't start stringing up us old intellectuals from the nearest lamppost.'

'You're not being serious, are you?' Dr Downes seemed genuinely taken aback.

'Of course not.' Campion grinned. 'I may be old but I'm far from being an intellectual. I should be quite safe as long as I don't put my foot in it with the student body. I've met one of them already and she seems jolly nice.'

'Most of them are,' said Dr Downes, and there was no disputing his sincerity, 'and though we go out of our way to encourage applications from the less privileged sections of society – where the child is the first from a family to go to university – and actively recruit from the comprehensive schools, the majority of our intake does come from decent, middle-class homes. Of course the Sociology department would say that is exactly where you find the most radicalized young mind, the students who become political activists but are really rebelling against their parents.'

'Well, the very pleasant young first-year I met is studying geology, not sociology, and seemed more intent on impressing her tutor than fomenting revolution.'

'Would that be Tabitha King?' Dr Downes's eyes narrowed like dipped headlights.

'No, her name was Bev, short for Beverley, Gunn-Lewis. Quite distinctive, I thought, and she's a New Zealander, and Kiwis aren't usually the first to man the barricades.'

'I meant her tutor. Tabitha King is a senior lecturer in earth sciences.'

'Sorry, but I've no idea on that score. Why? Is she a dangerous radical?'

'Certain people may think so, I could not possibly pass an opinion,' said the vice chancellor diplomatically. 'I doubt you'll come across her, but you should meet the head of her department, he's one of our prize assets. He's joining us for lunch, as is the pro-vice-chancellor, who is responsible for student discipline. You'll also be meeting our founding professor of sociology. I should warn you, he is not one of the bishop's favourite people.'

'I think *that*,' said Campion, 'is a very short list, and I doubt I am on it either. In fact I am sure I got the position of Visitor as a result of mistaken identity.'

'Oh dear,' sympathized the vice chancellor. 'Why did you accept?'

'It seemed churlish to refuse the honour, and I am cursed with good manners, though I am still not clear as to what a Visitor does, or what is expected of one.'

'We will discuss that over lunch. Suffice to say, your duties will not be onerous, and we are, of course, delighted to have you on board. We've put you up in one of the guest rooms here at the Dudley. Only my wife and I live here, above the shop, so to speak, so it's quite secluded, but all staff and students are encouraged to mix on campus. We do not have senior or junior common rooms, and our bar, restaurant and coffee bar are open to all. It can get quite lively on campus in the evenings.'

'I may well investigate later,' said Campion, 'but I would like a wash and brush-up before lunch, so if you could point me in the general direction of my room, I'll nip and get my case out of the car.'

Dr Downes showed the palms of his hands. 'Please, you are our guest. Let me summon Meade. He will get your luggage and show you to your room.'

'Meade? I presume you do not mean the drink made from honey which has caught many a West Country monk unawares.'

The vice chancellor laughed politely. 'Meade is our head porter and, effectively, our head of security. The students call him "Big Gerry" because his real name is, unbelievably, Gerontius. He has the distinction of being the first member of staff to be appointed here, so he pre-dates all of us. In more ways than one, actually, as he's a local chap, lives in White Dudley and is fiercely loyal to the house.'

'Meade, did you say? Why does that name sound familiar? Distant, but familiar. Where can I have come across it before?'

'I think such a thing unlikely, Campion. Dear old Gerontius doesn't own a passport and hasn't travelled further afield than Ipswich, as far as I know. In fact, I'm pretty sure he's never been out of Suffolk in his life. He sort of came with the place, part of the fixtures and fittings. I think his mother worked here before the war.'

'Oh, goodness me,' breathed Campion as realization dawned. 'He must be the son of the ferocious Mrs Meade.'

'You knew Big Gerry's mother?'

'Briefly, I'm glad to say, if that does not sound too ungallant. I seem to vaguely recall being trapped with her in an attic here. We were somewhat under siege at the time – I'm sure you've heard the story – and Mrs Meade wasn't exactly helpful. She kept on about her son, who seemed to like nothing more than a good punch-up and who would sort everything out. An awkward woman, prone to bouts of religious evangelism, I seem to recall. The sort who would have got on well with the bishop, I fear.'

'Funny you should say that, as Gerontius came with a solid gold testimonial from the bishop.'

'I did not realize the bishop was responsible for recruiting the staff here,' Campion observed.

'He's not,' said Dr Downes with a trace of bitterness. 'He just doesn't accept the fact. I sometimes wonder how we got any of the academic staff appointed in time to teach our first students, but we did and now they're a unified, well-drilled, dedicated team of top minds working to a single goal: to make this the best university in the country.'

Mr Campion bit his lip, not wishing to douse Dr Downes's clearly sincere pride and enthusiasm, even though the temptation was great to declare that he had never heard the words 'unified, well-drilled and dedicated to a single goal' applied to any group of academics, as those characteristics tended to go against the species' mentality. And just what was the collective noun for a group of academics? A *flock*? A *gathering*? A *senate*?

Instead he remembered his manners and said: 'I look forward to meeting them. I do hope one of them is clever enough to tell me what my duties are.'

Eight Years Previously . . .

'Naturally we recognize Dr Downes *nem. con.* as chairman of the Initial Appointments Sub-Committee, and of course we welcome him today as the vice-chancellor-in-waiting, as it were, of the University of Suffolk Coastal.' The bishop drew breath, leaving the meeting in no doubt that there was a 'but' coming. 'And while the *lay* members, if I may call us that' – he paused for laughter, but received no more than a polite titter – 'have no direct responsibility for academic appointments, I do hope that any observations and input we may have to offer will be given due consideration.'

'But of course, Bishop,' said Dr Downes, who for this encounter with the bishop felt on totally firm ground, 'all views would be welcome. I would, however, remind the committee that I personally have been charged with supervising the appointment of the heads of our first three academic departments, and two of those posts will be the first professorial chairs offered by the university.'

'Why not all three?' asked the chairman of the county council, thinking he ought to at least attempt a contribution to the discussion, preferably one which would not antagonize the bishop.

'Budgetary constraints, I'm afraid,' said Downes. 'Until we have actually attracted some students and, hopefully, some external research funding, the university is limited to the number of chairs it can offer at salaries which would attract the best candidates from other institutions.'

The bishop exhaled loudly, a warning sign to the others around the table. 'You make it sound, Vice Chancellor, as if we are in the football transfer market.'

'In a way, Bishop, we are. As a new institution, we have no track record or tradition of excellence, so we must attract the best people sometimes by commercial means.'

'Why not blow the budget on a footballer then? They seem to increase in value; just look at that Scottish chap Denis Law. Went from Manchester to Italy then back to Manchester, the price going up each time. Obscene amounts of money, they were.'

Dr Downes remained calm, preserving his strength for the battles to come. 'A very good example, my lord. Two institutions – in this case two *different* Manchester teams and one Italian one, Torino, I think – competing for a player who is at the top of his field. Albeit a football field,' he added, and that did get a polite laugh. 'I'm glad to say that for our first three appointments, I am confident we have the top men in their fields. Their academic CVs are in front of you, gentlemen, but I will give a brief description of each before putting their appointment to the committee.'

'For rubber-stamping.'

'For approval by consensus, I hope.'

Dr Downes put his head down and shuffled his papers. 'You are all aware that I regard the teaching of languages, modern languages, as one of the primary functions of the university,' he said, scanning the faces of the committee for traces of surprise or dismay, 'and that a considerable amount of investment will go into providing the most advanced language laboratories in the country. My first recommendation then, I am delighted to say, to be head of the Language and Linguistics department and, effectively, my second-in-command, is Dr J.K. Szmodics, currently professor of Finno-Ugrian studies at Birmingham.'

The bishop grabbed the top typewritten sheet of paper in front of him on the table and brought it up to his face, as though examining it for fingerprints.

'Isn't there a spelling mistake here?'

'No, bishop, the spelling is accurate, but the correct pronunciation is "Smoditch",' Dr Downes answered crisply.

'No, the other thing. What's a Finno-Ugrian?'

'It is the group of languages which include Finnish and Hungarian, two of the most distinct and difficult languages in Europe.'

The bishop lowered the paper slightly, so that his eyes emerged over the top of the sheet.

'And there is a demand for learning such . . . unusual . . . languages? You'll be telling us next that students should be learning Mandarin for when the Chinese take over the world!'

'That is an interesting idea for the future, Bishop,' said Downes smoothly, 'and should be noted in the minutes, with due credit to yourself, for future reference. In the meantime, I would point out that Dr Szmodics is pre-eminent in his field and will, in fact, be taking a slight drop in status in joining us as we cannot as yet offer him a professorial chair.'

Dr Downes reached for a new sheaf of papers and the rest of the committee, with a loud rustling noise, followed suit. 'Now to the first of our inaugural chairs, and I am delighted to say we have attracted a very bright star indeed. As head of the Earth Sciences department, we will be welcoming one of the world's youngest and most dynamic geologists, Professor Pascual Perez-Catalan.'

'Another foreigner,' said the bishop, not quite as *sotto voce* as he could have.

'Pascual brings with him some fascinating, ground-breaking research, if that's not an oxymoron when describing the work of a geologist.' Now there was polite laughter around the table. 'And he joins us from the Catholic University of Chile in Santiago.'

The laughter stopped immediately as the bishop, his *voce* hardly *sotto* at all, muttered, 'Catholic?'

Dr Downes pressed on regardless. 'Our third appointment, and second chair, will be the head of the department of Arts and Humanities, and again we have managed to attract one of the top men in his field, Professor Yorick Thurible.'

'Now that is an unusual name,' said the bishop, sounding relatively optimistic for once. 'Quite rare, I think.'

'Not if you know your Shakespeare,' said Downes, sensing common ground with the turbulent prelate. 'Comes from the Greek – the name, that is, not the professor.'

'No, his other name,' the bishop argued. 'Thurible. I don't think I've come across anyone with that name before, but it has a curiously devotional reverence to it, a definite sense of religiosity. Sounds just the man to teach our young people the arts.'

Dr Downes, for once, was lost for words, but his raised eyebrow signalled that his brain was working overtime.

'Er . . .' he began hesitantly, 'Professor Thurible is an eminent . . . sociologist.'

The bishop was utterly speechless.

THREE
The Ghost of Black Dudley

'Did you meet Meade on your previous visit?'

'Definitely not; once met, never forgotten,' said Mr Campion. 'You must remember, it was more than forty years ago and Gerry – I'm sorry, I cannot bring myself to say Gerontius – was probably no more than a teenager, and a pretty fractious one if his mother was to be believed. She gave the impression that her son was a bit of a scrapper, always spoiling for a fight; made him sound quite as terrifying as his mother actually was.'

The teenage hooligan of yesteryear had matured considerably in both temperament and girth into the smartly uniformed head porter who had helped Campion extract his suitcase from his car and offered portage to Black Dudley. Whatever sort of 'rare fighter', as his mother had called him, he had been in his youth, he was now clearly in the heavyweight division, a big, lumbering figure with a deep bass voice who, Campion thought, could certainly put the fear of God into misbehaving students, though the cleverer ones would soon realize they could outrun him.

The uniform, grey woollen serge jacket and trousers with razor-sharp creases, plus a peaked officer's cap, gave him the appearance of a modern security guard rather than the top-hatted, stripe-trousered bulldogs who had ruled with an iron fist wrapped in immaculate politeness over Campion's generation of students.

'I'm Meade, sir,' he had introduced himself. 'Gerry to them likely to stand me a pint or give me a game of darts down The Plough, Big Gerry to them that thinks I can't hear 'em, and Mr Meade to the lower classes who want to keep on the right side of me.'

'Well, that's all very clear, Mr Meade,' Campion had said deliberately. 'Have you worked here long?'

'From the start – of the university that is, not the house – but the family's always lived in Dudley, White Dudley that is, though my mother used to work here, off and on, at the Black before the war. I'm told you may have come across her during the trouble they had with those gangsters and the dagger ritual that went wrong.'

'Our paths did cross but only slightly,' Campion had replied. 'It was a pretty hairy situation, but I believe Mrs Meade's faith saw her through the drama.'

'Most exciting thing ever happened to her, her being kidnapped and locked in the attic like she was. She talked about it until the day she died,' Meade had said in a matter-of-fact tone. 'Even on the day she died.'

Mr Campion had expressed polite sympathy and Meade had shrugged his massive shoulders, as if to say that life must go on. To fill the silence, Campion felt he had to ask: 'What would your mother have made of the changes around here? All these modern buildings, all these young people?'

'Not a lot, sir, if you don't mind me saying so. She would have railed long and hard about the godlessness of what goes on here – all the new-fangled ideas, long-haired boys who look like girls, girls who dress and behave like strumpets, loud music at all hours of the day and night, not to mention the comings and goings in the halls of residence. And the politics! Sometimes you'd think this was a summer jamboree for Bolsheviks. I'm thankful in a way that she's not here to see this; she would have had plenty to rail about.'

'Was she a friend of the Bishop of St Edmondsbury by any chance?' Campion had asked mischievously.

'Couldn't say they were friends exactly,' Mrs Meade's loyal son had replied, 'but they corresponded regular like and it was the bishop who put me forward for this job when the university came to Black Dudley.'

'He seems a solid enough chap,' Mr Campion said to his interrogator, 'and no doubt good at his job, but I suspect your enquiry was not about my friendship with the Meade family, but about my part in the ritual of the Black Dudley dagger. Dr Szmodics, isn't it?'

'Forgive me for snooping, Mr Campion, but we are all intrigued by the story; and yes, it is Szmodics, and thank you for getting the pronunciation right. Do you speak Hungarian?'

'Not at all, other than the words *Egri Bikaver*, which appear on the label of a perfectly acceptable red wine called Bull's Blood. I notice that your little supermarket here on campus has a small off-licence section which stocks it at six shillings and sixpence a bottle. I'm sure it must be popular with your students.'

Dr Szmodics allowed a frown to float across his face, momentarily disturbing his solid good looks. 'I am afraid certain other stimulants are becoming more popular among the student population.'

'I'm sorry to hear that,' said Campion genuinely. 'Are such things within your remit as pro-vice-chancellor?'

'If they fall into the rather vague description of student discipline, then yes, I'm afraid they are, though in an institution which proudly and loudly proclaims its liberal values, there is limited support among the younger academic staff for upholding some of the accepted social values.'

Campion concealed his surprise at Dr Szmodics's forthrightness. Perhaps being father confessor to the academic staff was part of his all-too-vague duties as 'Visitor'. And he had not expected confessional to commence before they had given him a good lunch.

'Does Gerry Meade act as your chief of police? Even on very brief acquaintance, he seemed much concerned about the morals, and the politics, of the student body.'

'That sounds like Big Gerry.' Dr Szmodics allowed himself a smile, something Campion guessed was an all-too-rare occurrence. 'He can come across as a bit of a martinet, but most of the porters are approaching retirement age and they hardly constitute a police force, at least not an effective one.'

'I suppose that depends on your definition of "effective".'

'Keeping the peace and protecting life and property would be my base line.'

'That sounds a reasonable rule of law,' said Campion, 'and does not appear to impose moral judgements on anyone.'

'In a wider social setting, perhaps, but here in our rarefied little world, not so easy to enforce. We had a sit-in here last term, you may have heard.'

Campion bit back the urge to quip that the news had not made the pages of the *Racing Post*, but neither would he admit to being briefed at length on the subject by the Bishop of St Edmondsbury, so he merely nodded and tried to appear to be enjoying the cup of weak, milky instant coffee provided by a bustling, slightly fearsome middle-aged secretary.

'Some of our more militant students occupied the Earth Sciences department, effectively the whole of Piazza 3, and barricaded themselves in there for ten days. We were given ample warning that they would do this – the Students' Union even issued a press release – but at the appointed hour, Big Gerry Meade and his merry men were nowhere to be seen. We were actively avoiding confrontation, that was the official line, for we naturally could not be seen to be stamping down on peaceful democratic protest. In fact, Gerry had conveniently organized a union meeting for all porters and ancillary staff, held at The Plough in White Dudley at exactly the time the students occupied the buildings.'

'What was the protest about?' Campion asked. 'Vietnam? Apartheid?'

'An increase in bar prices in the refectory,' said Dr Szmodics ruefully. 'They were objecting to the fact that Norwich Bitter had gone up a penny a pint to two and threepence.'

'I've known barricades manned for less noble causes,' admitted Campion, 'but still, it must have been embarrassing for the university.'

'There was a lot of bad press, that's for sure. We had to get an injunction and the police and a squad of bailiffs in order to evict them. We found several of our younger lecturers camped in there with them when we did, but fortunately it does not seem to have affected student applications for this year.'

'So no lasting damage done?'

'I wouldn't say that. The vice chancellor, on advice – but not mine – cancelled the price increases in the bar, so our more militant students are now convinced that direct action works.'

'And you think that could lead to more trouble in the future?'

'I'm sure of it.'

Mr Campion beamed his most vacuous grin.

'Then *my* advice would be to keep the bar open for as long, and the prices as low, as possible.'

The official, though informal, luncheon to welcome the university's new Visitor was held in what had been the Great Hall of the house. Dr Szmodics – 'Please call me Jack, as my first names are even more difficult to pronounce than my surname' – escorted Campion from his first-floor office down the grand staircase to the main doors of Black Dudley, although Campion remembered the way, and the hall, perfectly well, in spite of the cosmetic changes to the house's décor and furnishings.

The Great Hall was still as vast as a barn, but it had been shorn of its dark oak panelling and its two rather majestic fireplaces. Its windowless gloom had been harshly alleviated by fluorescent wall-lighting strips replacing the giant iron candle-ring candelabra which had once hung from the ceiling festooned with twenty to thirty candles, each as thick as a man's wrist. There were large framed photographs along the walls, depicting the birth pangs of the campus from the mechanical diggers in what appeared to be an empty field, excavating the man-made lake, to the building of the piazzas from the foundations upwards to the 'topping out' of the pyramidal student residences photographed at sunset, giving them the silhouette of a row of shark's teeth.

Mr Campion's eye, however, was drawn to the space above where one of the fireplaces had been. Now it displayed a not-quite-in-focus colour photograph of Black Dudley with the lake and its wooden bridge in the foreground, taken as far as he could judge from the roof of the north side of Piazza 2. It was not, he decided, a particularly good or interesting photograph, but it was preferable to the circular display of spearheads and pikes, not to mention the infamous Black Dudley dagger which had hung there on his previous visit.

The hall, now re-consecrated as a board or committee room, was furnished with functional modern furniture: plain rectangular tables which could be placed end-to-end, and stackable plastic chairs currently lining the long walls. Campion assumed that all the important meetings concerning the governance of the university took place in there, though he felt that, in atmosphere, it had more in common with the waiting room of a municipal bus station than the council chamber in the Doge's Palace in Venice.

One of the tables featured three large plates loaded with sandwiches, all triangular, all white bread with the crusts removed, and one platter of cheeses, at least two different types, both English, surrounded by a circle of water biscuits and crowned with a small bunch of green grapes. On another table was a tray of wine glasses and three bottles of white and three of red wine. Campion deduced nothing from the labels other than the fact that the wine had probably originated in Spain.

'I hope Jack has been keeping you entertained,' Dr Downes greeted him, 'now please come and meet the other movers and shakers of the university – and grab a sandwich before they start to curl. There's egg and cress, cheese and tomato and what would be salmon pâté if pâté was spelled p-a-s-t-e. I hope you don't mind slumming it, but we don't go in for formal dinners and claret cellars here.'

Campion picked up a small plate, selected a brace of sandwiches, politely refused a glass of wine in order to keep one hand free and attached himself to the vice chancellor's coattails as the meet-and-greet began. First in the firing line was the only female in the room not wearing an apron or carrying a tray.

'Let me introduce Dr Woodford,' said Downes. 'Heather Woodford – Albert Campion.'

The handshake was firm, but did not outlive its welcome. The woman behind it was a brunette wearing a plain blue wool dress and an open, fluffy pink cardigan with enormous pockets, both of which came down to her knees. She was most likely in her mid-thirties, but trying to look ten years older.

'I'm a doctor,' she said, making sure she would be overheard. 'A real one. The only real doctor on campus.'

'You must be the medical officer. I promise not to pester you with my symptoms.'

'It might make a change,' said Dr Woodford. 'During term time my surgeries tend to resemble kindergartens and I spend an inordinate amount of time educating the kids about sex or hangovers or persuading them that the common cold isn't necessarily fatal. The most common disease I treat is loneliness – young people living away from home for the first time.'

'I am sure that is a very worthwhile use of your time, but it must make a change from general practice.'

'No house calls, that's one advantage. Most of my patients are within two minutes' walk of my office, and because students tend to be late risers my mornings are blissfully free, and I can put my feet up and listen to the radio. I shall certainly miss that aspect of university life.'

'You are leaving?'

'At the end of this academic year, to work in a hospital, to treat a wider variety of patients with more challenging ailments.'

Dr Downes, anxious to progress along the receiving line, intervened. 'Don't let Dr Woodford fool you, Campion. She does a wonderful job keeping our students fit, healthy and thirsting for knowledge.' Dr Woodford's expression did not necessarily endorse the vice chancellor's assessment, but she flicked a thin smile at Campion as he was moved along.

'And this is the man who keeps our students fed and watered, as well as ensuring that the lights stay on and the plumbing works – Mr Gregor Marshall, our estates officer.'

'A man with a plan, I presume,' mugged Campion, 'and I bet you'd be a rich man if you had a pound for every time you'd heard that.'

Mr Marshall sniffed loudly, and his saturnine face contorted into what Campion presumed passed for a smile.

'Mebbe I'd be comfortable, but not rich. Most of the kids round here wouldn't know the Marshall Plan from a bus time-table and they've got their own names for me – plenty of 'em.'

He spoke with a northern accent which no length of time living down south or among intellectual minds drawn from the four corners of the world would ever dislodge. He was a tall man, with slicked-back black hair shiny with Brylcreem and the sort of pencil moustache Campion hadn't seen since VE Day.

'If the students have thought up a nickname for you, you must be popular.'

'Hardly. They call me Marshal Ney, like that general of

Napoleon's, because I have to say "No" to all their crackpot demands.'

Given his accent, Campion could see where the name came from.

'As I understand it, the role of estates officer has great power over the students' living conditions: rents in the halls of residence, the food in the refectory, prices in the bar . . .'

'And a hundred other things, but I have no power, only great responsibility. If a light bulb goes in an office or if a student floods a bathroom because they've left the taps running or if the lifts stop working in the library or the telephone boxes get vandalized, it all ends up on my desk.'

'Where it is handled with supreme efficiency,' Dr Downes interjected with diplomatic skill. 'Mr Marshall makes the place tick like clockwork, allowing the academic staff to concentrate on teaching hungry young minds.'

'If only that were all they concentrated on . . .' muttered Mr Marshall, but Campion was already being pulled out of earshot.

'Now this is one of our rising stars,' enthused Dr Downes, determined to spare no one's blushes. 'A world leader in his field already, who will bring fame, glory and hopefully fortune to the university. More importantly, as far as you are concerned, he's from Chile and has never heard of the ritual of the Black Dudley dagger.'

Professor Pascual Perez-Catalan was a small, hyperactive man with a thick brown beard and a helmet of massively curly auburn hair. Campion could see him in a beret adorned with a red star badge doing a fair impersonation of Che Guevara, although he acknowledged that he might be guilty of subliminal suggestion following Dr Downes's revelation of his South American origin.

'I am geochemist,' said the Chilean, shaking Campion's hand vigorously, 'what are you?'

'By inclination I am a layabout,' said Campion. 'By profession I am a retired seeker-after-knowledge, and the particular piece of knowledge I currently seek is what the deuce is a geochemist?'

The young professor's face went blank and was then turned

to appeal to Dr Downes, who spoke in quiet bursts of rapid Spanish, smiling at Campion as he did so.

Eventually the Chilean, who had been listening intently, nodded and declared 'English humour', as if that explained the bulk of the world's mysteries.

The vice chancellor attempted to illuminate matters further.

'Pascual holds the founding chair in our department of Earth Sciences and is a noted pioneer in the field of plate tectonics.'

Campion looked pointedly at the plate, holding his half-eaten egg sandwich, balanced on his fingertips, but resisted the urge to confirm the professor's suspicions about English joke-telling.

'Please educate me,' he said. 'I am vaguely familiar with the terms earth and science, but plate tectonics is well beyond the brain of this poor old soul.'

'It is a relatively new field of study,' said Dr Downes, 'but I will let Pascual explain.'

The trail-blazing scientist stroked his beard and stepped into the breach as if he had been charged with leading a seminar of nervous first-year students.

'You are familiar with the term continental drift perhaps?'

'Vaguely, from a safe distance,' said Campion. 'It's why, when you look at an atlas, all the continents seem to fit together like jigsaw pieces; a jigsaw that's been dropped from a great height.'

'Precisely. The fact that the continents split apart seems incontrovertible. The geology matches up, the plant species match and the fossils match, but . . .' Mr Campion flinched as the professor became more animated, describing the shifting of continents with sharp slashes of the flats of both hands, movements which suggested horizontal karate blows, '. . . until relatively recently the physicists said it was not possible, that there was no force in nature which could exert such power. But now it has been proved that there is, that the sea floor can move and spread. One of your British marine geophysicists, Fred Vine, was at the forefront of this work.'

Sheepishly, Dr Downes made to interrupt, but it was not to save Mr Campion's scientific blushes, rather his own.

'You may have heard of Fred Vine; he's another rising star and we would have loved to have him here working with Pascual, but he was poached by those upstarts in Norwich at the University of East Anglia.'

Perez-Catalan coughed, far from discreetly. 'May I continue?'

Dr Downes graciously bowed out.

'What do you know of the Andes, Señor Campion?'

'They are not in Africa,' said Campion before he could stop himself, and then burst into a fit of giggles, as did Dr Downes, but both recovered their composure within a few red-faced seconds.

'I do apologize, Professor, that was rude, but you see there is a famous fictional English schoolboy . . .'

'Nigel Molesworth,' offered Dr Downes, straining to keep a straight face.

'Who thought an exam question was "Are the Andes?" because he hadn't turned the page to read the subordinate clause "in Africa?" but by that time, Nigel neither knew nor cared.'

Despite the vice chancellor nodding enthusiastically, Professor Perez-Catalan did not look convinced that he was in the presence of serious, hopefully sane, people. He decided the best thing to do was to abandon the concept of an intelligent tutorial and resort to the formal lecture which, in his case, involved a delivery of machine-gun rapidity and many swooping gestures using the flat palms of both hands.

'So!' he resumed dramatically. 'We are agreed that there are a series of plates on the earth's surface which move around over geological time. In some places they are coming apart, in some places they are rubbing together, in some places they are pushing together.

'My research is into the geochemistry of the subduction zone, or Benioff zone, after Hugo Benioff, between geological plates along the coast of my native country, Chile. In simple terms, that is where the oceanic, Pacific, plate is thrust under the thicker continental or South American plate. Where the two meet, the lighter rocks of the continental plate are crumpled and thrust upwards and at the same time there is much volcanic activity, and so the Andes are formed.'

'I see,' said Campion politely if not convincingly. 'And this

. . . subduction zone . . . is a sort of no man's land between the plates? I am guessing it is not an easy thing to find – otherwise you wouldn't be a professor.'

'We find the subduction zone by using seismography. We can locate the epicentre of earth tremors in the region – and we are blessed, or cursed, with frequent earthquakes in Chile – and we have found that they all fall on a plane which runs parallel to the coast and dips down at forty-five degrees to the horizontal.'

'This sounds frighteningly complicated and I'm sure I'm only understanding half of what you're telling me.'

'It is complicated by the amount of seismographic data we need to collect. Many, many readings are needed; so many that it is necessary to use the latest computers. Analysing them, combined with a study of the geology and the chemistry of the region, will produce a predictive algorithm.'

'I'm not terribly sure what an algorithm is,' said Mr Campion, avoiding the stern gaze of his clearly disappointed Chilean tutor.

Dr Downes came to his rescue. 'It's a sort of formula you give a computer to solve a problem. You input a series of steps and it maps the way to a satisfactory solution. Think of it as a recipe. You list the ingredients and their quantities, and you know roughly what each one contributes to the finished dish, but the recipe or algorithm is the pathway to getting there.'

'My expertise as a geologist is rated many rungs lower than my skill in the kitchen, Vice Chancellor, so I am afraid your analogy butters no parsnips with me, as my mother used to say.' Campion assumed an air of total distraction, one of his most accomplished poses. 'Now she was pretty accomplished in the kitchen though, as far as I know, knew nothing of geology.'

'Geochemistry,' corrected the professor.

'I do beg your pardon. Can I be clear, as politicians are apt to say, though rarely in the context of asking for advice, but this algorithm of yours: is it a method of predicting earthquakes or perhaps volcanoes?'

'No, Señor Campion, I leave those to the seismologists and the vulcanologists.'

'I am sure that's wise,' Campion demurred, but the professor was in full flow.

'My algorithm does not predict the future, but identifies the past – the very distant past. My algorithm should be able to predict the presence of valuable minerals, particularly heavy metals such as palladium, vanadium, rhodium, manganese, zinc, lead and tungsten.'

'My goodness, how interesting,' said a genuinely surprised Campion. 'I actually know what some of those are, and they're more than worth their weight in gold.'

'Very true, señor, but we can predict deposits of gold also.' He paused for dramatic effect. 'As well as thorium and uranium.'

Mr Campion was aware that his mouth must have fallen open but no sound was emerging. Dr Downes had noticed too and once more felt obliged to rescue his guest.

'I see you find that absolutely fascinating, Campion.'

'Indeed I do, Vice Chancellor, and I suspect rather a lot of other people will too.'

Mr Campion managed to finish the last of his sandwiches as the vice chancellor eased him towards the last of the VIPs he was to be introduced to. He had been briefed – too briefly he felt – that these would be the three kingpins; the three legs of the academic tripod which held the university aloft. Mentally he had filed them alongside the geographical locations of their own personal empires. Dr Szmodics, in addition to his duties as pro-vice-chancellor was also the head of the department of Languages and Linguistics which, for reasons he did not fully appreciate, also included the Computing Centre. His bailiwick was clearly Piazza 1, complete with the outdoor chessboard and its almost life-size pieces.

The excitable South American geochemist, who claimed to have invented a new method of divining valuable minerals, if Campion had understood correctly, was the head of Earth Sciences, which made his fiefdom Piazza 3; when, that is, it was free of Freshers' Week markets or student sit-ins.

Which left the Arts and Humanities department and the overlord of Piazza 2, the splendidly named Professor Yorick Thurible, who did not look anything like the tweedy, pipe-smoking Victorian clergyman Campion, in a flight of fancy, had imagined.

At first sight, he did not think this was a full professor, rather a student who had wandered into Black Dudley lured by the free sandwiches, and although he would never claim to be a dedicated follower of fashion, Mr Campion guessed that the younger man's dress sense had been inspired by pop-music magazines at least three years out of date.

'By a process of elimination, you must be Professor Thurible, and I realize I must be getting old when the professors look so young.'

'Why, thank you. My students keep me young, though many of them would say I should not accept compliments from a member of the privileged ruling class.'

'The privilege I cannot, nor will not, deny, but I rule nothing,' said Mr Campion with perfect good humour. 'I cannot deny that I have always fancied reigning over a few acres of scenic Ruritania, or being the governor of a Caribbean island, or even being the hereditary laird of a magical Scottish village which appears only once every hundred years, but I cannot imagine any government stupid enough to appoint me and certainly no electorate would ever vote for me. Please call me Albert, for I insist I must call you Yorick. I've never met a Yorick before, at least not one who looks so handsome and so . . . alive.'

Professor Thurible's pink, fleshy face became even more babyish as he smiled. 'Albert it is, then; although that's not your real name, is it? I've done my homework, you see.'

'So have I,' said Campion, returning the smile, 'and you are not at all what I expected.'

Everything Campion had learned about Yorick Thurible in a short but intense period of research comprising telephone calls to, and in one case, a very liquid lunch with, journalists who covered higher education for the national newspapers, had suggested a leather-jacket-and-jeans-wearing firebrand Marxist. Instead the professor had opted for a softer, far less threatening, almost dandified mode, with his dark blue velvet blazer, a purple shirt with a frilled frontage and matching satin cravat, light blue denim jeans with flares and black Chelsea boots with a good inch of heel. Had his hair been shoulder-length and luxurious, he might have passed as the modern equivalent of a seventeenth-century rake, but it was cut short and almost puritanical; far more Roundhead than Cavalier.

But Thurible seemed both good-humoured and charming, as far as Roundheads went.

'I trust I have lived down to your expectations, Albert, and that everything you have heard about me is scurrilous, disapproving and vituperative, in which case your sources are incredibly accurate.'

'I did read that you were once labelled "The Tottenham Court Road Marxist" by the popular press, though I dismissed that immediately,' said Campion.

'You did? That's jolly decent of you, old chap.' Thurible's voice was lightly laced with sarcasm. 'I suppose that eased your liberal conscience.'

'Not a question of conscience, liberal or otherwise, but of history. My grandmother, an eminent Victorian in her own right, always maintained that Karl Marx was the one and only Tottenham Court Road Marxist. It seemed he used to get plastered in the Pillars of Hercules on Greek Street and then stagger home via the Tottenham Court Road, smashing the street lamps as he went by throwing bricks at them. Clearly a dangerous revolutionary, dedicated to the overthrow of bourgeois street lighting.'

Professor Thurible gave an appreciative chuckle and fumbled in both pockets of his blazer until he found a pipe, which he made no attempt to light but which he waved to illustrate a point and then tapped the mouthpiece against his teeth like a metronome as if to keep time. 'Given who your grandmother must have been . . .'

'Or whom you assume to have been.'

'Assumption is the mainspring of academic thought, my dear chap, and far more interesting than hard logic or historical fact. All I was about to say was that, here at USC, I am the sworn enemy of street lighting, or rather the cause of anything which may go wrong. Sit-ins, student riots, bad publicity, plummeting moral standards, drug addiction, free love on campus: it's all my fault. Sociologists are to blame for everything.'

'I get the distinct impression that you are rather proud of your reputation as the professor of misrule.'

Thurible twisted his pipe to hold it like a pistol, the stem pointed at Campion's chest.

'I like that. You don't seem a bad sort, Campion, not at all stuck up, as some of my students would say.' He raised his pipe hand and tapped the stem against his right temple. 'Come to think of it, some of my students would love the chance to quiz you on a few things.'

'Oh, I doubt I could teach your students anything,' Campion said quickly, 'but I'm sure they could teach this old poodle a new trick or two.'

'I'm sure they could.' There was a twinkle in the professor's eye. 'I have a seminar group of second-years who are looking at the dynamics of class distinctions in the inter-war period. They would find it very useful if you had the time to sit in on a session and let them interview you; a living witness of a bygone age.'

'You make me sound like a fossil: "My life in the Jurassic period" sort of thing? Much as I would like to accommodate your students, my visit here ends after our pep-talk to the freshers tomorrow, and term proper doesn't start until Monday, I believe. In any case, I suspect your students would really only want to hear the details, as gruesome as possible, on the murder here at Black Dudley way back when.'

'To hell with my students,' grinned Thurible, 'if you've got gruesome details of the ritual, you must tell *us* – and make the details as X-rated as possible. As the only living witness we have, now that Meade's mother is gone, it's almost your duty to do so!'

Mr Campion shook his head gently. 'I may be the official ghost of Black Dudley, but I have – honestly – little of value to offer the enquiring minds of your students, either criminologically or sociologically. Forty years ago, some young people – yes, well-to-do and privileged, I admit – gathered for a weekend house party mainly with a view to impressing the opposite sex and entertaining the rather mysterious owner of the house, who turned out to be anything but the innocent, wheelchair-bound old man we assumed him to be.

'We gay young things participated in that ridiculous party game of a ritual which involved the lights going out and the circulation of an ornate dagger supposedly used in a murder around the year 1500. It was a cross between "Sardines" and "Pass the Parcel" but done in rather poor taste. An accident was bound to happen; in fact a murder took place. Any proper investigation was handicapped by the fact that the house was invaded by a platoon of gangsters and we party-goers, not to mention Gerontius Meade's mother, were in effect besieged.

'The cavalry rode to our rescue, quite literally, in the shape of the Monewdon Hunt. I suspect some of your students will be anti-fox-hunting types, but it really was they who saved the day. I returned to my life of privilege and leisure and the murder at Black Dudley eventually dropped out of the headlines.'

'And the murderer was never caught?'

'Not caught, as such, no; but my part in the affair was over long before the case was closed, if it ever was officially closed. So you see, I have not much of a story to tell.'

'What a pity,' said Thurible, wrinkling his nose. 'I was so hoping we might establish a tradition. Universities need traditions and new universities have to invent them. In fact, we are encouraged to do so.'

'You are? How? With a suggestion box?'

'The Bishop of St Edmondsbury issued an edict some time ago demanding that senior staff come up with traditions the university can be proud of. His own contribution was to provide Gerry Meade with a pony and trap.'

'A *what*?'

'A pony and trap, which he stables or garages, or whatever you call it, over in White Dudley. The bishop's idea was that important visitors to the campus – present company excepted – will be met off the London train at Darsham Halt by our head porter and driven here in stately progression, waving royally at the adoring peasantry labouring in the fields.'

'Good heavens,' Campion breathed, 'that's appalling.'

'Ostentatious, I agree,' said Thurible.

'No, appalling that I wasn't offered such a courtesy and had to drive myself here. It's a disgrace! I am the official university Visitor after all!' Campion lowered his voice to a conspiratorial level. 'By the way, do you have any idea what is expected of a Visitor?'

The professor stroked an imaginary beard, as if deep in thought, and his eyes twinkled with mischief.

'Based on the track record of our *first* Visitor, then one should have studied at Oxford, taught at a public school, joined both MI5 and MI6, then become a Labour MP and a junior minister, while all the time being a double agent selling secrets to those dastardly communists in Czechoslovakia. On being uncovered, the ideal Visitor would then plead that it was all the result of an unhappy childhood.'

Mr Campion shook his head in bemusement. 'Dear me, I hardly qualify at all. My childhood was extremely happy, and I like to think still continues. I have never stood for election to any office which would accept me as a representative, on the same basis that I would never join a club which would have me as a member. I think that it is a Marxist trait, but of the Groucho tendency rather than Karl. And to cap it all, I went to Cambridge which, as we all know, is blissfully free of scandals involving security matters.'

'How disappointing,' the professor said with a broad smile, 'but I think you will be just fine. A few choice words of welcome to the first-years is all that is required of you tomorrow, and you'll be among friends – or at least, not enemies. The vice chancellor will do the formal, dignified bit about how important higher education is; Gregor Marshall will tell them about their residences and how much rent he wants to screw out of them; Dr Woodford, without a trace of humour, will embarrass all the young males by telling the young females about sexually trans-mitted diseases and why they should think carefully before going on the pill; Jack Szmodics will bore them half to death about the importance of foreign languages, even though he has no students wanting to learn the languages he teaches; then our diminutive South American genius will jump up and down in an animated fashion trying desperately to get us all interested in rock formations. Even Big Gerry Meade gets to say his piece on campus safety. We call it his *Dixon of Dock Green* bit.'

'And what will your contribution be?'

'Me? Little old me? I will do what is expected of me, which is to corrupt young minds and morals, incite rebellion and demand social revolution.'

'But you cannot take the credit for that. Surely, some of it must be down to pop music and television.'

Professor Thurible turned his pipe stem on himself and jabbed the frilly frontage of his shirt.

'I agree, but as a sociologist I will take the blame, for I am the bad influence around here. If the ritual of the Black Dudley dagger was still going as a parlour game, then I'd be the one you'd find stabbed in the back when the lights came back on.'

FOUR

Pep-Talk in a Threepenny Bit

The welcoming lecture by the official university Visitor went rather well, even if Mr Campion said so himself, which he frequently did in the few days of peace which followed.

It took place in the twelve-sided building to the south of Piazza 1, which the architect had probably called The Dodecagon but normal humans, even the Bishop of St Edmundsbury, referred to as the 'Threepenny Bit'. Officially it was the lecture-theatre complex, which actually comprised six theatres of varying sizes, and greeting the new intake of students took place in the largest, the stage of which had been laid out with a semicircle of plastic chairs, so the ranked layers of fresh-faced first-years could get a good look at the speakers. They would have, Mr Campion thought, the same view as the plebs in the upper tiers of the Colosseum, but hopefully without the accompanying thirst for blood.

He worried unnecessarily, for the audience displayed no mob-like behaviour and did not bay or howl, but listened in polite, nervous silence to what wisdom the hierarchy of the university, with Dr Downes acting as MC, could offer, even accepting Gerontius Meade's homilies on why bicycles should be padlocked when not in use and left in the racks provided. Had the campus not been a pedestrianized area, Campion felt, Meade would have followed up with a demonstration of the new Green Cross Code.

After the doctor had done her 'sex bit', as she called it, and Gregor Marshall had pointed out, with a wolfish smile, that as most of the new intake would be paying rent for the first time, he had made their lives easier by charging by the term and in advance. Then came the three academics: Szmodics and Perez-Catalan emphasizing the thrilling opportunities on offer for learning and research in exciting new fields of study with the aid of state-of-the-art language laboratories and computers, and finally a clarion call from Thurible to 'question everything, always answer back and, now free from parental control, behave badly'.

Naturally, it was Thurible's exhortation which went down best with the youthful audience, and Mr Campion realized that he had a hard act to follow.

'You are all very intelligent,' he proclaimed, 'otherwise you would not be at university. You are also all very young and probably have excellent eyesight. Consequently, you will already have observed that I am very old. Not just older than you, but even more ancient than your distinguished professors who have allowed me to share a stage with them despite being totally unqualified to do so.

'They say that with great age comes great wisdom, although I am aware that I am currently disproving that theory. I do not claim to be wise, but I have experienced more of that strange thing called *life* than anyone else in this room; probably more than any three put together. That is, I'm afraid, the only thing I bring to this shiny new campus in my role as Visitor. It's a new role for me and I am still finding my feet, but from what I can gather I am expected to act as a sort of United Nations peacekeeping force in the unlikely event of any disputes between the student body and the university.

'Such disputes will be rare, hopefully unknown, and I will be gainfully unemployed. In the meantime, as I have the stage and your undivided attention, I will pass on one piece of wisdom.

'You have been urged to throw yourselves into your studies, and that you should certainly do, but also told' – and here Campion glanced pointedly at Professor Thurible, who responded with a very knowing smile – 'that you should question everything and protest at every opportunity. As the younger generation, that is absolutely your right and privilege and I would fight to the death – preferably someone else's death – to defend that right. But please be aware that the student next to you on the protest march today could be the chief of police of tomorrow.'

It was not an occasion where speeches were greeted with thunderous applause, or low-pitched boos, for the audience, most of whom were fresh from school, was too innocent and nervous at their first experience of university life. Still, Campion thought, the event had gone well; no one had cried, heckled or thrown things at him.

As the greeting party filed out of the lecture theatre through the flood of students who had already learned one valuable lesson – where the exit was – Professor Thurible came up behind him and spoke softly in Campion's ear.

'I knew I could rely on you to give the Establishment viewpoint. Don't rock the boat, let us spoon-feed you with what we think you should know and protesting can get you arrested.' He patted Campion lightly on the shoulder. 'But I don't hold it against you.'

'I am grateful for that,' said Mr Campion, 'but I was merely offering the advice any caring uncle would. In the absence of a brief from any higher authority, I have decided that the role of university Visitor should be that of the university's universal uncle.'

'But you don't like the idea of your nephews and nieces going on protest marches?'

'If the protests are peaceful and in a just cause, not at all, but you and I are well aware that there is a growing tendency to violence in student protests, and often it is violence initiated by a fanatical few. I certainly do not approve of that, nor of those who encourage such lawlessness but themselves sit back in safety and observe the chaos as if monitoring some sort of experiment.'

Thurible's voice was little more than a whisper. 'Do you mean a *sociological* experiment?'

'I am not equipped to answer such a question, Professor,' said Mr Campion, 'and I would have to refer you to an expert. Yourself, perhaps?'

From the entrance lobby of the lecture-theatre building, which reminded Campion of the foyer of a modern cinema minus the ability to purchase ice creams and tropical fruit drinks, paved footpaths pointed pedestrians to the right towards Piazza 1 or to the left to a concrete and glass, oval-shaped building. Dr Downes took Campion's arm and guided him towards the brightly lit oval, from which wafted the mingled scents of frying onions and boiled vegetables.

'You must come and see the Circus, Campion, though I don't expect you to eat there.'

'Circus?' said Campion, but then the penny dropped. 'Ah, of course, the elongated oval shape which mimics a Roman racecourse.'

'Yes,' said Downes with a sigh. 'Our architect had a bout of whimsy when he designed the non-teaching buildings, and they have all got nicknames. The Threepenny Bit for lectures, as you've seen; The Circus for the refectory and bar and shop complex; and, unfortunately, for our library, the shape reminds people of a toilet roll.'

As they walked past the top curve of the refectory, Campion nodded in the direction of the four unavoidably large concrete and glass pyramids which totally filled the eyeline.

'And this must be your Valley of the Kings,' he observed.

'Our beloved pyramids, for which we are more famous than we are for our teaching; but that, I hope, will soon change.' Dr Downes adopted the air of a weary public relations man who could not wait for the press conference to end. 'We had to give our students somewhere to live as there is simply not the accommodation available to rent in neighbouring towns. In fact, we have no neighbouring towns and all available houses, rooms, stables and garden sheds in White Dudley were snapped up by the staff, so our student residences have to be modern and fully furnished to attract students.'

Mr Campion adjusted his spectacles and looked up to the apex of the nearest pyramid. 'I believe they are – what is the phrase? – co-educational? Although our mutual friend the bishop tends to refer to them as "hives of sex" – a very unfortunate term, in my opinion.'

Dr Downes drew a deep breath in order to answer the question he had been asked, it seemed, a million times.

'The buildings are mixed-sex, but each floor is single-sex. There are twelve rooms on the ground floor, decreasing proportionally up to the sixth floor and then, at the apex, a single flat for the member of staff willing to take on the job as block warden. Each floor has its own very basic kitchen with a hotplate, a kettle and fridge, a bathroom and toilets, and is single sex, though there is a central staircase allowing easy access to all floors.'

Campion made a show of raising his eyebrows in pretend horror.

'At the moment, a majority of our applicants are female; around fifty-five per cent of them.'

'Once that news gets out,' said Campion, 'I suspect you will have far more applications from young men, but I am delighted at your statistics. My own university treated women abominably. I am glad the academic world has changed. Might I ask what attracts the young ladies?'

'I would like to think it is our approach to teaching languages, which will be invaluable should we ever get around to joining the Common Market,' answered Dr Downes.

'But not specifically Finnish or Hungarian?'

'I see you've been listening to gossip; Yorick Thurible, perhaps? It is true, those languages are not in the demand we had hoped for, but our language labs are state of the art and a major in French or German language, with a minor in French or German literature, is one of our most popular degrees among young women.'

'And sociology?' tempted Campion. 'Is that popular?'

'Yes, it is, and particularly so among a certain strata of teenage girls who have, shall we say, issues with their parents. Now, are you up to clambering up one of our pyramids? The view from the top is worth the climb.'

Mr Campion peered over the top of his round tortoiseshell glasses. 'I have admitted in public this very morning that I am old, but I have never so much as dropped a hint that I am infirm, so lead on, Vice Chancellor. Last one to the top of the pyramid gets to be mummified!'

Mr Campion stretched out his long legs and strode towards the entrance to the nearest pyramid, which resembled the gloomy opening to one of the older London Underground stations rather than a Regal or an ABC cinema. Campion half expected to find a newspaper vendor shouting "*Hee-vening Stanar*'" from the shadows.

Yet sprightly as he was out of the blocks, Mr Campion sensed a figure, a burly, grey-suited figure, at his shoulder, intent on overtaking him in the inside lane.

'I've asked Mr Meade to go on ahead and clear the way,' said Dr Downes, trying to keep pace.

'In case of booby traps?'

'I'm not expecting any, as only a few second- and third-years are back, just the ones helping out with Freshers' Week, although we might find a bicycle inconsiderately parked in the stairwell. Big Gerry will be clearing the way diplomatically – I hope. We don't like to drop in on students unannounced, and it might give them a few minutes' grace to make the kitchen presentable.'

Campion shot his cuff and checked his wristwatch. 'They'll be cooking their lunch?'

'Probably cleaning up from breakfast if I know students, but speaking of lunch, you are of course invited to join my wife and me in our quarters.'

'Thank you, but I must decline,' said Campion as they began to climb the neon-lit central staircase. 'I am already booked for a late lunch with my wife and her sister over at Monewdon. We're staying there with the Randalls for a long weekend. Catchin' up with the family; can't really get out of it.'

Two flights above them, a large grey figure loomed in front of the wall-mounted lights on the landing.

'Floor six is clear, Vice Chancellor – nobody home.'

'Thank you, Gerry,' said Downes, then to Campion he added, 'The freshers will be getting their library cards and signing up for seminars and tutorials today, which should keep them out of trouble until the bar opens this evening. The Students' Union are putting on a welcoming disco.'

'A welcome to the world of hangovers, I suspect.'

'For many of them, yes – first time away from home and parents.'

'They're young,' said Campion, 'their livers will survive. I am constantly amazed that mine did given the amount of beer I drank as an undergraduate.'

'I did my PhD in Spain,' said Downes with a smile, 'which involved an awful lot of Rioja.'

Gerontius Meade, standing to attention, interrupted their

Bacchanalian reminiscences by pulling open a door and holding it for them. Only a salute was missing.

'This is a standard kitchen, shared by everyone on this floor,' said the vice chancellor with pride, 'and, you have to admit, the views are spectacular.'

They were indeed. Through the large sliding windows of reinforced glass, Campion got a seagull's-eye view over the three interlinked piazzas and, beyond them, Black Dudley and the coastline and the deceptively calm North Sea off to the east.

'What is that, Vice Chancellor?' Campion asked. 'That little building on the shoreline. I noticed it yesterday when I arrived. I don't remember it.'

'That be St Jurmin's,' said Meade, while pacing the kitchen as if conducting an inventory of the fixtures and fittings.

'And what might a St Jurmin's be? Should I know?'

'It's a chapel,' Downes explained, 'named for Saint Jurmin, sometimes known as Hiurmine, of Blythburgh. He was of the Wuffingas, the royal family of East Anglia in Anglo-Saxon times, and the chapel is said to date from around AD 670, and to be built on the foundations of a Roman fort, though as far as I am aware there is absolutely no archaeological evidence for that.'

'Fascinating,' said Campion, 'something older than I am. Is it in use?'

'There's them in White Dudley who process up there every Palm Sunday for a service and for a midnight mass on Christmas Eve, with the local vicar officiating,' said Meade, 'and we keeps the grass cut and the roof on now it's in the university grounds.'

'Our friend the bishop,' Dr Downes said wearily, 'was keen on making St Jurmin's a chapel of contemplation for our students when he realized there were no plans for a chaplaincy, but nothing came of it, though I believe some students do visit it for . . .'

'Quiet contemplation?' Campion suggested.

'I hope so. Now, what else can we show you?'

'Well, I would love to challenge your computer to a game of chess, but I fear that may be a contest spread over several days and I have a lunch date, so I must take my leave of you. Perhaps on my next visit you could show me your language laboratories. I'd love to learn Albanian or, say, Swedish, in two easy lessons.'

'I'm not sure we can manage that,' said the vice chancellor, 'but you would be more than welcome to a tour.'

Campion moved closer to the window until he had his nose almost pressed against it.

'While we have the high ground, as it were, can I just make sure I have my bearings. Down there, nearest to us, is Piazza 3, which is where the students held their Freshers' Fair yesterday. Correct?'

In the reflection from the glass, he saw Dr Downes nod agreement.

'I noticed the fountain in the middle, which is a nice Italianate touch, apart from the fact that it no longer functions as a fountain; in fact it has been filled in and now holds less water than the average goldfish bowl.'

'Safety reasons,' growled Gerontius Meade from behind Campion's back. 'When it was a fountain it had a depth of about four feet and that proved just too tempting for some of our young gentlemen who couldn't hold their liquor on Saturday nights.'

'There was an incident, an accident,' said Downes hurriedly. 'A first-year found himself out of his depth, quite literally, and almost drowned. It was a drunken prank; his pals had dared him to dive in and he knocked himself out when he hit his head on the concrete.'

In the reflection from the glass, Meade pulled a face expressing his disgust.

'Lad was the son of an MP,' he snarled through curled lips, 'so naturally there was a stink and we had to fill the thing in. That's when the trouble started.'

'Started? How?' asked Campion.

'Once we poured concrete, we ended up with a fireplace, not a fountain, and that's exactly what the little bleeders used it for.'

'It was the time of the big Vietnam protests,' said Downes, 'and after one protest march, the students had the bright idea of burning all their banners in the old fountain. It started an unfortunate tradition. Every time the students wanted to make a point, they started a bonfire in what was effectively a firepit we had created for them, so we dug out a couple of inches of concrete and put some water back, to dampen the flames as it were.'

'It still seems to be a hot spot,' said Campion, stubbing a forefinger against the window. 'That's Professor Perez-Catalan down there, is it not?'

Below them, in the centre of the piazza, just to the left of the fountain/firepit, was the unmistakeable figure of the diminutive, bearded Chilean scientist in what, Campion assumed, was for him his natural stance of agitation. The thick curls of his head were thrown back and his arms rotating like windmill sails and, even at that distance, he was clearly engaged in a frenzied debate with a slim, tall, blonde woman dressed in a blue denim jacket and matching jeans.

'Those two again,' sighed Dr Downes, shaking his head. 'Still, at least they can argue in their own language and there is less collateral damage on innocent ears.'

'The blonde lady is Chilean?' Campion asked casually.

'No. Stephanie Silva, or Estephanie, to be precise, is a lecturer in Spanish and linguistics, and those two are always having rather heated arguments about academic priorities. I just wish they would have them in private.'

'I thought academic dispute was one of the cornerstones of a university education,' said Campion. 'Not that it was ever very high on the agenda at my *alma mater*.'

'They be fighting over that blasted computer again,' Meade contributed, now drawn closer to the window to get a better view.

'Computer? Are they teaching it Spanish?'

'Mr Meade means computer *time*,' explained Dr Downes. 'Our Computing Centre may be state of the art, but with so many demands on it . . . Access to the mainframe has to be rationed.'

'And some want a bigger ration than others,' said Gerontius in a tomb-side voice.

'And the striking Miss Silva down there,' Campion's forefinger thudded against the glass again, 'who seems to be getting more and more agitated by the second, needs the computer to teach students Spanish? What have you got down there? Some sort of electronic Tower of Babel?'

'Not to teach the language,' Downes said patiently, 'but for research into linguistics. Textual analysis by computer programme is the coming thing.'

'And it vies for computer time with the professor's plate tectonics? No, please do not try to explain any further, I am already out of my depth and was never a good swimmer in technical waters.'

'Jack Szmodics says the rows between them two were something to behold last year,' Meade continued in sepulchral tone. 'Almost came to blows, some say.'

'I think it just has,' said Campion calmly.

Down below in the piazza, the taller blonde woman suddenly drew her right arm back and swung the open palm of her hand against the bearded cheek of the smaller man, who appeared to be in mid-rant. The whole pantomime was conducted in silence to those watching from the sixth-floor kitchen, but when the blow connected, Perez-Catalan's head snapped to the side and he took an involuntary step backwards. It was clear, even from their elevated observation point, that the slap had at least stopped the professor talking. There would have been little point in him continuing as the woman immediately stalked off and disappeared into the throng of students and staff crossing the piazza, almost none of whom gave the altercation a second glance.

'Academic disputes can get a little heated sometimes,' said Downes weakly. 'Shall we make our way down to ground level?'

'Yes, I really must be making tracks,' said Campion.

To save the vice chancellor's blushes, Mr Campion did not remark further on the incident, though he was sorely tempted to say that, while his experience of academic fisticuffs was limited, when a woman slapped a man like that in public, there was far more to it than the distribution of computer time.

As the trio left the kitchen and began to descend the windowless stairwell, a door behind and above them opened and Campion caught the murmur of soft female voices.

'There's a stroke of luck, Campion,' said Downes, looking over his shoulder. 'You must meet Tabitha, one of our lecturers.

She has the flat at the top of the pyramid, so technically we are in her domain.'

Campion paused his descent of the stairs and, leaning back against the concrete wall, turned to see the outline of two female figures busy locking the door of the flat they had just left while whispering to each other. When they saw the three men several steps below them, they paused and, had the lighting been less harsh, Campion was sure he would have seen them blushing.

'Tabitha, come and meet the new university Visitor, Albert Campion,' Downes called.

'Yes, of course, Vice Chancellor,' the taller of the female shapes answered – somewhat nervously, Campion thought – as they descended.

'This is Tabitha King, one of our youngest and brightest lecturers,' said Downes, clearly with pride.

'A geologist if I'm not mistaken,' said Mr Campion, shaking her hand and noticing the strength of the woman's grip. Standing a step above him, she was as tall as Campion and faced him at unblinking eye level. Her dark brown hair had been cut short, almost military style, so that any grooming required could be done by splayed fingers.

'You are not, but how did you know?'

Campion picked up a trace of an accent; northern, possibly Lancashire, but an accent that had been deliberately diluted.

'The vice chancellor mentioned your name yesterday; in utterly glowing terms, I might add, as a shining light in earth sciences – or should that be a diamond? Plus, I have already met your loyal student, Bev.' Campion waved a hand to indicate the second female – smaller, younger, bespectacled and definitely blushing – to Dr Downes. 'And, Vice Chancellor, allow me to introduce one of your keenest first-years, Beverley Gunn-Lewis, all the way from New Zealand. Bev, this is Dr Downes – he's a good bloke and not hard *yakka* at all, as I think you'd say.'

The girl nodded, said a barely audible 'Hello', then looked towards her companion.

'Bev and I were going over her timetable and seminar choices,' said Tabitha King. 'Now I was going to show her the

Circus, where she is welcome to be appalled at the food on offer.'

It took Campion a moment to recall that the Circus was the refectory complex, which housed the canteen, pub and a coffee bar.

'I'm sure the food's not that bad. It can't be worse than the school dinners I had to suffer.'

'Try being a vegetarian,' said Tabitha grimly.

'You have my sympathies. Let us not delay you,' said Campion, indicating that the two females should precede them; as they squeezed by, he noticed that young Miss Gunn-Lewis refused to meet his eye, keeping her ornate spectacles firmly pointed downwards towards the lobby. When he spoke to her, it was to the back of her descending head.

'Settling in all right, are we, Beverley? Get your accommodation sorted out?'

'After a fashion,' the girl said without turning her head. 'I wanted to be here in Hutton, but that plan went down the gurgler 'cos I didn't get on the waiting list early enough. So they put me in Babbage.'

'Babbage is almost next door, my dear,' said Dr Downes sympathetically, 'and I'm afraid Hutton is our most popular residence.'

In Campion's ear, Mr Meade whispered, 'It's nearer the bar.'

They reached the lobby and the women quickened their pace and took the path to the right without a cheery wave, let alone a formal goodbye.

'I think I understood most of that, Vice Chancellor,' Campion mused. 'Hutton is the name of this pyramid block and presumably Babbage is the name of another one.'

'Quite correct. Allow me to show you the others, it won't take a minute and we can walk back to the car park via the library. Gerry will nip on ahead to get your bag from the house if you really need to get off.'

'Be a pleasure, sir,' intoned the head porter, as if it was anything but.

Dr Downes led the way along the path which linked the four pyramidal halls of residence, enjoying his role as a tour guide.

'Hutton you have seen, then comes Chomsky, Babbage and

finally Durkheim. Hutton is the most popular being, as Meade implied, closest to the refectory and Durkheim probably the least popular because it's nearest the library, though perhaps that's too cynical a view of the modern student.'

'Cynical, but accurate,' Campion said with a smile, 'but not limited to today's undergraduates. I was at the end of my second year before I realized there *was* a library, and it has clearly left my education wanting. Noam Chomsky I've heard of, though please don't test me on his theories of linguistics. Émile Durkheim was one of the founders of sociology and possibly French, I believe, but again, no questions please. Charles Babbage, I know, is said to have invented the computer, though I came across a couple of chaps in the war who could perhaps claim a share in that honour, though they weren't allowed to talk about it and neither should I. But Hutton is, I'm afraid, a new one on me.'

'James Hutton was an eighteenth-century Scotsman and is thought of as the father of geology.'

'Hence Beverley's interest – she's clearly dedicated to her subject. Remiss of me I know, but I never thought of geology as a popular subject among young ladies.'

Dr Downes paused, turned on his guest and screwed up his face in mock puzzlement. 'But isn't your wife, the Lady Amanda, quite a famous aeronautical engineer?'

'Yes, I'm afraid she is.'

'Surely that was an unusual career choice for a woman of her class?'

'Well, yes it was, but I'm immensely proud of her achievements and she has always had my undying support. I never really had a choice in the matter because I was – and still am – in love with her.'

Dr Downes coughed, as if with embarrassment. 'I have to admit that love – no, not love, infatuation – has something to do with female applications for courses in our Earth Sciences department, where we have a far higher proportion of girls than any other similar school in the country.'

'I'm afraid I don't follow,' said Campion, 'unless you mean that Professor Perez-Catalan is some sort of heart-throb or sex symbol.'

'That's exactly what I do mean,' said the vice chancellor. 'The man is a magnet for the opposite sex.'

'Really?' Campion could not keep the surprise out of his voice.

'I know,' said Downes with something of a cross between admiration and resignation, 'you wouldn't think it to look at him, would you? Yet he has an amazing success rate with the ladies. Short, hairy, and can't string three words together without flapping his arms around like a demented windmill, plus he has absolutely no morals.'

'Perhaps that's the key.'

'I really wouldn't know. Even my wife says he has an air of dynamism,' said Downes with a nervous laugh, 'which makes him attractive, plus a radical bent, always saying that science should be "for the people", whatever that means. He also has, I am led to believe, quite a success rate with the ladies, and seems to have no compunction about stringing one, or even two, along while stepping out with a third. Of course, we discourage liaisons with undergraduates, but one never knows . . .'

Mr Campion regretted – briefly – that Big Gerry Meade had left them, for he was sure the head porter would have had an opinion on the matter, if not certain juicy details. He dismissed the thought, reasoning that details of such thing, however juicy, were beyond the remit of a university Visitor and it would be indelicate to pursue the subject further, so he changed it.

'Your architect has a fondness for basic shapes,' he said airily. 'From the air the campus must look like one of those baby's shape-sorter toys, where they have cylinders and squares and triangles and polygons, and a frame with the appropriately shaped hole through which to push them. Sometimes you get a little wooden hammer with the set, so the child can bash them if they don't fit. Keeps a toddler happy for hours, though it can get noisy for the parents.'

'I never thought of the campus that way before,' Downes replied, 'though one right-wing newspaper did call the university "Dr Downes's Playground" because we offer modern rather than traditional courses.'

'Yes, I read that piece in *The Times*,' said Campion. 'The bishop sent me a cutting.'

The vice chancellor's shoulders sank, as if under the bishop's weight.

'He sent me one too. The consensus, however, was that a modern university should have modern architecture. There was absolutely no point in trying to mimic Oxbridge colleges or Ivy League universities, plus, with other new universities setting up, we had to be distinctive. I think our pyramids – four for now but others are planned as we grow – are certainly distinctive.'

'That they are,' Campion agreed, 'and their shape and proximity to each other make them an ideal amplifier.'

'I beg your pardon?'

'Just a theory, but if one had a trumpet or perhaps a cornet, and played it out of a window at a certain height, the sound would bounce off the neighbouring pyramid and carry all over the campus, even as far as Black Dudley.'

'Oh dear, you suffered from our Phantom Trumpeter. Did he wake you?'

'Midnight, on the dot. Got to give him marks for punctuality, and he had quite a nice tone, though I hope his repertoire extends beyond the "Last Post". However well executed, it's far too sad and funereal for young students who should have no reason to be sad.'

'You're not suggesting he takes requests, are you, Campion? The chap's a damn nuisance, but you're right about the acoustics. Mr Meade and his porters tried to pin the little hooligan down all last term but failed to locate him.'

'If you really want to catch him,' grinned Campion, 'then I'd look for someone who has a room on the third floor of one of the pyramids, almost certainly a male, is a third-year – he's established enough to have flyers printed – and is likely to be connected to the student Jazz Club.'

Dr Downes blinked twice before responding, 'I'll pass that on to the porters.'

'Oh, I wouldn't be too hasty, Vice Chancellor; it could be the start of a university tradition, and you know how keen the bishop is on those. Also, our Phantom Trumpeter is fairly harmless. It's only old goats like myself who need their beauty sleep and are tucked up in bed before midnight. Young people are far more nocturnal.'

'It's decent of you to take it like that; I'll overlook it this time. Now let me walk you to your car. At least with your family at Monewdon, you'll get a good night's sleep.'

And Mr Campion did. In fact, he had three consecutive nights of undisturbed slumber but, very early on the Monday morning, he was woken by the ringing of a telephone somewhere in the depths of Monewdon Hall, Guffy Randall's home and the hub of his farming empire.

Fumbling for his watch and spectacles, he consulted the luminous dial and discovered it was 4.45 a.m. At least it wasn't midnight, and the ringing telephone was nowhere near as dramatic as the 'Last Post' bugle call. The ringing, which had now stopped, had not disturbed his wife, who slept on serenely beside him, and so Mr Campion settled down to try and remember where he had been in the rather exciting dream – where he was sure he had cut an heroic figure – that had been interrupted.

He was dozing off satisfactorily when there was a gentle knocking on the bedroom door and then the door creaked open.

Campion reached for his glasses again and saw a dressing-gowned Guffy Randall shuffle into the room.

'Albert!' hissed his old friend. 'Sorry to disturb, old chap, but believe it or not that was the Bishop of St Edmondsbury on the blower and he was in one heck of a state. It's about the university. There appears to have been a bit of a murder.'

FIVE

The Body in the Lake

'What on earth makes you think you have to get involved?' scolded Lady Amanda.

Until breakfast that Monday morning, the weekend had gone splendidly to plan. Campion had driven the ten or so miles from the university to Guffy and Mary Randall's farm at Monewdon, where his wife was waiting, listening patiently to a lecture by her sister on the best ways of raising good crackling on a joint of pork. After an excellent lunch and the forced march across fields with several Labradors in attendance needed to walk it off, the Campions had just enough time to recover before the Randalls hosted a small cocktail party in their honour which involved meeting virtually the entire membership of the Monewdon Hunt and talking about horses, hounds, pigs and pork. The Saturday had offered the chance to fish in a pond on Guffy's land which he had stocked with carp and tench, though both Mr Campion and Mr Randall were comprehensively outwitted, and they returned to Monewdon Hall empty-handed to settle for a hot dinner of pig's liver, onions and mashed potato and large whiskies. Sunday morning meant morning service at St Mary's in the village, which Mr Campion realized – through a brief conversation with the incumbent vicar – had put him back in the See of the bishop of St Edmondsbury. He was not quite sure how he felt about that.

'There is no reason at all why I should, other than the bishop thinking I should,' said Campion, concentrating on the clearly compulsory thick slice of Suffolk ham and two fried eggs which had been placed before him. 'But then he probably wasn't thinking straight at that time in the morning.'

Guffy Randall, sitting at the head of the kitchen table, was already one egg and half a slice ahead of his oldest friend. He

spoke between mouthfuls: 'It was a bit of a rum do, him calling
so early.'

'Before the cock crowed twice, as it were,' suggested
Campion, 'or is that heresy? Perhaps he was just being the early
bird wanting to catch the worm – that would be me – while
the worm was still in Suffolk.'

'Who told the old goat you were staying with us?' asked
Mary Randall, circulating with a teapot and milk jug.

'Somebody at the university,' said Guffy, chewing heartily.

'I wonder who?'

'No idea, Albert. Cut me some slack, old boy. It was the
middle of the night, or just about, and I didn't think to ask too
many questions. When the bishop rings you out of the blue like
that – and it was him, I recognized his voice from a dozen
boring sermons – well, you stand to attention and do what he
tells you.'

'Which was to volunteer my services, it seems,' said Campion,
deftly buttering a slice of toast.

'Didn't get much of a choice. "Tell Campion it's happening
again and make sure we don't have another scandal on our
hands" was what he said, and it sounded like an order, not a
request.'

'I can imagine it did, but he didn't let on *who* had been
murdered, or where or when?'

'No, he didn't, and I didn't think it my place to ask. Might
have come across as being nosey.'

Mr Campion beamed affection across the table. 'Good old
Guffy, you keep clear of this mess, until you have to gather the
hunt and ride to my rescue as you did forty years ago.'

Guffy's ruddy face glowed even brighter at the memory, but
the rekindled fires of youth were instantly damped by his long-
suffering wife.

'Augustus! You haven't been on a horse for ten years on
doctor's orders and you haven't ridden with the hunt for twenty
on mine. You are too old and too . . . too . . . *sedentary* to go
gallivanting after Albert on one of his adventures.'

'No one has said anything about an adventure, Mary,'
Campion chided his sister-in-law. 'I hold the position of
university Visitor, which is in the gift of the bishop, who

appears to think that a visit is required. I cannot refuse, but I have no intention of doing anything other than making soothing noises, offering platitudes and letting the police get on with their job.'

'You make sure that's all you do,' said Lady Amanda, in a voice which brooked no argument.

'Darling, the only function I will be performing is to make mugs of tea for the boys in blue, who will surely have the situation under control by now. I am sure I cannot be of any other possible use as I'd never seen the place until Thursday, or not since that previous reincarnation forty years ago, and I don't even know who's supposed to have been murdered.'

'Neither did the bishop,' said Guffy, 'not that he was making much sense at that time of the morning. Said he'd been telephoned and told that a senior member of staff had been found murdered and the police had been called. He felt – he was quite insistent – that as Albert was still in the county, he should get back over there and act as the bishop's eyes and ears at the scene of the crime.'

'Could it be a student prank or a rag-week stunt?' Amanda suggested suddenly.

'The murder, the phone call to the bishop, or both? I doubt it. Term only starts in earnest today. The second- and third-years will only have come back over the weekend and will have had little time to organize anything for rag week; not that it sounds like an amusing fundraising scheme. It could be a prank phone call, I suppose, but it's in very poor taste.'

Mary Randall began to gather up plates and cups. 'Well, I for one don't believe it,' she said primly. 'I mean, who would want to murder a university academic?'

Mr Campion allowed himself a reflective smile. 'My own Sancho Panza, dear old Lugg, would have something to say about that.'

'Lugg?' exclaimed Amanda. 'What in the name of sweet reason could he have to contribute?'

'Given his innate distrust of higher education and all things academic, if you asked him who would want to murder a university academic, he would simply say: "Form a queue".'

* * *

Mr Campion drove himself back to the university, Lady Amanda having given him an ultimatum: if he was not back in Monewdon by two p.m., then her sister would drive her to Darsham Halt where she could get a train back to London and he would have to fend for himself. She tactfully reminded him that while he might be considered to be retired, she was not, and she had a board meeting to attend in the City the next morning, plus they both had tickets to previews of *Lie Down I Think I Love You*, the new West End musical at The Strand which featured their thespian son Rupert and his wife Perdita, appearing on the same stage together, albeit in very minor parts.

Campion naturally felt guilty about disrupting his wife's plans, but less so about the possibility of missing *Lie Down I Think I Love You*, which he had heard was an English version of the notorious show *Hair* and involved sex, drugs, nudity and a bomb at the BBC. While the latter plot point sounded quite interesting, Campion felt that, at his age, he could manage without the other ingredients.

He arrived at the campus to discover very little different, at least at first sight, even managing to park the Jaguar in almost exactly the same spot as five days previously. True, there were more cars in the car park now term was officially under way and, true, three of them were marked police cars.

It was only as he walked from the car park towards the piazzas, over grass which still had dew on it, that Campion noticed something rather incongruous. By the artificial lake between the concrete campus and Black Dudley, near the curved wooden bridge, had been erected a circle of brown and yellow striped material concocted from two beach windbreaks, the sort which could be hired for sixpence a day by families willing to suffer a British seaside summer holiday. Campion knew instantly what the windbreaks must be concealing, but could not resist wondering whether they had 'Property of Great Yarmouth Town Council' printed somewhere on the material.

The windbreaks may have been incongruous, situated well away from seashore or beach, but then so too were the pair of uniformed policemen standing guard over the gently flapping material. No doubt stranger things had graced modern university campuses, but here Campion observed a complete lack of interest on the part of the student body. Through the long line of windows bordering Piazza 3, he caught glimpses of figures moving in offices, seminar rooms and laboratories, proving that the university was in business and open for the pursuit of learning and the advancement of young minds even if, that early in the day, student minds tended to be rather sluggish.

As he approached the lake, Campion rehearsed what he would say to the brace of constables, who would surely challenge him once he got too close to whatever it was the windbreaks were hiding. He decided that 'I'm here at the request of the bishop' would make him sound like a minor character in a bad play in provincial rep; 'I am the Visitor and I am just visiting' sounded inane and assumed that the Suffolk constabulary knew what the role of a university Visitor was when he himself did not; and that old standby, 'Hello, hello, what's goin' on 'ere?' would earn him a well-deserved rap across the knuckles with a truncheon.

He was saved from any direct confrontation with the forces of law and order by a shout – 'Campion! What are you doing back here?' – from the doorway of Black Dudley, and he swerved smartly and strode towards the house.

Campion removed his fedora and held it to his chest, a standard mark of respect when bad news is about to be shared; but it wasn't quite the bad news Campion was expecting as he greeted Dr Downes.

'You sent for me, Vice Chancellor.'

'I most certainly did not!'

'Well, technically it was our mutual friend the bishop, who was on the telephone before dawn in quite a state. I presumed it was you who told him where to find me.'

'I have not spoken to the bishop for several weeks, and I certainly did not pass on your whereabouts to anyone. To be perfectly blunt, I have not given you a single thought since you left on Friday.'

'In a bizarre way, Vice Chancellor, I take that as a compliment. Sadly, I was clearly in the bishop's thoughts in the watches of the night. He is under the misguided impression that I may be of some use in your hour of need. I take it this is an hour of need?'

'You could say that, and it would be the understatement of the year, but I'm still not sure how the bishop knew anything about our . . . unless the police . . . but why should they?' Dr Downes took a deep breath. 'Look, Campion, I'm sorry you're involved, but I am rather glad you are here, and you may be able to help out, even if it is only to keep the bishop off my back.'

'That seems a noble cause,' said Mr Campion, 'but the last thing I want to do is interfere with a police investigation. I'm assuming we are in the middle of a police investigation?'

'Indeed we are. A murder enquiry, and I don't think you have much choice about being involved.'

'Really, why ever not? I don't even know who's been murdered.'

'The detective in charge of the case saw you walking down from the car park and muttered something about "Not him again", and demanded that you report to him immediately. He's taken over my office as his headquarters.'

'Does our Suffolk Sherlock have a name?'

'Detective Superintendent Appleyard, of Ipswich CID.'

'Oh, dear,' said Mr Campion, following the vice chancellor into Black Dudley.

When Superintendent Appleyard had identified the tall, thin figure walking from the car park and seemingly on a collision course with the lake and its wooden bridge – which was now an official scene of a crime – he did so with an oath and the dismissive description: 'He's no more than a fribble!'

Gerontius Meade, who as head porter automatically assumed that the senior investigating officer would require him at his shoulder at all times, was one of the few people in Black Dudley that morning familiar with the word 'fribble' to describe a nonentity or unimportant person. This was sufficient justification, he felt, for offering advice even though it had not been asked for.

'He was here the first time, sir,' he said to the policeman, 'at Black Dudley, when there was that other murder before the war. Name's Campion, and now he's the university's Visitor. It's an honorary post, I'm told.'

The policeman snorted and turned on his enthusiastic assistant. 'I know who he is; I've read the file. Used to go by the name of Mornington Dodd. Ridiculous fellow.' Having vented his spleen, Appleyard relented somewhat and tossed his faithful hound a bone. 'Not that Campion's his real name either, though it was when he crossed my path and that was more than once. Only a couple of years ago he got in the way of some enquiries I was making down at Gapton. Turns out he has friends in high places, so high even a detective superintendent needs an oxygen mask. He's a meddler by both trade and inclination, a born interferer, a nosey parker who always likes to put his thumb on the scale, and we don't need his sort here muddying the waters.'

As if on cue, Mr Campion was shown into the vice chancellor's office by the vice chancellor, whose desk had been commandeered by the senior policeman while a uniformed, very junior one perched on a chair nearby, notebook resting on a blue serge knee, pencil poised. Behind Appleyard's left shoulder, Gerry Meade stood to attention, his arms clasped behind his back and a fourth man also wearing a grey porter's uniform occupied another chair and attempted to stop the cup and saucer he was holding from rattling in his nervous grip.

'So, it's Campion, isn't it?'

'Good morning, Superintendent, I do hope I am not intruding.'

'I'm sure you will.'

Appleyard was a large man with a featureless face, apart from thick, slug-like black eyebrows. Sitting down with his shoulders hunched and his elbows skewering the surface of the vice chancellor's desk, he made no move to stand when Campion entered, but gave the impression that he could, animal-like, spring over the desk in a blur. It was a pose he had practised and one designed to frighten criminals and children alike, especially when he smiled.

'I am here merely as an observer, Mr Appleyard. Not through idle curiosity or a ghoulish taste for murder, but because I was requested to act in that capacity by the Bishop of St Edmondsbury, one of the guiding lights behind this fine university and its self-appointed moral guardian.'

Campion noted the strangled cough which convulsed Dr

Downes. 'If you wish to confirm my credentials, I am sure the university switchboard knows the bishop's number by heart.'

'There'll be no need for that,' said the policeman in a tone which suggested that he had crossed swords with the bishop before. 'Just make sure you keep out of my way.'

Appleyard's caterpillar eyebrows crawled into a chevron shape on his forehead, a sure sign that a thought had just occurred to him.

'But for form's sake, I would have to officially eliminate you from our enquiries before I let you stay on the premises,' he said with relish.

'I expect no preferential treatment, so eliminate away,' Campion replied. 'I take it you have questions for me?'

'I do.' Appleyard raised a finger; the signal for his constable to begin taking notes. 'Where were you around midnight?'

'Safely tucked up in a comfortable bed with my wife, at Monewdon Hall about ten miles away, where I have been since Friday afternoon. At the hall, of course, not in bed.'

'Did you know the deceased?'

'My dear Mr Appleyard, I don't even know who the deceased is, so how do I know if I know him? Or her. Who is supposed to have been murdered?'

'The most unpopular man on campus,' said Gerry Meade unbidden, which drew a severe glance from Appleyard and another choking cough from Downes.

'Professor Thurible?' Campion hoped he had put the right amount of surprise in his voice, but in Appleyard's reply the surprise was genuine.

'Who's he? The chap fished out of the lake is a foreigner, Professor Perez-something-or-other. A South American gent by all accounts, which means we could have a diplomatic incident on our hands.'

Mr Campion removed his spectacles and with practised sleight of hand produced a clean white handkerchief to polish the lenses with slow, circular motions.

'That is terribly sad news,' he said. 'Are we sure it is Perez-Catalan?'

'Formally identified by the vice chancellor here at—'

'Oh-six-fifteen hours, sir,' supplied the constable, consulting his notebook.

'And we are sure it was murder? He didn't fall in the lake and drown perhaps?'

'*We* are certainly sure, Mr Campion. Given the amount of blood on that fancy wooden bridge out there, he was dead when he went into the water.'

'Any ideas on a murder weapon?'

'Oh yes, it was a knife. He was stabbed in the back. That's how they do things at Black Dudley, isn't it?'

At eleven o'clock, the vice chancellor's wife and several of the university's senior secretaries produced coffee and biscuits for the growing number of people gathered, some willing and curious, others nervous and sullen, in Black Dudley. The reason they were there – the body taken from the artificial lake – had been quietly removed by two policemen who had covered it with blankets and carried it on a stretcher to an ambulance waiting in the car park. The professor's final exit from the university was watched, no doubt, by dozens of pairs of eyes from behind windows in the library, the Administration block and the pyramids beyond, but the scene of the crime was clearly regarded as a quarantine zone. The two uniformed constables, now guarding a pair of redundant windbreaks, remained on duty to deter the inquisitive, while a police photographer took photographs and a forensic science officer scraped shavings from the wooden bridge into a series of envelopes and filled a flask with water from the lake.

In effect the university was cut in two, those isolated in Black Dudley living under a police regime, while in the academic buildings the teaching timetable was being adhered to, at least as far as the vice chancellor could tell from the frequent reports he received from departmental secretaries on the internal telephone system.

Superintendent Appleyard demanded to interview anyone who had contact with the late Professor Perez-Catalan, and Meade's faithful porters were sent scurrying to fetch them, escorting them back to the house via the library and the car park rather than the direct approach over the off-limits bridge across the lake.

As staff arrived in an irregular procession, once their official interrogations were over, Campion tempted them into the committee room that had once been the Great Hall with the lure of coffee and biscuits and the promise of an opportunity, free of policemen, to exchange gossip to which Campion hoped to act like a charming magnet.

If Appleyard had turned the vice chancellor's office into a police incident room, Mr Campion preferred to think of the Great Hall as a *salon* which offered refreshment and wide-ranging discussion, hopefully indiscreet.

Very quickly he began to learn things.

The porter who had been sitting nervously in Appleyard's presence was called Bill Warren and he had the unwanted distinction of being the person who had found the body. He did not revel in that distinction and, given that he was of an age where a pension was rushing over the horizon to embrace him, Bill Warren would have much preferred a quiet life.

He was a Suffolk man; a White Dudley man, and had got the job at the university thanks to his old darts-playing partner Gerry Meade, and a character reference from the formidable Daisey May Meade, God rest her soul. Being one of the older members of the portering staff, and having done a fair bit of both gamekeeping and poaching in his time (a big conspiratorial wink to Campion here), Warren had been happy to take on more than his fair share of the night-duty roster. In practice that meant a couple of tours of the campus making sure that doors which should be locked were locked; that fire escapes could be escaped from (and that there were no obvious fires anywhere); that there were no drunken students wandering loosely around the place (not that they could fall in the fountain any more – those were the good old days); and that young tearaways from White Dudley (and there were a few of those) had not attempted to steal a car from the car park and go joy-riding.

Warren had been on patrol in Piazza 3 at midnight, torch in one hand and walkie-talkie in the other. (Connected to whom? Campion wondered.) He knew it was midnight because there was that blasted Phantom Trumpeter belting out the 'Last Post' and given that Mr Meade had offered a gallon of cider down at The Plough in White Dudley for anyone who could catch the little beggar red-handed, he headed for the pyramid residences from where the bell-like notes had echoed out. But yet again, the Scarlet Pimpernel of the B-flat trumpet (or perhaps cornet) had escaped the authorities.

With no other emergency requiring his immediate attention, Bill Warren meandered around the refectory Circus to make sure no after-hours drinking was going on (it wasn't) and then the Threepenny Bit lecture-theatre complex, which was an important stop on the regular round during term time as students attending the last lectures of the day had been known to nod off and get locked in. From there, Bill Warren's route took him across Piazza 1, which involved a quick count of the oversize chess pieces on the outdoor chessboard, popular targets for kidnapping and ransom during rag weeks. All pieces being present and correct, he took the footpath, illuminated by yellow sodium lights set into the edging bricks every ten yards, towards Black Dudley, where the porters' lodge – a small anteroom off the entrance hall – was fully equipped with the necessities of life: to whit, a kettle and a goodly stock of tea bags and sugar.

His mind had nothing more on it than the prospect of a cheering brew as he crossed the curved wooden bridge over what the student newspaper called 'the fake lake' until he felt his feet sliding from under him. Startled, he grabbed at the handrail to his left and instantly recoiled as his palm made contact with something wet and sticky instead of solid wood.

Recovering his footing and employing his torch, Bill Warren's hitherto untrammelled mind confirmed that he was standing in, and touching, blood, and small traverse of the beam over the rail showed, in the still water below, the source.

'I know now I shouldn't have touched the body,' he told Campion, 'and Mr Appleyard gave me considerable grief for having done so, but it was just instinct. During the war I was an ambulance man in London during the Blitz, the second one in '44 when we had the doodlebugs. You saw fresh blood and a body, and you went to help, to see if they were still alive. So I didn't think twice. Didn't think at all really, just splashed into the water and pulled him to the bank. It's not deep at the edges, but I'll be putting in for a new pair of shoes.'

Conscious that Bill Warren, as the finder of the body, had been continuously interviewed by professionals since before dawn, Campion had no wish to keep him from a long-delayed breakfast or add to the shock he had suffered, so he asked only a few questions and as gently as he could.

'He was dead when you got him out of the water?'

'As a doornail. I knew straight off there was nothing I could do for him, so I ran up to the Dudley and got on the phone to Mr Meade.'

'You rang Big Gerry first, before anyone else?'

'Them's standing orders,' Warren said, surprised at the question. 'Gerry told me to ring the vice chancellor on the internal line and *he* told me to dial 999.'

'Could you tell it was Professor Perez-Catalan?'

'Oh yes, straight away. We've had run-ins with him before.' Campion chose to let that one go – for the moment. 'It was the vice chancellor who did the formal identification for the police, but I knew who it was right enough, and so did Doc Woodford when she arrived.'

'Dr Woodford was on the scene?'

'She turned up before the police did. I remembered we had those windbreaks in the lost property cupboard – some students had nicked them for a laugh last summer after a trip to Yarmouth beach – and figured they would keep prying eyes away. Miss Woodford just appeared coming over the bridge. Gave me a bit of start, to be honest. I just reckoned the vice chancellor had called her, her being our medical officer.'

'She responded pretty quickly, didn't she?'

Warren had shrugged his shoulders. 'Didn't have far to come, did she? She lives in one of the pyramids – Chomsky, I think, or one of them other daft names.'

'And how did Dr Woodford react?'

'React? Well she was shaken up, that's for sure. Actually shaking she was, like she'd seen a ghost, which in a way she had. Still, she didn't get hysterical or anything. She's a doctor, after all, and must be used to bodies. Did a quick examination, felt for a pulse under his chin and said he was a goner, though I could have told her that. In fact, I did.'

'Could you see how he died?' Campion asked quietly.

'Have to be blind not to see that bloody great carving knife sticking out of the back of his neck,' said Bill Warren ruefully.

As Dr Woodford had given her statement to the police earlier and did not seem inclined to gossip, she had been allowed to return to her surgery in the Administration block, where several hundred new students would be waiting to register with her service. There were, however, plenty of other members of the university's staff who were willing to offer information, or at least an opinion, to anyone who would listen.

Estates Officer Gregor Marshall had adopted the air of a harassed businessman irritated by the last-minute cancellation of one meeting but anxious to move on to the next.

'Everyone on campus had a good reason to kill him,' he told a surprised Campion who had not asked a question, 'apart from his students, that is. They seemed to adore him, God knows why.'

'I thought the professor was a shining star, perhaps *the* shining star in the university firmament; a brilliant scientist in a ground-breaking new field.'

'Well, he certainly thought so, and never did he miss an opportunity to tell all and sundry that he was.'

'And that put some of his colleagues' noses out of joint, did it?' Campion probed.

'You bet it did, but then they're all *prima donnas* if you ask me. He has papers in all the scientific journals, wins prizes and gets on the telly whenever there's an earthquake or a volcano anywhere that requires a resident expert. Students queue up to get into earth sciences, from all over the world as well. Do you know how important foreign student fees are to the university?'

'So academic jealousy is a possible motive then?'

'Not directly, at least not within his field. The other disciplines just have to be more outrageous to get the same amount of recognition. Like Thurible, the charming middle-class face of revolution, who goes to posh parties where they drink fine wines and gossip about their *au pair* girls. Next thing they know, Thurible has written a sarcastic article in the lefty press lambasting them for being *petty bourgeoisie* and not sending

their kids to comprehensive schools. And he'd give his eye teeth
to be a television expert like Catalan; on any subject, it wouldn't
matter to Yorick as long as it was controversial.'

'That sounds like a clash of egos, which is part and parcel
of the academic life. It is, though, in my humble opinion, rarely
a motive for murder,' said Campion, feigning disinterest.
'Academics tend to be quiet, reflective beasts who chew things
over carefully before resorting to violence; rather like cows, I
suppose.'

Gregor Marshall snorted in surprise. 'You wouldn't say that
if you were caught in a stampede!'

'Probably not,' Campion conceded, 'but university professors
rarely stampede.'

'They do if they want to get computing time,' said Marshall,
clearly convinced he was stating the obvious.

'I'm sorry, I don't understand what computers have to do
with anything.'

'They have everything to do with why just about every
academic outside of the Earth Sciences department, and maybe
one or two in there, had it in for Perez-Catalan. Didn't he tell
you what his pet subject was?'

'Plate tectonics and something about an algorithm, though I
can't pretend I understood much of it, except that by studying
seismographic readings he can somehow predict where there
are deposits of heavy metals in the Andes.'

'Yes, that's about it, and all we mere mortals need to know
is that it's big stuff in scientific terms and the professor came
here because of our brand-spanking-new Computing Centre,
which he treats as his personal property. His research project
takes up eighty per cent of our computing capacity, leaving
very little for all the other departments to fight over, and that
causes resentment. You should have heard Jack Szmodics
arguing with him about it last term, how important work in
linguistic analysis – whatever that is – was being held back due
to lack of computer time.'

'Just because the late professor was not diplomatic in dealing
with his colleagues doesn't mean he made enemies, though,'
Campion argued but with little conviction.

'Ask Roger Downes about that!' Marshall was as indignant

as a Mothers' Union secretary being told by the local vicar that her jam was substandard. 'The vice chancellor has had his hands full since that little beggar arrived. Not just the squabbles between the academics and the political pressures, but also the scandals involving some of the campus wives.'

Marshall leaned in and lowered his voice. 'He fancied himself with the ladies, you know. Had some success by all accounts.'

Mr Campion tactfully refused to pursue this saucy morsel. 'You mentioned political pressures. Where did they come from?'

'Our government, his government back in Chile, plus every other South American country with the Andes in their back yard, not to mention the proper Americans who regard South America as *their* back yard. That algorithm he's working on is hot stuff in some circles. His death could be a diplomatic incident unless things get sorted out quickly.'

'I should have been more aware,' said Campion, 'or paid more attention, but I'm afraid I have an off switch when it comes to things mathematical. It seems there are quite a few people with an interest in the life of our professor, not to mention at least one with an interest in his death.'

'Like I said, he had a lot of enemies.'

'Well you certainly implied that.' Campion looked over the rims of his glasses. 'How about the Estates Office, Mr Marshall? Did Perez-Catalan rub you up the wrong way?'

'No more than any of the other whining academics around here, always wanting more resources because their work is more important than the chap's in the next office. And then they notice that the office next door is bigger than theirs, so that goes on their shopping list, along with a reserved parking place, direct phone lines, tape recorders, slide projectors, electric typewriters – the list is endless. They cause me more trouble than the students. At least they go home at the end of a term.'

'And the porters?'

'What about the porters?'

'They are under your command, part of your empire, are they not?'

'I wouldn't put it like that, but yes, the portering service is part of my responsibility. Do you have a problem with them?'

'Personally, not at all.' Campion smiled his most innocent smile. 'It's just that earlier, in front of the police, Gerontius Meade offered the opinion – an unrequested opinion – that Professor Perez-Catalan was the most unpopular person on campus. I wondered what the professor had done to upset such a fine body of men.'

Once more Marshall leaned his head in towards Campion's face as if imparting a state secret.

'We had a sit-in here last year,' he said in hushed tones.

'I know,' Campion whispered back. 'I read about it in the papers. It even made the *Hampstead and Highgate Express*.'

'It made *everywhere*,' Marshall said through gritted teeth. 'The professor saw to that, claiming that the occupation of the Earth Sciences department was disrupting valuable scientific research which was vital to the third world.'

'The bad public relations I understand, but why did Gerry Meade seem to take it so personally?'

'The students were objecting to price increases in the bar . . .'

'Which you authorized.'

'I most certainly did. With inflation running at nine per cent, I have to balance the books. The academics don't care about such things and the students just want cheap beer. Anyway, we all knew when and where the sit-in was coming, and we could have – should have – prevented it, even though Professor Thurible and his acolytes would have claimed that we were reactionary fascists crushing free speech. Gerry Meade decided that complete absence was the best way to avoid confrontation, and called a union meeting down at The Plough in White Dudley at exactly the time the Students' Union just walked in and started their siege of Piazza 3. Took us eight days and an injunction to get them out.'

'And Perez-Catalan took this badly?'

'You bet he did; he was furious with the university for allowing his vital research to be interrupted, and afterwards he demanded that Gerry Meade be disciplined for abandoning his duties. Called him a coward to his face and lobbied the vice chancellor for him to be fired. He would have put old Gerry up against a wall and taken charge of the firing squad himself if he could.' Marshall showed a mouthful of wolfish teeth as he grinned at the thought. 'That's the way they do it in South American universities, isn't it?'

'I really wouldn't know,' said Campion airily. 'We never used firing squads at Cambridge, but for Oxford I cannot speak.'

SIX
Sorcerer's Apprentice

Mr Campion was clearly shocked, his complexion a deadly shade of ivory, his hand trembling then searching in vain for the cigarettes he had forsworn years ago.

'Are you all right, Campion?' Dr Downes was genuinely concerned. 'For a minute there, I thought you were having a stroke.'

'As good as, Vice Chancellor. Your secretary just put a phone call through to me from our mutual nemesis the bishop.'

'I'm so sorry. She has specific instructions to divert him when he rings.'

'Unfortunately, I was not the diversion, I was the objective. It was me he wanted to talk to and when I say talk I mean sermonize. I'm afraid you are likely to be stuck with me for a day or so. The bishop is demanding daily reports from his university Visitor, whom he regards as something of an expert on crime at Black Dudley, though I cannot think why.'

With so many other larger problems on his mind, Campion felt guilty about adding to the vice chancellor's housekeeping woes.

'I have no wish to impose on you, or Mrs Downes,' he said, 'and I suspect Superintendent Appleyard would not wish me to stay in the Dudley itself as I think he fancies it as his head-quarters. So, is there anywhere nearby I can camp? Is there a bed-and-breakfast or a pub with rooms in White Dudley?'

'There's The Plough, but they don't have guest rooms and any house which could do bed-and-breakfast will have already rented its spare bedrooms to our students or junior staff. But if you don't mind roughing it . . .'

'Not at all,' grinned Campion, 'my needs are few and my wants mostly imaginary.'

'If you don't mind heights and are prepared to have your

slumbers disturbed by loud music late at night, then the staff flat at the peak of our Durkheim pyramid is vacant at the moment. It was allocated to a new member of staff, a Dr Gourvish, who has had to delay his arrival after breaking his leg by falling down a mountain on a climbing holiday.'

'Not the Andes by any chance?'

'Good heavens, no,' said Downes with mild astonishment. 'Snowdonia actually. Why would you think the Andes?'

'Absolutely no sane reason, Vice Chancellor,' said Campion, shaking his head. 'Flippancy brought on by a looming sense of dread.'

'You're not still worrying about the bishop's telephone call, are you?'

'No, not about that, but about the phone call I now have to make. To my wife.'

Mr Campion's fear of incurring his wife's displeasure was, as it always was, misplaced. Usually this was because Lady Amanda, after thirty years of marriage, knew her husband better than he knew himself, and partly because she was incapable of remaining angry at him for any significant length of time. On this particular occasion, Amanda saved her husband any discomfort by successfully pre-empting his telephone call by the simple expedient of not being at Monewdon Hall when it came through at one o'clock – exactly the time she had expected it.

Campion felt a guilty relief when he discovered that it was Guffy Randall on the other end of the line.

'She's gone, Albert. Mary drove her to the station to catch an earlier train. Left me having to forage for my own lunch. Thank you very much.'

'Was she cross with me?'

'Amanda? No more than usual, which is to say not seriously. More resigned than anything. Knew you just couldn't resist poking around at Black Dudley if there'd been a murder and, anyway, she spotted that you'd taken your overnight bag with you. She doesn't miss much, that gal.'

'I know,' said Campion affectionately, 'that's only one of her many qualities. She was wise to head off without me as I have, as she anticipated, been unavoidably delayed, and I will be lodging on campus for the next couple of days.'

'She said that you'd say something like that and to tell you to be careful. You are not to engage in any student pranks or beer drinking competitions, stay away from politics and do not – she repeated not – go on any protest marches or start any revolutions.'

'That pretty much curtails my freedom, doesn't it? Not to mention my enjoyment.'

'She was quite strict about it, Albert. She said that if you did any of those things, or even thought about doing them, she would embarrass you in front of your young audience and you'd never be able to show your face on campus again. She sounded as if she meant it.'

'I'm sure she does, Guffy. In fact I know she does.'

Around one o'clock Superintendent Appleyard and most of his detective team left Black Dudley, the police presence reduced to two constables on watch to make sure the crime scene was not tampered with or visited by ghoulish souvenir hunters. The official reason for their temporary departure was to search Professor Perez-Catalan's house in White Dudley, to which end Gerry Meade was acting as an enthusiastic gundog. Campion suspected that Big Gerry had tempted them into trying a plough-man's lunch at his local pub, a service for which the landlord no doubt rewarded him with liquid commission.

'Dolores will happily rustle up some lunch for you, Campion,' said Dr Downes, as policemen and the staff who had given statements began to drift from the house. 'Mr Appleyard said no one could leave the campus, so you might as well make yourself at home.'

Campion, still fortified by the residual effects of a Monewdon breakfast, had not really thought about lunch, though he had thought about Dolores Downes.

He felt guilty for not having taken more notice of the vice chancellor's wife on his earlier visit, when she had been an immaculate hostess and he was sure he had been a perfect house guest. That morning, with all the chaos and confusion that comes with a dead body virtually on the doorstep, the arrival of the police and the disruption of normal routine, she had behaved with a cool, quiet efficiency; perhaps too quiet.

A bout of hysterics would not have been out of place, Campion considered, as the poor woman had experienced a murder on what was, in effect, her front lawn; had had her house invaded and occupied and surely must have thought of the possible consequences for the university and her husband's career.

Dolores Downes was, as Amanda had warned him, a strikingly beautiful woman who would have graced the fashion pages of a society magazine, and the stoicism she had displayed that morning as her world collapsed around her added to her nobility. Her interview with Superintendent Appleyard had been short, which could mean she had nothing to contribute to the investigation, and presumably painless, though Campion had observed that she emerged from it with a slightly quivering lower lip and a moistness in the eyes. He was confident he had been the only one present who had noticed this crumpling of her mask and was willing to bet that Appleyard had not.

'No, thank you,' Campion said at last, 'I have imposed on your wife – we all have – too much already. I must say she is taking all this very well.'

'Dolores is a strong woman,' said Downes, 'and she was kind to Pascual when he first came to the university. He didn't know anyone, so Dolores took him under her wing somewhat, organizing dinner parties and Spanish evenings with wine and *tapas* so he could meet people. She's more upset by his death than she lets on.'

'The professor must have felt quite at home with all the Spanish speakers around here.'

'He insisted we always spoke English,' said Downes with a brief smile of memory. 'He said advances in science would only be recognized internationally if they were in English, plus him speaking English with a sexy Spanish accent would be a sure-fire hit with the ladies.'

'An interesting fellow all round,' said Campion. 'I wish I had paid more attention the other day when he described his work. Is there anyone I could talk to, to get an idea of what he was like to work with?'

'Nigel Honeycutt would be your man,' said Downes without hesitation. 'He's – he was – Pascual's second-in-command for all intents and purposes. The sorcerer's apprentice, so to speak, though a bit left-wing. Just got tenure as a lecturer, but the professor was supervising his PhD.'

'Has he been called in by Appleyard yet?'

'Not yet. I think Appleyard is going to descend on Earth Sciences this afternoon. If you want to chat with Honeycutt before then, you could catch him in our little pub in the refectory. He usually takes his lunch there with his student friends.'

Mr Campion raised his eyebrows. 'You said that, Vice Chancellor, as if you disapprove of members of staff having friends among the students.'

'The sort of students Honeycutt attracts, yes. What you might call the radical elements.'

'I take it you do not mean radical elements in the scientific sense?'

'Sadly, no, rather the political; the extreme political.'

'Is the School of Earth Sciences a hotbed of left-wingers?'

'Not really. Most scientists are naturally conservative. Our lefties tend to study sociology under Yorick Thurible, but Pascual had a touch of the Che Guevara about him, making him ideal as a romantic lead, a bit of a matinee idol, in fact.'

'Wouldn't that make Professor Thurible just the tiniest bit jealous?' suggested Campion.

'Almost certainly it did,' said Dr Downes, 'but Yorick has such an ego, he would never admit to being jealous of another academic, or any mere mortal.'

'So no grudges or feuds there then?'

'Not on Yorick's part, I would think. He would only feud with an equal, and he's yet to meet one of those. As for Pascual, he would challenge anyone who tried to take away his computer time to a duel to the death, but I don't think he would hold a grudge.' Downes paused and studied Campion's face. 'I'm sorry, Campion, have I shocked you? You look quite stunned.'

'I was just considering, Vice Chancellor, that it's a wonder you haven't had a murder here long before now.'

*　　*　　*

Mr Campion found Nigel Honeycutt in the refectory bar with little difficulty. Being the first day of lectures and seminars of the new term, and new students having yet to realize that attendance was not compulsory, the bar was half-empty and only one customer was seated alone at a table reading the *New Scientist*. His clothing also made him stand out from the over-dressed first-years, still unsure of what fashionable uniform to adopt, and the returning second- and third-years who had dressed in whatever had come to hand without a thought to the last time it had been laundered. Apart from Campion, he was the only one in the bar wearing a tie, a thick black woollen affair over a blue shirt with a button-down collar, and a brown corduroy suit which shone where it had seen better days. He was drinking what appeared to be a pint of bitter and picking at the remains of a ploughman's lunch.

'Mr Honeycutt? My name is Albert Campion. Do you mind if I join you?'

'Nobody's stopping you, so you might as well,' said the scientist, laying his journal down and edging his way along the bench seat to make room.

'I am the university Visitor,' said Campion, 'but this is my first visit to the refectory. Could you recommend anything from the menu?'

'I would if there was a menu, but in this bar they only do ploughman's lunches. They're not bad, actually; bit of French bread, two pats of butter, two bits of cheese, one white one red, pickled red cabbage and two large pickled onions. Not bad for two-and-six, though the university will put the price up to fifteen *p* with decimalization next year.'

The younger man spoke with deliberate world-weariness and without a trace of humour or irony.

'I'm not sure that bar prices are in the remit of the Visitor,' said Mr Campion, 'but I'll take your advice. Can I get you another drink?'

Honeycutt emptied his glass and rapped it down on the table.

'Pint of Adnams if you're buying. They don't keep it well, but it's the only real ale they stock.'

'Are the other ales *un*real then?'

'They're all keg beers, national brands made in factories, all fizz and chilled to hell. The big brewers are adulterating the workers' pint, just like they always did, except now they do it through advertising on the television.'

'How interesting,' said Campion, picking up Honeycutt's empty glass, 'I hadn't thought of it like that before now.'

'You wait, there's a revolution coming. A revolution in beer-drinking.'

Mr Campion turned towards the bar.

'Then I'll make sure I'm on the right side.'

Whatever Honeycutt's view of the optimum beer to accompany it, the university's attempts at a ploughman's lunch were very acceptable; the portions generous and the cheeses distinctive once freed from their cellophane straitjackets.

Campion ferried his meal – and a pint of bitter for Honeycutt and a bottle of stout for himself – from bar to table, sat down and folded his long legs away so that he could carefully decant his Guinness into a glass, producing the perfect creamy head. He took particular care to drain the bottle; the last few drops, delivered with a flick of the wrist, plopped into tiny brown spots in the centre of the foam head.

'Perfect!' Campion said as if to himself, although he had made sure that young Mr Honeycutt's attention had been tweaked by his little pantomime.

'What is?' asked Honeycutt, who was after all a scientist and therefore intrigued by natural phenomena.

Campion relaxed back in the bench seat then extended a forefinger to indicate the red and white cheeses on his plate and the black and white stout in his glass.

'The French say that wine is the assassin of cheese. I feel that cheese is the assassin of most beer, so to give one's beer a fighting chance, one has to choose a heavyweight beer like a stout, and I have been especially lucky in my choice today.'

'How?' Honeycutt was now as interested in Campion's diet as he had been in his *New Scientist*.

'See those little brown spots in the middle of the head? Those are dark truffles of yeasty goodness and you get them in the last of a bulk brew to be put into bottles. They are like the meat juices left in a roasting tin; they make the best gravy.'

'You know about beer,' said Honeycutt, impressed.

'Not really,' smiled Campion. 'I have an acquaintance at Brewers' Hall in London who acts as my advisor and, more often than not, my official taster. But I am not visiting the campus to try the beer.'

'You're here because of Pascual.'

'Inadvertently. My official visit was last week, but I was too slow in making my getaway and so I'm back to offer any help I can.'

'And can you help? Is that what Visitors do – investigate murders? I heard your talk to the new intake. You seem to have been hired to frighten the first-years, warning them not to go on protest marches.'

'That's a touch unfair,' said Campion, buttering a fistful of bread and slicing his oblongs of cheese into manageable pieces. 'I was only suggesting that they think before they act when it comes to trying to overthrow society. That rarely ends well, and for students enjoying all the benefits of university life, responsibility-free for three years at the taxpayers' expense, it's hardly a realistic goal.'

'You should have told them, Mr Visitor, to be realistic and demand the impossible!'

'Do I detect an echo of the Paris riots of '68? *Soyez réalistes, demandez l'impossible* was one of the popular slogans, wasn't it? The sort of sentiment I would have associated with a radical sociologist rather than a hard-headed earth scientist, if you don't mind me saying.'

'Pascual has a poster in his office with it in Spanish under a picture of Che Guevara.'

'Ah, the sainted Che.' Campion raised his glass in a silent toast. 'Does that mean that Professor Perez-Catalan was a Marxist revolutionary?'

'Not a Marxist, he despised organized politics of all shades, but he had a revolutionary approach to his research. He believed the results of his work should benefit the poorer people of his country.'

'A noble sentiment, no doubt.' Campion seemed intent on chasing a pickled onion around his plate. 'They've just had an election in Chile, haven't they?'

'Yes, a close one. Pascual was delighted to hear that the socialist Allende won – he was a big supporter.'

'I believe there was speculation that his campaign was funded by Russia and the KGB.'

Honeycutt responded as if stung. 'I think you'll find that America's CIA contributed more than twice as much to Allende's opponent, as well as a few dirty tricks along the way.'

'I'm sure you are right,' Campion said affably, 'but Chile and Chilean politics are such a long way away. How was the professor going to help the poor and needy of his country from here in darkest Suffolk?'

'With his algorithm,' said Honeycutt with astonishment that such a question needed asking.

'Oh yes, his famous algorithm.'

'It's not famous yet, but it will be.'

Campion abandoned his pursuit of pickled onions, placed his hands in his lap and turned to face Honeycutt head-on. 'He did try and explain it to me when I met him briefly last week. I followed as best I could and for a moment I thought I'd grasped it, but then it was gone, and I realized I was a bear of very little brain when it came to science.'

Honeycutt sighed the sigh of a put-upon man, but it was half-hearted, for few dedicated scientists can resist explaining their work, however stubborn or stupid their audience, and he soon warmed to his task.

'Pascual came to this country, and this university specifically, because he needed computer power which was not available to him back home in Santiago. To work out his algorithm, he has had to analyse thousands of seismographic recordings taken along the subduction zone where the Pacific and continental plates collide.'

He paused to examine Campion's face, but Mr Campion was nodding enthusiastically.

'With you so far.'

'Pascual's theory,' Honeycutt continued, gathering pace, 'was that by looking at them in conjunction with known geological strata and mineral deposits, plus chemical samples taken from existing mines, he could come up with an algorithm, a formula,

for predicting the presence of valuable minerals, particularly
the heavy metals such as zinc lead and tungsten.'

'I think he mentioned uranium and gold.'

'Yes, those too.'

'So essentially this algorithm of his, if it worked, could be
a sort of computerized divining rod?'

'Putting it very crudely . . . you could say that.'

'However crudely, could I say that if I were, for example,
an international mining company or perhaps even a government
interested in securing supplies of such heavy metals, then the
professor's algorithm would be high on my Christmas list?'

'You could, but it wouldn't be something you could go out
and buy.' Honeycutt appeared somewhat disturbed by Campion's
question.

'Why not? Please correct me if I'm wrong, but this algorithm
is something like a formula, isn't it? If I had come up with a
chemical formula for, let us say, turning sea water into four-star
petrol, wouldn't I be tempted to sell it to the highest bidder?'

'You might; Pascual wouldn't. His priority was to publish
his findings in the scientific journals for peer review and, if his
theories are correct, they would be put to use improving the
economies of some of the poorest countries in the world.'

'And in doing so increase the profits of multinational mining
companies.'

'As long as capitalism retains its stranglehold on the Western
world, probably yes.'

The younger man jutted his jaw, as if daring Campion to
counter-punch physically rather than verbally.

'Do I take it you would prefer a more communist philosophy
to prevail?' Campion said quietly.

'I make no secret of it!' Honeycutt picked up his glass, toasted
himself and drained it. 'I am a member of IS, the International
Socialists, who will be in the vanguard of social change in this
country when it comes.'

'While we are waiting for that,' said Mr Campion, 'would
you allow this old, reactionary capitalist to buy you another
drink?'

Honeycutt put the flat of his hand over his empty glass. 'No, better not. I have a lot to do this afternoon, seeing students and sorting out Pascual's teaching commitments.'

'And you'll be continuing his research, I presume?'

'As best I can, and it will probably fall to me to finish off the paper he was writing and get it published.'

Campion was pleased to discover that Honeycutt's academic responsibilities took precedence over the impending socialist revolution.

'I have no doubt you will do a splendid job, Nigel, even though I haven't really got a clue what your job is, but the vice chancellor referred to you as the sorcerer's apprentice, so I am sure you will work your magic.'

Honeycutt allowed himself a brief smile and a slight shake of a modest head.

'Pascual was certainly the sorcerer when it came to handling vast amounts of data and theories from different disciplines. His colleagues in Chile called him *El Mago* – The Magician. I can only hope a little of his magic has rubbed off on me.'

'You held him in high regard, I sense.'

'The highest. He was supervising my doctorate, he was a great mentor and a good teacher. It was an honour to work under him.'

'Can I ask if your high opinion of him is shared by your colleagues here in Earth Sciences?'

'Oh, I get it; this is the third degree, is it? Who had a motive to do in poor Pascual?'

'Not at all,' soothed Campion. 'You'll get that from Superintendent Appleyard this afternoon – and, word to the wise, don't volunteer any information on your political affiliations unless it seems germane to the enquiry.'

'Typical fascist pig, is he?'

'I'll have you know, my young friend, that several of my oldest and dearest friends are policemen, and they would react most strongly to being labelled fascists, though in the case of Mr Appleyard, I could be tempted to make an exception. He will certainly ask you about the professor's politics.'

Honeycutt's expression had gone from truculence to nervousness. 'I've told you, Pascual was not into organized political movements. He certainly had a socialist view of the world, but he was not committed to any party or movement, but the coppers will still call him "dangerously left-wing" when they talk to their lackeys in the press.'

'I'll have you know,' Campion said with a huge grin, 'that several of my oldest and dearest friends dislike journalists too.'

There was a pause while Honeycutt registered a smile, then Campion continued.

'You will forgive me, for I am very old and set in my ways, but I did not expect to find any left-wingers, dangerous or otherwise, among the staff of the science departments. I naturally assumed that the sociology department would be stuffed to the gunnels with them, but perhaps I have been misled by those lackeys of the fourth estate. My point is, I am sure the police follow a similar thought process.'

Honeycutt waggled a forefinger to indicate that he had picked up on Campion's meaning.

'They won't find Earth Sciences a hotbed of revolution – more's the pity. I'm the only one who takes any interest in what's going on in the world outside the laboratory. I think that's why Pascual took me under his wing. The rest of the department are straight-laced Conservative voters to a man.'

'And woman?' Campion made it a question, but then elaborated. 'I met one of your geology lecturers last week, a popular one judging by the reaction of one of her students.'

'That would be Tabitha King,' said Honeycutt. 'She's one of our rising stars. Pascual thought highly of her. Academically that is, even though she rebuffed his advances in no uncertain terms. Pascual just took it in his stride. It was just his way to try it on with anything female.'

'A ladies' man, as my mother might have said?'

'They didn't call him The Magician just for his science.'

'I see,' said Campion diplomatically. 'Did that generate any ill-feeling . . . any jealousy . . . within the department?'

'Not that I was aware of. We were all delighted to have Pascual as our leader; his work was trail-blazing and we were proud to be associated with it, and willing to put up with the fact that his research tended to monopolize our allocation of computer time.'

'So all is sweetness and light in Earth Sciences?'

'If you are asking, in a roundabout way, whether any of his colleagues in the department could have been responsible for his death, I would have to say absolutely not. In fact, I cannot think of anyone who would harm Pascual.'

Campion pushed his spectacles back on his nose with a forefinger.

'A magician who can predict where to dig for gold and silver and uranium? I'm sure there must be a few candidates . . .'

Campion followed Honeycutt's example and carried his empty plate and glass back to the bar as they made to leave, pausing to acknowledge the polite, 'Thank you, m'dear' from the middle-aged barmaid in nylon work coat crackling with static electricity, who already, on the first full day of term, looked suitably harassed. When Campion returned her thanks and complimented her on the perfect ratio of bread-to-butter-to-cheese in his ploughman's, it put a spring in her step.

Honeycutt had simply slammed his plate on the bar and turned for the door which would take him out of the refectory, but his exit was blocked, and deliberately so, by a tall blonde female figure.

Campion only had to take two paces to be within earshot of the exchange between them, which was short, sharp and far from friendly.

'Now that *El Brujo* is out of the way, what are the chances of the rest of us getting our fair share of computer time?'

The woman spoke quickly, and her tone made Honeycutt, rocking back on his heels, recoil from her. Campion was sure he could detect an accent not totally English.

'That's not up to me,' Honeycutt said nervously. 'Take it up with Jack Szmodics.'

'Oh I will, have no fear. There are plenty of us with research which needs computer time and we're not frightened of golden boy Pascual any more.'

And then the woman had gone from in front of Honeycutt and out of Campion's line of vision and, without turning around, Honeycutt also disappeared.

The left-leaning geologist had clearly opted for discretion

rather than valour, which Mr Campion felt was the sensible course of action, for the last time he had seen the blonde woman confront a member of the Earth Sciences department, it had resulted in a resounding, very public, slap against the face of the late Professor Perez-Catalan.

SEVEN
Spanish Practices

M r Campion followed the footpath into Piazza 2, the campus home of the Arts and Humanities department, where he blended in remarkably well with the bustling population of students, despite being half a century older than most. Perhaps, he ruminated, they thought he was a distinguished visiting professor rather than an undistinguished Visitor just visiting.

To his right, in Piazza 1, he could see the outdoor chessboard with its oversize pieces standing idle by the Computing Centre. Clearly none of the new intake of students had the confidence yet to challenge the computer to a game, or were not yet sufficiently off the parental leash to steal one of the pieces as a souvenir to decorate their room. It was an inescapable fact that such a rural setting away from main roads did not offer the traditional temptation of collecting traffic cones.

To take advantage of the vice chancellor's offer of accommodation, Campion was required to register with the Accommodation Office in the Admin building, and he pointed himself in its direction and began to traverse Piazza 3. Halfway across, he swerved to the left of the defunct fountain in a vain attempt to avoid contact with George Tinkler, the university chaplain, who was coming from Administration, walking swiftly with his nose in the air, an affectation born of years of precariously balancing *pince-nez*.

'Campion! Just the chap I was looking for,' said Tinkler, across the fountain-turned-firepit-turned-birdbath, the inside rim of which bore traces of scorching.

'I can't think why you should be, Mr Tinkler. I'm not really supposed to be here.'

Campion touched the brim of his fedora in the chaplain's general direction but kept walking. To his dismay, Mr Tinkler rounded the fountain and fell into step – or as near as his much shorter legs could manage – alongside his prey.

'Ah, but the bishop says otherwise. He telephoned me this morning and said you were acting as his eyes and ears on campus during the present . . . difficulties.'

'I would not put it that way,' said Campion, his eyes fixed on the archway entrance to the Admin block and the library beyond, 'but it seems that the bishop has a remarkable faith in my ability to be a reassuring presence in a time of strife. I cannot think why, but I wish he would share some of that faith with my wife.'

'He said you'd be the man to ask,' said the chaplain plaintively.

'Ask what?'

'About the funeral arrangements.'

'Excuse me?'

'For Professor Perez-Catalan.'

Campion looked askance at the smaller man buzzing around him. 'Oh good, I thought somebody else had died,' he said drily. 'As I understand the situation, the professor was murdered not much more than twelve hours ago. The legal ramifications of that should be clear even to the bishop. There will be no question of a funeral until the police have finished their enquiries.'

'The bishop is not expecting the university to bury the poor man,' Tinkler said, though Campion suspected the words were the bishop's, 'but he feels the formalities should be handled by an officiate of his own faith.'

'Are you presuming the professor was a Roman Catholic?'

'Well they all are, down in South America, aren't they?'

'I simply could not say, and I really do not understand what you – or the bishop – expect of me.'

Tinkler clasped his hands together, but in a wringing movement rather than in preparation for prayer. 'The bishop is most insistent that no aspect of this unfortunate incident should reflect badly on the university. He realizes that there has to be a police investigation, and what comes of that is out of his hands, but there must be no suggestion that the university neglected the spiritual side of things. Professor Perez-Catalan was, after all, a guest in our country, and a long way from home with no family here. The least the university can do is take notice of his religious needs.'

Campion scowled at the chaplain. It was something he did rarely and was not convinced that he was any good at it.

'I believe that is what is known in public relations as "covering all the bases" but what, pray – if that's not blasphemy – am I supposed to do about it?'

'The bishop thought you might know a local Roman Catholic priest who could advise us.'

Campion shook his head in genuine bafflement. 'And you don't?'

'Suffolk is predominantly Anglican, with very few Catholics. With your long-standing family connections to the county . . .'

'The nearest Catholic church will be Our Lady's in Stowmarket which, until this year, was one of the few, if not only, first-floor churches in the country.' Tinkler looked suitably confused and had he been wearing his *pince-nez* he would have adjusted them. 'I think the church was designed to incorporate a school on the ground floor, but that has eventually proved impractical,' Campion continued. 'I only know this because I read an article about it. Do we know if the professor worshipped there?'

'No.'

'Do we know if he worshipped anywhere or if he was at all religious?'

'I did not know him well,' the chaplain conceded, 'and we never discussed religion, but I assumed he had spiritual beliefs because of his retreats.'

'His what?'

'It was common knowledge that the professor would use the old chapel of St Jurmin, up beyond Black Dudley on the beach, for his private contemplation.'

'Did he now?'

Mr Campion was surprised.

Mr Tinkler had said something interesting.

The estates officer himself, Gregor Marshall, was in the Accommodation Office to ceremonially hand over the key to Campion's temporary lodgings.

'The vice chancellor has told me to put you in our spare staff flat, which you'll find at the top of the Durkheim pyramid; that's the one nearest the library. There's only the one key for the flat itself – the entrances to the pyramids are open twenty-four hours a day; just walk in and climb the central staircase until your head hits the ceiling, then you're there.'

'I had my introduction to tomb-raiding last week, so I think I can find my way,' said Campion, pocketing the serrated steel comb which resembled an elongated Yale key.

'Tomb-raiding?'

'I do apologize, it was my first thought when Dr Downes showed me inside one of the pyramids last week. Howard Carter and the tomb of Tutankhamun, but without the associated curse.'

'Yes, well . . .' Mr Marshall did not seem keen to pursue that image. 'As you will not be a permanent resident with a tenancy agreement, and therefore covered by the university's insurance policies, I'm going to have to ask you to sign a legal waiver exonerating the university in case of accidents, including falling down the stairwell or from the windows, plus an acknowledgement that you have been made aware of the fire regulations and acquainted yourself with the fire drill.'

'It suddenly sounds more dangerous than I thought, but if a legal waiver also protects me from a pharaoh's curse, then pass me a pen,' said Campion cheerfully as he scrutinized the sheaf of printed forms being thrust in front of him.

While still reading the fine print he said, almost as an aside: 'By the way, could I ask – and I realize this is a foolish question in a university specializing in languages and with a vice chancellor who is a Hispanist – but is there anyone reasonably adjacent who speaks Spanish?'

'Hundreds of 'em, down in the language labs. They speak every language under the sun and a couple not yet discovered,' said Marshall. 'Regular Tower of Babel it is down there, but they'll be up to their eyes in it this afternoon, with the new students trying out the equipment like kids in a sweetshop.'

'I wouldn't want to interrupt a class or a lecture, it's only a minor thing.'

'Well, there's the vice chancellor of course, though I think he's got his hands full up at the Dudley now the police are back there asking more questions.' Marshall paused, and his eyes narrowed. 'You could always try Mrs Downes, of course; she is Spanish after all.'

'Thank you, that's an excellent idea.'

Campion beamed his most innocent smile, to disguise his unease at the tone in which Marshall had suggested it.

He approached Black Dudley via the car park where a constable informed him gruffly that no one could remove a car without the superintendent's written permission. Campion assured him that he wished merely to retrieve his overnight bag from the boot of his Jaguar as he was staying on campus; hinting, if not saying outright, at the request of Mr Appleyard. The policeman nodded approval in a that's-all-right-then sort of way, and went back to rocking on his heels and surveying the campus and the parkland for illegal activities and no doubt sending messages telepathically to his two comrades still guarding the bridge over the artificial lake about the possibility of claiming overtime.

Suitcase in hand, Campion strode across the grass towards the house, tasting the salt on the air from the breeze coming off the sea to the east, fancying himself as looking like a door-to-door salesman a considerable way off his usual round.

Gregor Marshall had been correct in that Dr Downes was tied up with the police enquiry and simply could not see anyone, or so Campion was assured by his secretary, who had graduated from harassed to vexed as her daily routine continued to be sabotaged. Mrs Downes, however, was available, and was in her sitting room on the first floor if Mr Campion thought he could find his own way up there.

On Campion's original, dramatic visit to Black Dudley forty years previously, the Downes's sitting room would have been one of several dark and draughty north-facing bedrooms. Campion may well have been in it on that eventful weekend, perhaps entered it by one of the ridiculous secret passages which riddled the upper floors. He might even have been held prisoner there briefly or knocked unconscious by a burly gangster in a furious fistfight – it had been that sort of a house party.

He certainly could not remember the view from the large

sash windows, over parkland to the sea and the curve of the coastline, and had a vague recollection that the area had been given over to pine woodland, not that house guests on that infamous weekend had been encouraged to explore the grounds. For most of the time they had been forcibly confined to the gloomy Black Dudley itself.

Dolores Downes had welcomed Campion in with an automatic apology that her husband was busy helping the police with their enquiries, but did not appear reassured when Campion proclaimed that she was the reason for his visit. In fact, Dolores Downes looked faintly alarmed.

'I'm sorry to trouble you with so much else going on, but I need your help in a small matter.'

'Help? My help? How? Please, have a seat.'

'No, thank you, I will not outstay my welcome. It's a simple matter of translation as my Spanish is not presentable outside of a *tapas* bar. How would you say "The Sorcerer" in your native language?'

'*El Hechicero*,' she said uncertainly.

'Rather than *El Mago*, which I think is more the equivalent of "Magus", as in Greek or Persian and in English when we refer to the Magi – the Three Wise Men who followed the star to Bethlehem in the Bible.'

'Yes, I would agree,' said Mrs Downes. '*El Mago* would be a wise man, a teacher with mystical powers.'

'As opposed to a sorcerer who dabbles in magic and spells?'

Dolores's fingers went to her face and nervously flicked her long black hair back until it looped behind her ears before she answered Campion.

'You are talking about Pascual.'

'Yes, I am. He has been described to me as a sorcerer, or a magus, when it comes to his work. The Americans would probably call him a "whizz-kid" and the BBC might use the term "scientific wizard" when it is in one of its more informal moments.'

They had gravitated to the centre of the room and stood, rather awkwardly, a foot apart, Campion holding his hat by its brim and Mrs Downes touching her hair as if to get every jet-black strand in its rightful place.

'Have you heard Professor Perez-Catalan referred to as a sorcerer?' Campion asked to break the silence.

'Yes,' said the woman quietly.

'How about as *El Brujo*?'

'I have never heard him called that!'

Dolores Downes's eyes flashed, startling Campion into an instant apology. 'I do hope I have not offended. That was certainly not my intention. I am not even sure what the word means.'

'*Bruja* is a witch; *El Brujo* is a man who is a witch.'

'A warlock. I see. That's rather more sinister than sorcerer and definitely not as reverential as magus.'

'Who called him that?'

Now those big brown eyes were piercing into Campion's bland and unassuming expression. 'Absolutely no one of any consequence. It was merely something I overheard and was confused by. I'm sure no disrespect was intended.'

Mrs Downes did not appear convinced, but her gaze dropped away.

'One other thing while I am here,' Campion began carefully, 'and if it is not too personal, may I ask if you are a Catholic?'

'You may, and I am.'

'And the professor, was he a Catholic too?'

'Yes, he was.'

'Did you by any chance use the same place of worship? I was thinking Our Lady's in Stowmarket would be the nearest Catholic church.'

'I have been to mass there many times,' said the woman, and there was a dreamy quality about her voice, 'but Pascual was not a good Catholic and his place of worship was elsewhere.'

As Campion took his leave, his brain hummed with the last phrase Mrs Downes had spoken. She could, of course, have meant that the professor's chosen site for religious devotions was his scientific laboratory or perhaps the Computing Centre which he was said to monopolize. But those very feminine brown eyes had betrayed her by automatically focusing on the window as she spoke; and through the window, in the distance, the chapel of St Jurmin.

* * *

Suitcase in hand, Mr Campion was almost out of the Dudley's main door when he was stopped in his tracks by the command 'Campion!', at a volume which in the open air would have graced a parade ground and indoors was loud enough to rattle the window panes.

'Yes, Superintendent? What can I do for you?' said Campion without turning around.

'Wondered if you could spare me a minute. In here.'

Mr Campion put down his case near the door, took off his hat and placed it on the case, then reluctantly followed the voice into the vice chancellor's office, where Superintendent Appleyard had made himself very comfortable behind the vice chancellor's desk, the notetaking constable seated to his side now a firm fixture.

'Dare I ask how the investigation is going, Superintendent?' asked Campion.

'I wouldn't if I were you, at least not before you've told me if your snooping and sniffing around has turned up anything interesting.'

Campion threw up his hands in mock horror. 'Snooping and sniffing, Superintendent? What must you think of me? Goodness, I feel positively faint. May I sit down?'

'Only if you've got something to tell me,' snapped the policeman.

'In that case, I'll stand. I had no idea I was supposed to be freelancing for your investigation, Mr Appleyard. Should we draw up some sort of contract or hire agreement?'

Appleyard's face remained a slab; not even those thick hedgerows of eyebrows signalled emotion.

'Just cut it, Campion. Don't waste police time. You're a born meddler and a team of Suffolk Punches couldn't pull you away when you've been this close to a juicy murder.'

Campion did a passable double-take worthy of a television comedian. 'Not *too* close, I hope. Not close enough – Heaven forfend – to be considered a suspect?'

'And you can cut the music hall act. I know full well that you're conducting a private investigation for the Bishop of St Edmondsbury.'

'I am?' Campion's surprise was clearly genuine, if not obvious to the superintendent.

'So I am reliably informed.'

'By whom? No, don't tell me, the bishop's been on the phone, hasn't he?'

'Frequently. He seems to have spoken to just about everyone on campus except you, his gundog. He hasn't been able to get hold of you.'

For a split second, Appleyard's face softened, as if a pleasurable memory had intruded on his thoughts. 'Maybe you're not as daft as you look.'

'I hold no specific commission from the bishop, Superintendent, and I see my role here as a buffer, not a gundog, between His Lordship and the university. The vice chancellor seems a decent chap, and if I can relieve some of the pressure on him, then I will try and do so.'

'So what have you managed to sniff out?'

'Very little, so little I really do not deserve the bloodhound analogy. I have merely been trying to ascertain the character of the late, lamented professor. Investigating a few Spanish practices, you might say.'

'Spanish what?'

'I'm sorry,' said Campion, 'that's misleading. As I am sure you know, "Spanish practices" are what our friends in Fleet Street call the rather dubious working practices of the printers' unions. Men clocking on for two shifts or more at the same time under different names, one of the most popular being Mickey Mouse.'

'You've found that going on here?'

'No, not at all. I was being stupid and said the first thing that came into my head. It was pure word association and meaningless. What I meant was I seem to have spent the day trying to discover something of the habits and practices of our Spanish victim.'

'And what did you turn up?'

'Nothing that wasn't public knowledge, I suspect. The professor was a wizard in his academic field, doing valuable research which could produce real economic prosperity for his native country. He was at the top of his game and an asset to the university, attracting many students here and, I suspect, the prospect of considerable grant funding. I admit, though, that I have not yet got a feel for the private life of the poor professor.'

'Catholic, was he?'

'Yes, why do you ask?'

'I didn't, the flaming bishop did. Somebody mentioned he used to visit that old chapel down on the seashore. That would have been Catholic, wouldn't it?'

'When it was built, yes, but I do not think it has been used much since the Reformation, and I did not get the impression that the professor was a religious man.'

'Bit of a commie, you reckon?'

'I don't think so. A socially minded sort of chap, I'm told, but not a card-carrying political animal.'

'Unlike his faithful sidekick . . .' Appleyard turned to the constable acting as his stenographer, who flipped a page in his notebook and supplied the name.

'Honeycutt, that's it. We've had our eye on him for some time.'

'Nigel Honeycutt? I thought him the loyal assistant and dedicated scientist. A bit of a lefty, I grant you, but surely not a suspect.'

'Academic jealousy not a good enough motive for you?' Appleyard snorted in disgust. 'There's plenty of that around here, but we've had Honeycutt down as a troublemaker for some time, selling the *Socialist Worker* on the streets of Norwich, always in the front line of anti-Vietnam demonstrations, suspected of associating with members of the Angry Brigade. Know what that is?'

'I've read about them; a rather violent spin-off from the Paris student riots. Misguided fanatics who fancy themselves as urban terrorists, with counterparts in Germany and probably other places in Europe. I can't see them staging a successful revolution in this country.'

'I hope you're right there,' said Appleyard. 'Bunch of dissolute middle-class spoiled brats if you ask me. Cambridge drop-outs who tore up their Finals papers as a protest.'

'Do you know if they've been recruiting here on campus?'

'Wouldn't surprise me, but Gerry Meade says there are some strange goings-on after hours, so to speak, both here and in White Dudley.'

'And I'll bet Big Gerry is the sort who keeps an eagle eye peeled at all times,' said Campion without a trace of irony.

'He does, and more power to his elbow. Wish I had a few in blue who were as keen as he is.' Appleyard narrowed his eyes in the direction of his secretary constable, who made a great play of licking the end of his pencil then writing slowly in his notebook, silently mouthing the words of his superior.

Campion felt he could warm to the young constable and hoped he would get out from under his superintendent as soon as possible.

'Good to have a man like Meade on the ground, I should think.'

'Oh, it is,' said Appleyard with a twitchy grin. 'It's even better to have two.'

Leaving what the dramatist would call a pregnant pause, Campion bowed to the inevitable. 'I presume you mean me, Superintendent.'

'Well, as you're here, you might as well make yourself useful. Big Gerry has an ear to the ground when it comes to the below-stairs staff and taproom gossip, but there's others – bolshie students and them that fancy themselves as intellectuals – who would clam up as soon as he appeared. You can smooth-talk your way in with the professors and come across as a harmless old granddad to the students. All you have to do is keep your ears open.'

'So I'm to pick up a better class of gossip, is that it?'

'If you like. There's some would say you were born to it, plus you have another advantage. You were here back in '28 when Colonel Coombe got murdered, that gives you a certain . . . a certain . . .'

'*Cachet*, sir?' suggested the constable, pencil poised.

'I prefer *mystique*,' said Campion, suppressing a grin.

'I was going to say *notoriety*,' scowled Appleyard. 'There's people who will talk to you, and not to the police, because of your previous experience of murder most foul. It's only human nature, but I want to know what they tell you.'

'Is this exchange of information, should I glean any, reciprocal?'

'I'm willing to share to a certain extent, as long as it's not likely to break the chain of evidence in any future prosecution.'

'So there is evidence?'

'Not a shred that would stand up in court.' Appleyard's caterpillar eyebrows curled in anguish. 'We've searched his cottage down in White Dudley and his office. Not a clue as to who might have had it in for him. Lots of fingerprints taken, no matches as yet.'

'The weapon?'

Appleyard shook his head. 'No prints on the knife, which was of fairly standard kitchen issue. Good quality, mind, Sheffield steel and all that.'

'A professional job?'

'Still waiting for the official autopsy but from what I saw it could have been somebody who knew what they were doing or a complete fluke. The fatal stab could have been delivered by a man or a woman as long as they were taller than a dwarf.'

'Not much to go on.'

'That's where you come in. We've got the means – the knife – and the opportunity – middle of the night, on a bridge over a lake with nobody else around. But we don't have a motive, and I have a feeling in my waters that once we know the motive, we'll have the murderer. So you get out there and start snooping.'

'Do I have any choice?'

The constable with the notebook caught Campion's eye and silently shook his head. 'Not really,' said Appleyard, 'and there's one other thing I need you to do.'

'Let me guess. You want me to telephone the bishop at regular intervals to get him off your back, and I suspect the chief constable's back as well.'

'If you wouldn't mind,' said the superintendent with sarcasm rather than gratitude.

Once dismissed by the superintendent, Campion found Gerry Meade standing guard over his case and hat.

'Mr Marshall told me to show you to your room,' he said with a curt nod and an expression which suggested he had many far better things to do.

'How kind,' said Campion. 'I'm sure I can manage to find my way into Durkheim – the pyramid that is, not his books. I don't think my addled brain is up to that. Still, I would be glad of some sturdy company as I might need a bodyguard.'

'Really?' Meade's ox-like face glowed with curiosity. 'Why would that be, Mr Campion?'

Campion leaned forward conspiratorially and lowered his voice, although he and Meade had the entrance hall to themselves. 'Well, between you and me, I seem to be working for the police now, unofficially of course and' – he tapped a finger against the side of his nose – 'confidentially. I understand Superintendent Appleyard regards you as a useful pair of extra hands as well.'

'Hands, eyes and ears,' said Meade with pride and a disturbing gleefulness, 'and I'm more than glad to be of service, but I don't get why you might need a bodyguard.'

'Radical elements, anarchist groups and militant students who don't like the police or police snoopers. The superintendent seems quite worried about them and I will be living among them.'

'Don't you worry about that, Mr C. I know most of the troublemakers by sight and they know me. If they see you with me, they'll know not to trouble you.'

'That's very comforting,' said Campion, convinced that Meade would not recognize a dangerous anarchist if one ran up and handed him a round, black cartoon bomb with a spluttering fuse.

Having confirmed his suspicion that Gerry Meade would be a direct conduit back to Appleyard, and hopefully having convinced him that they were both on the same side, Campion began to extract information as the pair walked towards the campus. Meade indicated that they should take the path to the wooden bridge, where the constables on duty would allow them to pass as they regarded him as 'one of their own' now. This they did, one of them simply acknowledging them with a non-committal 'Gerry' as they crossed, the structure creaking gently under their weight.

'Do we have any idea what the professor was doing out here at midnight?' Campion asked, emphasizing the 'we'.

'There was no reason for him to be going to Black Dudley, not at that time of night, so he was probably heading for the car park. His car was there, we found it this morning.'

'So where was he coming *from*?'

'Probably his office or the Computing Centre; he had his own keys for both.'

From the middle of the bridge, Campion surveyed the low-lying concrete campus before him and the peaks of the residential pyramids behind the line of the piazzas.

'Or indeed anywhere on the campus,' he said as they walked on. 'Would that be unusual, working late on a Sunday night?'

'Not really. The professors and them with research projects work funny hours, especially those wanting to get on the computer.'

They were entering Piazza 1, where the large wooden outdoor chess pieces formed a formidable obstacle to anyone attempting to enter the Computing Centre by walking in a straight line.

'I get the impression that allocation of computing time is something of a touchy subject in the university.'

'You can say that again,' said Meade. 'They fight like cats and dogs over the bloody thing, them professors do. They're like kids pulling at a favourite toy.'

'Any of them likely to pull hard enough to kill him over it?'

'Oh, plenty of 'em threatened to knock him off at one time or another, but I reckon it was mostly fresh air.'

'What about the students?'

'They loved him. He was their very own scientific genius, in line for a Nobel Prize, they reckon. Quite something to say you've been taught by a Nobel Prize winner. Even the students he didn't teach liked him. The lefties because he reminded them of that Che Guevara feller and the girls because he was their idea of a randy Latin lover.'

They were through the piazza, following the paths around the Threepenny Bit and the Circus to the pyramids, an odd couple of elderly men, one in a grey uniform and one in a pinstripe suit and fedora, on a late afternoon *passeggiata* through some of the oddest architecture ever to grace the Suffolk countryside.

The students they passed on the way to the fourth pyramid gave them only cursory looks, Campion's fedora attracting far more admiring glances than Meade's uniform, but none seemed surprised or objected to their presence. Overall, they seemed a polite and trusting crowd, Campion thought, and frightfully young.

'The professor lived in White Dudley, I believe,' said Campion as they entered Durkheim and began to climb the stairwell, 'as you do.'

'Yes, what of it?'

Meade was ascending the stairs at a fair clip and was somewhat surprised to discover that Campion's long legs were keeping pace.

'Oh, I just wondered if he played a part in village life; joined the cricket team, grew vegetables on the allotment, frequented the local pub, that sort of thing.'

'Couldn't really say. Kept himself to himself. Here we are. Don't bother with your key, I'll use my master set.' He produced a bunch of keys on a ring as big as an orange and selected one. 'I'd better explain the lock. It's the latest in modern technology.'

The lock, said Meade, was a doorknob type, the long, thin key being inserted in the centre of the metal orb of the door handle itself. One turn of the key opened the lock and the door. Close the door and it locked automatically. For added security there was a button mechanism on the inside which could deadlock the knob.

'All the keys might look alike,' said Meade, enjoying the chance to lecture to a captive audience, 'but they only fit one lock. This being Durkheim and the top-floor flat, you'll find D1 embossed on your key, so it only works on this lock and there's no danger of you going into somebody else's room by mistake.'

'Or roaming the corridors with a view to a little breaking-and-entering,' said Campion as Meade held the door open. 'Thank you. I will sleep easier knowing I'm so secure.'

Campion dropped his suitcase in the middle of the room and went immediately to the window which gave a spectacular view of the library and the length of the campus. But Campion looked downwards, not at the panorama. Once he saw Big Gerry Meade exit the pyramid and begin to stride towards the Admin building, he took out his long, calfskin wallet and, from a narrow sleeve incorporated in the spine, he withdrew a thin metal nail file of traditional design, the pointed end curved like an upturned comma.

He went out to the staircase, closing the flat door behind him and testing the doorknob which refused to budge under his grip.

Checking he was alone in the stairwell, he dropped to one knee and inserted the comma end of his nail file into the key slot and turned it gently first left then right. A tumbler clicked, and the door swung silently open. The whole exercise taking less than five seconds.

Campion stepped back into the room and replaced the file in his wallet. 'Modern technology my foot!' he said to himself. 'We oldies can still show them a thing or two.'

EIGHT
The Mild and Bitter Brigade

M r Campion surveyed his new accommodation and was delighted to find that the wall-mounted telephone was clearly marked: *Internal Calls Only, No Outside Line*. If it offered few of the home comforts he was used to, that alone would have been worth the rent – had he been paying any for it – as it meant that, with a clear conscience, he could remain incommunicado from the bishop. There would come a day, if science-fiction television dramas were to be believed, when in the future there would be personal 'communicators' assigned to every individual to enable them to make and, worse, to receive telephone calls at all hours of the day and night. There would be no escape; it was an awful prospect.

The staff flat was compact, ergonomically designed and fitted with all mod cons; or so an estate agent would have said, all the time emphasizing the magnificent views over the campus to distract potential tenants from the tiny bathroom where it was physically possible – in fact, necessary – to use the shower and the shaving mirror over the washbasin simultaneously.

The Estates Office had provided bed linen and blankets, even making up the narrow bed which doubled as a sofa (clearly too short for Campion's elongated frame), along with a pair of towels, for which Campion was grateful, and after a thorough wash and brush-up requiring his previously unknown skills as a contortionist, he turned to the inner man.

Once he had deduced that the strange water-filled plastic container with a red switch and a stubby metal spout fixed to the wall above the doll's-house sink was in fact a space-age kettle, his opinion of the university dipped when he realized he had not been provided with tea, milk, sugar, or even a cup. As it was unlikely that the internal telephone was linked to anything resembling room service, and as he did not wish to impose on either Mrs Downes or Superintendent Appleyard at Black Dudley any further, he decided to explore the library, of which he had a bird's-eye view, and which might have one of those ghastly machines which dispensed ersatz tea in flimsy plastic cups.

If it had, he did not find it, but he soon forgot all about his need for the cup that cheers but does not inebriate (a homily he had never had much faith in) when faced with the task of gaining admittance after being confronted by a formidable middle-aged lady whose bird's-nest hairstyle acted as a quiver for several no doubt recently sharpened pencils and who wore a grey woollen cardigan like a flak jacket.

Campion knew he had little chance of pretending he was a new student. Not even his son Rupert, an actor, would attempt to with such a grim-faced audience, and this gatekeeper of the university's repository of knowledge would surely know all members of the academic staff by sight. There was nothing for it but to tell the truth, so when asked who he was, he replied with dignity just short of pomposity, 'I am the university Visitor.'

'Can you prove it?' asked the librarian, clearly a woman dedicated to her job.

'Would I admit to such a thing if it were untrue?' charmed Campion and then, realizing that the big guns might have to be produced, added: 'A telephone call to the vice chancellor or, even better, the Bishop of St Edmondsbury could confirm my appointment.'

At the mention of those names – or perhaps just one of them – the dragon at the gate relented and allowed Campion to enter her den, even pointing him to the lifts and a large information panel which showed, as in the best department stores, what was available on each floor.

Ignoring the first and second floors which concentrated on the sciences and languages and linguistics, he headed for the third floor where he thought he would feel more at home among literature, history and philosophy. Specifically he was looking for a minor enclave in the history section, and one which he felt sure would not be overcrowded with students on the first day of term, if ever.

To call 'Local History and Donated Archives' an independent

section would be flattering to say the least, as it comprised no more than four shelves of material – books and box files – and Mr Campion had it all to himself.

After amusing himself for a good half-hour reading a sheaf of yellowing press cuttings held together by a rusty bulldog clip on 'The Shocking Events at Black Dudley: Murder, Gangsters and Rescue by the Monewdon Hunt', he found what he thought he might be looking for in a box file containing parish magazines, programmes from amateur dramatic productions and flyers for Christmas fayres.

Some kind soul with an eye on posterity had deposited a dozen four-page pamphlets priced optimistically at sixpence per copy, with a brief description and history of St Jurmin and his chapel. They dated, Campion guessed, from the 1950s, and told him little that he had not gleaned from Roger Downes and Gerry Meade when he had spotted the chapel while on his official tour of the pyramid residences.

Jurmin, or alternatively Jermin or Hiurmine, was the son of Anna or Onna, a seventh-century king of the East Angles, part of the Wuffinga royal family. He had been, as far as Campion could tell, a 'good king', and his son Jurmin had been a saintly and holy chap, both of them receiving honourable mentions in the chronicles of the Venerable Bede, who Campion remembered with a giggle was better known to schoolboys now as the Venomous Bede.

Sadly, the Wuffinga father-and-son team were less well thought of by the aggressive Penda, ruler of the Midlands kingdom of Mercia, who had an eye on East Anglian territory and who duly invaded around the year AD 653. It had been far worse than the invasion of Stoke or West Bromwich fans to a football match at Ipswich, and had culminated in the battle of Bulcamp Hill just outside Blythburgh. Both Anna and his son Jurmin were killed, the battle marking the end of the kingdom of the East Angles and the dominance of the Mercia, but at least St Jurmin had a small church named after him and a feast day, 24 February.

There had been much debate (among whom? Campion wondered) as to whether St Jurmin's was one of the seventh-century churches generally known as the 'Kentish group' – churches built on Roman sites and usually out of reused Roman material.

While the structure contained dressed stone, bricks and roof tiles that almost certainly came from a Roman coastal fort or watchtower, no Roman structure had been positively identified nearby; if there had been one, it was probably under the sea thanks to coastal erosion.

The pamphlet had little further useful information to add, though the bottom half of the fourth page comprised an advertisement for The Plough public house in White Dudley, a 'welcoming local' which offered ales, stouts and cordials from the brewers Steward & Patterson.

And there was one final line of detail, advising the potential tourist that the key to St Jurmin's chapel could always be found at 8 High Street, White Dudley, in the care of Mrs Daisey May Meade.

As dusk fell and lights came twinkling on all over the campus, Campion found the view from the top floor of the library almost hypnotic. The childlike geometric shapes of the buildings had become indistinct as the eye was drawn to the patterns of orange lights blurring their outlines. Only Black Dudley itself, with every possible light burning, stood out as an unmistakeable point of reference. Beyond the house, between shore and sea, the chapel of St Jurmin, which had intrigued Campion, had disappeared completely into the gloom, but then his eye was caught by the movement of lights in the main university car park.

Unmistakably, cars were on the move, engines being revved and headlights illuminated, which meant that the police had allowed movement out of the grounds and, in turn, that suggested they had either made an arrest or had abandoned any idea of containing overnight the staff and students who lived off-campus.

Mr Campion suspected the latter and considered that, as teatime was now a memory, he should be contemplating the possibility of dinner, or at least a drink before dinner; perhaps at a 'welcoming local' within easy driving distance.

There were police cars still in the car park, but no on-duty policemen to challenge him as he manoeuvred the Jaguar out of its parking bay and, at the end of the campus slip road, turned left towards White Dudley, some three miles away according to the signposts.

From what the Jaguar's headlights – irresponsibly turned on full beam – could uncover, the village was a single-street affair straddled by short terraces of houses, cottages and bungalows, and Campion even thought he spotted a couple of pre-fab structures dating from the post-war housing crisis. There was a shadowy outline of a church, but the only building showing un-curtained lights and offering any sort of welcome was the pub The Plough, which actually had a real iron plough as an inn sign, dangling precariously from a scaffold in the small parking area at its frontage. Campion noted that of the few cars outside the pub, none had been parked directly under the suspended ironmongery and, valuing the Jaguar's bodywork and unwilling to file an improbable insurance claim, he followed the strategy of the locals.

He had thought little about White Dudley, other than making assumptions about its name based on his knowledge of East Anglia, where it had been common practice to give adjoining or divided villages the designation 'White' if it represented a community which had survived the Black Death and 'Black' if the inhabitants had not been so lucky. He had no justification for this theory other than a vague memory of once being told that the Black Dudley house had been built on the foundations of a long-abandoned fourteenth-century monastery, which would fit his speculative timeline, and it was perfectly possible that a medieval monastic community might decide to settle out on this part of the Suffolk coast where, thanks to St Jurmin, there was evidence of a spiritual track record.

Campion read the legal declaration above the door, which informed him that a Mr H. Hopewell was licensed to sell all the necessary liquors one might reasonably expect to find, before opening it to be greeted by music of anything but a spiritual bent. It was coming from a brash American jukebox, which seemed to take up one wall of a brightly lit saloon bar where each table had, as a centrepiece, a large green plastic ashtray, around which beer mats had been dealt out as if by a careless poker player.

The bar had perhaps a dozen customers and was clearly the result of two or perhaps three small rooms being 'knocked into' one. The one-bar pub was, Campion knew, something of a controversial modern development among traditionalists, although in truth it harked back quite accurately to the years before coach (and then rail) travel, which introduced the class system to the democratic British pub, demanding a division between saloon and public bars.

The Plough had, it seemed, adopted modernity in almost every aspect. The lighting came from harsh neon strips, the bar counter was made of shiny fake wood and armed with a variety of garish plastic boxes holding small dispensing taps for the keg beers. There was not a horse brass or a smooth mahogany beer pump handle in sight; only the music coming from the jukebox showed any sense of history in that it seemed to come exclusively from the 1950s and the era of skiffle, trad jazz and primitive – very primitive – rock and roll.

Although by no means a dedicated follower of musical fashions, even Mr Campion appreciated that the musical repertoire on offer was unlikely to attract any business from a young student population to whom the musical stylings of Lonnie Donegan, Chris Barber or even Bill Haley were ancient history.

But yet there were younger customers, who Campion presumed were students, a group of four seated around one table as far away from the jukebox as it was possible to get. The telltale signs were that they were all sipping from half-pint glasses while the rest of the clientele, almost exclusively middle-aged males, were quaffing full pints of Norwich Mild. It was not the only thing which distinguished the two castes of customer. While the male clientele stood within reach of the bar and talked, or at least nodded, among themselves, or shared a newspaper or played darts, the students were also distinguished by the fact that they sat in silence, smoking hand-rolled cigarettes with copies of the same, unopened, paperback book in front of them on the table.

At the bar Campion ordered a bottle of Worthington White Shield and, relieved to see that the landlord appeared to know how to pour it properly, summoned up the courage to ask if any food was available.

'You be from the university then?' the landlord demanded in an inquisitive, not unfriendly, Suffolk sort of way.

'I am indeed visiting that splendid institution,' Campion replied truthfully, and his answer acted like a password to provisions if not gastronomy.

'Then I suppose Gladys can rustle you up some vittles. Pie and chips be good enough for you?'

Campion rapidly assumed that Gladys was Mrs Hopewell and that to demand a more expansive menu might not be diplomatic. 'That sounds most suitable,' he said with a smile. 'What sort of pie?'

'Meat.'

'Perfect. I'll be sitting over there.'

The landlord nodded to signify that some form of contract had been entered into, and disappeared through a curtain into the private quarters of the pub. From the sounds which emerged as a door was opened and a television could be heard, it seemed that Mrs Hopewell was being dragged away from *Coronation Street* for kitchen duty. Campion hoped it wasn't her favourite programme.

He took a sip from his beer and thought briefly about dear old Lugg, who had once decanted twenty perfectly clear glasses of White Shield in a row, leaving the yeasty sediment in the bottom of the bottles. It had earned him the award of a tie from the White Shield Pourers' Club, which had a vaguely military design and, to Lugg's delight and sometimes advantage, was often mistaken for the regimental tie of 42 Commando of the Royal Marines.

'Do you mind if I join you?' he addressed the student enclave.

His request was met with sullen silence from three of the company, all male, but the fourth, a girl with long, straggling hair in need of a wash, blew smoke from a roll-up in his general direction, picked a shred of tobacco from her lower lip and said: 'They say it's a free country.'

'They do indeed,' said Campion, grinning and reaching for a spare chair from the neighbouring table, 'but they rarely mean it. Hope I'm not intruding. I'm at the university too, in a sort of way.'

'What makes you think we're students?' one of the boys reacted sharply.

Campion could have said many things, all of which would have been expected from a man of his age, but instead he pointed to the paperback books labelled Penguin Classics on the table.

'*Don Quixote* is not the usual early evening reading material for a Suffolk country pub, fascinating book though it is. Did you know that it is supposed to have been translated into more languages than any other book apart from the Bible? Another interesting fact: most of its first editions were exported to Spanish colonies in South America, but the bulk were lost in a shipwreck and only seventy copies made it to Lima in Peru.'

'So you've read it?' the girl asked.

She was, like the boys, not long out of her teens, twenty-one at the most, and like theirs her fashion sense extended only as far as a uniform of jeans and an anorak or parka bought from the Army & Navy Stores. Campion had already spotted that two of the boys wore long hooded jackets with the West German flag embossed on the shoulder.

'A long time ago,' said Campion jovially. 'Wonderful book, a great inspiration to dreamers like me. I even had my own Sancho Panza, of a sort.'

Campion was confident that Lugg would have taken that as a compliment.

'That'd be your butler, would it? Or your batman?' snapped the boy who had snapped before. He was, Campion thought, a callow youth trying desperately to look older than his years by growing a ragged brown beard to match his shoulder-length hair, which made a poor job of camouflaging a bad case of vibrant acne.

'Don't be rude, Kevin,' said the girl, draining her glass of clear liquid. 'This nice gentleman was just about to offer to buy a poor student a drink.'

She had turned away from Campion as she spoke, and he suspected that she was giving her companions a conspiratorial wink.

'In the absence of any nice gentlemen, I suppose that honour falls to me,' said Campion, playing along. 'Though I insist on introductions as one should never buy a round for strangers. That's something I learned from *Don Quixote*. My name is Albert.'

The girl offered up her empty glass. 'I'm Angie and these three are Joe, Brian and chopsy Kevin. They're drinking beer so they can relate to the working classes. Mine's a gin and tonic. Have you really read Cervantes?'

'Yes, I have, but a long, long time ago, way before any of you were born, so please don't ask me to help you with your homework, at least not before I've got the drinks in.'

Mr Campion went to the bar and placed his order with Mr Hopewell, who confided that his 'dinner' would be another five or perhaps ten minutes. Campion assured him there was no rush and that he would take it at a smaller table, not at the one he was buying drinks for.

Campion returned to his students with a metal tray on which he balanced three pints of bitter and a double gin and tonic, Mr Hopewell even managing to find an ice cube and a slice of preserved lemon for the latter, indicating with a nod and a wink that the recipient would appreciate such luxury, which she did.

'Wow! What a treat!' said the girl called Angie. 'A proper G and T. Thank you, Mr Albert. Now if you could write my seminar paper for me, you really would be my knight in shining armour.'

'I'm not sure that would be allowed,' said Campion, handing out the drinks, 'even if such a thing were remotely possible, for I am a poor scholar when it comes to judging literature.'

'Actually, Joe, Brian and I are studying linguistics. Kevin there is doing sociology, but his thing is really politics.'

'Goodness,' said Campion, 'as if sociology wasn't enough. Why the Cervantes?'

'Textual analysis,' said the boy next to Angie, who might have been Joe or possibly Brian, raising his glass in salute to its provider. 'You didn't get one for yourself.'

'I'm driving,' said Campion, 'and I no longer have the capacity of youth. Plus, I need to keep a clear head if I am in the company of intellectuals who know what "textual analysis" means.'

'We analyse texts by means of a computer programme,' offered the boy, warming to his subject.

'If you can ever get time on the bloody thing,' interposed Kevin.

'Well, we might this term,' said the girl, 'once our sanctions start to bite.'

'Sanctions?'

'We're boycotting lectures and tutorials until we get more computer time,' said the boy Campion had decided was Brian.

'Isn't that rather cutting off one's nose to spite one's educational face?'

'It's a protest,' Angie explained, as if explaining thunderstorms to a nervous child. 'Our next step will be direct action, but at the moment it's a formal protest.'

'May I ask against what?'

'Against the mad scientist, of course!' Kevin blurted, loudly enough to attract questioning stares from a group of locals propping up the bar. 'The South American heart-throb,' he added, lowering his voice and glaring at Angie, 'who monopolizes the Computing Centre for his precious research for the CIA.'

'Are you referring to the late Professor Perez-Catalan?'

Campion spoke quietly, so that his words could not be heard beyond the table, but the effect on his audience was as if he had shouted down a megaphone. The four students stared at him in amazement, drinks paused between table and lips, and Angie's mouth fell open to reveal a perfect set of white teeth. Only Kevin made a sound – a snort, but whether in surprise or derision, it was not clear.

The girl reacted first. 'Pascual is dead?'

'I'm afraid so,' said Campion. 'Have you not been on campus today?'

'Not much point if we're boycotting lectures.' The girl fluttered her eyelashes over the rim of her glass like a silent movie vamp. 'Did we miss anything exciting?'

'Alarums and excursions all round; everyone is in quite a state about it.'

'He didn't pop his clogs *in flagrante*, did he?'

'Kevin! That's a loathsome thing to say!' Angie's eyes now flashed in anger.

'Woops! Hit a sore spot, have I?' Kevin replied with a sly

smirk. 'Wouldn't it be a hoot if he'd conked out during an orgy with first-year virgins in his love shack.'

Mr Campion decided that the time had come to inject decency and decorum into this saloon bar Brains Trust. 'The professor's body was found late last night by the porters, near Black Dudley,' said Campion with gravitas, only to be taken by surprise by the reaction of the girl sitting next to him.

'Got you!' she squealed, awarding herself a large slurp of gin and tonic. 'You're the university Visitor, the chap who was here when there was a murder at the Dudley back in the last century.'

'Not quite that long ago,' Campion chided, 'though it must seem like it to you.'

'How did you know that?' Kevin accused her.

'Because I keep my eyes and ears open instead of reading pamphlets and plotting the revolution,' she shot back, before turning to Campion as if she had just remembered something. 'Hang on . . . does your being here mean there's been another murder? That Pascual's been murdered?'

'I'm afraid it does.' Campion adopted his sternest expression. 'But lest that should be taken as the starting gun for the revolution, I would point out that the campus is positively crawling with policemen.'

'Then we're well out of it here,' said the youngest of the group, who by a process of elimination must be Joe.

'Rubbish!' Kevin almost spat at him. 'If the pigs are on campus giving our comrades the third degree, we have to go and stand by them. Solidarity! United we will not be defeated!'

'I don't think anyone is getting the third degree,' said Campion, 'nor even the second, but I am not privy to the police investigation.'

'I'm surprised they haven't descended on us here,' said Kevin with a hint of regret. 'They'd love to put us in the frame for something serious.'

'Oh, but the police have been here – if you mean White Dudley, that is. They came to search the professor's house around one o'clock.'

'Ah.'

The girl Angie buried her face in her glass, but a telltale bloom on her cheek gave her away.

'I take it that was too early for you,' said Campion gently, 'not having lectures or classes to go to.'

'A bit. We must have missed all the fun. Pascual's cottage is just down the road from our house. We're practically his nearest neighbour.'

'Really? So you probably got on with him quite well.'

'Not bloody likely!' Kevin warmed to his theme. 'The work he was doing was funded by the CIA and the results would have ended up with some big American mining corporation.'

'Are you sure of that?'

'It said as much in *Socialist Worker*!' Brian blurted in support.

'Then it must be true,' Campion said dryly, proving yet again that fanatics have underdeveloped senses of irony. 'Although I did hear that the professor supported the new socialist government in Chile.'

'He wasn't that interested in politics,' said Kevin, glaring at Angie. 'He was mostly into women – as many and as often as he could get.'

'And that's why you called him the South American heart-throb; somewhat pejoratively, I thought.'

'He made men – and boys – jealous,' Angie intervened, 'because he was so charming. There was definitely something of the Latin Lover about him.'

As she leaned into Campion to confide in him, he noticed that the girl's unkempt hair had a suspiciously botanical odour, which had not come from her Virginia hand-rolled tobacco alone.

'The Randy Gaucho,' Kevin sneered. 'That's what we called him.'

'I think gauchos live in Argentina rather than Chile,' said Campion, 'but I may be wrong. Still, he sounds like quite a character. Did you say you were neighbours?'

'We share a house just down the street from his cottage,' said Angie, sensing the need to distance herself and her friends from Pascual. 'Not that we saw him much off-campus, and we're none of us his students.'

'We would have got more computer time if we were,' said Brian sulkily, at which the other three flashed warning glances at each other.

'Yes, I understand there has been a certain amount of bad feeling at the university about the allocation of the resources of the Computing Centre.'

'You can say that again!' Young Brian was clearly not picking up on the unease of his housemates. 'Just ask Jake Zee or Steph – they were always rowing with him.'

'That would be Jack Szmodics – Dr Szmodics – and Stephanie Silva, wouldn't it?'

Angie looked at Campion through narrowed eyes. 'You're quite the detective, aren't you? Are you sure you're not with the police?'

Mr Campion was grateful that, at that precise moment, Mr Hopewell appeared from behind the bar holding a steaming plate with a pair of obviously burnt oven gloves.

'My dinner is served,' he said. 'Let me leave you, with Cervantes, in peace.'

Campion settled himself at the small table the landlord had laid for him and began a forensic examination of what he had been served. He had hardly started the autopsy on his meat pie when the students, having rapidly finished their drinks, stood up and trooped out of the pub. As they passed Campion, Angie winked at him, Brian nodded sheepishly, Joe said, 'Thanks for the drink', and Kevin gave him the clenched-fist salute of the international revolution. He acknowledged all of them.

He had just determined that the meat in the pie on his plate was lamb, and actually was quite palatable, when he noticed that he was being observed by one of the locals playing darts. By some unwritten law of pub or darts-playing etiquette, Campion was allowed to finish his meal before one of the players approached him, a pint of mild in one hand and a set of 'Norwich woods' – the short, stubby, native dart of East Anglia, made from pine and weighted with lead, with stiff white 'feathers' – in the other.

'I know you,' said the darts player when he stood immediately before Campion's table.

'Indeed you do,' said Campion. 'We met earlier today. It's Mr Warren, isn't it? I didn't recognize you in your civvies.'

The uninvited guest looked down his front as if to make sure he was still wearing the blue pullover and brown corduroy trousers he had started the darts match in. 'Oh, the uniform,' he said, the penny dropping. 'Glad to be out of it after a day like today. Mr Meade has pulled me off the night shift after my midnight patrol . . . discovery.'

'That's perfectly understandable, Mr Warren. University porters see many things which would melt the eyeballs of normal men, but your experience was well beyond the call of duty.'

Bill Warren nodded in agreement. ''Course I ain't supposed to talk about it, so the p'liceman said. Saw you with them students. We call 'em our local branch of the Angry Brigade.'

'Oh, they're hardly that,' chuckled Campion. 'No more than a Slightly Cross Platoon, I would say.'

'Were they bending your ear?'

'I suppose they were, but not about the . . . about your discovery. They were in blissful ignorance as they hadn't been up to the campus today.'

Mr Warren clicked his tongue against his teeth.

'Don't surprise me, that bunch. Layabouts they are, and hooligans.'

'I don't mind lazy hooligans,' said Campion, 'they cause less trouble than energetic ones. I've known some distinguished hooligans in my time.'

'Aye, you're 'im,' said Warren with satisfaction.

'Yes, I probably am,' said a confused Campion, 'but who do you think I am?'

'You're Albert Campion, of course, friend to hooligans, minor royalty and criminals of most persuasions. No time-wasters, please.'

Campion sat back in his chair and reached for his glass and the last drops of his ale.

'That sounds awfully familiar, Mr Warren, and rather like a testimonial, one I might have written myself. May I ask where you heard it?'

Bill Warren took a contemplative sip from his pint.

'It was during the war, up in Lunn'un, when I was in the Ambulances.'

'I believe you mentioned your service this morning, but how on earth did I crop up?'

'There was a whole street got flattened by a V-bomb down in Chelsea and it was a three-day job digging the survivors out. Got chatting to a bloke in Heavy Rescue. Once I said I was from Suffolk, you couldn't shut him up about how he thought it was "pure nachure" out here and how he loved the countryside.'

'A big chap, built like a wrestler,' said Campion wearily, pinching his nose between finger and thumb, 'bald head the size of a beach ball? Moustache like a walrus's perhaps? Good with children but you wouldn't trust him with the keys to your coal cellar?'

'That sounds like him. Good man to have next to you when the beams start creaking and the gas main's leaking. Funny name, though.'

'Magersfontein,' supplied Campion.

'No, that wasn't it. Major Lugg I think it was. Must have been a major in the war previous, as he was too old for active service.'

'You can say that again,' Campion said quietly.

'Anyway, this Lugg said he was partners with a toff – pardon my French – called Campion, though that wasn't his proper name, and they got up to some right old larks together before the war. He was looking forward to getting his junior partner back in harness after the war for a bit of "private narking", as he called it. That was you, wasn't it?'

'In a bygone era, it might have been, but I retired a long time ago.'

'You don't happen to know what happened to Major Lugg do you? I heard he kept pigs during the war and he looked the sort who could wrestle one to the ground with ease.'

'He could certainly eat one into submission,' said Campion.

'I hope he got through the war in one piece,' said Mr Warren wistfully. 'He saved a dozen or more civilians to my knowledge.'

'Oh, he's still around,' Campion admitted. 'He survived the war all right, but sadly lost his mind worrying about the Festival of Britain. The poor old soul is quite mad nowadays and is only allowed visitors on Wednesdays if there's an "R" in the month.'

'Sorry to hear that.'

'A sad fate, but the logical outcome of low living, I'm afraid.

Now, tell me about those students I was drinking with. Why are they layabouts and hooligans?'

Bill Warren wetted his lips with his pint. 'The four of them share a house in the village and you wouldn't believe the goings-on that go on there.'

'Oh, I might,' said Campion casually. 'I'm very broad-minded.'

'Loud music, visitors at all hours, rubbish strewn all over the front garden, drugs probably; visits by the police and I bet they never bought a round.'

'Well, they were certainly guilty of that, but I didn't expect them to, being poor students living on toast and baked beans.'

'Pah! Don't you be taken in. That Angie, she's got expensive tastes and comes from a good family. When she came to the university a year ago, her parents drove her down here in a Rolls-Royce. They took one look at the pyramid residences and said "our darling daughter's not staying *there*" so they came over to White Dudley and bought the first cottage they saw for sale. Paid cash for it and a price none in the village could match. 'Course rich old mum and dad have never been back to see what a mess's been made of the place.'

'My goodness, I can see why they may not be popular in the village, but I have to ask, Mr Warren, how do you know all this?'

'Gerry Meade lives here, don't forget.'

'And Mr Meade likes to keep an eye on students who live off-campus?'

'Not so much him as Mrs Meade.'

Campion did a double take. He could not help himself. 'Daisey May Meade?'

'No, goodness me, she passed on ten years since,' Warren reassured him. 'I was meaning Edwina Meade, Big Gerry's missus. She doesn't miss much that goes on around here. I'm surprised the police haven't co-opted her to help them, instead of you. No offence, of course.'

'None taken,' said Mr Campion. 'None at all.'

Back in his temporary lodgings in the staff flat atop the Durkheim pyramid, Mr Campion stood, with the light off, taking in the sights and sounds of the campus at night. His brain ticked over in neutral, wondering idly what the electricity bill of the university must be, for the library and all three piazzas were lit up, as were the footpaths, as if indicating the location to a passing spaceship. Even Black Dudley had light showing, though beyond the house was only inky blackness.

The library was, of course, closed, and there was little sign of human activity in the piazzas, though occasionally a figure walked over to the car park and Campion noted that everyone who did so had come armed with a torch. In the morning it might be worth asking Superintendent Appleyard if the professor had carried a torch on his midnight ramble to the car park. The important question, however, was still where was he rambling from?

Almost imperceptibly the background noise from the residences – doors slamming, muted music from record-players, the occasional inebriated shout – declined and Campion began to consider carefully the problem of how he could comfortably bend his elongated frame into the short and narrow bed provided.

Painful decision-making was delayed by the very audible sound of a trumpet playing the mournful first notes of the 'Last Post'.

Campion consulted his watch. Dead on time; and for once the Phantom Trumpeter's choice of tune could not have been more appropriate.

NINE
Mainframe

M r Campion was delighted to find that part of the refectory was open for breakfast at seven thirty but not altogether surprised to discover he was the first customer. The matronly figure behind the counter who served him rewarded him with an extra rasher of bacon on condition that he didn't tell anyone, and recommended the coffee 'before it got too stewed'. When Campion thanked her he tipped his hat before sliding his tray towards the cash register and she declared in a loud voice how nice it was to serve a gentleman for once.

Gradually the cafeteria began to fill with middle-aged women wearing nylon house coats and, from their dawn chorus chatter, Campion gathered that they were the cleaning staff who had completed their allotted tasks in the academic and administrative buildings and were taking a well-deserved break before steeling themselves for the grim task of tackling the student residences.

The first actual student he saw that morning was as he traversed Piazza 2 heading for Black Dudley, where he was sure the police would be wide awake and open for business. There was little doubt it was a student; as Rupert Campion would have said, he could have come straight out of Central Casting. He wore jeans, baseball shoes, an old school blazer over a T-shirt bearing a famous Disney character behaving completely out of character, and a scarf in the colours of a relatively well-known public school. He was clutching a sheaf of papers, clearly a handwritten essay, and was sneaking up on the entrance to the School of Arts and Humanities in the hope that it would not notice him. Campion guessed this was an attempt to sneak in a piece of coursework for marking even though the deadline had long passed; in fact, Campion realized, this being the first week of term, the deadline must have been sometime in the last academic year which, given the long summer vacation, meant that the essay could be up to three months better-late-than-never.

He sauntered out of the piazza, taking the footpath to the artificial lake and the curved bridge, now free of its police guards. Once free of the buildings, he buttoned up his jacket as the salty tang of sea breeze struck him. The Suffolk coast was throwing one of its hissy fits that morning, and from the bridge Campion could see, in the distance, white flecks on the grey water. Before it was masked by Black Dudley, he also caught a glimpse of the chapel of St Jurmin jutting up like a broken tooth from the shoreline.

Superintendent Appleyard had made himself comfortable in the vice chancellor's office; indeed he had occupied most of Black Dudley as he had brought reinforcements. Every nook and cranny of the ground floor of that gaunt old house seemed to have been crammed with uniformed constables sitting at folding card tables, pecking at the keys of portable typewriters to copy notes on to Rolodex cards. Flitting between the temporary desks, rather like overkeen exam invigilators, were half a dozen plain-clothes detectives, occasionally leaning over a constable to read or correct a card, or to drop cigarette ash all over his uniformed colleague's painstaking work.

'Glad to see somebody else is up with the milkmaids, even if it's you,' Appleyard greeted Campion. 'If you've got something useful to tell me, you're welcome. If you haven't, keep out of my hair and don't pester my officers.'

Not to be cowed, Mr Campion ignored the superintendent's threat completely.

'You seem to have increased the size of your staff,' Campion observed. 'Special Branch helping out, are they?'

'Who said . . .? What makes you think they're Special Branch?'

'I would be very surprised if they weren't. An officer of your experience would surely have called them in given the sensitivity of Perez-Catalan's work and the local gossip about student politics and the Angry Brigade.'

'I don't class such things as gossip, and we have reason to believe there is an active cell operating within the university.'

Campion shook his head slowly, and set his face with his most beatific smile.

'Oh, come now, Mr Appleyard, if you're referring to that knitting circle of young radicals over in White Dudley, I've met them, and they don't strike me as dangerous. They may be living in a commune or squatting or whatever young people do these days, and no doubt they are a drain on the rates and not good for property prices, but they seem a mild rather than wild bunch.'

Appleyard strained his neck muscles as if his shirt collar was strangling him. 'Our sources on the ground beg to differ.'

Campion had no doubt he knew who those sources were. 'I'm sure you know best, Superintendent, and I don't presume to teach you how to do your job,' he said. 'I am here to help if I can.'

'Have you phoned the bishop?'

'Not exactly, but he is constantly in my . . . thoughts.'

'And you're in his, or you were at seven o'clock this morning when he rang the chief constable.' Appleyard's face strained to adopt an expression of bemusement. 'And guess who *he* phoned at two minutes after seven? If you've nothing to tell the bishop, have you got anything for me?'

'Very little, I'm afraid, scraps mostly, and to make sense of things I need to ask a question and a favour.'

'As long as you realize I am under no obligation to either answer or grant.'

'Understood. I was interested to know whether Professor Perez-Catalan was carrying a torch when he was assaulted.'

Appleyard considered the question for half a minute before deciding it was harmless. 'If he was, we haven't found it. Could be in the lake, of course, like his body.'

'You haven't dragged the lake yet?'

Appleyard bristled. 'I am having to spread my resources across a number of fields of enquiry,' he said stiffly.

'I quite understand,' Campion soothed. 'Now, my favour. Would it be possible for me to examine the professor's cottage down in the village?'

'I don't see why not; we've finished with it and technically it's not a crime scene. You won't find anything because we didn't. Big Gerry Meade has a set of keys; he'll let you in.'

'I would rather act independently,' Campion said, perhaps too quickly.

The superintendent shrugged. 'Suit yourself. The professor was carrying a set of keys. I'll get one of my lads to peel off his house key, but I must have it back – chain of evidence for the inquest and all that.'

'I understand and thank you. In return, can I offer you a snippet of what may be scurrilous gossip? I am given to understand that there was an article in the *Socialist Worker* claiming all sorts of conspiracies involving the CIA and the professor's research. I'm not sure when it appeared, but it might be worth getting one of your lads to dig it out.'

Now the superintendent did the completely unexpected. With some difficulty, he forced half his facial muscles into producing what could pass, if one was being generous, as a smile.

'I can do better than that – I can give you a photostat of the article. It's quite interesting – and so is the author. A certain Nigel Honeycutt, no less, the loyal assistant of the very professor he's accusing of being one of capitalism's running dogs, or hyenas, I forget which. We seem to be way ahead of you, Mr Campion.'

'It won't be the first time, Superintendent, and probably not the last.'

Campion strode from Black Dudley, altering his planned day as he walked back towards the campus buildings. He was sure that there was much in the late professor's private life that was germane to his death, and the starting point for that would be his cottage in White Dudley. But what the superintendent had told him – and what he had not said – made Campion think that a visit to the Earth Sciences department was now the priority, and his route there, back over the curved bridge – the real scene of the crime – gave him the chance to do something he had forgotten to do on his first traverse.

This time he was heading south, and pointed in the right

direction to observe the triangle peaks of the pyramid residences. From the middle of the bridge he could clearly see the top three floors of each pyramid and certainly the top-floor flats at the peaks. Logic dictated that if he could see those rooms, or at least their windows, then someone inside looking out would have a clear line of sight of him on the bridge. Whether they could see him, or anyone else, at midnight, unless he was waving a torch around, was another matter.

Over the bridge he took the path which ran alongside the lake until it turned into Piazza 3, where the student population had reluctantly come to life and were shambling towards lectures and seminars. He also noted, with a mixture of disapproval and amusement, a row of empty bottles of light ale arranged neatly on the edge of what had been the central fountain before it became a firepit; now, it seemed, it was being used as a 'midden', which Campion was sure was what a rubbish dump was called in an academic setting.

Through the main doors of the School of Earth Sciences, Campion was confronted by a floor-to-ceiling sign pointing him to a bewildering choice of offices, seminar rooms and laboratories, most of them dealing with a specific subject or subset of geology, geography, minerology, climatology and numerous 'ologies' which were new to him, plus the specific offices of members of staff. Here he felt on safer ground and followed the arrows to the staircase which, he was assured, would lead to the second floor and room 2.21 which was the office of the late Professor Catalan-Perez.

Room 2.21, he found, was guarded by Room 2.21A; a small, open-plan affair occupied by a prim, middle-aged secretary wearing a powder-blue twin-set and a string of pearls, who sat behind a large electric typewriter giving every indication that she knew how to use it in anger. She had, to Campion's eye, arranged her office furniture using the blueprint of a machine-gun nest, but when she looked up as he entered her field of fire, he saw that she had made several botched attempts with her morning make-up to hide the fact she had been crying.

'Yes?' she said, daring Campion to answer. 'I know you don't have an appointment, so don't pretend you have. You press people are all the same.'

Campion removed his fedora and held it over his heart for protection. 'My name is Campion.'

'I don't care what newspaper you're from, no one here has anything to say to you. The police have told us not to talk to the likes of you.'

'I fear you are labouring under a misapprehension on two counts,' Campion said gently. 'Firstly, I am not a member of Her Majesty's Press Corps in any shape or form; and secondly, the police have wisely told you not to talk to strangers, but they have insisted that I talk to you.'

'To me?' she pointed an index finger at herself at pearl-necklace level.

'Well, not you personally; I'm not even sure who you are, but my remit is rather wide when it comes to anyone who had contact with the late Professor Perez-Catalan.'

'Contact?' the woman bristled. 'I am the departmental secretary. My contact with the professor was purely professional and took place within office hours. I was never party to his extra-curricular activities and was certainly never invited to his private conclaves.'

'My dear lady,' Campion began to protest, but was rescued by the opening of the connecting door to Room 2.21 proper, through which poked the head of Dr 'Call-me-Jack' Szmodics.

'Is there a problem, Sheila?'

'Not at all, Pro-Vice-Chancellor. This is Mr Champion, but he hasn't said why he's intruding.'

Dr Szmodics raised his eyebrows as he acknowledged the intruder.

'Oh, hello, Campion, do come in. Sheila, I don't believe you've met the university Visitor, Mr Albert Campion.'

'No, I haven't,' said the woman, and though Campion advanced a pace towards her extending his right hand, she dropped her gaze and busied herself inserting a new sheet of paper into her typewriter.

'The pleasure was almost mine,' said Campion under his breath.

'Were you looking for me, Albert?'

'No, Jack, but since I find you here, you can certainly help me in my unofficial capacity as one of Superintendent Appleyard's unpaid and under-appreciated bloodhounds.'

'Delighted to help if I can, but how?'

'You can start by inviting me into Professor Catalan-Perez's office. You see, I need to search it.'

Dr Szmodics opened the door wide. 'By all means, please enter.'

As he did so, Campion was sure he heard Sheila emit a deep sob, but over the furious sound of typing it was difficult to be sure.

Dr Szmodics took Campion's casual announcement that he wanted to search the dead professor's office as if it was the most natural request in the world, and seemed more worried about the reputation of the university staff.

'You'll have to forgive Sheila. She can be very protective, and she's been the queen bee in this department since before Pascual got here.'

'I'm presuming the police have interviewed her?'

'Of course, she kept Pascual's diary among other things; not that there was much of interest in it.'

'Really?'

'Well, other than departmental meetings, his teaching schedule and his computer allocation. General academic stuff, nothing out of the ordinary. The police have it now, of course. Were you looking for anything specific in there?'

'I wasn't looking for it at all,' said Campion. 'I wanted to try and get a feel for his work, but now you mention a diary, I would be interested in any . . . shall we say . . . social entries, and by that, I mean entries of a *very* social nature.'

Dr Szmodics stiffened as if a metal rod had been threaded down his spine.

'What do you mean by that?'

'I'm trying to ask the indelicate in as delicate a way as possible.' Campion turned away to avoid the pro-vice-chancellor's disapproving stare and found himself taken with the view from the late professor's office window. 'You see, every time I mention Pascual's name, the subject drifts to his . . . social life, and terms such as Randy Gaucho and Latin Lover get thrown into the mix with a total lack of decorum.'

'Tango Trousers,' said Szmodics.

'I beg your pardon?' spluttered Campion, turning back to face him.

'It's what the student newspaper christened him two years ago and the nickname sort of stuck. He took it as a joke and actually bragged about it.'

'As both the tango and gauchos are more relevant to Argentina than Chile, he was probably amused at your students' lack of geographical awareness.'

'That is a worry, I admit, but Pascual was quite unashamed about his reputation as a likely lad who chased the girls.'

'Was he discreet about his conquests? I am presuming he had conquests?'

Dr Szmodics moved to the connecting door to the secretary's fortress and, with the flat of his hand, made sure it was firmly closed. 'By all accounts, females found him irresistible, but he was discreet about his conquests, I'll give him that; he didn't flaunt his relationships.'

'I take it you did not approve.'

'I'm no prude, Campion, but there is always the good name of the university to consider.'

'And the bishop.'

There was a gleam in Dr Szmodics's eyes as he said, 'Who I understand is your personal problem.'

'I'm afraid so.' Campion sighed. 'I am supposed to report progress regularly to His Lordship, but so far there has been little to report that would not enrage him.'

'Is that why you wanted to snoop around his office? Were you looking for smut?'

Campion did his best to look outraged. 'I take exception to that word, Dr Szmodics. I do not *snoop*, I *peruse*; admittedly, I may have given the impression that in this case I was perusing for smut, but my intention was to learn more about the professor's work.'

'Then you're in the wrong place. Pascual used this office for departmental matters only. All his research work took place in the Computing Centre where he also has an office.'

'I see . . .' said Campion, as if inspiration had arrived direct from heaven without passing 'Go', '. . . so that explains your presence here; the Computing Centre coming under your remit as part of Language and Linguistics if I'm not mistaken.'

'I'm not sure what you're getting at, Campion. The vice chancellor asked me to make sure the department keeps running smoothly. Why else would I be in here?'

'No reason at all, other than admiring the view.'

He nodded towards the window, which framed the picture Constable might have painted had he been still alive and offered a decent fee, containing the length of the artificial lake, the curved bridge and, as a backdrop, Black Dudley. Constable, he was sure, could not have resisted the urge to add in a few oak trees, some black-and-white cattle and a horse-drawn cart or two.

'You think I was here removing evidence, don't you?' Dr Szmodics spoke as if his own revelation had just arrived at the platform, albeit a few minutes late.

'My dear chap, the thought had not occurred to me – until just now. You weren't, were you?'

Mr Campion could still hear Dr Szmodics's loud and robust denials ringing in his ears, and feel the metaphorical tracer bullets fired from the secretary Sheila's eyes – both barrels – thudding into his back as he left the Earth Sciences department.

The piazzas were filling up with students clutching books and ring-binder files and notepads, hurrying between the buildings. They were dressed in an eclectic mixture of styles and although flared jeans were almost *de rigueur* for the boys, many of the girls were still participating in the ongoing fashion debate as to whether the mini or the maxi was 'in' this autumn.

As he threaded his way through the bustling crowd, Mr Campion was heartened by the air of self-confidence given off by those young, fresh faces, even though he knew that the majority were probably the new intake and were alone and away from home for the first time. But then young people were resilient and resourceful and it was such a shame they had to grow up into adults. Most impressive of all was the fact that none of them found anything odd in a tall, thin, seventy-year-old wearing a suit, tie and fedora, walking among them. Perhaps they thought of him as a distinguished, though of course eccentric academic, looking for someone to give a lecture to. Campion took it as a compliment and, as he entered Piazza 1, decided to play the part.

The open-air chessboard in front of the doors to the Computing Centre had been in use that morning, for the freshening breeze coming straight off the sea could not have moved the plywood pieces so neatly without divine intervention. To one side, several pawns the size of dustbins and a white knight had been removed from the 'board', which made Campion think the game had been abandoned, but a brief survey of the remaining pieces showed an obvious next move, if it was black's turn.

'Let boldness be my friend,' Campion said aloud, and stepped on to the board. He grasped the black queen, which came up to his chest, around the collar and, with the side of his shoe against the square wooden base, he advanced it diagonally towards a gap in the ranks of the white enemy. When satisfied he was in the ideal position, he stopped pushing and released his hold on the queen. Retiring to the side of the squares, he admired his handiwork, briefly touched the rim of his fedora towards the queen, and stepped towards the glass doors on which was painted the legend 'Computing Centre'.

The doors opened before he got there and a long-haired, bearded male wearing a dark blue pullover dotted with holes and trailing loose threads of wool, jumped out to meet him. 'How did you do that?' he demanded.

'I'm awfully sorry if I've spoiled your game,' said Campion. 'Was it white's move?'

'No, it was black to move,' admitted the chess player.

'Then I must apologize for putting you into check.'

'But how did you do it?'

'It seemed a logical move and really rather obvious. I make no claims to be a grand master.'

'But you didn't give it time!' the chess player wailed.

'I didn't realize I was playing anyone.'

'You weren't! I was playing the computer. I was white and the computer was black.'

'Oh dear, and I suppose the computer would have come up with a much better move.'

'I doubt that,' said the young man, whom Campion would henceforth always refer to as 'Mr White'. 'Putting me in check is a good move, but you didn't give the computer time to work it out. I'm still waiting for the printout; you were just too flaming quick for it! That's just not fair!'

Mr Campion found himself in a room full of metal coffins all standing to attention, as if awaiting a good dusting from a house-proud robot undertaker; something which would be totally superfluous as the room was spotlessly clean and dust-free, the temperature in there held at that constant level technically known as chilly by the air-conditioning. Some of the upright boxes had Perspex panels through which blinked small green lights, and some had pairs of large spools which whirred and spun seemingly at random. The whole room throbbed with a quiet humming noise as the machines went about their mysterious business, only occasionally disturbed by the frantic clatter of a printer spewing a torrent of broad green paper into a shiny metal bin like a demented weaver's loom ejecting bolt after bolt of finished cloth.

'Mr White', whose chess game Campion had hijacked, was in fact a postgraduate student called Oliver Brownlee, and once he had accepted that he was firmly in check, with 'mate' in three moves (although Campion thought two), he agreed to escort the Visitor into the Computing Centre. Dr Szmodics had rung ahead and warned the centre of an approaching VIP, and the centre's manager, Charles Fowler, was expecting him.

'But do have your cigarette first,' Campion said.

'What makes you think I smoke?' asked White-Brownlee, his hand going automatically to his trouser pocket, from which he produced a squashed packet of ten Embassy cigarettes and a box of matches.

'A good guess,' said Campion. 'I know little about computers other than they tend to be hermetically sealed in their own private atmospheres, whereas the chessboard gives you a good excuse to nip outside and move the pieces from time to time. The holes in your jumper are burn marks caused by sparks from a cigarette being enjoyed in a breezy location and this is a breezy location. No wonder the chess pieces are weighted at the base.'

'Are you Sherlock Holmes?' asked Oliver Brownlee, extracting a cigarette from the packet, having first removed to his other pocket the blue gift coupon which the brand offered.

'Good Lord, no!' exclaimed Campion. 'Mr Holmes would know why a campus of open piazzas had been built facing east, into a wind coming straight from the Urals; I don't.'

Once inside the technological sanctum, Charles Fowler welcomed the Visitor in the way Campion suspected he welcomed all non-technical visitors, with a well-rehearsed opening line delivered with thinly disguised boredom.

'So how much do you know about computers, Mr Campion?'

'Less than nothing up until five minutes ago, when I realized I could beat one at chess.' Campion beamed. 'Which one did I best?'

'We have only one computer. All these machines are connected together by intricate wiring under the floor, and technically, you didn't beat it. The computer was playing black.'

'So I helped the computer beat young Mr Brownlee. I call that a win.'

Fowler waved for Campion to follow him and walked over the spotless tile floor to the large metal bin near the printing machine. He delved into it and emerged with an armful of green paper with perforated edges folded at regular intervals along its length, the resultant pile being at least a foot thick.

'The computer was suggesting the black queen's move when you pre-empted it and it went on to predict checkmate in two moves. It's all here in the printout.'

Campion gazed in wonder at the stack of paper Fowler was holding as delicately as if it was a newborn baby. 'Goodness, and to think a tree had to die just for that.'

'I can see you are determined not to be impressed,' said Fowler.

'Oh, I am willing to be impressed. It is just that I start from a very low base. At school I had a mad maths teacher. Well, they're all mad, aren't they? And he would insist that algebra was a language and made us put full stops at the end of quadratic equations, like sentences. For a while it seemed to make sense, but then something shiny must have caught my eye, for it suddenly all slipped away . . . as did calculus. A bit of geometry did come in useful later in life, I admit, as did arithmetic, which is invaluable when scoring at darts, but on the whole, I was a bit of a dunce when it came to mathematics.'

Charles Fowler inflated his cheeks like a frog and exhaled through pursed lips. Campion resisted the urge to tell him that was exactly the same exasperated expression he had produced from his mad maths master at Rugby all those years ago; and he too had worn a tweed jacket with leather elbow patches.

'Let me rephrase my question, Mr Campion. How much do you need – or would like – to know about computers?'

Campion smiled. 'I *need* to know about Professor Perez-Catalan's work with your computers. As to how much I *want* to know about computers, I am too long in the tooth to appreciate anything more than a simple – a very simple – explanation of what they do.'

Mr Fowler returned the smile. 'Good. To be honest, I'm fed up with explaining things to new students who seem to think the computers are here to do their coursework for them and will respond to voice commands, because they've all seen far too many science-fiction films. So can I give you the idiots' version?'

'The more idiotic the better; preferably small words delivered in a slow monotone.'

'Excellent.' Mr Fowler waved an arm at the humming metal boxes which surrounded them. 'You are now standing in the middle of an electronic brain which stores data and makes calculations many times faster than any human.'

'While playing chess,' said Campion slyly.

'Yes, well, you caught it at a very busy moment. If you give it time, it can beat any above-average player, but that is really just a flippant add-on to its main function, at least at the moment. I can foresee a time when you'll be able to play a computer at lots of games.'

'Good lord, I hope *that's* science fiction,' said Campion. 'What if your electronic brain turns out to be a bad loser?'

Mr Fowler was not distracted and moved to one of the

cabinets which had an open metal drawer at hip height. From it he plucked a thick wedge of cards the size of postcards and held one up for Campion to see the holes punched through it.

'It looks as if someone's been using them for target practice with a twelve-bore.'

'Not quite. These punch cards are how we put information in. The computer crunches the numbers and prints out the answers on those green sheets.'

'Number crunching,' Campion said airily. 'I like that, though it conjures up an image of rows of poorly paid clerks wearing armbands and eyeshades, working rhythmically at a battery of adding machines.'

'Those days are long gone; the future is computing.'

'I am sure you are right, but forgive me if I do not rush to embrace it. I take it that Professor Perez-Catalan was an enthusiast.'

'You can say that again; he thought he owned the place. His work took up to seventy per cent or more of our capacity at times, which didn't go down well with the rest of the university.'

'I can see that,' said Campion. 'The professor must have had a lot of numbers to crunch.'

'He did,' Mr Fowler agreed. 'He would get seismic recordings and geological data, vast amounts of it, from all over the world.'

'And he would feed it into your machinery and the end result would be his algorithm?'

Mr Fowler raised a quizzical eyebrow, much as the young Campion's maths master had. 'You know about his algorithm?'

'Only what the professor told me, and I admit not all of it sank in. I wouldn't recognize it if it ran up and bit me in the leg. Does it come out of your machines on a stream of green paper?'

'No, his workings might, but the algorithm is his own personal brainchild. As I understand it, he was writing a paper for publication and peer review which would announce his algorithm to the world.'

'But I was under the impression that his algorithm was a formula which could be of great value in commercial terms.'

'That's as may be, but I'm happy to say it's not my problem.

All I do is make sure the numbers get crunched and the academics don't kill each other over the allocation of computing time.'

Mr Fowler stopped himself and dropped his gaze. 'I'm sorry, I shouldn't have said that.'

'Don't worry,' said Mr Campion gently, 'we're all thinking it.'

TEN
Staff Appraisals

On entering what Mr Fowler had described as the professor's 'inner sanctum' – a tiny, windowless office, its door sandwiched between two humming green cabinets – Campion recalled how he had often remonstrated with his contemporaries who claimed that because of the fashion for long hair 'you couldn't tell the boys from the girls these days'. Now he found himself guilty of a similar, but reverse, ridiculous simplification, for when the two figures working at a tiny metal desk turned to see who had entered, one of the faces to greet him was female.

'We were told someone would be coming to check up on us,' said Nigel Honeycutt. 'Thought it might be the coppers again. This is Tabitha King, one of our geologists.'

'We've met,' said Campion with a short bow. 'In fact, we're neighbours.'

'We are?'

Tabitha King's brown trouser suit and short-back-and-sides haircut had momentarily fooled Campion, and when she and Honeycutt rose from their plastic chairs and stood side by side, he noticed that even wearing sensible shoes she towered over her fellow scientist.

'Sort of. I am temporarily housed in one of the pyramids, but further down the Valley of the Kings in Durkheim. Convenient for the library, but miles away from the pleasure beach and donkey rides.'

He edged his way into the cramped space, carefully placing his feet between the piles of green computer printouts, until he could get a good view of the desk which was covered in loose sheets of white paper to a depth of three or four inches. Some of the sheets were handwritten, some typed, and Campion thought that in the middle of that snowstorm of paper he could just make out the outline of a portable typewriter. The shelves above the desk were equally frosted with loose papers, but also textbooks, badly folded maps and various rock samples ranging from ping-pong to rugby ball in size, several of them balanced rather precariously.

'And I am not here to check up on you,' he continued, 'rather I wanted to make sure that the professor's magic algorithm was safe and secure, though to be honest I wouldn't recognize it if it jumped up and bit me in the leg.'

Tabitha King took a half-pace back and turned sideways to give Campion a better view of the desktop. 'Well, there it is. Help yourself.'

'Really? I've seen neater burglaries. What exactly am I looking at?'

'Pascual's rough notes and first drafts of a paper explaining his algorithm,' said Honeycutt. 'We're trying to make sense of it, so we can submit it for publication and peer review.'

'So you're writing a posthumous scientific paper.'

'I know what you're thinking!' snapped Tabitha.

'I'm rather glad someone does,' Campion said disarmingly.

'You think we're stealing the professor's work. We most categorically are not. If anything, we're protecting his legacy.'

Honeycutt waded in to Tabitha's defence, not that, to Campion, the woman needed defending.

'The paper will be in Pascual's name which, being honest, carries far more weight than either of ours. We will take credit only as editors, along with the translator.'

'Translator?'

The pair shuffled uneasily, like guilty schoolchildren, in front of Mr Campion.

'It was Pascual's wish that his paper be first published in Chile through the University of Santiago,' said Honeycutt, 'although publication in an English journal would be almost simultaneous.'

'So his algorithm is to be made freely available to the scientific world?'

'And so it should.'

'Ethically, I am sure you are right, but I was under the impression that the algorithm, to put it crudely, was a formula for finding deposits of valuable minerals; a positive treasure map for mining companies and, indeed, many a government.' Campion paused and reached into the inside pocket of his jacket for the photostat he had been given at Black Dudley. 'According to a recent article in the *Socialist Worker*, which therefore must be true, the professor's work was attracting interest, perhaps even funding, from certain non-academic sources such as the CIA; and in my limited experience, where the CIA are involved, the Russians will not be far behind.'

'You idiot,' said Tabitha under her breath, and Campion was glad to see that her displeasure was aimed at her colleague. 'You just couldn't resist, could you?'

'I stand by what I wrote!' Honeycutt was far from cowed, almost pugnacious. 'Pascual wanted the poorer countries of South America to benefit from his work, but are the imperialist Americans going to let that happen? Not likely! Not if there are deposits of heavy metals in their own back yard for the taking. They've already tried to interfere in the elections in Chile, and a socialist government with access to resources such as gold, silver, tungsten, thorium . . .'

'And uranium,' Campion inserted.

'Well, the capitalists are just not going to let that happen, are they?'

'Do you have any proof of this?'

'Of course he doesn't,' said Tabitha.

'But it stands to reason! The CIA have probably infiltrated agents into the university already. I tried to warn Pascual, but he wouldn't listen.'

'Warn him about what exactly?'

'That he could be intimidated, a target even. That his research could be stolen.'

'And has it?'

'Not as far as we can tell,' said Tabitha, 'but there is a problem.'

'I can think of several,' said Campion, 'but which one exercises you most?'

'Pascual wrote large chunks of the first draft of his paper in Spanish.'

Campion waited for further details but none were forthcoming.

'I cannot see that as a problem in a university which has a dedicated, top-notch language department, or so I'm told; I haven't seen it myself yet. The vice chancellor himself is a Hispanist of some distinction. Why not ask him to translate?'

'Couldn't do that,' said Honeycutt with relish. 'Downes would be seen as trying to take credit for another academic's work, one that he appointed to the chair of Earth Sciences, and it was a controversial appointment at the time. Pascual was a foreigner for a start, and little known outside South America.'

'I can see how that could be embarrassing in certain circles,' Campion conceded, 'but what about Dr Downes's wife Dolores? She's Spanish.'

'No, that would not be a good idea.' Campion noticed that any trace of relish or smugness had gone from Honeycutt's voice. 'She's not a scientist, not an academic of any sort, and that would look like nepotism.'

'Is there nobody in Earth Sciences who speaks and reads Spanish?'

Campion's question was answered by a pair of shaking heads.

'But there are in other parts of the university. What about Stephanie Silva in Linguistics? I was drinking with some of her students last night.'

'No!' Tabitha spoke far too sharply, but quickly retracted her claws. 'She had issues with Pascual over the allocation of computing time.'

And perhaps other things, but Campion kept that thought to himself.

Mr Campion would have liked to pose one or two questions to Tabitha King in private, but she and Honeycutt were adamant that they needed to work on the professor's papers before the tiresome demands of having to teach students intervened. Campion had the distinct feeling that neither totally trusted the other alone, either with the work or to talk to him about Perez-Catalan. Realizing that he could not help them and was probably taking up valuable oxygen in that tiny room, he wished them 'happy hunting' and took his leave.

As he walked out via the mainframe, trying not to think he was actually strolling through a *brain*, he formulated half a plan for the rest of his day's itinerary. It was only half a plan, but it was still too early for lunch and he needed to know the position of various people on the campus before his expedition to White Dudley armed with the key Appleyard would provide to the professor's house.

He was, he thought, arranging his chess pieces on the board, but realized that perhaps that image had come to him because he was now out of the Computing Centre and standing on the edge of the outdoor chessboard, where the plywood pieces were swaying in the breeze and a new game was clearly under way.

'Please don't,' said a voice behind him.

Oliver Brownlee was leaning against a concrete pillar sheltering from the wind off the sea, a cigarette cupped in his right hand held close to his chest.

'I promise not to interfere with your game, on condition you tell me where I can obtain a timetable for a member of staff.'

'In Computing?'

'No, Earth Sciences.'

'In that case, you want the departmental secretary, Sheila Simcox, over in Piazza 3.'

'Ah, yes, Sheila,' Campion said slowly. 'I know where her office is, thank you. Are you playing white again?'

'No, I'm black this time.'

Mr Campion took a moment to study the layout of the chessmen. 'You are?' he said. 'Well, good luck then.'

'And good luck with Sheila,' said Oliver Brownlee to Campion's back as he strode away.

He knew he was unusually dressed and inappropriately aged for a modern university campus, but the trick in such fish-out-of-water situations, Campion decided, was to look as if you owned the place. With his fedora at the traditional jaunty angle and his back ramrod straight, Campion marched through the university precincts with the precision of a guardsman. Only a gnarled walking stick – or better, an RSM's swagger stick – could have made the image more distinctive.

By the time he topped the steps leading into Piazza 3, he still had only half a plan formed, now with the added problem of how to approach Sheila Simcox, on whom he had left a less than positive impression earlier that morning. The solution to that difficulty came unexpectedly in the form of divine intervention, although the university chaplain would have considered such a description heretical.

'Campion! There you are!' bellowed George Tinkler, loping across the piazza towards his prey.

'We really can't go on meeting like this,' said Campion, as the smaller man, his face twisted to keep his *pince-nez* in place, came within range.

'I was hoping to catch you in the Computing Centre. Jack Szmodics told me you might be there.'

'Let me guess; the bishop's been on the phone again.'

'Oh my, yes he has. He's *very* anxious for a progress report.'

'And I was just on my way to give him one.' Mr Campion felt sure that Mr Tinkler's spiritual boss would forgive a little white lie, even if his temporal one would not. 'Do you know if Dr Szmodics is still in Earth Sciences? I was going to ask if I could use the telephone in the departmental office.'

'No, I ran into Jack over in the Admin building; he was off to a meeting. But don't worry, Sheila will help you.'

'Sheila?' Campion probed innocently.

'The departmental secretary. If I had what you might call a congregation, Sheila would be the most loyal member of my flock. She's a good Christian soul and a great admirer of the bishop. She corresponds with him regularly, often appealing for him to give moral guidance to the university, or just complaining about the lack of morals at the university. Simply mention you are on an errand for him and she'll be delighted to help.'

Campion had been prepared to deploy all of what he liked to think of as his 'old-world charm', but which Lugg, disparagingly, would call his 'schoolboy smarm', on Sheila Simcox but now the chaplain had provided a new plan of attack.

'I fear we may have got off on the wrong foot earlier, Miss Simcox,' said Mr Campion, holding his hat by the rim in front of his stomach, presenting himself as a true penitent. 'I realize I should have introduced myself properly. I am here on campus as the special envoy of the Bishop of St Edmondsbury.'

Miss Simcox's eyes had been fixed in a stare which had

unnervingly reminded Campion of tiny icebergs, but at the mention of the bishop, those icy crystals began to melt.

'I believe you know the bishop.'

'We have corresponded,' said Miss Simcox pertly. 'The bishop was kind enough to respond to some genuine concerns I had about the moral image that the university was projecting.'

'He told me you had made many invaluable suggestions and he was seriously considering including some of your points in a future sermon.'

'Really? How kind, but then he is a kind and Christian gentleman.'

'One would certainly hope so,' said Campion deadpan, 'given the position he holds. He suggested I could turn to you for help in a crisis.'

'You have a crisis?'

'A minor one, or possibly two. Firstly, I would like to have sight of the teaching timetable of Tabitha King, to see when she has free time, and secondly, I would like to borrow your telephone if I may. The bishop is expecting me to call him.'

'Then you must,' said Miss Simcox, her eyes now melted pools. 'I can get you the timetable and you can use the telephone in the professor's office. Simply dial nine for an outside line, unless you would like me to connect you?'

She reached eagerly for the telephone on her desk and Campion had to think quickly to forestall her.

'Please, allow me,' he said, stretching a hand towards the instrument. 'I'm putting you to too much trouble as it is.'

Miss Simcox stood and moved from behind her desk, something Campion suspected she did only with reluctance, and went to open the second drawer of the metal filing cabinet against the wall. When her back was safely turned, Campion twisted the telephone towards him, lifted the receiver and began to dial.

'My dear bishop, it's Albert your faithful gundog reporting progress, such as it is,' Campion said into the mouthpiece. As Miss Simcox resumed her seat in the stronghold that was her desk, Campion made sure he caught her eye.

'No, the vice chancellor is still tied up with the police,' he said, 'and I am imposing on the departmental secretary of Earth Sciences for the use of a telephone. Yes. Why yes, it is

Miss Simcox, and I certainly will pass on your best wishes. I am sure she keeps you in her prayers too.'

Miss Simcox averted her eyes, casting them downwards into the bowels of her electric typewriter. It was simply not done to eavesdrop on the telephone conversations of others, even when it was physically impossible to get out of range, and though she pretended deafness, the pink blushing on her cheeks when her name was mentioned gave her away.

'I've spoken to several people here on campus,' Campion continued. 'No, my lord, I would not call any of them the "usual suspects", as you put it. Today I have been trying to educate myself on Professor Perez-Catalan's work and it's been jolly difficult for a dullard like me. Everyone thinks the professor was something of a genius and, do you know, I think they were right. As far as I can tell, his research is intact and secure, and his academic colleagues are already working on a posthumous scientific paper which I am assured will enhance the university's reputation internationally.'

Campion paused as if listening intently, and turned slightly away, as much as the telephone cord would allow, from Miss Simcox's desk.

'Really, Bishop? Well, no, I have not . . . What was that? You really think I should? . . . Oh, I see, you think I must . . . Well, of course I agree that the moral reputation of the university is just as important as the academic, but I simply do not feel equipped to . . . Yes, I have heard things about the professor's social life . . . You have too? . . . Oh, I agree, that is shocking if true . . . But really, Bishop, how do I start to ask questions about the professor's private – very private – life? I simply wouldn't know where to begin . . . Excuse me, what was that?'

Again Campion paused, this time dramatically, and he flashed a look of shock and surprise at the bewildered Miss Simcox.

'Are you quite sure, Bishop? I mean, it's a very indelicate thing to ask of a lady . . . I would not like her to think I was simply trawling for salacious gossip . . . Yes, I understand we must establish if there are likely to be . . . problems of morality then we should be aware of them, but . . . Very well, Bishop, if you are sure Miss Simcox will not mind me asking her some rather crass and crude questions, then . . . I'm sure she is,

Bishop, and also that she shares your concerns. Very well, I can but ask. I will of course treat any information in complete confidence. Yes, thank you, Bishop, and goodbye.'

Campion replaced the receiver and took a deep breath, but before he could speak, Miss Simcox looked up at him with deadly seriousness and said, 'I will help in any way I can.'

A few miles away in Monewdon Hall, a confused Guffy Randall looked at the telephone in his hand buzzing the dead line signal, shook his head and said to his wife Mary: 'That was Albert playing silly buggers again. No idea what he was on about.'

Although more than willing to be a cooperative witness, Miss Simcox turned out to have more speculation than substance to offer her interrogator.

It was certainly true, she volunteered between blushes and fluttered eyelids, that the late Professor Perez-Catalan had been a 'ladies' man'. For reasons which she failed completely to understand, women found him irresistible, and he seemed to have an insatiable appetite for women. There was not a female member of staff nor, may the bishop forgive her for saying so, the wife of an academic who had not been at least considered, if not pounced upon, by Pascual.

Except perhaps one, Campion thought, remembering her emotional sob that morning.

Surely a devout and upright person such as Miss Simcox must have found it intolerable to have to work for such a lothario?

One has to allow genius the freedom to flourish, said Miss Simcox, repeating a mantra she did not sound as if she believed, but there were, of course, limits. While the professor did not flaunt his conquests, neither did he make any secret of them and, judging by the smug expression on his face some mornings, he was quite proud of himself. But that was probably the South American idea of manliness: crude and ungentlemanly and certainly un-British, but somehow attractive to a certain type of female.

It was her Christian duty to report the rumours to the bishop.

Rumours? Were there allegations that the professor was philandering with his female students?

No, not at all, Miss Simcox had protested, that would be gross moral turpitude and probably grounds for dismissal, as the university was supposed to be acting *in loco parentis*, wasn't it?

Unsure of the law on such matters, though he was quite sure he had read somewhere that 'gross moral turpitude' related to the mass raping of nuns in medieval times, Mr Campion allowed Miss Simcox to continue.

That wasn't to say the students were not at risk – risk of seeing corruption and decay in their moral values when they saw those in authority behaving immorally.

Mr Campion asked if the professor's – he refrained from adding 'the late' – behaviour was blatant enough for the student body to notice it. Oh yes, it had been. The student newspaper had come up with some disgracefully rude nicknames for him, and that irritating pest they call the Phantom Trumpeter had even started playing the tune 'South of the Border' whenever the professor made a new conquest.

With admirable, almost superhuman, restraint, Campion retained a straight face and confided that he had heard rumours of 'private conclaves' held by the professor. These he took to be trysts or assignations with his lovers. When Miss Simcox nodded her agreement, he pressed her on where these conclaves could be located.

Logically, most would have been at the professor's house in White Dudley, though there were stories of 'dirty weekends' in gruesome seafront hotels in Great Yarmouth. However, in the summer term, when the weather was warmer and the daylight hours longer, there was always talk that the professor's periods of retreat and prayer in St Jurmin's chapel on the seashore involved more than private contemplation.

The only question remaining was with whom did the professor enjoy such 'contemplations'? Now that, Miss Simcox could not or would not say, and she tightened her lips and set her jaw accordingly.

How about Tabitha King? Mr Campion had tried, and was surprised by the woman's explosive 'Not her!' as she, everyone knew, would be the last female to fall for the professor's charms. In fact, she would be violently repelled by them.

The one person best equipped to provide a list of the professor's partners, and with few scruples about doing so, was to be found in White Dudley, not on campus. That was a woman who kept a close eye on the professor's house and, as it happens, was the key-holder for the chapel of St Jurmin.

'Daisey May Meade,' Mr Campion had said aloud without meaning to.

'No,' Miss Simcox corrected him. 'Edwina Meade, Big Gerry's wife.'

Campion took the long path from Piazza 3, walking along the south side of the artificial lake towards the curved bridge. The windows of Black Dudley were like a spider's eyes observing his approach and he made a mental note to check the functions of the first- and second-floor rooms whose windows offered a clear view of the bridge. Could there have been someone at one of those windows, at midnight on a Sunday, who might have seen something?

As he got nearer to the house it reminded him of a dark skull, a haunted house, even though uniformed and plain-clothed policemen flitted in and out of the main door carrying boxes of documents rather like tropical ants trooping leaves to a nest.

The focal point of all this activity was Superintendent Appleyard, ensconced behind the vice chancellor's desk, a veritable queen ant – if ants had queens (somebody on campus would know, Campion thought) – instructing her soldiers.

'Another visit from the Visitor: we are honoured!' Appleyard groaned aloud at the sight of Mr Campion. 'Unless you've got something useful for me, I'm busy.'

'I see you are, Superintendent, and it is a good thing to see,' said Campion as the policeman scrutinized him for signs of sarcasm. 'Earlier this morning you promised me a key to the professor's house in White Dudley.'

Appleyard sucked in his cheeks, an obvious aid to memory, then grunted at the uniformed constable seated at the side of the desk who had clearly inherited the duty as his personal secretary. 'Peters?'

'In your in tray, sir,' said PC Peters, and made to stand and reach over the desk to the wire-basket filing tray less than twelve inches from his superior's right hand.

'I can get it,' snapped Appleyard, plunging his hand into the tray and rummaging through the papers piled in it. 'I'm not help-less. There you are, Mr Visitor; one key, front door for the use of, number eleven, High Street. You can't miss it as there is only one street in White Dudley. Make him sign for it, Peters, and make sure you sign it back in. Got that? Good. No other requests, I hope?'

'A question,' said Campion, pocketing the Yale key. 'Were there any other keys found on the body?'

'A whole bunch of them, heavy enough to weigh down the body if that lake had been deep enough.' Appleyard caught Campion's look of distaste. 'Oh, sorry if I've offended your delicate sensibilities. What about them?'

'Can I have a look at them?'

Appleyard turned to his personal assistant. 'Well, Peters, can he?'

'Sergeant Walters is doing the rounds with them at the moment, sir. He's checking which key goes where.'

'Needles in haystacks in a place like this,' muttered the super-intendent. 'Trying them in every lock on campus? There must be thousands.'

'He's got Gerry Meade with him, to show him the ropes so to speak. Gerry knows roughly which key fits which lock in which department.'

'Rather him than me. Still, it gets Big Gerry out from under my feet for a bit.'

And mine, thought Mr Campion. Now to achieve the same advantageous position with the superintendent.

'There is one line of enquiry I might suggest, Mr Appleyard, as I am in no position to follow it up.'

'Really? Something the humble police force can do that you can't? Do tell.'

'The professor's research could prove invaluable to certain commercial concerns and to certain governments,' Campion started.

'Yes, I've got that. Even a humble Suffolk copper who never went to university can see that.'

Campion bit his tongue, as he always did when someone insisted they had been to 'the university of life' or described themselves as humble, a sure-fire way of conjuring the ghost of Uriah Heep.

'Well, it has been suggested to me that the Central Intelligence Agency may have been taking an unhealthy interest in Pascual's algorithm. I'm sure there's nothing concrete in such dramatic speculation, but have you considered the possibility that there might be an American agent on campus?'

The superintendent's natural expression – a mixture of indifference to and disinterest in any new concept put to him – was enlivened by the merest twitch of those bushy eyebrows.

'Americans? They're on our side, aren't they?'

'Occasionally and sometimes tardily,' admitted Campion, 'though their involvement in Vietnam is generally protested by the younger generation.'

'I know all about the long-haired protest-march mob,' snorted Appleyard, 'but who is this American agent?'

'I haven't a clue. I'm not even sure there is one. It may be militant student paranoia, just like they see undercover policemen in plain clothes joining their protest marches.'

'Well, that does happen,' Appleyard admitted, 'and usually they stick out like a sore thumb and are quickly spotted.'

'You should let them grow their hair longer. But we digress. I simply thought it might be worth checking the staff records to see if the university has any Americans on the books, or academics who have studied or spent time in America.'

'Staff, not students?'

'Perhaps postgraduates, but most of the students here on Sunday were probably first-years who had never heard of Perez-Catalan.'

'I'm starting to wish I never had. American. You're sure?'

'Not at all. Oddly, as the campus is a veritable United Nations in miniature, I've not come across an American – well, not so far. Therefore, I would look at academic track records to see who may have worked there before being appointed here. It would, of course, have to be done diplomatically and in strict confidence by a senior officer.'

'Like me I suppose. Strewth, that could take ages.'

Mr Campion certainly hoped so.

'Go fetch the vice chancellor,' the superintendent said to Constable Peters. 'Tell him I need to see him pronto.'

When the constable had left the office, Appleyard leaned forward and planted his elbows on the desk, his arms forming two pillars topped by clenched fists on which he rested his chin.

'You're a rum cove, Campion. You've come to Black Dudley twice in forty years and there's been a murder both times. I've checked up on you and I know you've mixed with some dodgy people up in London and now you're after uncovering American spies, which I can't think is going to please our chum the bishop. How on earth did you get to be university Visitor?'

'That, Superintendent,' said Campion deliberately, 'is a mystery.'

One Year Previously . . .

'The situation really is intolerable. If one cannot rely on a Member of Parliament, and a junior minister at that, who can one rely on? When I appointed him Visitor, the last thing I expected was that he'd turn out to be a Russian spy. That's no good for the image of a new university, no good at all.'

Detective Chief Inspector Bill Bailey had never seen the bishop so agitated. It was as if he had contracted St Vitus's Dance; such were the fits and starts of his uncontrollable arms that he was in danger of spilling the sherry he had just poured.

'Nothing has been proved against him, Bishop,' he said soothingly. 'The security services will be investigating, but all they have at the moment is the word of a defector, who is Czech actually, not Russian.'

'Czech, Russian, what's the difference? They're all communists, and the Visitor to the University of Suffolk Coastal, which is supposed to be a jewel in the crown of our county, has been in their pay for years. A traitor!'

Thankfully the bishop put the two glasses of sherry down on to the safe surface of a coffee table, then he hitched up the hem of his purple cassock and settled himself in a deep leather armchair, the twin of the one in which Bailey had taken shelter.

'The minister has resigned his post and his parliamentary seat,' Bailey said calmly, 'and will no doubt face charges under the Official Secrets Act in due course. It could be quite a while before the case comes to court.'

'But it's all over the papers right now,' the bishop's voice was almost a wail, 'and I have to find a new Visitor for the university before the start of the next academic year.' He stretched out a hand for his sherry, changed his mind, and patted Bailey's knee instead. 'That's where you come in, Bill.'

'I do?' Bailey was startled enough to decide he really needed that sherry after all, despite the fact that it was still two hours short of lunchtime. 'I can't think how.'

The bishop took up his glass, sipped enthusiastically and smacked his lips before leaning forward intently.

'You know Black Dudley, where my . . . the new university is based, I take it.'

'I know of it, Bishop, but it's not on my patch; it comes under Ipswich and East Suffolk for policing.'

'Yes, its geography is annoying as I find the campus is not on my patch either.' The bishop sipped more sherry to ease his frustration. 'Are you familiar with its rather colourful history before the university adopted it? Before the war, in fact.'

'I take it you mean the murder of Colonel Coombe and that gangster business. Yes, I've read about it, but surely that's all old history now, if not folklore.'

'So there would be no taint on the character of someone involved in that incident?'

'Forty years ago? Were they a suspect?'

'Not as far as I know, but they were involved in what must have been an unsavoury incident.'

'Well, if they weren't murdered and they weren't a suspect, I don't see the problem. Who are we talking about?'

'A man called Albert Campion, though that's not his christened name. It is not uncommon for persons of his . . . lineage . . . to avoid titles and adopt *noms de plume* when moving among the common folk. I believe his aliases included Mornington Dodd and Tootles Ash among others, so he seems to have a rather dubious sense of humour. He could just be a bit simple, I suppose.'

Bill Bailey risked another slurp of sherry to fuel his courage. 'I've met Campion, Bishop. We had dealings over that business with the Carders gang at Lindsay Carfax. The last thing I'd call him is simple, and if you get that impression of him, it's because he wants you to.'

'So he's a reliable sort of chap? What I would call a stout fellow?'

Bill Bailey suspected that the bishop's definition of 'stout fellow' was a man who agreed with him and did his bidding without question. From what he knew of him, that was a bill Campion did not fit, and it might not be wise to sing his praises too loudly. Bailey was the one, after all, who had to live on the bishop's patch.

'Charlie Luke speaks very highly of him,' he said after due consideration.

'Who?'

'Commander Charles Luke at Scotland Yard. He knows Campion of old, mostly in London but also here in Suffolk; he would be the best person to speak to if you're looking for a character reference. I'm assuming Campion is in the running for the Visitor job.'

'It's not a job, it's an honorary appointment,' said the bishop, 'and his name has been mentioned, but what about this Commander Luke? You hinted he had Suffolk connections . . .'

'I think his wife was from around Pontisbright.'

'*Was?*' The bishop was instantly *en garde*.

'She died giving birth to a daughter,' said Bailey, and when the bishop brightened at the revelation of widowhood rather than divorce, he added, 'but a senior serving policeman couldn't take on such a position, however honorary, and it could only inflame the more radical students.'

'You have a point, Bill. Student protests don't go down well with ratepayers and there are . . . elements . . . only too keen to confront the police.'

'Don't I know it,' said the policeman.

'Quite so, but you think Commander Luke would speak up for Campion?'

'He's far more qualified than I to sing Campion's praises,' said Bill Bailey, thinking that Luke would also be well out of range of the bishop's wrath if anything went wrong with the selection process.

'Then I may very well call in on Commander Luke when I'm up in London next.'

Bailey had no doubt that the bishop would demand an appointment with the commander, even if Parliament was on fire and the streets a sea of rioting crowds.

'I look forward to seeing a puff of white smoke emerging

from the roof of New Scotland Yard,' said Bailey without thinking.

The bishop scowled. 'White smoke? I'm not picking a pope. That would be highly Catholic!'

Charles Luke had realized, from his very first day on the beat as a uniformed constable, that the lot of the policeman was to deal with difficult people. As his career had progressed and he had advanced in rank, the people he came into contact with changed but they always came with difficulties; just a better class of difficulty.

He had agreed to see the Bishop of St Edmondsbury because commanders of the Metropolitan Police are expected to grant such requests out of politeness and good public relations. There might also, in this case, be an operational necessity, in that the See of St Edmondsbury, for peculiar reasons lost in London's smoky history, happened to own the freehold on two venerable seventeenth-century public houses in the city, both of which were within a few minutes' walk of Fleet Street, which made them important cogs in the wheel of public opinion.

The bishop, who was not unaware of his responsibilities as a nominal licensed victualler, soon made it clear that his visit to Commander Luke had nothing to do with the licensing law (or the lack of its observance given the proximity of Fleet Street). It was a private matter, though professional not personal, and he was sure he could rely on the commander's discretion.

When the call of duty did not draw him away from the building, Luke preferred to take his morning coffee in the canteen with his officers, where he often learned much to his advantage, but the visit of a bishop called for the best crockery and the fanciest biscuits served in his office. At least there he could set an alarm clock in the form of his secretary, who was primed to interrupt him with an important telephone call after exactly seventeen minutes – the odd number being selected to divert the suspicions of his visitor.

'It's about this chap Campion,' said the bishop, once his coffee had been sugared and his Bourbon biscuit dunked. 'I believe you know him.'

'Albert Campion? Yes, I've known him for nigh on twenty-five years and for most of them I've been proud to call him a friend,' said Luke, settling himself into his broad uniform jacket, which a colleague had once said had been 'tailored to fit an oak tree'.

'*Most* of them?' The bishop raised an eyebrow.

'I won't deny there have been times when he's infuriated me to the point of wanting to strangle him, but that was invariably when he turned out to be right on the money over something I'd missed. He's a clever boy is our Albert and, though it often looks as if he's playing the idiot, just remember, he is *playing*.'

'Would you say you knew him well, then?'

'Apart from his wife – and she had him pegged from the moment she first set eyes on him – there's only one other person who really knows him. Albert likes to keep a low profile and does so, which is remarkable considering what he gets up to. Amazingly, given his society connections, he manages to stay well under the radar of the gossip columns.'

'Good,' said the bishop, 'that's very good. Would you know if he has an interest in the university sector of higher education?'

'Well, he's a Cambridge man . . .' Luke began.

'Excellent,' breathed the bishop.

'St Ignatius College, I believe . . .'

'Oh well, never mind.'

'And his son Rupert went to Harvard over in America, but if you're looking for a brainbox in that family, Lady Amanda's got degrees and honours from three or four universities.'

The bishop fondled another biscuit as he considered this. 'Lady Amanda . . . one of the Fitton family . . . she became some sort of aeronautical engineer, didn't she?'

'Quite a successful one,' said Luke. 'She advises numerous companies and even the government.'

'Odd choice of career, for a woman.' The bishop's tone suggested that he rarely used the words 'woman' and 'career' in the same sentence.

'She would make a very impressive Visitor for your university,' pressed Luke. 'I know she does talks in schools and technical colleges encouraging young girls to take up more of the science subjects.'

The bishop shook his head slowly in a passable imitation, thought Luke, of genuine regret. 'Oh, I don't think so,' he said slowly. 'The University of Suffolk Coastal has a very liberal policy when it comes to admitting females, but we do not offer degrees in engineering and I think Lady Amanda's talents would be wasted on us. The Visitor does not have to be an academic; goodness knows we employ plenty of *them*.'

'Then what are you looking for in a Visitor?' asked Luke, desperately resisting the urge to look at his watch to see if seventeen minutes had passed.

'Someone more diplomatic than academic. Someone personable rather than intellectual. In fact, they don't actually have to be that bright at all, just someone who gets on with people.'

'Well, Albert certainly gets on with people – all sorts of people – but I've no idea if he's looking for a new job. He's supposed to be retired now and he's got his seventieth birthday coming up next May.'

The bishop waved a biscuit-less hand in dismissal. 'Oh, it's hardly a *job*. The Visitor's duties are hardly onerous. He would be expected to say a few words to new students at the start of the academic year and perhaps at congregation when the third-years get their degrees. Other than that, they can be called on to adjudicate if there are any minor disputes between the university and the staff or students. They don't have to have the wisdom of Solomon, just a fair amount of common sense, and to be able to show a sincere empathy with the younger generation.'

'Well, Albert always said that sincerity was an important trait, and if you could fake it successfully, you could get away with murder.' Luke caught the frown appearing on the bishop's face. Surely his seventeen minutes must be up by now. 'He was joking, of course. He's a bit of a joker is Albert.'

'Not too much of a comedian, I hope,' said the bishop uncertainly. 'He sounds a likely candidate but, if you'll forgive me, Commander, I will seek a second opinion just to reassure myself. You said there was another person, apart from his wife, who knew Campion even better than you . . .'

'Yes, there is, and you really should talk to him,' said Luke
with a smile that was positively wolfish.

Michael Dillon, the custody sergeant at Love Lane police station,
had earned the nickname 'Sweetheart' for his willingness to
supply restorative beverages to those unfortunates who found
themselves in his charge, often in distressed circumstances. His
ability to provide, at exactly the most felicitous moment, a
refreshing mug of sweet tea, instant coffee, Bovril or even, on
the night shift, cocoa, had elicited the standard expression of
the incarcerated Londoner grateful for small mercies, 'Thanks,
sweetheart', on occasions without number.

But Sergeant Mike 'Sweetheart' Dillon could not recall ever
having to put the kettle on for a bishop, or certainly not a real
one.

Yet there, standing before his desk as if waiting, as so many
had before, to be charged, or for at least the prospect of a warm
cell and a bed on a winter's night, was a bishop. The Bishop
of St Edmondsbury, no less; and though Dillon was not terribly
sure where St Edmondsbury was, other than beyond Epping,
this was not a con-man, a passing cheapjack or even a resting
actor, but the genuine article. Of that he had been assured by
Commander Charles Luke, whose reputation had spread across
all layers and divisions of policing in London, and whose word,
especially on the subject of bishops, was gospel.

'Good morning, my lord, we've been expecting you.'

'Good morning, Sergeant. I hope I'm not putting you to too
much trouble.'

'Not at all, sir. I'll just grab my helmet and take you round
the corner. It's only a step and a half.'

'This whole area is unrecognizable since the last time I was
here, though that was before the war.'

Sergeant Dillon adjusted the chinstrap on his helmet and
lifted the counter flap to allow him to step from behind the
desk. The bishop stifled a gasp of surprise as he realized how
tall the sergeant was. With his policeman's helmet taken into
account, he measured almost seven feet in height.

'It was the Blitz what did it,' said Dillon, holding the station
door for the bishop. 'December 1940 when this area copped it.

Took out St Mary Aldermanbury completely. Just a few bits left to mark the spot where it was.'

'It has been resurrected – in a sense – across the Atlantic,' said the bishop, adopting a favourite role as a lecturer. 'It was a Wren church and the stones were taken by our colonial cousins and reassembled in somewhere called Missouri five or six years ago.'

'The Brewers' Hall got flattened at the same time, but at least they rebuilt that instead of selling off the remains as souvenirs to rich Americans.' Sergeant Dillon turned his head and looked down at his portly companion. 'You sure you've got the right place, sir?'

'That's what Commander Luke said. The person I need to talk to has an important position at Brewers' Hall, and you were volunteered as just the man to effect an introduction.' He paused as if suddenly remembering something. 'In fact, he was most insistent that I took someone in uniform with me.'

Somewhere above the bishop, the sergeant nodded wisely. 'I can see the sense in that,' he said thoughtfully. 'You sure you've got the right chap though? He's never struck me as one who has much truck with gentlemen of the cloth.'

'He doesn't have to be. I am merely asking for his opinion on a third party, someone he knows quite well, I'm told. I'm hoping he will give me a good character reference on this third party. You know the sort of thing, speaking up for his morals and probity.'

Sergeant Dillon broke stride, almost stumbled, in surprise. 'You're asking Lugg to vouch for somebody's morals? Who's vouching for his?'

In anticipation of the bishop coming to call, Mr Magersfontein Lugg had dressed, as he thought, appropriately, in black jacket, pinstripe trousers, wing-collar shirt and black tie, with his stomach constrained by a favourite grey moleskin waistcoat, in whose back an understanding tailor had inserted a 'v' of material to allow a more comfortable fit.

The bishop certainly approved of his host's formalwear, along with the setting for their meeting, the magnificent Livery Hall, where chairs had been placed at either end of a table polished to mirrored perfection on which was displayed a small selection of the hall's silverware, mostly large, gleaming tureen-like objects of impressive silver content but little practical value.

It occurred to neither of the participants in that duologue that as they faced each other over the length of that silver-strewn table, they would have reminded an outside observer of a pair of Toby Jugs in a pawnbroker's window.

'I am told you are an office holder here,' was the bishop's opening gambit, indicating that he approved of their surroundings.

'You could say that,' Lugg replied warily.

'Commander Luke tells me you are a man of probity and ideally placed to help me in a rather delicate matter.'

'Charlie – Mr Luke – always was free and easy, bright and breezy, when it came to selecting volunteers. Still, a good character reference from him must be worth something in court.'

'You've hit upon it, Mr Lugg, gone straight to the nub and crux of the matter.'

'I 'as?' Lugg's slip might not have been showing, but his accent was certainly slipping.

'It's a character reference I'm after, purely verbal, nothing will be put in writing and the whole matter, naturally, treated as completely confidential.'

'And 'oo exactly would I be sticking up for?'

'I'm not expecting you to defend him against anything,' the bishop tried to be reassuring, 'merely give me your considered opinion of his character. I'm referring to Albert Campion. I believe you know him.'

Lugg relaxed back in his chair, which creaked ominously in protest.

'I've known Albert through the reigns of two kings and our present Queen. Two-and-a-half kings if you count the Abdication. I think you can safely say that if I was his strong right arm, he was my left-hand man. We've been through it, thick and thin – mostly thick, come to think of it. Anyhow, what can I tell you about Albert Campion? I've got forty years' chapter and verse on him and I've never thrown away the negatives. Is it for a job or something? He was supposed to be retired, but he likes to keep his hand in.'

'I am considering him for an honorary position; he would

be a figurehead, nothing more. It's not a job as such and will only take up perhaps two days out of a year; there's hardly anything to it.'

'Pah!' Lugg snorted. 'That's a red rag to a cross-eyed bull for a start. If he takes your 'onorary posting, he'll find something to do to stir things up. If life gets too easy for him, 'e gets suspicious and quite often agitated.'

'Oh dear,' said the bishop, 'perhaps I've miscalculated . . .'

'Don't let me put you off,' said the fat man. 'My manners may leave a lot to be desired, but 'is are h'impeccable, and you can trust him with your life. Come to think of it, he'd probably be very happy to do a favour for a bishop. He 'ad an uncle who was one once.'

'Yes, the late bishop of Devizes, I believe. That's certainly a point in Campion's favour. Would you know how he feels about young people?'

''E can take 'em boiled or fried, even scrambled, but not coddled if you follow me.' The bishop was not sure he did. 'He doesn't approve of the ton-up boys on loud motorbikes and thinks the Carnaby Street fashions are just a joke gone wrong, but on the whole, he's probably got more in common with the younger generation than he has agin them. There's them that would say Albert never really grew up himself. He once persuaded a bank manager that he'd won a gold medal at the Olympics for tiddlywinks and there was his time at Cambridge when he told his tutors that he was a werewolf and that's why he had to roam the streets after dark.'

'Now that's interesting,' said the bishop, seizing an opening. 'Would you say Campion got on well with students?'

Mr Lugg's face folded into an expression of puzzlement which left it resembling a crater on the lighter side of the moon.

'If they're marching down Whitehall chucking bricks at policemen, certainly not. If they're sitting in a tin bath of custard for rag week, he'd give 'em a fiver or, most likely, take his boots off and jump in as well. This 'onorary position of yours, it involves students does it?'

'Yes it does, at USC.'

'In California? I don't know if Albert would fancy that. He's no spring chicken.'

The bishop contained both his annoyance and surprise at Mr Lugg's knowledge of geography. 'No, not that one. The new University of Suffolk Coastal based on Black Dudley.'

'Black Dudley, eh? That'll ring a few bells with him. What's the job?'

'The *position* is that of university Visitor. It would be mainly ceremonial, but he could be called upon to arbitrate minor disputes between students and the university. I see the role partly as setting a good example and partly being what the Scandinavians call an ombudsman.'

Lugg's eyes narrowed to shadowy slits. 'The current incumbent didn't exactly set a good example from what I read in the papers, did he? I take it 'is is the position wot needs filling?'

Again, Mr Lugg had surprised the bishop. It would not be the last time that morning.

'Yes, well, that was a most unfortunate experience for all concerned. The man was an MP and a junior minister; a bit left-wing, but then aren't all politicians these days? How were we to know he was spying for the communists?'

'Albert had his doubts about him and said so on several occasions over a pint down the Platelayers' Arms, but that's by the by. One thing's for sure, Albert couldn't be a better bet for this visitation lark of yours.' The big man gave the idea some thought. 'He could certainly keep your students amused with some of his anecdotes. He's good at telling jokes and they're mostly clean.'

The bishop was not sure he was reassured. 'Would you say Mr Campion has led a colourful life?'

'Technicolour.'

'I see,' said the bishop. 'Could you tell me anything more about him? His character, his career, his values, perhaps his outlook on life?'

'I could tell you enough to fill a book – half a library of books – but that sort of thing is best done over a glass of something, don't you fink?'

For the bishop, the morning was starting to look up and his response was immediate. 'Well, we wouldn't be in the Brewers' Hall without being offered a glass of beer, would we?'

'Oh we can do better than that.' Lugg grinned, reaching into his jacket pocket. 'We can offer you ale, certainly, but you look like a claret man to me, my lord, and as Beadle of this h'establishment, I 'appen to be in charge of the keys to the wine cellar.'

The bishop's eyes brightened. 'Lead on, Mr Lugg, lead on.'

It was almost five p.m. when probationary Police Constable Osgood checked in at the Love Lane station at the end of his shift and reported to Sergeant Dillon on the incident he had witnessed around the corner on Aldermanbury Square.

'Has there been a do on at Brewers' Hall, Sarge?'

'Not that I'm aware of. Something amiss?'

'Not really,' said the constable. 'There was a taxi outside and Lugg, the beadle, was helping a very jolly gentleman into the back of it, but it was like the gentleman – a substantial chap, though not in Lugg's weight division – didn't want to go as he'd been having a good time. Lugg had to manhandle him and it was like he was trying to put an oyster in a slot machine.'

'Nobody hurt? Nobody in tears? Did they frighten the horses? Did the cabbie object to the fare?'

'Didn't seem to. Lugg shouted, "Liverpool Street, toot sweet" and gave the cab a cheery wave as it set off.'

'Well then, nothing for us to worry about.'

'What was going on?'

Sweetheart Dillon drew on his years of experience as policeman and diplomat. 'Some sort of job interview, I think. Let's just keep this to ourselves, eh, lad?'

ELEVEN
The Crime at White Dudley

M r Campion had not seen White Dudley in daylight before and quickly concluded that as Suffolk villages went, this one was unimpressive. It was not that the brick-and-tile cottages or even the more modern bungalows were out of character, it was just that the houses individually and collectively were not very characterful. The only building of any distinction was The Plough, with its huge hanging inn sign, which in the light of day looked more like a medieval implement of torture than a ploughman's sturdy tool, and which was likely, in a high wind, to fall and decapitate anyone walking underneath it.

Campion drove slowly down the single street, observing house numbers; odds on the left side, evens on his right, until he spotted number eleven and parked the Jaguar outside a green garden gate leading up a short path to a front door painted bright blue. Even as he climbed out of the car, he was aware that the curtains in a ground-floor room of the cottage opposite had begun to twitch.

Just as he had been determined to show the students on campus that he had every right to be there despite being clearly a fish out of water, now was the time to ooze confidence, act boldly and literally as if he owned the place. He had the key in his hand, aimed at the front door Yale lock even as he strode towards it, so that gaining entry to the cottage was swift and smooth.

Once inside he consulted his watch and only then began to explore his surroundings. The front door had opened into a small lobby, the sort of area used in country cottages for storing outdoor shoes and gumboots, walking sticks, raincoats, torches and the occasional shotgun.

The late Professor Perez-Catalan had left only a sheepskin

coat hanging from a wall hook, and used the remaining space as a makeshift wine cellar with three cases of Rioja Alta Viña Arana, the top case opened and half full, with empty bottles having been replaced in most of the slots from which they had been plucked. Pascual had certainly liked his wine, mused Campion as he idly went through the pockets of the hanging coat and, unable to obtain supplies of Chilean red in England, had opted for Spanish.

Finding nothing in the coat but a small battery torch, and noting from the way the dust on the tiled floor had been disturbed that the police had presumably checked the stack of wine cases, he concluded that Appleyard's men had conducted a thorough search. As he entered the living room, he decided that he must search where a policeman would not look if he was to find anything hidden. If, that was, there was anything to hide.

The living room had exposed beams and a fireplace with an iron dog grate containing logs, laid but not lit for some time, given the amount of dust surrounding it. There was a television set in one corner and a modern record player with stereo speakers on the floor in another. The furniture, chintzy and mismatched, had probably come with the cottage, and the only indication of the professor putting a personal stamp on the place was in the contents of a small bookcase against one wall.

There were three shelves to the bookcase and none was full, but then Pascual had come from the other side of the world and books are heavy and expensive to transport. Besides, he had at least two offices on campus, and no doubt his own section in the university library for academic texts, so this collection, however small, might give a clue to his private existence; and Campion was becoming more and more convinced that his death was a very private matter.

Campion dropped to one knee and scanned the bottom shelf, running a finger along the spines of large reference books on geology and computing theory filed indiscriminately with a well-thumbed *AA Book of the Road*, several Spanish–English dictionaries and three cookery books published by a well-known women's magazine, which appeared never to have been opened. There was also a copy of *Len Deighton's Continental Dossier*, with ribbon bookmarks marking a recommended driving route from Madrid to Badajoz, but whether that meant anything was another matter. Moving up on to the middle shelf, Campion found himself in the fiction section, mostly paperbacks, the majority being garish thrillers in something he translated as 'the library of spies', published in Barcelona, almost all being Spanish editions of English crime writers, some of whom he had heard of. There were, inevitably, a smattering of Agatha Christie and Peter Cheyney titles in English, which did not surprise him as he had come across many a foreigner who claimed to have learned the language by reading Christie and Cheyney, which could explain a lot.

The top shelf was obviously the serious, read-for-betterment section, with a newish Bible (Revised Standard Catholic edition) an elderly Complete Works of Shakespeare, a battered paperback of *Bleak House* and an almost pristine two-volume set of *War and Peace*, plus a thick hardback copy of *Don Quixote de la Mancha*, at which Campion allowed himself a chuckle, as he had now seen more copies of the adventures of 'that valorous and witty knight-errant' in the backwater of White Dudley than they probably had on display in the Spanish Embassy in Belgravia.

Out of nothing more than idle curiosity, he was reaching for it when he heard the lock in the front door being turned.

He consulted his wristwatch. Three minutes twenty seconds. In White Dudley it seemed you didn't get the regulatory four-minute warning.

'Who be you?'

'I am, madam, the university Visitor,' said Campion, rising to his feet, 'and I am, well, visiting.'

''Ow did you get in?'

'With a key, madam, as, it appears, did you, although I think you saw that with your very own eyes from behind a nervous curtain.'

'Are you now a policeman?'

'I am not of the police, but I appear before you with their blessing.'

The woman looked nonplussed, on the cusp of bemused. She

was a small woman, perhaps in her late fifties, with a weather-beaten, slightly simian face, and frizzy black hair which had suffered from too much contact with heated rollers. She wore a nylon housecoat which Campion suspected gave off enough static to power a street light and, incongruously, a pair of men's carpet slippers. Perhaps they had rubber soles and were useful insulators.

Mr Campion, realizing that an embarrassing standoff was in the air, opted to parlay.

'My name is Campion and I am here to take stock of Professor Perez-Catalan's personal possessions.'

'Ain't nothing missing!'

'My dear lady, I never suggested there was, but might I ask who you are and what your interest in this house is?'

The woman could not have looked more surprised if Campion had stood on one leg and recited the periodic table.

'I did for him,' she said.

'I beg your pardon?'

'I did his cleaning, sometimes his washing, laid the fire, kept an eye on the place.'

'That's why you have a key.'

''Course I do. Had to have one in order to perform my duties for the university.' Campion's quizzical look clearly required further explanation. 'The university owns this cottage. Bought up half the village when they came here and I does for all of them. The ones with students in are the worst, what with all their goings-on, as I often tells Gerry, but he says he can't do anything about it with it being off-campus.'

Campion held up a finger to pause the woman in mid-flow. 'Would that be Gerry Meade?'

'It certainly would. He's been my husband for better or worse these past thirty years.'

'And let me guess,' Campion said with a smile, 'you live across the road at number eight.'

'That's right,' said Mrs Meade, wide-eyed, as if Campion had done a magic trick.

'And going for double-or-quits if I may, that would have been Gerry's mother's house.'

'Well, it was until she moved out to the churchyard, so she

could be nearer to her God. After nigh on twenty years of married life with her under the same roof, it was a bit of a blessing, I don't mind saying. How come you knows Daisey May?'

'I don't – didn't – well, not really; I spotted her name in a leaflet recently saying she was a key-holder for the chapel of St Jurmin up beyond Black Dudley.'

Mrs Meade dug her fists into her hips and planted her feet apart, prepared to take a stand on the matter. 'Well, it had better say Edwina Meade now, not Daisey May, 'cos I inherited them duties, for which I gets paid a pittance, I might add, for my trouble. Not even a pittance – half a pittance!'

'I will make sure your efforts are reported to the proper authorities, Mrs Meade, though I have no powers of negotiation on the size of your pittance,' said Campion, displaying his second-best concerned face. 'But tell me, how often were you asked for the key to St Jurmin's?'

'Once or twice a summer maybe, not often, but it was the inconvenience, that's what I should get credit for.'

'Quite so. I totally agree, and I will make sure the Bishop of St Edmondsbury appreciates that.'

Edwina Meade's expression softened. 'You know the bishop?'

'You could say I represent him in the unfortunate matter of the death of the professor.'

Now Edwina was genuinely impressed. 'Gerry's mother, Daisey May, spoke very highly of him. They used to write letters to each other; proper pen-pals they were, according to Gerry.'

'The bishop remembers her fondly,' said Campion, another white lie, 'and has often said he could not think of a better guardian for the key to St Jurmin. Just out of interest, did the professor ever borrow the key?'

'Just the once, but he had it for nigh on a week before he dropped it back. Said he was always leaving it in his office at the university and forgetting to bring it home. I told him he could have given it to Gerry, but he was always rushing around keeping his head down too much to worry about such little things.'

Edwina's tone was tinged with disapproval and Campion decided to capitalize on it.

'Keeping his head down? Was the professor avoiding someone?'

'Probably all those women he kept entertained,' said Mrs Meade, but offered no further clarification.

'Did he do a lot of entertaining here at the cottage? Living just across the road you could hardly have failed to notice . . .'

'He always had students calling on him at all hours and the doctor came once when he must have been poorly, but he didn't spend much time here these last six months. He'd come back late at night and be off again by eight o'clock.'

'So when you said he kept women *entertained*, you meant in the biblical sense rather than entertaining by giving a dinner party or a bridge evening?'

For a moment Campion thought he had gone too far and certainly, from what he knew of her, he would not have risked any biblical reference in front of Edwina's late mother-in-law. The latest generation of Mrs Meades did not take umbrage or express outrage; she put her head on one side and observed Campion with sly cunning.

'How would I know what the professor got up to with his lady friends? You think I spent all my days watching his comings and goings?'

Mr Campion thought that was precisely what Edwina Meade had done to fill her days, and he wished he could remember who it was who had said: 'If cunning was equated with intelligence, then a cat would be Chancellor of the Exchequer.' He was sure the woman was itching to tell him something, but her animal instinct for self-preservation held her back.

'I merely thought that as his cleaner,' Campion picked his words carefully, 'you may have seen signs of lascivious or wanton behaviour. He did have a reputation on campus of being something of a ladies' man.'

'So I've heard.' Edwina's jaw jutted out defiantly. 'But it's not my place to pass judgement on them that 'as no morals, especially them that's supposed to know better – them that 'as positions and reputations they should be thinking about.'

'So the professor did have female visitors.'

'I never said that, and you can't prove I did!' Campion did

not have to, but already Edwina was on the attack. 'Anyway, 'oo exactly are you, coming in here snooping?'

'I told you, I am the university Visitor.'

'No, you ain't.'

'I assure you, madam, that I am, and I probably have references to prove it.'

'You can't be, the visitor's coming this aft'noon. Gerry rang and told me half an hour ago, so I can't stand here blathering, I've got to go and get the horse ready.'

You had to hand it to her, Campion thought. Edwina Meade's exit had been as dramatic and enigmatic as her entrance had been stealthy.

That the woman knew something about the late professor was clear, but how to extract it from her without breaking several clauses of the Geneva Convention was beyond Campion for the moment. He did, however, draw one conclusion. Edwina Meade's reaction to discovering a complete stranger in a house she was nominally responsible for had produced the required initial burst of indignation but that had quickly faded. To Campion this suggested that Mrs Meade was not in the slightest bit worried about anything he might find there. Given the impression she had left on him, Mr Campion was in no doubt that the woman had been through the cottage with a fine-tooth comb and could probably recite an inventory of the professor's sock drawer.

It seemed pointless to continue searching; but then, he had never really had an idea what he was looking for. Perez-Catalan's research and his valuable algorithm were safe enough back at the university and surely the police would not have missed any scientific papers left lying around? Unless, of course, Edwina Meade was an undercover agent for the CIA or the KGB and had spirited them away after bumping off the professor.

He resumed his examination of the bookcase, if only to take his mind off such fantasies, and his fingers strayed back to where they had left off, hovering over the sumptuous leather-bound edition of Miguel de Cervantes' most famous book – and, it seemed, one of the most popular works of literature in White Dudley.

Campion lovingly ran the tips of his fingers over the gilt embellishment on the leather and then hefted the book, all six hundred pages of it, in one hand, concluding that it was a substantial read, even though this was only Volume 1. The title page showed it was a 1930 Spanish edition, printed in Barcelona, and Campion guessed it would fetch several hundred pounds from an ardent bibliophile. It had therefore been an expensive present, but a gift it had certainly been, as the inside of the front carried a loving inscription – or had been defaced, if you were a book collector.

Reading that luxurious edition of *Don Quixote* might have been beyond Campion, but even his elementary Spanish ran to *Con todo mi amori*, written in a large, elaborate and blotchy red ink cursive script.

That anyone would desecrate a valuable book was always a disappointment to Campion. The signature which accompanied the rather splattered inscription, along with two 'x' kisses came as a surprise: *Estephanie*.

Yet that was not the only surprise the book contained.

Even as he held the volume, Campion knew – could feel – something wrong. It was not in the weight, which was considerable, but the fact that something seemed to be moving or sliding *within* the pages. He closed the book and examined the gold-painted edges of the pages, and when he could see nothing out of the ordinary, he put the book down on the nearest flat surface – the seat of a fiddle-back chair – and carefully began to flip the pages. At page 103 he discovered an even bigger piece of bookish vandalism.

'Poor old Don Quixote,' he said to himself, 'gutted like a fish.'

A square had been cut, almost certainly with a razor blade, in the pages to a depth of half an inch and a good half-inch in from the edge. It was an old trick, used to provide a hiding place for small valuables or secrets, and in this case the secret that fitted perfectly into its paper coffin was a small, one-ounce tobacco tin.

It was a tin worth hiding, thought Campion, as it was one of those embarrassingly jolly 'pin-up' tins, decorated with a picture of an attractive brunette sitting in a heart-shaped leather chair, wearing a low-cut but formidable basque and something flimsy carefully arranged to allow a generous view of long black nylon'd legs and stocking tops. Although attractive as a model, the pictured lady seemed the most unlikely of pipe-smokers.

Campion eased the thin square tin out of its hidey-hole and used a fingernail as a lever on the bevelled edge. The tin opened with a satisfying pop to reveal neatly folded squares of light green paper, six of them, and without unfolding them, Campion could see that they were cheques.

They were all cheques for twenty-five pounds, dated over a period of eight months, but the most recent was a year ago and therefore all had lapsed, a matter which almost certainly did not worry the Southwold branch of Lloyds Bank on which they were drawn. The amount was standard, as was the payee, a name which Campion was not terribly surprised at: Mrs Edwina Meade.

It was the signature of the account holder which caused him to draw a sharp breath.

Before he left the cottage, Campion consulted the copy of Tabitha King's timetable which had been given to him by departmental secretary Sheila. If she adhered to it, Tabitha King would be tied up teaching until six o'clock, which gave him time to fit in a surprise visit to another university department and to consider what action to take on the mildly erotic tobacco tin containing six folded cheques which was now in his jacket pocket.

As he climbed into the Jaguar, he waved cheerfully towards the windows of Mrs Meade's house, and as he turned the car in the road to head back to the university, he gave a cheeky semi-quaver toot on the horn as he said aloud: 'Why didn't you cash those cheques, Edwina?'

The campus car park had more police cars than he remembered from that morning and curiosity got the better of him, so he took the path towards Black Dudley only to find Dr Szmodics coming bustling out of the open front door and making a beeline for him.

'Jack, just the chap I need to pull a few strings for me,' Campion hailed him.

'Where have you been?'

'Down in White Dudley, why? Have I missed anything?'

'You might say that. The bishop's been on the phone again.'

'You surprise me,' said Campion calmly, then added: 'He didn't ring Miss Simcox in Earth Sciences, did he?'

Szmodics did a double take of confusion. 'No, he rang Gerry Meade direct, said he was sending somebody to keep an eye on you.'

'That sounds ominous. Do we have any hints as to who it might be?'

'None at all, only that Meade is meeting them off the train at Darsham Halt, but that's really neither here nor there now.'

Although almost bursting to divulge something further, Dr Szmodics played his advantage and waited for Campion to prompt him.

Campion made it a statement, not a question. 'I take it something more significant has happened.'

'Stephanie Silva,' said Dr Szmodics under his breath for dramatic effect.

'There's a coincidence,' said Campion, hefting the copy of Cervantes he held in his left hand. 'I was going to ask you where I might find her this afternoon. I need to have a word with her.'

'You'd better join the queue then. Superintendent Appleyard's men pulled her out of a seminar half an hour ago. I think he's going to arrest her.'

'Oh dear,' said Campion, crestfallen. 'I was hoping to discuss a book with her.'

Whatever Miss Silva was discussing with Superintendent Appleyard, it was not literature.

The vice chancellor's office was being used for the interview, or interrogation, depending on how it was going, and the door was guarded by PC Peters, the constable whose duties, Campion had assumed, were confined to being Appleyard's stenographer.

As Campion and Dr Szmodics approached, PC Peters stiffened his stance, the standard policeman's on-duty stance, hands in the small of his back, feet apart, knees flexing slightly.

'You can't go in there, sirs. The VC and the super are going to be tied up for some time.'

'With Miss Silva, I presume. I'm rather surprised you're not in there taking notes,' said Campion.

'Got a WPC up from Ipswich in there. Always best to have one present when it's a female suspect.'

'Quite right, Constable, that's a sensible and probably sensitive policy; very forward-thinking,' said Campion. 'So Miss Silva is a suspect, is she?'

The young policeman was impassive. 'You can think that, sir, but I never said so.'

Campion turned to Dr Szmodics. 'I think this young man has a great career ahead of him.' Then he turned his smile on PC Peters and reached into his pocket. 'I have no wish to disturb the superintendent, but I can trouble you with another matter. I hereby return the key to Professor Perez-Catalan's cottage which you made me sign for this morning.'

'Duly noted, sir, thank you.' Peters took the proffered key and slipped it into the breast pocket of his uniform jacket, where it clinked faintly against the police whistle already there.

'I also asked if I could see the other keys found on the professor's key ring. One of your detectives was trying to identify them with Mr Meade.'

'I remember, sir. They're back now, over in the incident room.' He nodded in the direction of what had been the Great Hall. 'There's a table with a filing tray marked "Evidence". They're in there.'

'Thank you, Constable; I just want a quick look to satisfy my curiosity.'

'I didn't know you read Spanish,' observed Dr Szmodics as he accompanied Campion across to the hall.

Campion patted the book tucked under his left arm. 'Oh, this. I don't, I just wanted to talk to Miss Silva about it.'

'I could find a translation for you easily enough,' Szmodics offered. 'We have lots of them kicking around the department.'

Campion saw an opportunity and took it. 'That would be incredibly decent of you,' said Campion, standing still and looking squarely into Szmodics's eyes.

'You mean now?'

'If it's not too much trouble.'

Mr Campion's luck held. The incident room was devoid not only of incident, but mostly of policemen, only two plain-clothes detectives pecking at typewriters in a far corner. Neither took any notice of Campion as he approached the table bearing filing trays with handwritten signs saying 'Evidence' sello-taped to them.

The professor's key ring was hard to miss, containing enough keys to distort even the most flexible pocket fabric, and if found on a certain type of individual in the East End of London would inevitably have led to a charge of going equipped for theft or burglary.

Campion placed the leather-bound book he had been nursing on top of the filing tray to mask the movements of his hands as they flipped through the key ring. The majority of keys conformed to the standard design of the cylinder locks used throughout the university; two or three looked as if they might fit a filing cabinet or a mail box, and two were thick, modern, double-edged security keys which Campion guessed allowed entry to the Computing Centre. One key stood out: a three-inch-long old-style iron mortise lock key, bigger and heavier than any of the others. In design, it was not all that advanced from something which could have been found on an archaeo-logical excavation of an Anglo-Saxon homestead.

With a dexterity which impressed even himself, Campion separated that key from its companions and, flipping open *Don Quixote* with a stage magician's flourish, he transferred it to the square paper grave which had been cut into the pages, closed the book and replaced it in his armpit.

Back in the lobby, he grinned inanely at PC Peters, who responded with a loud sigh and a flexing of the knees to indicate that the superintendent was still involved in giving Miss Silva a thorough grilling, and turned left to the staircase leading to the vice chancellor's private quarters.

It was Dolores Downes who answered his polite knock. 'Hello, Mr Campion, I'm afraid my husband is busy with the police.'

'Excellent, may I come in?'

'If you must; I'm rather busy preparing the guest room for your colleague.'

'My colleague?'

'I have been told to expect another visitor from the bishop,' she said, leaving no doubt that she had been instructed rather than consulted. 'So I am preparing the room you had. The police have no objections and Roger tells me they will soon be packing up and getting – how do you say it? – out from under our feet. Perhaps you should move back here instead of living with the students?'

'No, no, I'm perfectly happy where I am, but that's not why I'm here.'

Dolores waved a strand of hair from her eyes; she had beautiful, nervous brown eyes.

'Then why are you here, Mr Campion?' she asked with a quiver in her voice.

Campion drew a deep breath. 'To ask you why you've been writing cheques to Edwina Meade.'

As he was leaving Black Dudley, he met Dr Szmodics coming in clutching a paperback edition of *Don Quixote*. Campion thanked him and slotted the book next to the larger Spanish edition under his arm.

'Thank you, that's my homework for the week, though I had hoped to get a few tips on the texts from Miss Silva,' Campion said, and then answered Szmodics's unasked question. 'But that doesn't seem likely as she's still in there getting a grilling from Appleyard.'

'Do you think the police have a case against her?'

'For Pascual's murder? I have absolutely no idea. I've not even spoken to the woman. She was next on my little list.'

'You have a little list?'

'I have a little list but, please, let us not descend into Gilbert and Sullivan. I am totally in the dark as to what the police might have against her, other than that she and Pascual clashed over computer time. That seems to be fairly common knowledge.'

'It was,' agreed Szmodics. 'Some of the clashes were quite public which made her very popular with the students in my department and the more radical elements encouraged by Thurible among the sociologists. That's why there'll be trouble if they don't release her soon.'

'What do you mean, Jack?'

Dr Szmodics appeared surprised at the question, but remembered that Campion was new to student politics. 'The police made a big mistake arresting Stephanie while she was teaching a seminar group.'

'I think they "took her in for questioning" is the legal terminology,' said Campion. 'There's been no formal charge made against her yet as far as I'm aware.'

'That won't cut any ice with the angry mob forming down in the piazzas,' said Szmodics. 'In my time as dean of students, I know the signs. First they gather in groups, then they start making placards and banners, then they start sharpening the pitchforks and making torches. Then comes the marching and the chanting . . .'

'You sound as if you're predicting a riot,' said Campion, realizing that Dr Szmodics was being partly serious.

'We've had them before and this is a far more exciting cause than protesting about price increases in the refectory. They'll get a good turnout for this one.'

TWELVE
Riot Act

Mr Campion had always been of the opinion that anyone who encouraged others to run into battle, or march towards the sounds of the guns, was probably a staff officer quartered well behind the front line, but on this occasion that was exactly what he found himself doing.

'Shall we wander over to the piazzas to observe the enemy?' he said to Dr Szmodics. 'I haven't seen an angry village mob for a long time. Were you serious about the pitchforks and torches? If you were, they were a nice touch of local colour.'

'Are you sure about this, Campion? When students start protesting, they tend not to respect either age or manners.'

'Well, I won't hold them responsible for their youth and I'm sure I can be just as rude as they if the Furies take me. And remember, I am the official Visitor and it is my duty to mediate between the student body and the university authorities.'

'But your remit doesn't run to negotiating on behalf of the police, does it?'

'I'm sure Superintendent Appleyard can look after himself,' said Campion, 'but where are your police?'

'My police? What do you mean?'

'The university porters; they are in charge of campus security, are they not?'

Dr Szmodics snorted in surprise. 'You've seen them; they're nearly all of pensionable age and if they've any sense they'll stay out of sight. In any case, Gerry Meade has disappeared off to Darsham Halt to collect another envoy from the bishop, so I suppose Bill Warren is in charge and he's probably hiding back in the porters' lodge, crouched down below the window with the lights off.'

'I've met with Bill Warren,' said Campion, 'and I need another word with him before I forget. Look, we have reinforcements!'

As Campion and Szmodics walked down the path towards the lake bridge, a lone figure was hurrying up the path from Piazza 2. As he approached with long, athletic strides, the smart light brown, almost bronze, suit and blue paisley cravat suggested it was unlikely to be a student; very quickly he was identifiable as the handsome and fashionable Professor Thurible. The three met in the middle of the bridge.

'Jack.'

'Yorick.'

'Then I must be Horatius,' said Campion, 'if we are to defend the bridge. Black Dudley will have to stand in for Ancient Rome and the students can be the invading Etruscans, or whatever they were.' Campion noted the expressions on their faces. 'Or I could read an improving book to them. Do you think some Cervantes would calm them down, Professor?'

He held out the leather-bound Spanish edition but Thurible showed no sign of recognizing the book. 'This is no time for your upper-class manners or public-school humour.'

'That's pretty strong stuff coming from an old Harrovian,' Campion riposted.

Professor Thurible's eyes narrowed. 'You've done your homework.'

'A pure guess, old boy, a shot in the dark,' Campion grinned, 'but we really should not argue amongst ourselves. What is the situation down below? Are the natives restless and the war drums beating?'

'Stephanie's students are certainly furious and they've whipped up all their friends in your department, Jack.'

'With a little help from some of the professional agitators in Sociology, no doubt,' said Szmodics.

'Stephanie is very popular across the university and the students are going to demand her release,' Thurible retorted.

'If that's their noble cause,' Campion interrupted, 'why are you not marching with them?'

'I may yet be, but I want to be sure of a few things before I go up against the police. If Stephanie is being unjustly held or harassed in any way, then I'll be leading the charge, but if the boys in blue have a case against her . . .'

'It wouldn't look good to be seen defending the murderer of

a fellow professor, would it?' Campion suggested. 'I can't see that going down well in the world of academia.'

'Yes, well, what *is* the situation in Gestapo headquarters up at Black Dudley?'

'I hardly think Mr Appleyard is getting busy with a rubber truncheon,' said Campion, 'but it can't be pleasant for Miss Silva, whom we should presume innocent, at least for the moment. To be honest, Professor Thurible, we are in the dark as to why Miss Silva has been brought in for questioning. I do not believe she has been charged with anything yet, otherwise she would have been removed from the university.'

'Are you willing to tell a crowd of angry students that?'

'With you and Dr Szmodics beside me, certainly.' Campion looked at them both. 'Are you with me, gentlemen? Shall we hold the bridge?'

'We must try,' said Dr Szmodics.

Yorick Thurible asked a supplementary question with a sly grin.

'I'm not up on Roman history, Campion, so remind me. Did that Horatius bloke end up on the winning side?'

'Yes, he did, he was quite the hero, although it was a rather bloody battle from what I've read, and Horatius suffered several wounds including a spear in the buttocks in one account.' Campion looked at Thurible over the tops of his spectacles. 'But I assume that Miss Silva is a cause worth suffering the slings of outraged students for. I've never met her, so tell me, why is she so popular?'

'She's a good teacher and a first-class academic,' said Thurible, shuffling into position on Campion's left side. 'Those two things do not always go together.'

'She's a firebrand,' said Szmodics, assuming the role of Campion's right flank, 'always determined to get her own way.'

'She's also the most attractive member of staff in Language and Linguistics by a long chalk,' said Thurible mischievously.

'My, my,' Campion said, imitating a disapproving aunt, 'there seem to be sex symbols everywhere on campus. If Perez-Catalan was the Don Juan of Earth Sciences and Miss Silva is the pin-up of Language and Linguistics, who is the heart-throb of Arts and Humanities? You?'

'Oh, Yorick is way above such things,' said Szmodics. 'He keeps himself pure for the revolution . . .'

'Jack, please . . .'

'And has a career mapped out in politics, so he makes sure he has no dirty laundry in his baggage.'

'I thought that was a prerequisite for a politician,' said Campion, gazing down the sloping path which led to Piazza 2, 'but now is not the time for that debate. The natives appear to be restless, and restlessly moving this way.'

Thanks to the dimensions of the archway leading into and out of Piazza 2 rather than any nod to military history, the students had formed a column, five persons wide, and were advancing like Napoleon infantry towards the bridge. In place of muskets and pikes, they carried placards and hand-made signs on large sheets of paper or cardboard, and stretched across the midriffs of the front rank, a long strand of green computer printout paper which bore the message: FREE STEPHIE SILVA NOW.

Campion hoped there was no important formula or calculation on the other side of it, and secretly admired the students' initiative in manufacturing at short notice a banner they could literally march behind. Some of the placards, however, left a lot to be desired in terms of both sentiment and grammar.

Although the students could have easily marched around either end of the lake – revolutions were rarely deterred by 'Keep Off the Grass' signs – the column headed directly for the bridge and the three men, two of them twice and one three times their age, standing shoulder-to-shoulder in the middle of the span.

The nearer they got, the louder their chanting resembled that of a football crowd, if there was a team called 'Steph-ee', and placards were shaken furiously as if insisting they be read. Campion spotted Nigel Honeycutt in the throng, holding up a poster bearing the *Socialist Worker* masthead on which was neatly printed *End Police Aggression*, but the sign which caught his attention was being waved above his head by a student in the second rank, determined to deliver the message: NO FASCESTS ON CAMPUS.

'I apologize for the spelling,' said Jack Szmodics on Campion's right.

'He must be one of the number-crunchers from the Computing Centre,' Thurible said on his left.

'Actually, he's one of yours, Yorick,' said Campion, then he took off his fedora and waved it in a cavalier greeting. 'Hello there, Kevin! How go the sociological studies?'

'What are you doing, Campion?' warned Szmodics. 'Don't antagonize them.'

'He's not antagonizing them,' said Thurible with a broad smile, 'he's embarrassing them.'

'Coo-ee Angie! How nice to see you again. I've taken your recommendation and got myself a copy of *Don Quixote*. Two copies actually. Are Joe and Brian in there with you?'

In the middle of the column, a hand was raised as if in answer to a classroom question, and then, almost as quickly, retracted.

'How do you know these hooligans?' hissed Jack Szmodics.

'We drink in the same pub,' replied Campion. 'It's quite a good crowd for a chilly afternoon, isn't it? What would you say, fifty or sixty?'

'It's difficult to be accurate,' said Thurible, 'while they're still marching *straight towards us.*'

'Do you have your pipe on you?' Campion asked him out of the corner of his mouth and, when Thurible nodded, 'Then take it out casually and light it. Make like there's nothing untoward happening and you've just popped out here for a smoke. And you, Jack, whisper something important into my ear and then start looking anxiously back to the Black Dudley end of the bridge, as if you're measuring out the distance.'

'What do you think you're doing?'

'Don't worry, Jack, I haven't really become Horatius on the bridge, I'm going to negotiate. That's what a Visitor is supposed to do, isn't it?'

The first four ranks of students were already tramping on the bridge when Campion stepped forward and raised his hands. As he was still holding the two books in his left, he took on the guise of a revivalist preacher, which was not exactly the image he wished to project.

'Good afternoon, my name is Campion and first-years will know me from my brilliant welcoming speech on Friday. Others will have no idea, and probably care less, that I am the university Visitor, which actually means that you, the students, can come and visit me if you have problems.'

The student column, now on the bridge, stopped marching, but still shuffled forwards until the front rank was within a few feet of the three men defending the centre point. Thurible, playing his part, made an elaborate fuss of lighting his pipe then leaning his backside casually against the handrail, while Szmodics, in true pantomime fashion, whispered something vital in Campion's ear.

'You're here because of Miss Silva,' said Campion, and acknowledged the cheer that received. 'Well, so am I!' There was an even bigger cheer at that. 'You want to know what's going on – well so do I!' Now there was cheering and waving of placards.

'Careful, Campion,' said Thurible under his breath, 'or you'll be getting yourself elected to something.'

'Do you have a leader or a spokesman perhaps? It is rather difficult to talk sensibly to such a large, but appreciative, audience.'

'I suppose I'm the spokes*person*.'

'Hello, Angie, we must stop meeting like this. Can I suggest a solution to our rather dangerous problem?'

'I'm listening,' said Angie uncertainly, glancing nervously at her fellow students who were glancing quizzically at her.

'We all want to know what has happened to Stephanie Silva, don't we?'

'Of course.'

'Then what if I were to go up to Black Dudley and demand to speak to the most senior policeman there?'

There was a murmuring within the crowd and then a lone voice rang out.

'What's the vice chancellor doing about all this?'

'I know that Dr Downes is negotiating with the police on behalf of Miss Silva at this very moment,' Campion shouted over the heads of the student column.

'Is he really?' Professor Thurible spoke quietly under cover of a cloud of pipe smoke, but Campion ignored him.

'Let me go and see what I can find out on your behalf. Are you happy with that, Angie?'

'I suppose so,' said the girl, who was immediately surrounded by several fellow marchers muttering their dissent, but Campion quite clearly heard her declaim: 'No, he's a nice guy. He bought us all drinks down at The Plough.'

As testimonials went it was fairly limited, but Campion thought that, in the circumstances, it would do.

'Let me do that, Angie, and I promise I'll be back in fifteen minutes,' said Campion at full volume. 'One other thing, though. Dr Szmodics reminded me to tell you that this bridge, ornate and picturesque as it is, is not structurally safe with more than fifteen people on it at any one time. So unless any of you fancy a plunge-bath into water which recently had a dead body in it, I suggest some of you pull back. Professor Thurible and Dr Szmodics will remain here to ensure the structural integrity of the bridge and, if I don't return, you can take them hostage!'

A few of the placard-wavers cheered, while the bulk of the students began to edge their way carefully off the bridge, looking almost as confused as Professor Thurible and Dr Szmodics as Campion gave a cheery wave and set off towards Black Dudley.

'Would you mind holding these, Constable?'

Mr Campion pressed the books into PC Peters's hands and, while the surprised constable clutched both volumes to his chest, Campion reached a clenched fist over his shoulder and rapped loudly on the door of the vice chancellor's office.

'I do apologize, but I really need to have words. I take full responsibility. Have you read *Don Quixote* by the way? They made a musical out of it, you know, quite a good show. Saw it in the West End two years ago . . .'

To the policeman's considerable relief, the office door was opened by an irate superintendent. 'I thought I said we were not to be disturbed!'

'Please, Mr Appleyard, the fault is entirely mine,' soothed Campion, 'but there is a situation developing on campus of which both you and the vice chancellor really should be aware.'

'Campion! I might have guessed. What have you done now?'

It was a fierce and scowling Appleyard who stood holding the door, preventing Campion from entering but not from seeing into the office. A uniformed WPC sat primly, but clearly bored, at the vice chancellor's desk, a pencil poised over an open notebook. At a far corner, with his elbows on the desk, sat Dr Downes, head in hands as if in despair. In the middle of the room, sitting in a curved leather-effect armchair and looking the most relaxed person present was Stephanie Silva. She was wearing an electric-blue two-piece wool suit, the jacket three-quarter length, the skirt a very short mini. Her legs, sheathed in black stockings and shiny black leather high-heel boots, were stretched out in front of her and crossed at the ankles. Her upper body leaned back in the chair and she had her hands deep in the pockets of her suit jacket. From her feet to the top of her head, her body formed a diagonal at forty-five degrees, and she looked comfortable enough in the position that she might nod off for forty winks at any moment.

'I have not done anything, Superintendent,' said Campion firmly, 'but I'm afraid you have. The students are revolting – in the nicest possible way of course – or perhaps I should say protesting at your treatment of Miss Silva there.'

The Miss Silva in question, who was suddenly not in danger of dozing off, let out a cross between a laugh and an expletive 'Hah!', which seemed to shake Dr Downes into action.

'Are they sitting-in?'

'If that is their plan, Vice Chancellor, their chosen venue is probably this office. They were initially intent on storming Black Dudley and liberating Miss Silva from police brutality.'

'Careful, Campion, don't push it. Now what's going on?' growled Appleyard.

'The student population has risen in protest at your treatment of the popular Miss Silva and were on the way here to vent their spleen. Dr Szmodics and Professor Thurible have bravely delayed them on the bridge over the lake. If you look out of the front door, you'll see them, and I'm sure they'll give you a hearty cheer when they see you.'

The superintendent turned on his heels to accuse Dr Downes. 'Can't you control your bloody students, Vice Chancellor?'

'I resent that!' Downes shot to his feet, startling the police-woman, who was unsure as to whether she should still be taking notes. 'Our students are given the freedom to think for themselves; they are not schoolchildren. When they see something they regard as unfair or unjust, they protest, and within the law we encourage them to do exactly that, as we should.'

'Well said, Vice Chancellor.' Stephanie Silva spoke clearly and with sincerity, even though her immobile position gave the impression of a commuter on a railway station platform resigned to the fact that her train would be at least an hour late again.

Appleyard swung back to confront Campion, who was now easing his way into the room. 'Have you been stirring them up? I wouldn't put it past you.'

'I have been trying to calm the situation,' said Campion, relieving PC Peters of his books with a nod of thanks, 'and offered to perform my official duties as Visitor. So here I am, visiting and ready to mediate. I promised to report back to the student body and tell them exactly what was going on.'

'I'm not answerable to a mob,' blustered the superintendent.

'Well, in this case I am, and I'm on a promise to tell the students why you removed Miss Silva from them so publicly and, if I may say so, in such a ham-fisted manner.'

'Are you criticizing my methods?'

'I'm sure the bishop would,' said Dr Downes, in what Campion regarded as a stroke of tactical genius. 'I presume you will be bringing him up to speed on events, Albert. You know how he worries about the image of his university.'

'Telephoning him was the very next thing on my agenda,' said Campion. 'Of course I would be happier if I could tell him we have diffused the situation.'

Appleyard sprang into action. 'Peters! Stick your head outside and see what's going on, and you, lassie,' he turned on the policewoman who automatically sat to attention with her pencil poised, 'get all the lads together and lock down the incident room. I won't have a sit-in where there's evidence being stored.'

'And what about me?' Miss Silva said in a deep, vampish voice without moving a muscle.

'Yes, what about Miss Silva?' echoed Campion.

'Oh, throw her to the mob,' snarled Appleyard. 'Anything, just get her out of my sight.'

Mr Campion had expected a raucous reception from the student crowd as he emerged victorious from Black Dudley with Miss Silva on his right arm, but the cool, calm and collected Miss Silva herself seemed taken aback and slightly embarrassed by the whooping and ragged cheering.

'Let me show you off to your adoring fans, just to prove that you haven't been beaten up too badly,' said Campion as they walked towards the bridge, 'but then I really must have a private word with you.'

Miss Silva, who appeared perfectly happy leaning on Campion's arm for support, smiled and waved at the students gathered on the other side of the lake before answering.

'I suppose I owe you that, after you rode to my rescue in there.'

'I did very little, my dear. I'm assuming the police had no real reason to charge you with anything.'

'Only loose morals,' she said with a smile. 'The superintendent was very excited when someone told him that I had slept with Pascual. No prizes for guessing who did that, by the way, but he was positively shocked when I admitted it and told him what a good lover Pascual had been.'

'And now you're trying to shock another elderly gentleman.'

'Oh, I don't think I could shock you!' She laughed. 'Point is, that made me Suspect Number One for PC Plod back there, plus I don't have an alibi for the time of the murder, except that I was in bed well before midnight. The superintendent naturally assumed I was bragging about my sex life again.'

Campion levered his arm so that it acted as a brake on Miss Silva's progress and they stopped just short of the bridge. On the far side the student crowd had increased, but had assumed the air of an afternoon in the park, albeit a chilly one given the breeze coming off the sea, and in the middle, at the apex of the arch, Dr Szmodics and Professor Thurible were still on guard duty.

'Are you willing to follow my lead, Miss Silva?'

'As you've ridden to my rescue, I can hardly refuse, O Gentle Knight. And please call me Steph.' She wiped a loose strand of blonde hair from the front of her face and smiled a smile which made her popularity understandable. 'What did you have in mind?'

'I need to talk to you about rather personal and private matters; in fact I was on my way to see you this afternoon, but Mr Appleyard got there first. I am not with the police and have no authority to press you with questions, but I would appreciate it.'

'Sure, why not? My personal life is certainly not very private. Do you want to do it now?'

'No, not now.' Campion looked across the bridge to where many of the angry mob of revolting students were sitting on the grass and quietly chanting the mantra 'Steph-ee, Steph-ee'. One or two had actually produced books and were reading, several were smoking what Campion hoped were legal cigarettes, and four rugby types were passing a pint bottle of light ale between them.

'You need to go and talk to your loyal following,' said Campion, nodding to the far bank. 'I would appreciate it if you would keep it simple and say that the police have apologized for their rudeness in the way they took you in for questioning.'

'But they haven't apologized.' Miss Silva gave an outrageously fake pout. 'Do you want me to lie? Actually, I'm perfectly all right with that.'

'Thank you, Steph, you're a girl after my own heart. Now go and do that and hopefully this crowd will disperse before Mr Appleyard calls in the Riot Squad. I have something I must do in . . .' Campion consulted his wristwatch, '. . . the next hour, but then you could show me around the language labs, unless you have other commitments.'

'Suits me. My teaching schedule has been rather disrupted for the day, so I'll be in my office. I'll see you then.'

She gave Campion another winning smile and patted his arm, then set off across the bridge, the heels of her boots clacking like a metronome.

*   *   *

It had been Mr Campion's daughter-in-law Perdita, a blossoming actress with a flair for mimicry, who had taught him – and demonstrated – the word 'sashay'. Originally a term from American square dancing, it had come to describe a style of walk somewhere between a flounce and a strut, and was only applicable to females, usually when leaving a room. He could think of no other word to describe Miss Silva's walk as she clip-clopped across the bridge, sharing a smile with Thurible and a flick of blonde hair with Szmodics as she passed them *en route* to her adoring supporters.

Campion followed her at a respectful distance to the middle of the bridge, noting that Thurible and Szmodics were carefully observing that sashay rhythm from the rear.

'Successful outcome, Campion?' Szmodics asked as he drew level with them.

'No thanks to me,' said Campion. 'The police had simply jumped in where angels wearing size twelve boots should have feared to tread. They had no legal reason to hold, or charge, Miss Silva, and if they thought they could bully her into a confession, they made a dreadful misjudgement.'

'Dressed in that outfit she doesn't look like the victim of bullying, though the police would not have been the first to try,' said Thurible, puffing smugly on his pipe.

'Was that aimed at me?'

'Not at all, Jack, but you must admit she had a flair for the dramatic and could be a pain in your backside when it came to the allocation of computing time.'

'She was always seeking attention,' said Dr Szmodics through gritted teeth, 'but that hardly makes her unique around here, does it, Yorick?'

'Gentlemen,' Campion interrupted before any serious academic in-fighting flared up, 'would you do me a favour and stay here on guard for half an hour or so? I have an errand to run and I promised the vice chancellor that the bridge would continue to be defended until the students dispersed.'

'I think they're waiting for the bar to open,' said Jack Szmodics. 'Nothing else is going to budge them.'

'Can't you open the bar early?' Campion asked.

'Break the licensing law with all those police officers crawling over the campus?' Thurible feigned outrage then grinned inanely. 'I can't see that happening, Campion, but I like the cut of your jib. You'd make an excellent dean of students if Jack here ever fancied early retirement.'

'Don't let him get your hackles up, Jack. It wouldn't look good if the students were sitting on the grass behaving themselves and their professors were having a childish row. It would only confirm their suspicions. Toodles!'

Mr Campion strode to the end of the bridge and picked his way along the path through the crowd of students. Those he recognized from the previous evening in The Plough had surrounded Steph Silva, who seemed to be handling their questions about police brutality with great diplomacy, while the majority sat around, smoked and chatted, and two had fetched guitars from somewhere and were serenading their comrades in arms.

Unaccosted and unchallenged, Campion took the longer path to Piazza 3, but no sooner had he emerged into what appeared at first to be a deserted square, was both challenged and accosted.

'Mr Campion! Mr Campion!'

Campion immediately identified George Tinkler crouched down behind the firepit fountain, marched straight at it and without breaking stride towards the exit leading to the residences.

'Good afternoon, Chaplain. Playing hide-and-seek?'

'What's going on out there? The bishop will want to know.'

'Tell him everything is under control. Can't stop, I'm on a tight schedule. Don't forget to wave to your fans.'

Leaving the chaplain open-mouthed – and suddenly realizing that he was being observed by quite a crowd of staff and students at the windows of the Earth Sciences department – Campion quickened his pace around the refectory block and entered Hutton, the first of the pyramidal residences.

The timetable he had been given by Sheila Simcox told him that Tabitha King was teaching until six o'clock, which should, he felt, allow even this ancient and decrepit cat burglar enough time, and he set to climbing the central staircase with sprightly but quiet steps. Only the occasional sound of muffled voices or a burst of muted pop music from the corridors leading off the staircase indicated that the pyramid had any occupants in residence.

As with the room Campion had been allocated in Durkheim, the staircase narrowed so that access to the staff flat at the apex of the pyramid had to be in single file. On the door there was a small metal nameplate holder containing a square of cardboard with the name Tabitha King typed in capital letters and, like all careful burglars, Campion knocked three times to make sure there was no one home.

He allowed a good thirty seconds of silence, then eased himself down on one knee, laid his twin Cervantes' on the concrete floor and armed himself with his trusty nail file to attack the lock in the circular doorknob. A satisfying click followed almost immediately.

The flat was of exactly the same design as his, with a bed doubling as a sofa, a desk doubling as a dining table, a tiny corner of a kitchen with its space-age water heater and a wartime vintage hotplate and a door leading to the bathroom designed for, and by, a contortionist. Unlike Campion's, this staff flat at least looked lived in. Amidst the scattered papers and piled books on the desk/table, were a small cactus plant in a pink pot shaped like a pig, a hairbrush, a paperback of *Cathy Come Home*, a bottle of Miners runproof mascara and two copies of *Nova* magazine from earlier in the year, posing the questions on the front cover as to why Brigitte Bardot looked better at thirty-five and why we all loved Robert Redford.

A cursory glance suggested that Miss King had few secrets worth hiding; or had hid them extremely well. Certainly there was nothing resembling punch cards or green printouts which might suggest she had been taking work – specifically the professor's work – out of the Computing Centre.

It had only been a notion, Campion said to himself. Had he really expected to find Perez-Catalan's magical algorithm here? Would he recognize it if he saw it? Still, now he was here he might as well tick one other thing off his list of queries.

In the V-shaped window, which reminded him of the prow of a ship, he took in the view over the main teaching buildings towards Black Dudley. He had a good view of the students sitting around the south bank of the lake and, as they all seemed to be sitting rather than marching, he assumed they were, as predicted, waiting for the bar to open. The window also gave him a clear sight line of the bridge across the lake, which was what really interested him, as did the fact that his two sentries, Thurible and Szmodics, had been joined by a third, female, figure.

Campion was wracking his memory for her name when his thought processes were rudely interrupted by a voice behind him.

'What are you doing here?'

Without having to turn around or even check for a reflection in the window glass, Campion recognized the high-pitched, sing-song timbre of the voice. 'I might ask the same of you, Beverley.'

Miss Beverley Gunn-Lewis, who had emerged from the bathroom (seriously denting Mr Campion's professional pride as a burglar) stood motionless in the middle of the room, barefoot and dressed in a pair of men's pyjamas at least two sizes too big. Her cheeks were throbbing pink at Campion's counter-charge.

'Tabitha lets me sleep here,' she said, her voice regressing to her schoolgirl years.

'Is your room in – where was it? – in Babbage, unsuitable in some way?'

Her voice went quietly back to the pre-school nursery. 'I couldn't sleep.'

'Oh, come now, a brave Kiwi afraid of the dark? I don't believe it.'

'Not the dark,' sniffed Beverley, 'the noise. It was the noise that disturbed me.'

Mr Campion softened his tone. 'Typical students with their late-night parties and loud music. They can be so selfish at times.'

'No!' said Beverley with a flash of anger. 'It's that bloody trumpet player in the room below me. Somebody should throttle him.'

'Yes, I shared exactly those homicidal notions myself last night.'

'If I knew who it was signalling him, I'd do for them too!'

As well as being sympathetic, Mr Campion was now curious. 'Signals? What sort of signals?'

'Flashing a torch from down there by the bridge over the fake lake.' She pointed to the view through the windows. 'I thought that was what you were looking for.'

'Well, not during daylight, surely?' Campion said gently.

'Then what were you looking for? What are you doing in Tabitha's flat anyway?'

Campion thought quickly and held his dual *Don Quixotes* towards her.

'I wanted Miss King's opinion on a book.'

Beverley squinted through her glasses at the volumes as though reading a menu.

'Tabitha doesn't read stuff like that; she's into *Lord of the Rings* like me. Don't suppose you've heard of that.'

'Heard of it, read it and even met the author. There, thought that would impress you. Taught me some very rude words in Old Norse.'

Now Beverley turned her piercing squint, and those ridiculous red plastic 'cat's-eye' framed glasses on Mr Campion's innocently beaming visage.

'Are you for real?' asked Beverley, after shaking her long red hair as if to clear her head.

'Probably not,' said Campion cheerfully. 'Best put me down as a figment of your sleep-disturbed imagination and not mention my visit here to anyone, not even Miss King.'

'Not tell Tabitha there was a man in her room? Cripes to that!'

'Think carefully, Bev. What if someone was to tell the university that a member of staff was allowing a student to live in her flat?'

Miss Gunn-Lewis gave the idea a full three seconds of consideration, then, with a decisiveness Campion could only admire, said, 'OK, that's a fair cop. But what if someone saw you come in? Tabitha doesn't have men visitors.'

'I quite understand,' said Campion. 'Nobody saw me but, if asked, tell them I came in for a better view of the riot going on over by the lake.' He turned his head to the window. 'My goodness, something seems to have stirred them up again.'

The students by the lake were all on their feet suddenly. Placards were being waved and arms raised in clenched-fist salutes. At that distance, with the window closed, there was no sound from the assembled crowd and it was impossible to tell if they were cheering or howling in anger.

What had captured their attention became obvious when
Campion looked over to the left of Black Dudley. Coming out
of the car park and bouncing across the grass towards the house
was a pony and trap.

It was not just any old trap or gig, but a 'governess carriage',
where access is via a door in the rear and the passengers and
driver sit on bench seats down the sides facing inwards, and each
other. Much to the amusement of the student audience and
the dismay of the driver, the pony between the carriage shafts
began to veer down the slope towards the lake, probably dying
for a drink after a long haul from Darsham Halt with two
heavy passengers.

Campion knew the driver must be Gerry Meade and, even at
that distance, he was sure he recognized the bowler-hatted bulk
of the fare he was taxiing.

'What's all that in aid of?' asked the girl, her nose pressed
to the window.

'I think my governess has just arrived,' said Campion, then
burst out laughing as a solo trumpet, disturbingly close by,
blared out a familiar melody.

'Strewth! That bloody Phantom Trumpeter again. Hasn't he
anything better to do?'

'At least it's not the "Last Post",' chuckled Campion,
conducting in time to the music with a forefinger, 'and it shows
he has a sense of humour. Don't you recognize the tune? *Ta-da-
da-da, tah-da-da-da, rumpty-tum, rumpty-tum.*'

'No, should I?'

'You have youth as an excuse, though it's not a good one.
That's the "Cuckoo" song, sometimes called "Dance of the
Cuckoos" but better known as the theme tune of Laurel and
Hardy.'

'Who?'

THIRTEEN
The Visitor's Visitor

As he returned to the bridge through a thinning crowd of students, which suggested that either boredom or hunger had set in, Campion recognized the female figure who had joined the garrison on the bridge as the university medical officer, Heather Woodford, her hair tied up in a business-like bun, her hands thrust deep into the pockets of an ill-fitting beige duffel coat.

'Dr Woodford, how nice of you to join us,' said Campion, tipping his hat and nodding towards Thurible and Szmodics. 'I hope you have not been called out to treat any walking wounded.'

'Not at all,' said Heather Woodford with a weak smile, 'no casualties as far as I'm aware. I saw the crowd gathering and wondered what was going on. Most of them are drifting off now the show's over.'

She raised an arm and pointed towards Black Dudley, where the governess carriage had been parked and a feed bag had been put over the pony's head.

'I think it's jolly brave of you to return to the scene of the crime,' Campion said softly, but his words had the effect of an electric shock.

'What? How dare you? What are you trying to imply?'

'Only that you were among the first to find Professor Perez-Catalan's body and it can't have been pleasant.'

'I am a doctor,' she said with defiance.

'A very young doctor, who can't have seen many corpses yet. Tell me, what brought you to the scene so promptly? It must have been shortly after midnight.'

Campion was aware of Thurible and Szmodics edging quietly closer, so he turned away casually and manoeuvred Dr Woodford towards the end of the bridge.

'That damned Phantom Trumpeter woke me as he usually does during term time. The same hooligan who just gave us a signature tune for Gerry Meade and his mangy old pony. Though that was quite funny.'

'Yes, it was amusing,' Campion agreed, 'and I think Big Gerry is going to be stuck with that melody for quite a while. So you had an unplanned alarm call in the middle of the night. What made you venture over here?'

'I saw torches flashing.'

Campion turned his head back towards the distant residences. 'You live in the pyramids?'

'Yes, they gave me the staff flat in Chomsky, that's the second block from the left.'

'Between Hutton and Babbage. I'm in Durkheim myself, not to mention being rather proud of being able to remember all those names. Flashing torches, you say? Were they signalling to someone?'

'No!' said the doctor, rather too quickly. 'It must have been Bill Warren waving his torch around.'

'Ah, yes, the porter who actually found the body. But you were on the spot very quickly. This very spot, in fact.'

They had reached the north end of the bridge where the attack on Perez-Catalan had taken place.

'There was something odd happening, that was clear. Torches flashing, lights coming on in Black Dudley. I thought I might be able to help.' As she spoke, Dr Woodford glanced around, focusing on anything except the surface of the lake. 'But I was too late and the police were on their way.'

'Did you know Pascual?'

'Of course I did. He was a patient of mine.'

'And without breaking medical confidences, could you tell me if he was a fit and healthy person?'

'He was perfectly healthy, and I've already told the police that.'

'I hear he was quite a ladies' man . . .' Campion let his words drift out over the water.

'Meaning what?'

'Nothing, just that you were of a similar age, both intelligent, single, footloose and fancy-free, living and working in a liberal environment. Mutual attraction would surely not be out of the question, would it?'

Dr Woodford glared at her tormentor – and Campion was in no doubt that she regarded him as a tormentor.

'If it's gossip about Pascual's sex life you want, then talk to Gerry Meade's wife. She had him under constant surveillance since the moment he came here.'

The woman spoke through gritted teeth and did not wait for a response before hurrying back across the bridge, brushing aside Thurible and Szmodics as if they were cobwebs.

'You have a visitor, Albert,' said the vice chancellor, before Campion had managed to get both feet over the threshold of Black Dudley, 'and he is posing a slight problem.'

'If it is who I think it is, Vice Chancellor, I can assure you that the word "slight" is rarely used to describe him.'

Dr Downes frowned and patted the palms of his hands together in either silent applause or hesitant prayer.

'It's a question of accommodation. The bishop rather sprang the gentleman's visit upon us. In fact, he rang Gerry Meade with his instructions; I was tied up with the police at the time and the bishop is clearly unaware of the situation here.' He paused to allow Campion to comment on communication, or lack of it, with the bishop, but Mr Campion politely held his peace. 'He told Gerry to pick up our . . . guest . . . from the station with his horse and cart, which is a university tradition the bishop thought of and is keen to see established, and to arrange for him to stay here, in our guest room. Well, I'm afraid that simply isn't on, Albert, and you'll have to tell him that. Not only is my wife suffering badly from nerves thanks to this business, but Superintendent Appleyard has again forbidden any nonessential personnel to be here while the police have the run of it.'

'Is there not a room in the residences for him, like the one you put me in? I hasten to add that I am not offering to share. There are limits and I don't mean just the fire brigade's regulations.'

'We have none vacant,' said Downes, 'so I have suggested that Gerry Meade puts him up down in White Dudley. He has a spare room I gather, unless he keeps that fleabag pony in it.'

Mr Campion brightened instantly. 'That sounds a perfect solution, Vice Chancellor; couldn't be better. And don't worry about my distinguished visitor having to sleep in a stable if there's no room at the local inn; he's quite used to that and has even shared a sty before now. Do let me be the one to tell him. He will be wherever there is food being prepared and a kettle coming to the boil, but no policemen, so if I head for the kitchen I ought to be on the right track.'

Mr Campion's visitor had indeed taken command of the ground-floor kitchen, which provided light refreshments for those who worked in the house and committee meetings held in the Great Hall and was testing both the skill and the patience of the catering staff.

Mr Magersfontein Lugg was seated in all his black-jacket-and-pinstripe-trouser'd glory, his large bowler hat placed regally in front of him in pride of place on a table which also displayed a large metal teapot of the sort usually reserved for catering at fetes and Mothers' Union meetings, assorted crockery, and a three-tier cake stand groaning under the weight of doorstop-thick bacon sandwiches.

'Making ourself at home, are we?'

The fat man glowered over a thick crust stained with tomato sauce.

'Me stomach thinks me throat's been cut. No buffet carriage on the train and then I'm collected not by the promised limousine and uniformed chauffeur but by something out of *Steptoe and Son*, much to the amusement of that flamin' bugler out there. That wasn't you doin' one of your party pieces, was it?'

'Would that I had such talent,' said Campion, pulling out a chair and folding his legs under the table. 'Is there any tea left in that pot or have you drunk the whole gallon?'

With the bacon sandwich lodged between his teeth in a grip a Siberian wolf would have envied, Lugg poured milk from an open bottle and slid a cup and saucer towards Campion, then hefted the teapot one-handed.

'How kind of you to be Mother.' Campion toasted him with his cup. 'Welcome to Black Dudley. Now, what the devil are you doing here?'

'Been sent 'ere to find out what *you're* doing,' said Lugg

once the chewing had subsided, 'and I 'ad 'oped for a more discreet entrance. Got the shock of my life when the big feller met me at the station in his greatcoat and brown bowler.' He glanced at his own capacious regulation black bowler on the table. 'Thought he was taking the mick at first, then I reckoned he must be a brewery drayman, so naturally I follers him only to find he's driving that dog cart of his, which ain't big enough to carry a dog, leastways not one bigger than a Labrador pup, and as for suspension, I reckon the springs got taken out and donated during that Spitfire appeal which took all the railings during the war.'

'I hope you weren't expecting to arrive unnoticed,' said Campion when Lugg paused for breath, 'two bowler-hatted old fusspots trotting into the middle of a student protest like that. No wonder they pegged you for Laurel and Hardy.'

'Cheek! No respect for their elders, the younger generation.'

'And nobody ever said that about you when you were running around in knickerbockers with your hoop and stick, chucking mud pies at Mr Disraeli and that dangerous Liberal Mr Gladstone.'

''Ere, steady on, you're no spring chicken yerself; and anyway, the first prime minister I insulted was Lloyd George when he brought in our ridiculous licensing laws.'

'Yes, well, I was with you on that one, but back to business. I take it the bishop sent you.'

'In a way,' said Lugg, attempting to look coy. 'He asked if I could spare a day or two to check up on you, seeing as 'ow I helped get you the job. That makes you my protégé, don't it?'

'Only if "protégé" means superior in both intellect and moral fibre in ancient French.'

'Well, anyways, I turned His Lordship down as universities ain't my natural habitat, a little learning being a dangerous thing.'

'You're quite safe on that score, old chum, but what changed your mind?'

'I had a word with Lady A.'

'My better half?'

'Your better three-quarters, if you ask me. She said she'd no idea what you were up to, but she'd just had a call from Guffy Randall who was convinced you'd gone doolally and she'd appreciate it if I took up the bishop's offer pronto.'

'Yes,' Campion mused, 'she did threaten to embarrass me in front of the students . . . You made good time and now you're here, you can be useful.'

Mr Lugg sighed loudly and reached for another sandwich. 'No peace for the wicked. I suppose it's the murder of that foreign professor that's got your juices flowing?'

'I didn't realize it had been reported in the *Racing Post*.'

'Didn't have to be. I got the full SP and form from Gerry the wagon driver on the way over here. Sounds as if Pedro, or whatever his name is, was a bit of a lad when it came to the ladies, a regular Don Juan. You got any idea who topped him?'

Mr Campion drained his teacup and tentatively reached for the one remaining sandwich on the cake stand, but Lugg's massive paw was quicker and he inched it out of range.

'If this was a classic country-house murder mystery, which it isn't because this is no longer a country house, then suitable suspects would be identified first by who had means and opportunity; then there would be a lot of psycho-babble about motive. In the case of poor Pascual – not Pedro – we have an abundance of motives and quite a few suspects, but it's pinning down the means and opportunity.'

'Who's next then?' asked Lugg.

'Next? Next for what?'

'The chop. In yer traditional country-house whodunit, there's always a second murder, then the 'ero turns up in the nick o'time to stop a third, and catch the villain.'

'Don't worry your pretty little head about that. This isn't a country house any more, it's a university, a civilized place of learning and scientific research. I am confident there will not be a second murder and we will find that the motive for Pascual's murder was sadly really rather pedestrian.'

'Sounds like you've got it sorted out.'

'Far from it, chum, that's why you have to keep your ears open for me down in White Dudley.'

The fat man was taken by surprise and a surprised Lugg was usually a dangerous beast.

'What's a White Dudley when it's at home?'

'It's where you're staying, *chez* Gerry Meade, for tonight at least.'

'The bishop promised me the best room in the house. This house.'

'Unfortunately, the police are continuing to occupy the building and don't want civilians wandering about in their pyjamas. Incidentally, keep well clear of Superintendent Appleyard, their big boss; he's a prickly sort of fellow and the bishop's name cuts no ice with him. He's even had me thrown out and lodged in the student residences.'

'I pity the students, all except that saucy little sod with the bugle.'

'You'll be down in White Dudley, so you'll miss his midnight matinee when he plays the "Last Post".'

'Seriously?'

'Scout's honour. He's known as the Phantom Trumpeter and you can set your watch by him, but you'll be out of earshot. That doesn't mean your ears shouldn't be flapping. I need you to pick up anything you can in the way of local gossip, especially about Mrs Meade – her name's Edwina and she's the local snoop.'

Mr Lugg was immediately suspicious. 'What you got planned for me, a quiet night in front of the telly with Gerry Meade's missus?'

'Oh no, there's a local pub called The Plough. Get Gerry to take you there. You might even run into an old face from the war, a chap called Bill Warren, who's one of the porters here. He should be good for a drink.'

Mr Lugg brightened. 'Does this pub do food?'

'Yes, and you must try their pies.'

'What flavour pies?'

'Meat.'

Mr Lugg smacked his lips. 'My favourite.'

After briefing Lugg on who was who in the university hierarchy and offering a silent prayer that he would not come into contact with any of them, Mr Campion discovered that he was running late for his tentative appointment with Stephanie Silva. He felt, however, that as her knight in shining armour who had rescued her from the police dragon that afternoon, she would allow him some leeway. He promised himself that he would consult *Don*

Quixote, who was bound to have something quotable on the prerogative of elderly knights to be late.

At the quick march, he strode for the bridge over the lake again. Szmodics and Thurible had disappeared, no doubt in search of a warming drink as the afternoon was now distinctly chilly and the sun going down. Only a handful of students remained lounging on the grass, all thoughts of protest spent. No doubt taking inspiration from the Phantom Trumpeter, they began whistling the 'Colonel Bogey' theme to accompany Campion's progress across the arched bridge and, so as not to disappoint them, he stood to attention and gave them a parade-ground salute before stretching his long legs on the path to Piazza 1.

He spared the open-air chessboard only a cursory glance, noting that the last game had ended in a Pyrrhic victory for whoever had played black, before entering the department of Languages and Linguistics hoping for the customary wall notice for guidance. He found it easily enough and was amused to learn from it, thanks to added graffiti in felt-tip marker pen, that the language labs were on the ground floor, the departmental office and seminar rooms were on the first floor, staff offices were on the second floor, and 'lingerie and footwear' were, apparently, on an imaginary third floor.

He took the lift to the second floor and worked his way down the deserted, neon-lit corridor until he found a door marked, rather formally, 'Estephanie Silva, BA, BSc', which opened at the first tap of Campion's knuckle.

'I'd almost given up on you,' said Miss Silva, leaning in coquettish pose against the doorframe. 'Then I saw you doing your *Bridge on the River Kwai* act, taking the salute of your loyal fans.'

'*Your* loyal fans,' Campion corrected, 'and on the whole a cheerful, dedicated bunch. You are lucky to have students who adore you. I get the impression that the late Professor Perez-Catalan inspired similar feelings among students and colleagues.'

Miss Silva waved Campion into her office. 'Pascual was loved by everybody – except that can't be true, can it?'

'Clearly not, but were you among his admirers?' He held up the leather-bound Cervantes. 'And before you answer that, I own up to having read the inscription on this rather expensive volume.'

'I've told you I have already shocked the superintendent with honest tales of my sex life, so it would be stupid to deny now that Pascual and I were lovers. Very *passionate* lovers,' she added, with a deliberate flutter of her eyelashes.

'Latin lovers?'

'You've been quick to pick up the gossip, but it was not technically accurate. My father was Spanish, but he died when I was very young. My mother was British – no, not British, English, very English – and I was born and brought up in that famous Spanish coastal resort, the Costa del Brighton, then boarding school in Kent and university in London, which is why I have a British passport, struggle to get a tan and don't look particularly Latin, whatever that means.'

'I suppose the blonde hair fools most people,' said Campion.

'Not necessarily. There are blondes in Spain, probably as a result of some Viking raids a thousand years ago.'

Campion nodded sagely. 'Yes, those Vikings got everywhere. But you kept your Spanish name.'

'Why not? Estephanie is rather nice, my mother never remarried, so I saw no reason to change. Because I speak Spanish, teach Spanish and have a Spanish name, people assume I am Spanish. They probably think that explains my explosive bursts of temperament, but those are when I feel strongly about something, not because I'm hot-blooded Spanish. In fact, I'm more sort of cold-blooded Home Counties.'

'I have been here less than a week and I have already witnessed two of your public explosions. Are they common events?'

'Only if I don't get my own way.' She smiled at Campion and the word 'she-wolf' sprang into his mind. 'On academic matters, I should add. I take it you saw my little spat with Pascual in the middle of the piazza?'

'That and your assault on poor old Nigel Honeycutt in the refectory.'

'Nigel, that lily-livered pinko? I've no time for hero-worshipping acolytes, not when they stop me using the computer to teach my students.'

'So your emotional eruptions were over professional, academic matters?'

'Of late, yes. We stopped rowing about sex or whose turn it was to do the washing up or put the bins out well over a year ago.'

'That would be down in White Dudley, would it?' Campion asked. 'The row about the bins and the washing up, not necessarily the sex.'

'Why do you say that?'

'Pascual lived there, and I don't think you live on campus, so his place would be the nearest venue for scenes of domestic bliss – or outburst.'

'I have a flat in Saxmundham, so Pascual's place was more convenient for getting to work in the mornings. It had its drawbacks, of course.'

'Let me guess: Mrs Meade across the road.'

'Got it in one,' said Miss Silva, 'the nosey old cow. Oh, sorry, I hope I haven't shocked you.'

Mr Campion prodded his spectacles further up his nose. 'If your sex life fails to shock me, I do not see why your opinions on Edwina Meade should, particularly when I agree with them.'

The woman tilted her head and stared quizzically at Campion. With her face framed by her long blonde hair, Campion could see why men fell for her.

'There's a Spanish proverb,' she said, 'which, roughly translated, says: *Love is blind, but the neighbours aren't.* I never realized how true that was until I ran into Mrs Meade.'

Campion made a show of consulting his wristwatch. 'Look, Miss Silva . . .'

'Stephanie, or Steph. Please.'

'Steph, I've just realized a terribly important thing,' he said seriously. 'I missed lunch entirely and I really do not fancy chancing the menu down at The Plough in White Dudley again – well, certainly not tonight. I believe the refectory opens at five. Could I persuade you to join me? We can continue the character assassination of Mrs Meade.'

'The food in the refectory is truly awful,' said Steph Silva, 'unless you really like baked beans and chips with everything, and I do mean everything. But as those are the two main food groups of the average student, it gets quite busy in the early evening. So I suggest we go now and grab a table where we can gossip in peace.'

If there was a dress code in the refectory inside the 'Circus' building, Mr Campion and Miss Silva exceeded it by some considerable distance. Both drew inquisitive glances from student customers; in the case of Campion they were of mild curiosity from both sexes, in the case of Steph Silva the bulk were of embarrassed lust from young male eyes. Miss Silva seemed unaffected by them.

They queued together at the self-service counter and Campion realized that Miss Silva had not been exaggerating about the limitations of the menu. He settled for a brace of suspiciously orange fishcakes which came with the obligatory chips and beans and, as a treat, added a portion of 'spotted dick' sponge pudding and custard to his tray.

'You don't have to worry about your figure,' said Steph as Campion pointed a raised eyebrow at the plate on her tray which contained a splatter of limp lettuce, a tomato cut in half and a cold chicken breast, with a glass of water for dessert.

'Neither do you,' said Campion, 'judging by the admiring glances. You have the ability to turn male heads.'

'And I hope a few female ones too. I like to keep the opposition on their toes.'

She gave Mr Campion a lascivious wink and led him to an unoccupied table with four chairs, two of which she folded into the table to discourage any other diners from joining them. Campion put down his tray and placed the *Don Quixote* translation to one side. The leather-bound Spanish edition he placed in front of Steph's tray.

'It's awfully rude to read at the table, but I think this may be the one place it's allowed,' said Campion, 'and I'd like to start with that far from slim volume.'

'I've read it, several times. What do you want to know about it?'

'I told you, I'm nosey. I've read the inscription. When did you give it to Pascual?'

'Two years ago, when we were at it like rabbits. Do I shock you?'

'No, not yet, but please do not stop trying. You were lovers, but it ended some time ago, correct?'

'In a nutshell, yes; and before you ask, yes, it was a stormy relationship, shockingly public and often violent.'

'You seem neither sorry nor upset by that.'

'Should I be? Both Pascual and I were consenting adults and what we did in our private lives should have been private, except it was anything but. We started out trying to be as careful as possible, but that didn't last long. Prying eyes and flapping lips made sure of that.'

'Edwina Meade, I'm guessing.'

'You guess right, Mr Visitor. At first it was quite fun trying to shock her, but then it got nasty when she tried to blackmail Pascual and downright sinister when the gossip started on campus, suggesting I was some sort of Mata Hari seducing Pascual to get at his research. *That* one was started by the odious Gerry Meade and, sadly, quite a few of the academics here were starting to believe it.'

'So you wisely called it a day,' said Campion.

'Oh no, we called it a day when I found out he was two-timing me and then it became definite when I discovered he was three-timing me. I think that was when I threatened to kill him for the first time.'

'And Mrs Meade – or Gerry – they overheard you?'

'As I did it in the middle of Piazza 3, I think everybody heard me.'

'I see.'

'Now I have shocked you.'

'No, modern times mean modern morals. I try and keep up, not judge. My mother, on the other hand, would have had you shot.' Campion, realizing his meal was cooling and congealing, went to work with his cutlery. 'You said that was the first time you . . .'

'Threatened to kill Pascual?' Steph shrugged her shoulders. 'Yes, that was the first of many and the police knew about all of them, thanks to Gerry Meade. That's why they hauled me in today; when I didn't deny any of it, it rather stumped them. Being honest proved the best policy for once. All they had was gossip, and they couldn't charge me with gossip.'

'I'm sure Superintendent Appleyard would if he could,' said Campion without a trace of cynicism. 'He's been looking for someone with sufficient motive to commit murder.'

Steph Silva took a sip of water, put down her glass and smiled at Campion. 'I had two very good ones.' She held up one finger, then a second. 'Firstly, I discovered Pascual was a cheating little rat. Then his precious research took over the Computing Centre and no one else could get a look-in. That was screwing up any chance I had of developing my course on textual analysis in linguistics, which was seriously denting my career prospects.'

'With whom was Pascual cheating on you?'

Now the woman wagged a finger in front of Campion's face.

'I have my suspicions, but I won't share them. To be honest, I shouldn't have been surprised. Pascual spread his charm as widely as possible. He was a natural flirt but, to be fair, he stayed clear of the female students, even though many went googly-eyed over him. When it came to the staff or the secretaries, though, no woman was safe.'

'Would that include Tabitha King?'

Miss Silva burst out laughing. 'God, no! Not that he didn't try it on, and it clearly upset her, but Tabitha is not remotely interested in men. You know what that makes her, don't you?'

'A vegan?' said Campion gently.

Miss Silva laughed again. 'Delicately put. I think she actually is a vegan, but you know very well what I meant, because you knew already, didn't you? I think you're a bit of a dark horse, Mr Campion, and I like that. But you can rule Tabitha out of the homicide stakes.'

'Even though she stands to inherit Pascual's research? If she publishes, that's surely the making of her academically, isn't it?'

'You could be right – that would be a much better motive than the old "hell hath no fury" in her case. Still, it's a theory, and I suspect one that hasn't occurred to the police. Well done you! I'm so glad I decided to tell you the truth, the whole truth and nothing but.'

'Yet you won't tell me who your rivals were for Pascual's affections, however liberally they were spread.'

'I don't care who they were! There were always going to be

other women where Pascual was concerned. Once I realized that – which I did pretty quickly, by the way – it was time to cut my losses. If you want to know about Pascual's sex life after me, try asking Edwina Meade. She watched what went on in his house more than she watched television.'

'Scurrilous rumour has it that his house in White Dudley was only one of his – what should we call them? – love nests.'

Miss Silva's expression, which Campion was observing closely, showed no emotion.

'You mean his "love shack", the ruined chapel across the park on the beach? Worst-kept secret on campus. It would have appealed to Pascual, thinking if he was out of sight, he was out of prying minds, plus he had a thing about sleeping out of doors. He'd done a lot of climbing and camping in the Andes on his research expeditions. Sleeping bags and oil lamps never appealed to me, I'm a home comforts sort of girl.'

'Curled up in front of the fire with a good book sort of girl?' Campion said lightly, indicating the leather-bound book in front of her.

'You might say that,' said Steph, caressing the book's cover with her fingertips. 'But Pascual was really only interested in the physical side of things.'

'Have you looked inside?'

'I know what the inscription says. I wrote it.'

'Open the book,' Campion pressed.

Miss Silva did as ordered, slowly and carefully, noting her own handwritten dedication.

'Keep going.'

She began to turn pages and then her fingers became uncertain as she felt, as Campion had, something wrong with the density of the book. When she reached the hollowed-out section, where Campion had placed the key he had 'borrowed' from the police evidence table, Miss Silva's eyes widened.

'That's not right,' she breathed.

'An awful bit of vandalism,' said Campion, retrieving and closing the book. 'It must have cost you a pretty penny and Pascual made a hidey-hole out of it. I'll ask the police to return it to you when their investigation is completed. Unless the professor had relatives likely to claim his effects.'

'He had no one as far as I knew,' said Miss Silva, reacting as if a spell had been broken by Campion removing the book. 'There were certainly women back in Chile, but whether any had a claim on him I wouldn't know. As far as I'm concerned, I don't want it back, and it's in no fit state to give to the library, so tell the cops they can dump it.'

She wiped her hands on a paper serviette, as if washing her hands of the matter.

'That was a terrible thing to do to any book, but especially a classic like that one. Have you read it?'

'Not recently,' said Campion, reaching for the paperback translation Dr Szmodics had given him, 'but I intend to reacquaint myself with the old Don. I have always thought tilting at windmills was a noble, much derided, occupation.'

'I think you have always known exactly what you were tilting at,' said the woman. 'There is a passage in *Quixote* where the Don says something like: *It's true I'm pretty clever and I'm something of a rascal, but that's well hidden under this always easy and natural disguise of behaving like a fool.* In my opinion, Cervantes had you down to a tee, Mr Campion.'

FOURTEEN
The Conclave of St Jurmin

n the staff flat at the top of the Durkheim pyramid, Mr
Campion took off his shoes and his spectacles, lay on the
too-short bed and settled down to treat himself to a thirty-
minute snooze. It had been a long day and it was not yet over.
He awoke with a start, disturbed by the rhythmic thumping of
an electric bass guitar, coming from a record player somewhere
in the bowels of the residence, to discover that two hours had
passed. I am, he concluded, getting far too old for this lark.

The view from his windows was, if anything, more spectacular
by night, with the university buildings lit up like Blackpool's
illuminations. Campion could clearly see figures – students he
hoped – walking about and sitting at tables in the lighthouse
that was the library and even, at the other end of the campus,
two figures braving the night air and sea mist playing chess *al
fresco*. Even the windows of Black Dudley were lit up, as if
promoting the message that the police never slept, although
Campion suspected that any activity there was more likely to
be the university porters coming and going off patrol.

He washed his face to make sure he was awake, then
rummaged through his suitcase for a change of clothing. He
had not planned on needing attire suitable for going burglar-
izing, but he had thoughtfully – or rather Amanda had – packed
two ancient pullovers and a pair of corduroy trousers in case
Guffy Randall had needed help with his prize pigs at Monewdon
Hall. He changed his trousers and pulled on both pullovers, to
cover his white shirt and insulate him against the cold night
air, hung up his suit jacket in the tiny cupboard which served
as a wardrobe and laid his suit trousers under the thin mattress
of the bed to maintain a semblance of a crease for the morning.
It was, he felt, rather like being back at school.

Before he ventured out into the night, he removed the key

he had secreted in the Cervantes and placed it and his room key in separate trouser pockets, so they did not jingle as he walked, and his wallet in his back pocket. A final check in front of the long mirror on the wardrobe door satisfied him that despite the absence of a mask, a striped jersey and a sack with the word 'Swag' printed on it, he looked the part.

As he descended the stairwell of the pyramid, he experienced a wide repertoire of muffled musical styles coming from the corridors and his nose was assaulted by a variety of cooking smells worthy of a North African spice market, but somehow less appetizing, as well as what he would charitably refer to as the scent of herbal cigarettes.

Outside the pyramid he waited until his eyes became adjusted to the dark and his body became comfortable with the much lower temperature. He felt, he imagined, as a bee leaving a warm and snug hive on a frosty morning might feel and wondered, not for the first time, what the central-heating bills for the residences must be. Not to mention the electricity bill for keeping the central piazzas lit up all night, even though the campus was eerily deserted, though the fact that the bar in the refectory still had two hours of opening time probably accounted for a large proportion of the student population.

As a good burglar should, he shunned the illuminated buildings, taking a long, elliptical route to Black Dudley across the park, behind the curved outline of the library, up the slope to the car park and then across to the house where there were no police in evidence but, as he had hoped, the office which served as a porters' lodge was open for business.

He was slightly surprised to find that Bill Warren was the porter on duty.

'Have they got you back on night shift already, Mr Warren?' Campion said as he entered the porters' lair to find Warren sitting behind the desk, a mug of tea in one fist, a copy of the *Ipswich Star* spread out in front of him like a tablecloth.

'Oh, hello there. I'm filling in for Gerry Meade until ten o'clock, then Arthur takes over.'

'Arthur?'

'Arthur from Aldeburgh. He's Gerry's cousin, been with us for years, and he don't mind doin' nights, leastways not when

Gerry tells him he has to. By rights it should have been Gerry on tonight, but he's tied up entertaining a visitor – another visitor – a friend of yours, I hear.'

'And yours, from what you told me of your wartime experiences. A large gentleman, and I use the term loosely, by the name of Lugg. I suspect they will be well entrenched in The Plough by now.'

Bill Warren nodded enthusiastically. 'I'm hoping to join them for last knockings. Be nice to see Major Lugg again.'

Major? Campion bit his tongue at the rank but reasoned that it was at least shorter than Magersfontein as a Christian name.

'Anyway, what can I do for you, Mr Campion?'

'Do you have such a thing as a torch I could borrow? I fancy a bit of exercise, stretch the legs, take in the sea breeze, that sort of thing before bed.'

'In the dark?'

The prospect of voluntarily being isolated from central heating and a hot beverage clearly appalled Bill Warren.

'That's why I need the torch,' said Campion. 'I'd like to go along the seashore as far as St Jurmin's chapel, but I don't plan on going swimming.'

'Well, I'll give you the loan of a torch right enough, but you be careful, sir. The pebble beach up by St Jurmin's is treacherously slippy at the best of times, but at night you can easily turn an ankle.'

'I'll heed your sound advice, Bill. By the way, is there anything in the paper about our local difficulties?'

'That Superintendent Appleyard's been getting his name in the papers right enough, and he's declared the whole campus a crime scene.'

'Which is why we don't have reporters crawling all over us yet,' said Campion ruefully, 'though that can't last much longer.'

'The poor old vice chancellor's getting dozens of phone calls – fair driving him crazy it is. Not just reporters, but parents of students wanting to know if their little darlings are safe.'

'I suppose the bishop's been on the phone as well,' said Campion with a guilty wince.

'I don't know who pays His Lordship's phone bill, but I'm glad I don't. He must have phoned six times this evening, demanding to know what's going on. Fair upset Mrs Downes, it has. We've had to get the MO to come over and give her a sedative to calm her nerves.'

Campion was confused for a moment. 'The MO? Oh, you mean the medical officer, Dr Woodford.'

'That's right; nice lady, and it's really handy having her living on site.'

'She lives in the staff flat on top of the Chomsky pyramid, doesn't she?'

'That's right, sir, You can see her flat from here, standing outside and in daylight o'course.' Warren handed Campion a long, truncheon-like rubber-encased torch after testing that it worked. 'At night I always reckon that you could stand at the window and flash an SOS signal and Doc Woodford would spot it and come running.'

'How interesting,' said Mr Campion.

Campion turned back on himself as he left Black Dudley, walking towards the car park until he reached the end wall of the house, where he swung right and followed its dark shadow until he was in open parkland again. There were no lights showing on this side of Black Dudley, and this close to the house he was masked from the unearthly glow of the illuminated main campus.

Employing his borrowed torch, Campion followed the north walls until his beam picked up a pathway which pointed away from the house and into the darkness. Keeping a circle of torchlight playing on the path about a yard ahead of his feet, he followed his nose and ears as much as the path towards the salty tang and slaps and thuds of the sea lapping hungrily at the low coastline. If there was a moon, it was hidden behind cloud, and Campion could only distinguish the coast to his right by the faintest of changes in the thickness of the darkness surrounding him. It seemed unreal that something as big as the North Sea could be so close and yet indistinguishable from the land, and he hoped that the path, which was unlit and untended unlike the ones on campus, arrived at the chapel before it led him to a watery surprise.

It did so, but more suddenly than he expected. Without

warning the walls of St Jurmin loomed up out of the gloom in front of him. The path ended and, with the aid of his torch, Campion picked his way through a rough patch of fallen stones and bricks, which time and marram grass had turned into booby traps for the unwary pedestrian.

Campion raised his torch and saw a rough wall stretching up to the edge, he presumed, of a tiled roof. From his room in the pyramid residences, St Jurmin's had seemed a dark pimple on the horizon, and he had first thought it a ruin, but here, close up, it was solid enough; a rectangular building constructed of stone and bricks almost certainly reused from a Roman site fallen into disuse or destruction. Despite the second-hand building materials, the chapel had withstood the ravages of both time and the wind and tides coming off the North Sea, to which it was totally exposed, for over thirteen hundred years.

It had no doubt survived the intrusions of raiding Vikings, warring feudal knights, religious reformers and counter-reformers, perhaps even a greedy bishop or two, should such things ever have existed. But now it faced its greatest challenge in Mr Albert Campion, a burglar with a key. All he had to do was find the door.

A quick survey with his torch told Campion that he was three-quarters of the way along the side wall. As the sea was to his right and the east, where the 'business end' of a church was usually located, he deduced he would find the west-end wall and the door to his left, and he edged his way to the corner, his right hand gliding over the rough stone fabric to steady himself. If this was indeed a place where lovers met for secret carnal trysts, then the younger generation were, he decided, a hardier breed than he had given them credit for.

If there had been a porch on the chapel, it had long gone, but the door remained in place. It was not the original door, though it had considerable antiquity, and the lock was, in comparison, brand spanking new, perhaps less than one hundred and fifty years old, for which Campion was grateful as the original Anglo-Saxon key would have been hefty enough to fell a horse, never mind fit in a hollow book or a trouser pocket.

The professor's key fitted perfectly, the lock turned with a satisfying *clunk* and Campion was inside, out of the wind which had left the taste of salt on his lips, but into a cocoon of darkness even more impenetrable than the night outside.

If it had originally been a church, what remained to become a chapel was the nave, a rectangle fifty feet long and half as wide, and, Campion estimated, some twenty-five feet in height, though – by the light of a single torch – he put little faith in the accuracy of his measurements.

The most striking thing about the chapel of St Jurmin was its emptiness. There were exposed roof beams and, high up the walls, windows which during the day would have contributed little to lifting the gloom. There was an altar, a small rustic wooden affair, above which, suspended from a beam, was a large painted crucifix, and a wooden candelabra stand bearing the stumps of a dozen candles.

Campion walked the length of the nave, his heels echoing from the flagstone floor, sweeping his torch from side to side, the beam failing to pick up any sign of life; not a bat nor a rat, not even a mouse dropping. But there, tucked against the long north wall behind the wooden candelabra was something, and something definitely out of place.

It was a metal travelling trunk with a gently domed lid, carrying-handles at the side and a metal locking hasp secured with a padlock. The trunk was in good condition for its age, though it lacked the travel agent or shipping line stickers which would have made it a prize exhibit in an antique shop, and the padlock was almost brand new.

Campion appropriated the multi-headed candlestick, mentally kicking himself for not bringing any matches, and squashed his torch at an angle on to several candle stubs so that the beam pointed down on to the trunk, leaving his hands free.

He knelt down in front of the trunk and, pulling his wallet from his back pocket, extracted his trusty metal nail file. He was not sure whether to be pleased or worried to find that the padlock resisted for a full minute longer than the doors in the residences to his delicate probing, and when it yielded, he freed it from the hasp and opened the lid fully against the wall.

Campion's first thought was that the trunk was some sort of dressing-up box, and his second that he had committed sacrilege by disturbing a cache of religious vestments. On closer examination he realized he might have been looking at fabric, but it was not clothing, and there were two distinct layers of fabric, the top one thick and soft, the underlying one cold and rubbery. He reached in and began to unpack, pulling, unfolding and then pushing items behind him as he identified them, his nose wrinkling as he sniffed a mixture of damp and, he was sure, paraffin.

First came a green sleeping bag of Brobdingnagian proportions, which Campion quickly realized was in fact two quilted sleeping bags zipped together. From somewhere in the depths of his memory he recalled reading that Ernest Hemingway had owned such an item of *al fresco* slumber, or at least approved of the design. Next, a folded blue rubber inflatable mattress, which Campion presumed would be big enough for two and, under that, a variety of items which could have graced a vicarage white-elephant stall.

There was a concertina-like bellows foot pump for inflating the mattress, two antique storm lanterns, an empty bottle of Rioja which Campion recognized from the case he had found in the professor's house, and several plastic hand torches. At the very bottom of the trunk, numerous smaller items rattled around as he reached in and swirled his hand around, as if delving blindly for the mystery prize in a bran tub, as the angle of his torch, jammed in the candelabra stand, did not allow the beam to illuminate to the darkest depths.

His fingers identified three flashlight batteries, presumably exhausted, the unmistakeable bendiness of some plastic cutlery, a magazine of some sort and a small, hard box which Campion recognized as the sort of jewellery box he kept his cufflinks in. He held his find up into the torch beam to confirm his suspicions and levered the box open to reveal the curve of a silver or white metal ring with a cluster of sparkling stones.

He closed the box and palmed it into his trouser pocket. Whether it was evidence or not, it was the most valuable item in the trunk, and he was taking it into protective custody. As the police had clearly not searched the chapel, presenting it to Superintendent Appleyard would have to be done tactfully, as would explaining how the professor's key to the chapel came into Campion's possession, not to mention the opening of the trunk's padlock when the key to that remained on the professor's key ring.

Campion got to his feet and began to repack the items he had removed. He was struggling to refold the double sleeping bags, which had developed a mind of their own, when he was sure he felt a cold breeze on his cheek, a sea breeze, as if the outside elements had come inside. He turned instinctively to where he thought, in the disorientating darkness, the door was, but the light from his torch was still aimed downwards and did little to lighten the far end of the chapel.

He shrugged off the feeling of unease, and continued to try to stuff the sleeping bags into the trunk, with a growing feeling of frustration as they refused to behave; he even tried using a foot to squash them down while recognizing it as somewhat less than dignified behaviour for a man of his age.

Fortunately there was no one in that dark, lonely chapel to see him; except there was, and the first Campion knew of it was when he felt something small but solid pressed into the back of his neck.

'Kneel down,' ordered a muffled voice.

'I'm sorry if I appear to be trespassing,' said Campion, sinking down to resume his devotional position in front of the trunk, 'but I have every right to be here.'

His eyes flicked from side to side trying to catch a glimpse of the shadow – of anything – of the figure behind him.

'Whoever you are, I mean you no harm, and may even be of some assistance . . .' He knew it was important to keep one's enemy talking as long as possible, especially when the enemy had you at a disadvantage. 'If I have disturbed something personal then I apologize . . .'

He took a deep breath when he felt the pressure point on his neck was suddenly relieved. Had it really been the barrel of a pistol as he had automatically assumed? Surely it could not have been the old trick of making a two-finger gun to back up an enormous bluff?

'I am sure we can talk this through, whatever "this" is. I am not of the police, merely a gifted amateur. Well, perhaps not so gifted, for it seems—'

Campion felt a sharp scratch on his neck below his right ear.

His brain had just about concluded that he had been jabbed with a hypodermic needle when his knees folded under him and he collapsed forward over the trunk into a blackness darker than the interior of St Jurmin's chapel.

'Light another candle, 'e's coming back to us. Don't worry about the dopey expression on his fizzog, that's what passes for normal with him.'

Mr Campion returned to consciousness to find three torchlit faces looming above him like floating Halloween pumpkins. One seemed as large, as round and as expressionless as a full moon and was instantly recognizable. It took him a moment or two to identify a second face as that belonging to the porter Bill Warren. The third hovering visage he could not place, but he too was wearing a university porter's uniform, and Campion's befogged brain did what it did best and remembered the inconsequential before the necessary.

'You must be Arthur from Aldeburgh,' he said, and then looked around to take stock of his situation.

He was sitting – or had been sat – on the metal trunk, the contents of which were scattered across the flagstone chapel floor as if a bomb had gone off. He was able to identify all the items he was sure he had repacked by the light, now, of four torches and a handful of candles, and the substantial bulk of Lugg came into sharp focus as he stood before him holding the empty wine bottle as if offering Exhibit A to an unsympathetic judge.

'Been 'aving a good time, 'ave we? Quite a party from the looks of things.'

'Parties there have undoubtedly been,' said Campion, his throat dry, 'but I was not present and, as for that bottle of *vino*, not a drop touched my lips.'

'Pull the other one.' Lugg held something small up to Campion's eyeline. 'Like you pulled this cork.'

Campion took the cork from him and examined it before handing it back.

'That's interesting; as is the fact that you are here. What *are* you doing here?'

'Rescuing you, Mister Ingratitude.' Lugg turned to his companions in despair. 'See, not a word of thanks. Typical.'

Campion bowed his head and rubbed the back of his neck. 'Thank you, gentlemen, one and all. Now, help me to my feet, please, or alternatively, stop spinning this chapel on its axis. I take it I was found in a prone position?'

'Flat on your face, Mr Campion,' said Bill Warren a little too enthusiastically, 'with a bottle rolling across the floor. We naturally thought you'd been taken suddenly drunk.'

Mr Campion allowed himself a smile at the porter's descriptive powers. 'Not a drop has passed my lips, Mr Warren, but I'm betting Lugg here can't say the same.'

The fat man bristled. 'Well, you may have been at your devotions in this 'ere chapel; I was at mine down The Plough. When Bill turned up we swapped war stories for a bit and the subject came up of an elderly gentleman, who ought to know better, wandering off to collect seashells on the seashore in the dead of night. I told Bill here that you weren't supposed to be allowed out on yer own anywhere there wasn't street lighting, so he rang Arthur who said he'd not seen hide nor hair of you.'

'I could see Maj . . . Mr Lugg was worried,' said Warren, 'so we jumped in my car and shot back over here. Mr Meade offered to drive him, but he wasn't really in a fit state.'

'You had a good evening in the pub, did you?' asked Campion.

'It was steady,' Lugg said reluctantly. 'Gerry Meade might be a big man, but he's got no head for beer at all. Buys his rounds, though, and tries to keep up best he can. Anyways, what's been going on here?'

On his feet, but steadying himself on Lugg's extended and rock-hard forearm, Campion bowed his head.

'Shine a torch on the back of my neck, over towards the right, if you wouldn't mind, old chum. See if you can see anything.'

After a full minute of careful examination, Lugg said: 'Looks like you've been nipped by a flea or pricked by a wasp, but you ain't going to bleed to death. What was it, a poison dart from a blowpipe? I told yer: there's always a second murder in these country house affairs.'

'Clearly I haven't been murdered,' said Campion, straightening up and running a finger round the inside of his collar. 'Somebody took me off guard and put what I thought was a gun to my neck. I realize now it was that cork you found. It was new and virginal and didn't come from a bottle, but was protecting the tip of a hypodermic needle. The cork came off, the needle went in and I went out . . . What time is it?'

'Twenty past eleven, sir,' said Arthur from Aldeburgh, who seemed delighted to make a useful contribution to a confusing situation.

'Then it was probably an anaesthetic, not *curare* or any other exotic poison; perhaps that new ketamine stuff the Americans are using in Vietnam. It wasn't meant to kill, just incapacitate.'

Lugg did not appear impressed. 'What for? You nicking something? Is this a pirate's treasure chest? 'Cos it looks more like donations to a jumble sale.'

Without drawing attention to the movement, Campion dropped his right arm and patted his trouser pocket to reassure himself that the small jewellery box was still there.

'Nothing seems to be missing,' said Campion, manipulating Lugg's arm so that the torch he was holding played across the floor. 'So no harm done. I believe all this stuff belonged to Professor Perez-Catalan and the police need to be informed in the morning.'

'Shouldn't we report this now?' suggested Bill Warren. 'After all, you were attacked, and Arthur here is duty-bound to log that for Mr Meade. Really, we're supposed to phone him when anything out of the ordinary happens.'

'If you would be good enough to run Mr Lugg back to White Dudley, where he's staying with the Meades, you can tell him personally.' Campion adjusted his spectacles, which Lugg knew was a signal for him to play along. 'After he has escorted me to my room, that is, just in case there are bands of ruffians out there lying in wait.'

Lugg extended an elbow, as if he was asking a dowager duchess to accompany him in the last waltz on the dance card.

'Are you sure you are all right?' Bill Warren was genuinely concerned. 'You still look a bit shaky.'

'That's his natural colouring,' scoffed Lugg, but Warren persisted.

'I could call out the university medical officer.'

'No!' said Campion sharply. 'That wouldn't be a good idea at all.'

*   *   *

Bill Warren agreed to share a warming brew with Arthur from Aldeburgh in the porters' lodge in the entrance hall of Black Dudley, once Campion insisted that only Lugg need see him to the door of his room. Lugg would easily find his way back to the house. If there was a kettle boiling, he would find it.

They made an incongruous pair, and anyone watching from a distance would have put them down as an elderly married couple, perhaps a masochistic couple, out for a midnight stroll on a cold and damp evening. As they entered Piazza 3, Campion knew it was midnight without having to consult his watch as the first mournful notes of the 'Last Post' rang out and bounced off the buildings and across the campus.

'Strewth! You weren't kidding about 'aving your own Louis Armstrong on tap, were you?'

'I told you, he's as punctual as ever.' Campion made no attempt to keep the admiration out of his voice.

'He ain't got much of an audience; looks like all the kiddies have gone to bed,' Lugg observed.

'I think that's rather the point. The Phantom Trumpeter is telling them it's Lights Out.'

'Hoh, very droll, I'm sure. You any idea who this joker is?'

'No,' said Campion, steering Lugg out of the piazza and towards the pyramids. 'Not yet, but I have a good idea *where* he might be.'

Observing the four pyramidal residences close up, Lugg was speechless, but not in admiration.

'What school of ark-ee-tek-chewer do they call this, then? Lego with a hangover?'

'That's not bad, old fruit,' Campion admitted, grinning broadly as Lugg gazed up at the concrete structures towering over them, 'but to be safe, just call it "modern". Face it, it's far less brutal than some of the things going up in the old London docks, and the students seem to like them. The views from the top are spectacular; on a clear day you can see Walberswick.'

Lugg turned on him, instantly suspicious. 'Where's your room then?'

'Right at the very top.'

'And there's no lift, is there?'

'The pharaohs never needed lifts in their pyramids.'

'They wus already dead.'

Once Lugg had got his breath back after his exertions on the
stairs, observed that the swinging of a cat in the staff flat would
be impractical and grudgingly admired the view, Campion
insisted he sat down on the bed – assuming the bed could take
his weight – for his interrogation.

'So what have you to report from that hotbed of vice and
corruption that we call White Dudley?'

'Give us a chance,' Lugg complained in his schoolboy-in-detention
voice. 'I've hardly had time to get my feet under the table.'

'But you met the awesome Edwina?'

'Oh yes, once met, never forgot. Not a nice person in my
humble.'

'Your opinions are rarely humble, chum. Do go on.'

'You know the old saying, which I've just made up; the three
fastest methods of communication are telephone, telegram and
tell-an-Edwina. The woman lives for gossip, hoovers it up
wherever she can, then distributes it like one of them muck-
spreaders you see on the farms round here. Hardly got my hat
off before she was quizzing me about you and what you were
doin' here. She offered to show me round the dead professor's
house like she was running tours for Thomas Cook. And she
keeps a pair of binoculars on the windowsill in the front room,
just so she don't miss anything, the nosey old crone.'

'That's as neat a piece of character assassination as I've heard
since I got here,' said Campion, 'and universities tend to specialize
in them. I think you've got the measure of Mrs Meade.'

Lugg shrugged his shoulders in false modesty. 'Only saw her
for half an hour before Big Gerry dragged me off to the pub.'

'Define "dragged" – no, never mind. What did you glean
from Gerry?'

'He's an odd cove, no mistake. Kept mentioning his mother
and what she would have said or done. I got the impression
his mother was a bit of a strict Christian lady, though more
strict than Christian and probably not much of a lady.'

'A little unfair,' mused Campion, 'but I'd recognize her from
that description.'

'Well, according to Gerry and the ghost of his late mother, this university is an 'otbed of sin and debauchery and it's Gerry's duty to report it all to your friend and mine, the bishop. Though since the prof's murder, Gerry clearly fancies becoming the favourite in Superintendent Appleyard's class, pushing for milk monitor or to be teacher's pet. So, old cock, you be careful what you say in front of him.'

'Don't worry, I will. Now what I want you to do is chat up Mrs Meade – perhaps over breakfast and preferably on her own.'

'Do I have to?' Lugg sulked.

'Yes. Tell her you might be lodging with her for a week; don't worry, you won't have to. Say the bishop wants you to stay on and keep an eye on me, that should impress her. Add that the bishop thinks you shouldn't be a burden on her and that he insists she should take a week's lodging in advance. Whatever amount she suggests, stick on ten pounds for her trouble, but – and this is important – you have to pay her by cheque. You do have a chequebook on you, don't you?'

'No I don't.' Lugg was belligerent. 'Never occurred to me, this being a free board-and-lodging job as I was led to believe.'

'Well, in that case, you'd better take mine.'

Campion opened the sliver of wardrobe where he had hung his jacket and retrieved his chequebook in its brown soft leather case from an inside pocket. He held it out to Lugg but, before the big man's paw covered it, he pulled it just out of reach.

'I know you can forge my signature, though you're not very good at it and usually it wouldn't fool a blind cashier, but that shouldn't matter as Mrs Meade has no idea what my signature looks like.'

'But she'll notice the cheque's in your name, not mine.'

'Tell her it's a general account used by everybody who does special work for the bishop.'

'And she'll fall for that?'

'With your natural charm? I don't think you'll have any trouble with her. Just remember one thing.'

'What?'

'I've counted the number of cheques in the book and I'll count them again tomorrow.'

FIFTEEN
Trumpeter Voluntary

Despite his exertions the night before, Mr Campion was up, shaved, dressed and the first customer in the queue for breakfast in the refectory. Once again, he had the pick of the tables and was greeted by the cheery hellos of the cleaners in their nylon coats, all homely Suffolk ladies, taking a break between shifts, and the silent and suspicious glares of the few students around, if not fully awake, at such an early hour. Some may have had work to catch up on and were waiting for the library to open, Campion thought; some might be insomniacs or natural early risers, but at least two, he was sure, had not yet made it to bed, or certainly not their own.

He said his 'good mornings' and even tipped his hat when necessary and tucked into a brace of sausages, a greasy fried egg and two slices of toast, opting to wash it all down with a cup of tea, having tried the coffee the day before.

Suitably fortified, Campion bought *The Times* in the Students' Union shop next to the bar where the cleaners were getting to work with heavy machinery on the beer-soaked carpet, and made his way out of the oval refectory, past the Threepenny Bit lecture-theatre complex, and into the square that was Piazza 2. He was headed for the Administration building, which was a long, tall rectangle tacked on to the end of Piazza 3 at right-angles, but which did not have a nickname as far as he was aware.

Mr Campion, seated on the edge of the redundant fountain in Piazza 3, had completed twenty-five per cent of the crossword before estimating that the Administration block was open for business. Once inside he followed the signs for the Estates Office on the third floor and found it open and unguarded by a secretary, but with Mr Gregor Marshall already hard at work behind his desk or at least shuffling papers to give that impression.

'You're the early bird, Campion. What brings you into my domain?'

'An administrative matter, Mr Marshall. Do you have lists of the residents of the pyramids?'

'Of course I do,' said a surprised estates officer. 'The students pay rent and we need to know who to collect it from.'

'But you know which student lives in which room?'

'Naturally, we need to know where to deliver post or who is supposed to be where in case of a fire. What's your point?'

'No particular point,' Campion reassured him, 'I would simply like to look at a list of residents in the Babbage pyramid if that's at all possible.'

'It is possible,' Gregor Marshall narrowed his eyes, 'but it is a highly unusual request.'

'Have the police not asked for that information?'

'No they have not.' Marshall shook his head. 'I would, of course, make it available if they did.'

'Would you make it available to me? I don't want the complete census return, I'm really only interested in the current residents of the Babbage pyramid.'

'Anyone in particular?'

'An overseas student called Beverley Gunn-Lewis. She's from New Zealand and really rather sweet.'

'And you want to know which room she's in?' Marshall was torn between curiosity and suspicion.

'Actually I'd like a list of the students who live on the floor below her; and would it be possible to identify which are second- or third-year students?'

'I could do that,' said Marshall hesitantly, 'though I'm not sure if I should.'

'I will take full responsibility,' said Campion, 'and I will make sure the bishop is aware of how helpful you've been.'

'Oh please don't do that. I'll get your list; just promise me you won't do that.'

The police presence was back in force in Black Dudley and Superintendent Appleyard once more camped in the vice chancellor's office. Of Dr Downes there was no sign, and it seemed that Jack Szmodics had been left to represent the university authorities, or at least make sure the police did not steal the cutlery.

Surprisingly, Campion was invited into the superintendent's sanctum for a private 'chat'; surprising because Campion had spent the walk over from the Admin building trying to think of a way to negotiate such a meeting.

'You're up and about bright and early,' said Appleyard, waving Campion to a chair, 'considering your exertions last night.'

'So you've heard?'

'The night-shift porter logged an incident up at the old chapel just before midnight and Big Gerry brought it my attention as soon as he came on shift at eight o'clock. Care to enlighten me?'

'If only I could, Superintendent.' Campion removed his spectacles and began to polish the lenses lazily with his handkerchief. 'Where is Mr Meade, by the way?'

'He's in the porters' cubbyhole by the front door, having a bit of a lie-down, I reckon, judging by the state he was in first thing. It seems he had a bit of a night in the pub down in White Dudley last night, trying to keep up with that other visitor the bishop has wished on us.'

'That would have been a serious mistake,' Campion agreed, 'but I can assure you that Mr Lugg, the gentleman in question with the hollow legs, was in fine form at midnight. He and the portering staff rode to my rescue, you might say.'

'I might very well, if I knew what went on and what the devil you were doing up at that ruin in the first place.'

Mr Campion breathed on each large circular lens, rubbed them vigorously with a corner of handkerchief and slowly fitted them back on his face before he spoke.

'You never searched the chapel, did you? And, incidentally, it's not a ruin but perfectly weatherproof and watertight – though, I grant you, it is lacking in many a home comfort.'

'Why should we search it? There was no reason to.'

'You didn't notice that Professor Perez-Catalan had a key to the chapel on his key ring? It was quite distinctive.'

Appleyard went on the defensive. 'I had one of my lads go around with Meade and they checked all the keys on that ring to find out what they opened. There's a report on them in the file.'

'But you haven't read it yet, have you? Hardly surprising, you have had a lot on your plate the last few days. Take it from me, one of those keys was to the chapel, and I suspect Pascual had a copy made some time ago after he borrowed the original from Edwina Meade. He was a regular visitor to St Jurmin's, though I think more in the summer than the winter. Some on campus, such as Mr Tinkler, the chaplain, thought he went there for private contemplation, but others believed he rarely went there alone and was usually accompanied by a lady friend. Some cynics among the staff and the students referred to it as his "love shack".'

The superintendent's usually expressionless face struggled to contain both surprise and righteous indignation, eventually settling for a long, slow exhale through pursed lips and an angry flutter of his right eyelid.

'I don't have time to listen to idle gossip, I've been busy checking alibis and staff records, not to mention keeping the bishop and the chief constable and the press at bay. We've even checked all members of staff and students, and that's damned near a thousand files, for connections to Chilean politics, foreign intelligence agencies, big business concerns with mining interests, and so on, in case it was the professor's blasted secret formula they were after.'

'Algorithm,' said Campion patiently. 'It's an algorithm not a formula, and I believe it is perfectly safe and secure. In any case, if stealing his research was the object of the exercise, why kill him?'

'You tell me. I can see you're dying to.'

'I think we should be looking for a much more basic, more emotional motive.'

'Don't tell me, you've got a theory.'

'As a matter of fact I have.'

'And I said don't tell me.' Campion realized that the policeman was not making a joke. 'I know your reputation, Mr Gifted Amateur, and this isn't one where you help out the plodding coppers. So don't come to me with theories unless you have proof or at least solid evidence. Do you have any evidence?'

'Not just at the moment.'

'Thought not.'

'I have an idea where you might find some, but it would require an official police search, not an accidental find by a bumbling amateur. If it produces a result, all the credit goes to the police; if it turns up nothing, no one's the wiser.'

'I'm listening,' said the superintendent.

Campion found Dr Szmodics holding the university fort from a small makeshift office between the kitchen and the hall, occupied by police detectives, and he found the office by following the sound of two constantly ringing telephones. Szmodics was crammed behind a small table, juggling the two phones and attempting to take notes on a thick pad of ruled A4 paper.

'Busy?' Campion set his face with his most vacant grin and pushed it around the door.

Dr Szmodics, relieved at the interruption, snapped a curt goodbye into each receiver, replaced them in their respective cradles, then picked them up again and laid them on the table, the hum of their dialling tones filling the room with a soporific buzz.

'It's a madhouse, Campion, the switchboard must be near meltdown. I'm fielding calls from newspapers, scientific journals, the Chilean embassy, even the BBC television studio in Norwich. I can't tell them anything the police haven't, can I?'

'Of course you can't, nor should you,' said Campion, 'and I will try not to add to your woes. I need to find the vice chancellor.'

'Roger is upstairs in his apartments, handling the calls from the University Grants Committee, the county council, even the new secretary of state at the Department of Education, who sounds quite a difficult woman. Then there's the parents, all wanting to know if their offspring are at risk from some homicidal maniac.'

'Could you do me a big favour, Jack?'

'That depends. You have the air of a man who is plotting something.'

'Which is unusual, as most people say I look as if I'm not following the plot. What I need you to do is get the vice chancellor out of the way for ten minutes. I need to speak to Mrs Downes in private.'

'Dolores isn't in the best of health,' said Szmodics firmly. 'She's suffering from stress and nervous tension; even had the doctor out to her last night.'

'Really?' said Campion. 'That's very interesting, but I promise not to distress her further. In fact, I may be able to cheer her up. Please, Jack, it's important.'

Dr Szmodics exhaled slowly through his nose and reached for one of his purring phones. 'I suppose you'd prefer Roger not to know of your visit?'

'If possible.'

'Then go up the stairs to the first landing and hide in the Gents lavatory until Roger comes down. I'll find something to keep him occupied down here, but I don't promise more than ten minutes.'

Campion thanked him and hurried to the staircase and up to his designated hiding place, an action which brought back sudden memories of the harum-scarum of forty years before when the candlelit Black Dudley was a dark maze with frightened guests tearing hither and thither.

With the timing of an Aldwych farce, he watched Roger Downes leave his private quarters and pass the crack in the lavatory door to which he had his eye pressed. As he heard footsteps descending the stairs, Campion emerged from his hideout, strode over to the door of the Downes's flat, knocked twice and entered without waiting for an answer.

Dolores Downes was wearing a long woollen dressing gown, almost certainly her husband's, and was sitting in an armchair by the large sash window which looked northward over the park to the chapel of St Jurmin and the sea beyond. She turned her head as Campion appeared in the room but expressed neither surprise nor alarm.

'Oh, it's you,' she said weakly, then turned her head back to the window.

She was either clinically depressed, Campion decided, or a good actress playing the part of a dowdy heroine fatally afflicted by a terminal disease or a broken heart in a Victorian melodrama. Possibly a mixture of both, and for a very attractive woman, she did dowdy very well.

'Mrs Downes – Dolores – forgive the intrusion, but I need

to talk to you about those cheques you signed to Edwina Meade. May I ask what you have done with them?'

'I burned them.' She raised her face towards her intruder, her eyes moist and languid, as the stage directions would have said.

'Good show! That's exactly what I was going to suggest. I'm assuming you did not show them to your husband?' The woman, visibly brightening, shook her head. 'Excellent, then there's no reason for him to ever know. I doubt if Edwina Meade will mention the matter. How long was she blackmailing you for?'

'Just over a year,' said Mrs Downes, after clearing her throat and finding her voice, 'long after things had finished between Pascual and me. She's an evil bitch, once she got her claws in.'

'And Pascual was buying your cheques off her, to protect you.'

Mrs Downes shrugged her shoulders, but not in despair, rather in the way a weight-lifter prepares for a lift.

'Our infatuation ended some time ago, when Pascual met someone else; several someone-elses, I suspect. He was determined not to give Edwina any more scope for blackmail down in White Dudley.'

'Hence the love nest in St Jurmin's,' said Campion, noting that Dolores turned her head automatically back to the view out of the window as he said it.

'That was not a very well-kept secret, and then Pascual met someone really special.'

'Heather Woodford.'

'I never said that.'

Mrs Downes got to her feet, her strength returning, Victorian gloom slipping from her.

'You don't have to,' said Campion, his right hand involuntarily rubbing the back of his neck. 'She was here last night, wasn't she?'

'I needed something to help me sleep, but in many ways, Heather was in a worst state than I was. She took Pascual's death very badly, though she doesn't show it. They were going to be married, you know; that's why she'd given in her notice, as she couldn't really marry one of her patients. She's got a new job lined up at the Norfolk and Norwich Hospital.'

'Did their relationship make you jealous?'

'Not at all. For me, Pascual was a stupid infatuation; a fling, a dalliance to relieve boredom. I now fully accept that my future is with Roger. Heather knew about me, and it was she who told me that Pascual had bought those cheques from Edwina, to protect me.'

'You did not know he was buying the cheques off Edwina Meade?'

'Edwina Meade had her claws into me. I had no idea she would try and blackmail Pascual as well. When it was over between us, I was paying that wicked woman to protect Roger, not Pascual.'

'Did you not notice that your cheques had not been cashed?'

'Of course, but I put it down to Edwina not wanting to leave a trail which could be followed. She wasn't after the money, she just liked having a hold over people.'

'I wonder why he kept the cheques?' Campion asked without expecting an answer. 'Sentiment?'

'Pascual was not sentimental with his women,' said Dolores, staring vacantly out of the window, then her tone changed. 'Except perhaps with Heather. He had real feelings for her. Heather was the only woman, and he had many, to whom he proposed marriage.'

'Can you trust Dr Woodford to keep your secret?'

'I'm sure of it. She has no need to leave the university now and, if she stays, she has no reason to antagonize its vice chancellor.'

'And there is nothing Dr Woodford might have discovered about Pascual which might have suddenly turned her against him?'

Dolores Downes stiffened her spine and jutted her chin. The depressed invalid had gone, replaced by a strong-willed woman defending a fellow female.

'Are you suggesting . . .? Don't be ridiculous, Heather Woodford wouldn't hurt a fly.'

Mr Campion felt a twinge in the back of his neck.

'I wouldn't be too sure of that.'

With good theatrical timing, Campion made it down to the lobby and was hovering outside Appleyard's appropriated office as Dr Downes emerged from Jack Szmodics's temporary base of operations.

'I'm sure I can leave such matters in your hands, Jack,' he was saying over his shoulder with thinly disguised irritation. 'You are the dean of students; deal with the students. I'm busy dealing with everybody else. Oh, good morning, Campion, you're not after me as well, are you?'

'No, no, you're quite safe from me, Vice Chancellor; just checking in with my earthly masters.'

Campion jerked his head in the general direction of the policemen milling around.

'I wish you were as conscientious when it comes to liaising with your spiritual boss in St Edmondsbury.'

Doing his best to look crestfallen and perhaps just a little ashamed, Campion mumbled a schoolboy apology.

'Ah yes, the bishop. I have been remiss on that score, but I intend to placate him later this afternoon.'

'I'll be happy if you simply telephoned him,' said Roger Downes. 'Placating the bishop is probably beyond you; beyond all of us, for that matter.'

On his way out of the house, Mr Campion paused to peep into the porters' lodge where he caught a surreptitious glance of Big Gerry Meade slumped in a chair, the peaked cap pulled down over his eyes and moving up and down in time to his snoring. He did not disturb Mr Meade, for whom he felt a certain amount of sympathy, as having Lugg as a house guest was one of the tasks Hercules wisely avoided, though he would have liked to check with Meade that the old reprobate had made it back to White Dudley without incident.

As he emerged from Black Dudley, he realized his fears on that score – which were more curious whimsy than genuine worry – were unfounded, for there was Mr Lugg striding across the grass from the car park. He had dressed down into what he referred to as his 'country casuals' of dark gabardine trousers, a white roll-neck fisherman's pullover and, adding to the nautical theme, no doubt due to the proximity of the North Sea, a navy blue pea-coat.

Campion raised his hat in salute and pointed to the bridge

over the lake. Lugg altered course diagonally with the speed if not the grace of an oil tanker, so that their paths converged just before the bridge.

'A good night well spent in White Dudley?' Campion enquired.

'Don't know about that,' grumbled Lugg. 'Bill Warren drove me back there after I'd tucked you in and made sure the bed bugs weren't biting, and Big Gerry was sitting up waiting for me blowing the dust off a bottle of whisky he must have had for two Christmases.'

'I thought you said last night that he had a thin skull when it came to alcohol.'

'I did, and he does, but his liver just hasn't told his brain yet. I more or less had to put him to bed as well, but fair dos, he was up and out of the house by seven o'clock, though I bet his head was pounding something awful. That left yours truly with Mrs M. insisting I get a good breakfast inside of me, what with me being a "hemissary" from her beloved bishop. Know what she gave me? Fried Spam and baked beans. Spam! I ask you! Not even with an egg! To this day I can't eat Spam fritters without hearing *Hancock's Half Hour* on the radio. The walk up from the village has just about settled my stomach.'

They were halfway across the curved bridge before Campion thought it best to interrupt.

'Did you learn anything at all useful?'

'Only what you asked me to. I bent over backwards, offering to pay my way for bed-and-breakfast at her delightful hostelry, especially as it offered the delights of Spam for breakfast . . .'

'Yes, yes, get on with it.'

'But, anyway, she wouldn't take a cheque. Couldn't, shouldn't, wouldn't. Simple reason being she don't have a bank account, never 'as, never seen the need. So you might as well have this back.'

Lugg handed back Campion's chequebook. Campion paused, made a careful count of the number of cheques still in the book then, satisfied, tucked it into the inside pocket of his jacket.

'That all seems to be in order,' he said primly. 'Now let's crack on.'

'Where're we going?'
'To the rude awakening of a sleepy student.'

According to the list given to him by Gregor Marshall, there
were only two third-years among the male students on the fourth
floor of the Babbage residency hall, and only one of them lived
on the same side of the pyramid as Beverley Gunn-Lewis's
fifth-floor room. The inhabitant of Room 4, Floor 4 (Babbage
4:4 in university shorthand) was, according to the Estates Office,
a certain Anthony Judson, an undergraduate in the School of
Arts and Humanities.

After climbing four flights up the central stairwell, Campion
and Lugg took the left-hand corridor and examined the handwritten cards in the doorplates, until they stopped at the fourth
door along. Underneath the name 'Tony Judson', written in red
ink, was a line of tiny, but precise, musical notation, which
Campion followed with a silent whistle through puckered lips.

'Clever,' he said quietly. 'That's Louis Armstrong's opening
cadenza to "West End Blues". This is definitely our boy.'

Lugg flexed his right hand and turned it into a fist.

'Want me to bust his lip? Put a couple of teeth out? Trumpet
players can't function without their front teeth.'

'I'm not sure I could either,' hissed Campion, 'and don't be
a bully. Just keep quiet and look menacing.'

'I'll do me best,' said Lugg, folding his ham-hock arms and
turning his face to the wall, but glancing slyly down as Campion
knelt before the doorknob lock and went to work with his trusty
nail file. Only a raised eyebrow showed that Mr Lugg was
impressed; that and a whispered 'Ain't lost yer touch', as he
took Mr Campion's elbow and helped him to his feet.

They entered the room like ghosts; for perhaps the thou-
sandth time, Campion was impressed with the lightness and,
yes, grace, with which the big man could move when he put
his mind to it.

The accommodation was more basic here than in the staff
flats at the apex of the pyramids; basically a rectangular room
with a bed down one side and a desk and chair against the
opposite wall. On the desk, amidst an explosion of books, papers
and pens, was a silver-plated B-flat trumpet standing upright

on its bell. With the blind down, allowing the entry of a minimal amount of weak morning light, the room was in semi-darkness, but it was possible to discern a sleeping shape in the bed under a mound of tangled blankets, a protruding mat of curly black hair indicating which way the body was lying.

Campion swept the trumpet off the desk with his right hand and wiped the mouthpiece with his left before placing it to his lips and leaning over the mound in the bed. Behind him, Lugg placed a finger in each ear.

While he had some skill at the piano and had made a fair fist as a stand-in church organist on occasion, Mr Campion's previous experience with brass instruments was limited to a phase, during his own student days, when he carried a trombone with him to parties, sporting events and once, with consequences, into a second-year examination at St Ignatius College.

To his delight, he managed, using the first valve, to get a clear, loud, rising trill of notes out of the trumpet, though his delight was not shared by the sleepy head only a few inches away from its business end.

Mr Tony Judson, the owner of the head under fire, sat bolt upright as if electrocuted, and let rip a stream of obscene profanities peppered with a four-letter word he would have said was Anglo-Saxon in origin, but which Campion knew had its roots in Latin.

'Bet he's not studying Divinity,' Lugg observed.

'Good morning, Mr Judson,' said Campion, balancing the trumpet on the desk again. 'Sorry to disturb your slumbers, but as you clearly do not have a nine o'clock lecture scheduled, we thought you wouldn't mind a visit from the Phantom Trumpeter Fan Club.'

'Just who are you jokers?' The student attempted to swing his legs out of the bed, but seemed pinned there by a knot of tangled blankets and quickly gave up, sighed loudly and sat up in a cross-legged, Buddha-like position, his chest bare, the bedclothes protecting his modesty.

'Jokers is h'exactly what we is,' said Lugg at his most menacing.

Campion saw the unease flash across the young man's face and stepped in to calm the situation. 'We are helping the police make their enquiries, and we do so with, we feel, a good sense of humour, but for all our jolly japery, we would like you to answer a serious question.'

'All right, it's a fair cop, I am the Phantom Trumpeter.'

Campion exchanged grins with Lugg. 'I didn't know modern youth used expressions like that. It takes one back, doesn't it?'

'Shows respect, too, coughing up to it straight off,' Lugg agreed.

'But we know you are the midnight bugler, Mr Judson, and your punctuality impresses as much as your musicality, but answer me this if you would. Your midnight performances, are they to your timetable or do you respond to external stimuli?'

The student rubbed the sleep from his eyes with his fists and emitted the sort of huge lethargic yawn in which bored cats specialize.

'What are you talking about?' said the student, once his jaw had closed. 'Who are you guys anyway?'

'We are the official Visitors to the university. Because of the death of Professor Perez-Catalan, they thought it best to send us in pairs. Now, do you do your midnight stunt on your own initiative, or is anyone else involved?'

'How many people do you think it takes to play the trumpet?'

'Oi, cheeky!' warned Lugg.

'Let me simplify things before my elderly colleague has problems with his blood pressure,' Campion said reasonably. 'Did you ever time your nightly renditions in response to a signal, a flashing torch, say, from across the park?'

'Of course not, I have a watch and can tell the time.'

'But you don't 'ave an alarm clock to get you out of your pit in the mornings, do yer?'

'That shouldn't concern us,' said Campion, 'we're only interested in what young Mr Judson does around midnight. How he spends his mornings is of no interest to us.'

'You mean the flashing torch from the bridge across the fake lake,' Tony Judson volunteered.

'You saw it too?'

'I've seen it plenty of times, usually just before midnight in the summer term, earlier in the winter months. Thought it was Morse code at first, but it wasn't, just random signalling.'

'By whom, to whom?'

'No idea who was doing the sending, though it was odds on it was a woman. The receiver was Prof Pascual, the Latin Lover. I would have thought that was obvious.'

'Why was it obvious?'

'Because whoever was flashing that torch would have been pointing it at the window of his office in Earth Sciences, which looks out on to the park, the other side of Piazza 3. That was the professor's nookie call. Everybody knew.'

'And you've seen this before?'

'Oh yeah, loads of times last year, then again on Sunday night.'

'And it wasn't unusual for the professor to be working so late?'

'Not during term time; the lights were on in there most nights. Sundays . . . a bit unusual, but he was probably getting things ready for the new term. I don't know, you should ask somebody in Earth Sciences.'

'Oh, we will. Why didn't you tell the police that you'd seen the torch flashes on the night the professor was murdered?'

The student suddenly looked much younger than his twenty years.

'Nobody asked me, and I didn't want to get into trouble,' he said softly.

'What for? Playing a bum note?' snapped Lugg.

'Your playing,' said Campion, 'unlike your citizenship, is immaculate, but your location is now known so you may wish to restrict your performances. We will leave you to your studies.'

'Just who are you guys?'

Campion held the door for Lugg to squeeze by and through.

'You know Oliver Hardy here, and I'm Stan Laurel,' he said, tipping his fedora.

SIXTEEN
The Inelegant Solution

The three-mile walk from White Dudley and then the ascent and descent of four flights of stairs in the Babbage pyramid had restored Lugg's appetite which, he declared, could be satisfied by anything as long as it was not Spam. As it was only ten o'clock, which Campion described as 'dawn's early light' in new university terms, the restaurant in the oval refectory was still serving breakfast, and conveniently it was *en route* to their next destination.

Campion limited himself to a cup of tea, while Lugg fought to remove the memory of Spam with 'proper' bacon, eggs, tomatoes and fried bread. The restaurant was now much busier, with far more student customers than when Campion had breakfasted with the cleaners, and the sight of two elderly gentlemen so physically mismatched brought many a covert stare and at least one wag quietly whistling the 'Cuckoo' song, as made popular the day before by the Phantom Trumpeter.

When Lugg's stomach was finally appeased, Campion took him into Piazza 2 and then Piazza 1, where the outdoor chessboard immediately caught Lugg's eye.

'Strewth, they're real pieces! I thought this was just a statue when I saw it last night, or one of them silhouette puppet shows like they have out East.'

'No, it's a fully functioning chess set,' said Campion, patting a pawn on the head in passing, 'and you can give the computer a game if you fancy your chances.'

'Does the computer play Knock Out Whist or Find the Lady?'

'Probably not, but knowing you, I wouldn't fancy its chances.'

Charles Fowler, the Computing Centre manager, was surprised to receive another visit from the university Visitor, and positively speechless when he caught sight of Lugg squeezing his way between metal cabinets, apparently hypnotized by their small flashing green lights. The image of a bull in a china shop was somehow inappropriate, but that of a confused wildebeest lost in the lighting department of Selfridges sprang to mind.

'We don't mean to disrupt you, Mr Fowler,' Campion reassured him. 'We're looking for Tabitha King. Is she here by any chance?'

'She's here permanently these days, or it feels like it,' said Fowler, 'going through the professor's research.' He looked at Lugg speculatively. 'Is . . .?'

'Oh, this is Professor Magersfontein from South Africa. Doesn't speak a word of English. He's with me and I'll make sure he doesn't touch any buttons.'

Perez-Catalan's tiny windowless office was full to bursting without the addition of Campion's thin frame, and certainly could not accommodate Lugg's bulk. Nigel Honeycutt was standing to the right of the overloaded desk, Tabitha King to the left. Between them – seated on the sole chair for which there was room – was Beverley Gunn-Lewis, and all three stared in silence at Campion in the doorway.

'Beverley, how impressive! Been here less than a week and here you are in the nerve centre of the university at the heart of its most important research project.'

'Bev speaks Spanish,' said Tabitha King.

'I learned it specifically to follow the work of Professor Pascual and his team in Santiago,' said Beverley, blinking rapidly behind the winged frames of her glasses. 'I knew it would come in handy.'

'You are full of surprises,' said Campion jovially. 'It must be quite exciting to be helping out with his algorithm, but would you allow an interruption for a minute or two? I must have a word with Miss King here, and in private. Nigel, Bev, would you mind stepping out? You could, if you were feeling generous, show my associate Dr Lugg the wonders of the modern computer.'

Campion could tell from their expressions that a Lugg-sized shape had materialized behind him in the doorway.

'I suppose you're still acting as one of the police's running dogs,' Honeycutt snarled, 'but don't be too long. We only have Bev between her lectures.'

'I'm sure she's learning a lot from her time at university,' said Campion, noting that the student avoided eye contact as she and Honeycutt left the room. 'This is Dr Lugg. His field is criminology and he knows nothing of computers, so please introduce yourselves and educate him.'

When they were alone, and Campion had closed the door, he offered her the chair, but Tabitha King shook her head and leaned back against the overstuffed bookshelves, crossing her legs at the ankle and thrusting her hands into the pockets of the one-piece green garment she wore. Campion was unsure whether it was best described as overalls or dungarees and decided it was wiser to avoid the subject.

'Miss King, I need to ask you something which has nothing to do with geology, computers or algorithms.'

'Is it about Beverley?'

'Not at all, though I must say I find her quite charming and clearly she's full of surprises.'

'What do you mean?' asked Miss King, tight-lipped.

'It must have been a pleasant surprise to find she could speak Spanish and, of course, she knows the subject matter. I'm sure she'll prove very useful in getting the famous algorithm published.'

Miss King relaxed a little. 'So what can I help you with?'

'On Sunday night, the night Pascual was killed, did you see a torch flashing from over by Black Dudley, specifically by the bridge over the lake? It would have been near midnight.'

'Who told you about that?' she asked in a tone which reminded Campion to protect his sources.

'Believe it or not, the mysterious Phantom Trumpeter.'

Miss King was obviously relieved and somewhat impressed.

'Yes, I saw the same thing. From that high in the pyramids, you can see right across the park.'

'All the way to St Jurmin's chapel?'

She shook her head.

'No, not that far, not at night.'

'But you know why I mention St Jurmin's.'

'Everybody knew.'

'It was a signal from Pascual's lovers to arrange a meeting at . . .'

'Nigel called it his Love Shack.'

'So he did, I had forgotten how poetic Marxists could be. Do you have any idea who could have been signalling him on Sunday?'

'No, Pascual's sex life was a matter of complete indifference to me.'

'I understand that,' said Campion diplomatically, 'but did you not think it worth reporting the next day, when it was announced that Pascual had been murdered?'

Tabitha kept her hands deep in her pockets, but her forearms stiffened as her muscles tensed.

'I was not asked about it, and felt sure someone must have mentioned it, as anyone living on the fourth floor or above in one of the pyramids could have seen the signal.'

'But not necessarily known what it meant,' Campion pointed out.

'Everyone who lived on campus who wasn't a first-year knew about Pascual's women.'

'Naturally, all first-year students should be thought of as innocent,' said Campion, watching carefully for a reaction but getting none. 'You said *women*, plural, why?'

'Because there were at least two living on campus on Sunday who had used that method of signalling him in the past.'

Nigel Honeycutt escorted Lugg and Campion out of the Computing Centre – as Lugg put it later, to make sure they didn't steal the spoons – and as they traversed the mainframe, Campion asked about the addition of Beverley to the algorithm project.

'She's a real find,' said Honeycutt. 'Not only is she familiar with the terminology, even if it's on a basic level, but the fact that she can read Spanish is a godsend; not that I believe in God.'

'Of course you don't,' said Campion, 'but it sounds like Fate had a hand bringing her here just now, and of course, Tabitha. She's Beverley's tutor, is she not?'

'She is.' Honeycutt was suspicious. 'And she will make sure that helping us with Pascual's notes does not interfere with Beverley's coursework. Tabitha will keep her nose to the grindstone.'

'Well, I certainly didn't see either of them at the impromptu protest yesterday at the lake bridge. They were probably far too busy for such excursions, unlike yourself, Mr Honeycutt. I was quite surprised to see you demanding Stephanie Silva's release from captivity. I didn't think the two of you got on.'

'We don't, that's no secret,' said Honeycutt, 'and when I saw her dolled up like a *Vogue* model, I was sorry I turned out.'

Campion paused at the door leading out on to Piazza 1, forcing Honeycutt to halt as well. A yard or two behind them, Lugg was playing with a wad of hole-punched computer programming cards, casually shuffling them as if they were a deck of playing cards, until a gesture from Campion prompted him to put them down.

'What do you mean she was "dolled up"?' Campion pressed.

'You saw her, all dressed up, short skirt and boots. She must have known she was going to be arrested in full view of the university, so she dressed up for it.'

'Well, technically she wasn't arrested, merely called in for questioning.'

'But come on, Campion, you saw her; she looked a real dolly bird.'

'Do young people still say that, or only earth scientists? I admit she certainly looked smart . . . attractive, if you will, but then she's a very attractive woman.'

'She sure is, but she's not known for being a fashion model. Everyone thought she was cool the way she dressed like a cowgirl in denim jacket and jeans, like a student, or in her leather jacket, which made her look a bit of a Hells Angel. She always fancied being the centre of attention but we'd never seen her tarted up in her Saturday night disco best before yesterday.'

'Perhaps she just didn't have a thing to wear,' said Campion lightly. 'I cannot count the number of times I've heard that excuse over thirty years of married life.'

As they walked by the chessboard, Lugg said, 'What was that all about then?'

'The fashion sense of an interesting young woman, something I noticed yesterday, and which might be relevant if Superintendent Appleyard's boys have done what I asked.'

Lugg broke off from making a rather rude gesture at the white bishop on the chessboard.

'Got the police doing your legwork now, have you? Getting too old for it, are we?'

'Yes we are, both of us, but that's by the by. What I had in mind had to be done legally and with the full authority of the law, not a bit of casual breaking-and-entering by a pair of overactive pensioners.'

Lugg ran a giant hand over the globe of his bald head. 'So who is this interesting young woman with the fashion sense?'

'Possibly the most accomplished liar,' said Mr Campion, 'or perhaps the best actress I've ever come across.'

'Same thing,' said Lugg with conviction.

Campion had been, up until then, smugly pleased that he had been able to wander the campus and hardly draw a second glance from the youthful populace of the university. With Lugg in tow there was little chance of him going unnoticed. Heads turned, eyes were averted and then involuntarily drawn back, and female students carrying books and walking in pairs were seen to whisper and then shake with giggling. Lugg remained impervious to it all, and Campion was grateful that their visit to the Phantom Trumpeter had removed the prospect of the 'Cuckoo' song echoing over the piazzas.

'Where we going now?' Lugg asked, while taking time to scowl at a long-haired youth sitting cross-legged by the fountain that was now a firepit, strumming discordantly on a cheap Spanish guitar and so oblivious to his surroundings that he did not turn a hair when Lugg leaned over him and said, 'That animal's in pain, son; be a mercy to put it out of its misery.'

'We are going to borrow an office in the Administration building,' said Campion. 'That's that big square thing full of windows up ahead. Hopefully the estates officer will let us use his, otherwise we may have to impose on the chaplain, which I do not relish, as you and he would not get on.'

'I gets on wiv most people!' Lugg made it sound like a challenge. 'What do we need an office for, anyway?'

'A bit of privacy. A doctor won't examine a patient in public.'

'Doctors? Who's ill?'

'You are,' said Mr Campion. 'You're looking very peaky and I insist we get a professional diagnosis.'

Gregor Marshall, though not by nature a boastful man, was prone to say that no request presented to him in his role as the university's estates officer had ever surprised him, and that included the twenty-eight-year-old postgraduate who demanded a night light, the parents of a female fresher who wanted a private telephone line installed in their daughter's room, and the Swedish exchange student who was outraged that there was no sauna on campus. Never before, however, had he been asked to turn his office over to a virtual stranger for use as a doctor's consulting room, and never before had he seen a patient, or indeed anything, like Mr Lugg before. With some experience of dealing with student sit-ins, or 'occupations', as they liked to call them, Mr Marshall's first thought was that if Lugg wanted to occupy his office, for whatever reason, then it would stay occupied.

At least the chap Campion had some official standing as the bishop-inspired Visitor, and was polite enough in his request and in begging indulgence for not explaining the reason for it.

He made the internal phone call Campion had asked him to, and then vacated his office with, it had to be said, some sense of relief, as Mr Marshall had long ago learned that ignorance could, ironically in a modern university, indeed be blissful.

After seating Lugg on a chair in front of Marshall's desk, but turned so he faced the door and would be the first thing anyone entering the room saw, Campion took up a position in a corner between a tall filing cabinet and the window, leaning languidly against the wall. The filing cabinet distorted the outline of his body and, with his fedora tilted over his eyes, he was confident he could, at first glance, pass for a hat stand.

Not that he was hiding; his plan was that he would not be noticed, but it would be impossible not to notice Lugg, and in that way he would gain a tactical advantage, even if a small one.

There was a single light tap on the door, which then opened, and Heather Woodford, with a canvas army-issue medical bag hanging from one shoulder, stepped, business-like, into the office.

'You the doc, then?' mumbled Lugg, his jowls resting on his chest as he tried his best to look weak and feeble, perhaps even malarial.

'I'm Dr Woodford, the university's medical officer,' she said approaching the quivering bulk seated before her, 'and you must be Mr Lugg. Now can you tell me what's wrong with you?'

Lugg opened his mouth and emitted a cross between a low moan and a massive yawn but, before either could reach their full potential, Campion straightened up and emerged from behind the filing cabinet.

'A bad case of galloping lethargy,' he said, 'but I doubt it will prove fatal. Perhaps a reviving injection might be the cure.'

As the woman stared and recognition dawned, Lugg slid off his chair and, with a swerve worthy of a fly-half a third of his age and a quarter of his weight, he danced around and behind the woman and positioned himself between her motionless figure and the door.

'Just what the hell is going on?' said Dr Woodford through gritted teeth.

Although he knew her to be in her thirties, and that she must have spent at least seven years in medical training, Campion could see how Chaplain Tinkler had come to regard her as appearing no older than many an undergraduate. There was a youthful apprehension in that face, something of the naughty and rebellious teenager, but there was also a strand of steel in her demeanour.

'I wanted to get you alone, Doctor, as we didn't get time to chat out at St Jurmin's last night, did we?'

Heather Woodford's face remained a defiant mask. 'I have no idea what you are talking about, Mr Campion.'

'No,' Campion corrected her. 'What you meant to say was "You can't prove I was anywhere near Jurmin's chapel last night", and you'd be right, I can't, although the police might be able to. My companion Mr Lugg, who seems to have made a remarkable recovery, is much more experienced in these matters. Tell me, old chum, in your learned opinion, can their forensic whizz-kids take fingerprints from a cork?'

From his left jacket pocket, Mr Campion produced the pristine bottle cork and held it up between finger and thumb.

'Wouldn't surprise me if they could,' said Lugg. 'There's very little privacy these days.'

'I'm sure that's a terrible thought for someone with the keys to a wine cellar,' Campion said casually, tossing the cork to Dr Woodford, who caught it one-handed with aplomb. 'But it really is only of academic interest. The police need not be involved if you cooperate with me.'

'Cooperate? How?'

The doctor's expression had not changed, but the knuckles of the hand holding the cork had gone white with the pressure she exerted.

'I'll keep it simple. I will tell you what I know, or think I know, and you tell me where I have miscalculated or misconstrued. Agreed?'

'Do I need a solicitor?' she said in the same tone as if she was asking if she needed a coat in order to venture outdoors.

'I don't think so. If you do, then perhaps I have miscalculated completely, but I don't think I have. Would it reassure you if I said that anything said this morning in this room will remain in strictest confidence?'

'Can you promise that?'

'Yes, I can.'

'Then I accept your terms of engagement.'

Mr Campion nodded as if approving her turn of phrase. 'Very well, then. In summary, you were involved with Professor Perez-Catalan.'

'We were engaged,' Heather Woodford corrected him.

'Unofficially, I think, though I am not sure if that distinction still holds these days. Can we agree that it was not common knowledge on campus?'

'Agreed. I had given notice that I would be leaving the university at the end of this academic year, but not the personal reason behind the move.'

'Doctors having relations with their patients would be frowned upon, I suspect, even in this liberal environment, so you had to keep it quiet, hence your trysts at St Jurmin's, which I must say showed a considerable hardiness and commitment on your part. It must be one of the most Spartan love nests since the days of Sparta itself, and at least they had a decent climate.'

'It was far from comfortable,' the woman admitted, 'but it was secure from curious students in the residences, and prying eyes down in White Dudley.'

'Ah, yes, Edwina Meade. I was coming to her . . . and to the professor's previous liaisons.'

'I knew about them all,' said Dr Woodford. 'Pascual kept nothing from me. He told me that the odious Meade woman was blackmailing Dolores Downes following their brief fling two years ago.'

'How did Pascual know?'

'Because that damned woman took cheques from Dolores even though she didn't have a bank account! She didn't need or even want the money at first, she just wanted a hold over the vice chancellor's wife. Then she got greedy and wanted the money, and so she approached Pascual and got him to buy the cheques off her.'

'An enterprising lady – she was blackmailing them both, in a way.'

'But it stopped when Pascual said he would go to the police with the cheques; not that he ever would have.'

'But from then on, Pascual refrained from entertaining ladies at his house in White Dudley and set up his trysting camp at St Jurmin's, having had the key copied. Can I ask an indelicate question, Doctor?'

'This whole conversation is indelicate,' said the woman, turning to glare at Lugg, who was pretending innocence by fixing his eyes on the ceiling.

'Don't worry about my associate,' said Campion, 'he can be deaf, blind and mute when the need arises; all three wise monkeys rolled into one.'

'Then feel free to be indelicate, but allow me to be selective with my answers.'

Campion conceded the point. 'I cannot compel you to answer at all, let alone truthfully, although I think you owe me that courtesy. I was going to ask if you were the first female to share the rather chilly hospitality offered by the chapel of St Jurmin?'

'I will be honest,' said Dr Woodford in a quiet, girlish voice, 'and admit that I was not, but for the past year I was the sole object of Pascual's affections.'

'Because you were engaged,' said Campion, slipping a hand into his right jacket pocket.

'And we were to be married as soon as I moved to my new job at the end of this year. Would it sound terribly lame if I said I loved him, and he loved me? Well, I don't care, that's exactly how it was.'

'I believe you, Doctor,' said Campion, pulling the small square jewellery box from his pocket, 'because you went to extraordinary lengths to recover this from the chapel, as I know to my cost. This is your engagement ring, isn't it?'

Heather Woodford reached out a trembling hand, took the box and opened it to reassure her moist eyes that the ring was inside.

'How did you know to follow me to the chapel last night?'

'I was leaving Black Dudley after seeing Dolores when I overheard you in the porters' lodge asking to borrow a torch and telling Bill Warren where you were going. I assumed you had a key to the chapel.'

'You didn't?'

'Pascual had made a copy and that witch Edwina Meade had the only other one. I wasn't going to ask her for anything, but I wanted my ring back.'

'And you weren't averse to a spot of robbery with violence.'

'It looked as if you were in the process of stealing Pascual's things and I must have taken leave of my senses. I suppose I owe you an apology.'

'Do you always go around armed and dangerous?'

The young woman shrugged and patted the canvas bag hanging from her shoulder. 'I had my bag with me when I was called to see Dolores. I always carry small doses of anaesthetics in cases of emergencies.'

'In hypodermics with corks covering the needle points,' said Campion as Dr Woodford nodded, 'which I mistook for the barrel of a gun at first. Whatever you injected into me acted quickly.'

'Yes, it did. About that,' the doctor showed embarrassment for the first time, 'I think I misjudged the dose for a man of your age and slender frame.'

Campion stroked his chin as if pondering an alternative

scenario. 'It's a good thing you weren't confronted by my associate here – then you would have understood the meaning of a dosage big enough to fell an elephant. That's assuming you could get a needle through his thick hide.'

'Charming,' snarled Lugg.

'But I tried to make you comfortable before I left you,' protested the doctor.

'After you failed to find your ring,' countered Campion, 'which I had already discovered in Pascual's treasure chest. You didn't think to search my trouser pockets, did you?'

'I admit I was not acting rationally. I think Pascual's death made me mad.'

'That is quite understandable, especially with you being one of the first on the scene. I saw you on that bridge across the lake yesterday; in fact, I made sure we stood exactly where Pascual must have been attacked and I saw how uncomfortable you were being there.'

'Delayed shock, if I were diagnosing myself.'

'As I say, quite understandable. That particular spot was also where you signalled Pascual with a torch to request a . . . tryst, if that's not too ancient a word . . . at the chapel, wasn't it? A flashing torch from there would easily be seen in Pascual's office in the Earth Sciences department if he was working late, which I understand he did regularly.'

'Yes, that was our private means of communication. I would flash a torch two or three times and Pascual would answer by turning his office lights on and off twice. Ten minutes later we would meet at the chapel. There was nothing unusual about carrying a torch here. The campus may be lit up like a Christmas tree at night, but large areas of the park are very dark, especially if you're walking to the car park.'

'Unfortunately, your Aldis lamp signalling was seen by the residents of the pyramids, especially those living on the upper floors. It had been noticed before, and on Sunday it was thought to be a signal to the famous Phantom Trumpeter to begin this term's reign of terror at midnight.'

'That's ridiculous,' snapped Heather Woodford, 'there was no signal on Sunday, there was no need. Pascual and I had been to the chapel and he had walked me back to the residences and we had said goodnight. When he left me, he was heading for his car in the car park, as far as I knew.'

'And his natural route would not have taken him across that bridge, would it?'

'No.'

'But he went to his office after leaving you, didn't he?'

'He must have.'

'And while he was there, he saw a torch flashing a signal; a signal he was not expecting, and went out to investigate. It wasn't a signal, it was a lure.'

'But it wasn't me! I was in my room. I had just left Pascual after a lovely evening.'

'I believe you, Dr Woodford,' said Campion, 'but if you didn't flash that signal, which effectively drew Pascual to his death, who did?'

'So what was all that about?'

'That, my old fruit, was me providing what my old maths master would have called an inelegant solution to our little mystery here.'

Mr Campion and Mr Lugg were walking purposefully over the park towards Black Dudley. The university buildings behind them were, at that time of the morning, at their busiest, and students and staff scurried between lectures, tutorials and meetings like mice in a maze. If two elderly gentlemen of comically distinct proportions, striding across the grass, were observed, it provoked no noticeable reaction, not even a sarcastic phrase on a trumpet.

'What's your maths teacher got to do with the price of fish?' asked Lugg.

'He floated into my mind yesterday, funnily enough. Well, not funnily – there was nothing funny about him – and not so much floated as jumped out of memory, stage left, with a flash and bang like a pantomime villain. I was telling one of those bright young chaps in the Computing Centre how he wanted us to write quadratic equations like sentences, with good grammar and punctuation. We'd get whacked across the knuckles with a wooden ruler if we made a mistake or got a blob of ink on the page, or for not drawing a margin straight. Everything had to be absolutely precise, and all working had to be shown. Sometimes, you would get the right answer, but if your work was messy he would call it "an inelegant solution" and down would come the ruler. I never saw anything wrong with a solution being inelegant, as long as it was correct, for I saw myself as a student of life, not mathematics, and solutions in life are rarely elegant.'

Campion could almost feel Lugg's face straining to process thought into word.

'So what you're saying . . . It's like that Sherlock 'Olmes when 'e said that when you've got rid of every possible solution, however fanciful, however complicated, what was left was the bleedin' obvious. That's right, innit?'

Mr Campion sighed. 'Something like that,' he said patiently.

SEVENTEEN
Final Exam

M r Campion would have been the first to disparage anyone who suggested that Superintendent Appleyard's good humour had 'reached a crescendo', for such a statement was not only linguistically suspect but also assumed that there was a basic element of good humour which could gradually increase in the first place.

There was, however, no doubt that Mr Appleyard was in a cordial mood when he greeted Campion and Lugg and ushered them into his commandeered office; so cordial in fact that his face twitched into a passable imitation of a half-smile. If the policeman had possessed a more extensive portfolio of facial expressions, Campion felt sure he could summon up an impressively wolfish grin.

'Well, Campion, done what you had to do?' The superintendent's welcome was positively effusive, and he even gave Lugg a polite nod of greeting.

'I have had a very successful morning tying up loose ends, Superintendent,' said Campion. 'May I ask if your chaps have followed up on my suggestions?'

Appleyard clapped his hands and rubbed them together as if warming them on an imaginary brazier. 'They have, and with far better results than we could have hoped for.'

'Proof that will stand up in court?'

'Absolutely, one hundred and ten per cent certain.'

'You're not the only one who had trouble with maths,' Lugg whispered out of the side of his mouth.

Ignoring Lugg, Campion took advantage of the superintendent's good mood. 'And you are prepared to let me play it my way?'

'I've been considering that, and given what we've found, I don't quite see how it would be to my advantage.'

Mr Campion realized that the old Superintendent Appleyard was dangerously close to re-emerging. 'What have you got to lose? You may get a confession out of it. At least you'll get a clear idea of means, motive and opportunity, and it could all be wrapped up by lunchtime.'

'Now yer talking,' grunted Lugg.

'You are the professional here,' Campion pressed. 'I am only the amateur, albeit a gifted one. You will make the arrest, not I, but I will make sure the bishop knows where the plaudits should go. Plus, you would be in plenty of time for the evening edition of *Look East.*'

'Very well, Campion, you seem to have played a straight bat so far. We'll do it your way.'

'Excellent! Now let's gather all the suspects together in the library.'

There was a moment of awful silence before the superintendent said, 'What on earth for?'

'Absolutely no reason at all, I've just always wanted to say that.'

At Campion's suggestion, the vice chancellor made the required telephone call and was then allowed to stay in what, after all, was his office. Superintendent Appleyard insisted on the token policewoman on his investigating team being present, with which Campion heartily agreed. No one objected to Lugg's presence, though it did not go unnoticed, especially when his stomach began to rumble quite loudly.

And then there was a knock on the door, which was opened by Dr Downes to allow Stephanie Silva to enter with the air of a model on a catwalk. She wore a white leather miniskirt, shorter even than her blue suit skirt of the day before, a white cashmere roll-neck sweater, dark tan-coloured tights and brown knee-high boots, the whole ensemble partly wrapped in a maxi-length white, grey and black rabbit skin 'fun fur' coat, which flowed, unbuttoned behind her, as she swept in. The immediate mental image which flashed into Mr Campion's head was of something icy and Russian – a very modern noblewoman from the tsarist court dismounting from a sleigh, perhaps. No wonder they'd had a revolution.

'What's this, Vice Chancellor, another third degree or a kangaroo court? You said on the phone that we needed to talk about a career move,' said Miss Silva, coolly surveying the four men and the policewoman in turn, her gaze pausing longer when it landed on Lugg. 'Who's that? My careers officer?'

'Mr Lugg and Mr Campion represent the lay authorities of the university,' Dr Downes said formally. 'I, of course, represent the academic body and the university senate. Superintendent Appleyard and the constable represent the police, of course. Can we all sit down, please? There should be enough chairs.'

They sat in a semi-circle around Miss Silva, who crossed her long legs and flounced the skirts of her long coat back off her thighs, linking her fingers and resting her hands on her knee as she leaned forward, a confident candidate at a job interview awaiting the first question.

'This sounds like a hearing of some sort, if not a trial,' she said, 'so may I ask who is leading the prosecution?'

'I'm afraid I am,' said Mr Campion.

Stephanie Silva laughed. It was a very relaxed laugh, a cocktail party laugh, as if someone was pressing her to another canapé, and though she really shouldn't, she would indulge.

'Of course it was going to be you, the country-house murder specialist, who else? When the police are stumped, who else do they call in but the gifted amateur detective with all the right social connections. God! It's like being back in the nineteen thirties.'

'You are assuming we have called you here to discuss the murder of Professor Perez-Catalan,' said Campion before Appleyard could intervene.

'Well, of course you have,' said Miss Silva. 'I'm not stupid.'

'You most certainly are not,' said Campion. 'You quoted *Don Quixote* to me, something along the lines of "Although I'm pretty clever, I'm also something of a rascal and keep it well hidden". That was it, wasn't it?'

'The gist was that Quixote cleverly duped his opponents by acting the fool, and that reminded me of you.'

Campion was conscious that all eyes in the room were now focused on the duel between himself and Miss Silva.

'I'm not sure whether to be flattered or not. On reflection, I will take it as a compliment, but it was the first part of what you quoted, being a clever person but keeping it well hidden, that immediately reminded me of *you*.'

Stephanie's head tilted to one side as she observed Campion carefully, after slowly folding a tendril of blonde hair back into place behind her ear.

'Go on,' she said, her voice suddenly husky. 'You know you want to. Want to show off, that is. You think you know something and you're dying to tell me in front of your handpicked audience here, whom you regard as your inferiors. You feel you are cleverer than the vice chancellor and more efficient than Mr Policeman there, though that wouldn't seem to be too difficult.' She turned her head and glared at Lugg, who was straining to balance his bulk on a straight-backed chair. 'As for him, whatever he is, I don't think you need to impress him. I think he's here for moral support. Yours, that is, not mine.'

'You should regard Mr Lugg,' Campion continued, 'as my Sancho Panza, although he has fewer of the qualities of the Everyman and more of a propensity towards violence than the original. He is in many ways like me, a man out of his time, just as that marvellous man of La Mancha was.'

Stephanie Silva smiled at Mr Campion, but the smile was not mirrored in her eyes.

'I suppose you cannot resist tilting at me.'

'You could say that,' said Campion quickly, having noticed that Superintendent Appleyard's mouth was drooping open and forming the word *tilting?*, 'but neither of us really believe I'm tilting at windmills, do we?'

'Here it comes,' said Miss Silva, looking, if anything, more relaxed and comfortable than ever, 'the exposition; the solution to a mystery presented as a lecture based on supposition, conjecture, speculation and massive coincidences by the infallible detective. I'm surprised you didn't gather all the suspects together in the library!'

'I did suggest it,' said Campion with an innocent grin, 'but Dr Downes did not want me to disrupt the students studying there.'

'Or disrupt the university with another demonstration if I

was dragged out of there by the heavy mob. *That* wouldn't have looked good in the papers, or on television.'

'Interesting,' said Campion quietly.

'What is?'

'That your first thought was about the press and public relations and the possibility of television cameras on campus. We can all see that you have dressed for them, but were not to know that Superintendent Appleyard – and, I suspect, my mentor the bishop – have done a splendid job of keeping the press at arms' length. However, my point is that while you half expected all the suspects to be called together, whether in a library or a vice chancellor's office being neither here nor there, you never questioned or objected to the fact that you seem to be the *only* suspect.'

'And now you are going to tell me why I am the only suspect, using all your powers of observation and deduction and the cod psychology gleaned from a thousand country-house detective stories! Go ahead, the floor is yours.'

Mr Campion produced his handkerchief, removed his spectacles and began to slowly polish the lenses.

'I knew you would allow me to tread where angels should tread warily, and I thank you for that. It makes me feel as if I have earned my corn, so to speak, even though no payment in grain of any kind has been made, but I feel I must do something to justify the bishop's faith in me.'

Stephanie Silva looked decidedly unimpressed and her crossed leg began to bob impatiently.

'It is ironic that this thoroughly modern institution, with its modern approach to teaching, cutting-edge architecture, newfangled computers and algorithms which could change the future of entire countries, should host a murder the motive for which is one of the oldest in the book: love.

'Do they still sing "All You Need is Love"? I'm sure they do, and in my short time here I have seen lots of examples of it. Not just physical love between the sexes but love as passion for a field of research or academic study, admiration for a teacher or the simple joy of being young and the chance to be an irresponsible student. For the militant ones, the not-so-angry brigade and the left-wing members of staff, their passion for politics is something akin to a love affair, and even the dear old Bishop of St Edmondsbury feels love for this place in his own peculiar way.'

'That was better than your speech to the first-years.' Stephanie Silva made a silent clapping motion with her hands. 'Are you being paid by the word?'

Dr Downes was the only one to react to her insolence and spluttered, 'Estephanie, really . . .' only to be silenced by a withering glance from Mr Campion as he replaced his spectacles on his face.

'You are a good actress, Stephanie,' he said, turning back to the woman. 'I especially liked your performances in the piazza last week when you slapped Pascual in full public view, and then when you confronted Nigel Honeycutt in the refectory restaurant. The image you projected was that of a tough academic woman fighting her corner for her subject, a woman not given to hysterics or acts of sudden passion. When we stood on the bridge over the lake, on the exact spot where Pascual was stabbed, not a flicker of emotion crossed your face, reinforcing the pretence that there was iron in your heart.

'Yet it was well known that you had had an affair with Pascual – you were not reluctant to mention it yourself – but you were keen to present the façade that his death meant little or nothing. You even dressed to impress, as I believe the phrase is, in a most fashionable and stylish way, but I think your feelings for Pascual were far from dormant.

'You were certainly a visitor to Pascual's little love nest at St Jurmin's; you told me, in passing, that sleeping bags and oil lamps were not exactly your idea of home comforts, and you would be familiar with the system of torch signals to the professor's office; it seems to have been the worst-kept secret on campus.

'What convinced me that it was you who signalled Pascual on Sunday night was when I showed you the copy of *Don Quixote*, that expensive edition which you had given to Pascual and in which he'd carved out a little hidey-hole. His desecration of the book didn't seem to bother you, but the hidey-hole contained his key to the chapel, which you recognized, and you said: "That's not right".

'It was I who put the key there and you knew it wasn't right that it was in the book because it had been on Pascual's key ring when you killed him. You had seen him use it when he left the chapel that night with Dr Woodford. He walked her to the residences then called in at his office, as was his habit, before going home. There was no way in which that key could have got into the book which was on a shelf in his house in White Dudley.

'You were probably planning on confronting him as he went to his car, but when you saw the lights on in the Earth Sciences department, you tempted him out to the bridge with your torch signal. He would have been curious, having just left one lover, but from the little I know of Pascual, he would not have been able to resist a signal from another.'

Mr Campion looked at Miss Silva and Miss Silva looked at Mr Campion. The rest of the room did not breathe.

'Wonderful! Brilliant!' Stephanie showed a perfect set of teeth as she laughed. 'An elegant summation by the prosecution, but not one which would stand up in any court outside of the fantasy land you inhabit. You have absolutely no proof or concrete evidence at all, do you?'

'None at all,' said Mr Campion calmly, then he pointed a finger at Superintendent Appleyard, 'but he does.'

The superintendent was not slow to react to his cue. He nodded at the uniformed policewoman, who stood and walked to the office door, then cleared his throat and looked squarely at Miss Silva.

'Stephanie Silva, acting on information received' – his eyes flicked towards Campion – 'my officers searched your house in Saxmundham earlier this morning.'

'When I was not present? Is that legal?'

'According to the Estates Office, your house is leased to the university, and we therefore class it as university premises, for which I have a warrant to search for a murder weapon.'

'But you didn't find one.' Miss Silva's voice was rock steady.

'No we did not,' said Appleyard equally coolly. 'The murder weapon was in fact recovered with the professor's body; we were searching for *the absence* of a long-bladed kitchen knife.'

'A negative which proves nothing.'

'Sir.'

Four pairs of male eyes turned to the office door, which was being held open by the WPC to allow Constable Peters to enter, carrying a catering tray on which was a heap of blue and black material interlaced with charred foliage and burnt twigs, accompanied by the distinct smell of damp smoke. Peters placed the tray on the desk in front of his superior officer, as if presenting the main dish at a banquet, and then he and the WPC moved to stand behind Stephanie Silva's chair.

'We believe these were the clothes you were wearing on Sunday night,' said Appleyard, peering at the pile with distaste. 'Jeans, a denim jacket and a cotton blouse, all with considerable traces of bloodstaining. They were recovered from a compost heap in the garden of your rented property when a clear attempt had been made to destroy them by burning.'

The superintendent cleared his throat again. 'Estephanie Margaret Silva, I have to caution you that anything you say . . .'

Miss Silva ignored him and swung around on her chair to glare at Campion.

'It seems, after all, that hell really doesn't have a fury like a woman . . .' he said calmly.

'It wasn't love, it was jealousy; pure, uncontrollable jealousy.' Miss Silva's voice was the growl of a cornered big cat. 'If I couldn't have him, I wasn't going to let that dowdy bitch of a goody two-shoes doctor have him. How did you figure it out?'

Mr Campion exhaled slowly and showed the palms of his hands in supplication. 'Like the best amateur detectives in the best country-house mysteries, it was all down to one thing – pure guesswork.'

EIGHTEEN
Knight to Bishop

The vice chancellor, Mr Campion and Lugg stood at the entrance to Black Dudley and watched as a haughty and proud Stephanie Silva was escorted towards the car park and the awaiting police cars by Superintendent Appleyard and his minions. No one else on campus seemed to notice her going, to the relief of Dr Downes.

'Well, we seem to have got away with that without the students rioting and storming the ramparts.'

'It's coming up to lunchtime,' said Campion, 'and the bar will be open soon: that should distract their attention. In fact, I advised Dr Szmodics that it should be university policy to extend the licensing hours on campus whenever student rebellion festers.'

From a deep grunt next to him, Campion was assured that Lugg agreed with his proposal.

'I doubt the university council, and the bishop, would thank you for that suggestion, Campion, but I certainly thank you personally for what you did in there.'

'I did very little, Vice Chancellor; the police did all the real work.'

'You kept my wife's name out of it,' Dr Downes said quietly.

'You knew of Dolores's indiscretion?'

'I do now. She has told me everything. It was over, and she was sorry. You finding those cheques brought back unpleasant memories, but I have forgiven her. Indeed, I could understand why she did it; I was incredibly busy getting the university up and running and Perez-Catalan cut a dashing figure and was willing to pay her the attention I wasn't giving her. To err is only human.'

'And to forgive really rather rare,' said Campion, 'but I hope things continue to work in your favour. There will be a trial, of course, but I see no reason why Dolores needs to be mentioned. She was not the object of Miss Silva's jealousy, and in any case I have a feeling that Stephanie will plead guilty and claim a crime of passion after being used and abused by a swarthy lothario. She might even pull off such an act.'

'She will be a hard act to follow in the department, that's for sure. She was a very bright young woman and a good teacher.'

'Just unfortunately homicidal, but I'm sure you will attract a replacement. This is a fine place to work and study.'

'It won't be easy now that term has started,' said Dr Downes, 'and I may have to go back to the seminar room and do some teaching myself. I might have to brush up on my *Don Quixote*, but it's you who deserves to be called the university's knight-errant. Can I at least offer you lunch?'

Out of the corner of his eye, Campion saw Lugg girding his ample loins.

'Thank you, Vice Chancellor, but no, we must be on our way. I will get my traps from my room in Durkheim and hand in the key to Mr Marshall, then I will drive Lugg down to White Dudley to pick up his things from Mrs Meade's house. While we're there, I'll take the liberty of telling her the latest gossip and how the police are investigating the suggestion that Professor Perez-Catalan was being blackmailed.'

'Oddly enough,' said Downes with a wry smile, 'I was thinking of talking to Mister Meade and explaining the university's very generous early retirement scheme.'

'You know,' said Campion, 'I think Edwina Meade might just encourage her husband to jump at such an offer.'

Campion and Lugg took the path over the arched bridge and down into Piazza 1 where students and staff bustled about their business and the removal of Stephanie Silva seemed to have gone unnoticed. There was even a chess game in progress in the corner.

'What put you on to her?' Lugg asked as they walked towards the outdoor chessboard.

'It really clicked when Tabitha King said something. She's the geologist working on the professor's algorithm in there.' He indicated the entrance to the Computing Centre.

'The one with the little Kiwi friend.'

'That's her. She told me there were at least two women who lived on campus who wanted Perez-Catalan dead. She was wrong about that, but it made me think that there could be a female who lived *off*-campus who might have a motive. A silly little thing but it got the old brain working in mysterious ways. I was wondering whether I should pop in and say goodbye if they're in there. I took quite a shine to young Beverley Gunn-Lewis; I think she'll do well in life.'

'Strewth, with a name like that she better had,' said Lugg. 'But 'ang on, who's this? He's hailing you like you was a taxi.'

'Campion! Mr Campion!'

Campion knew instantly that he was being stalked by the chaplain, who was pushing his way through a flock of students to get to them.

'Quick, hide!' he said, diving towards the chessboard and filtering himself in between the pieces.

Lugg realized the futility of trying to conceal his bulk behind even the largest of the hardboard pieces, and stood on the edge of the board shaking his head in despair as the chaplain, breathless from his sprint across the piazza, closed in on his prey.

'Campion! I've just seen the most incredible thing: Stephanie Silva being loaded into a police car!'

Mr Campion raised himself to his full height from behind the black rook.

'Please keep your voice down, Mr Tinkler,' he commanded with as much gravitas as he could from his rather ludicrous would-be hiding place. 'Her arrest is not common knowledge and not even the bishop is aware of it yet. Someone should tell him before he hears it on the news.'

'Oh my goodness, you're quite right,' said Tinkler, running a hand through his thinning hair and automatically reaching to adjust the *pince-nez* he was not wearing. 'Do you think I should telephone him?'

'As soon as is humanly possible,' said Campion, 'if not sooner. Tell him that the murder of the professor was the result of a sordid love affair and loose morals, but it has so far been kept out of the jaws of the ravenous press. The police and the vice chancellor have done sterling work on that score.'

'Yes, yes, the bishop must be told, I must see to that immediately. I do hope it wasn't as a result of anything I said.'

Mr Campion stiffened. 'What did you say and when?'

'It was last week sometime, when I told her that Pascual and Heather Woodford were engaged to be married. I thought at the time that she didn't take it too well.'

'He's a right panic, isn't he?' said Lugg.

'Observant as ever, old fruit,' said Mr Campion.

'Who was that?'

'The bishop's inside man here on campus. No, wait: I'm the bishop's inside man on campus.'

'I thought I was,' said Lugg, aggrieved.

'No, you're really here to embarrass me on the orders of my wife.'

'Oh yeah, that's right. And a wife outranks a bishop.'

'In the case of my wife,' said Mr Campion, 'always.'

He turned on the chessboard and squared up to the cut-out figure of the black bishop, then put his fists up into a boxer's stance and delivered a strong right cross to the bobbled head of the chess piece, which wobbled and then toppled over, sending two pawns flying and rocking the black queen on her wooden base.

'Hey! Stop that!'

Campion recognized the voice as belonging to Oliver Brownlee, the computer chess playing supremo, who had indeed emerged from the centre and was glaring across the chessboard.

'You're ruining the computer's game – again!'

'I am so sorry,' Campion apologized. 'It was a moment of temporary insanity. The last thing on my mind was to disrupt the computer's programme.'

Normally happy to see Mr Campion caught 'on the hop', as he would have said, on this occasion Lugg was quick to spring to his companion's defence.

'Don't you worry about upsetting them computers,' he pronounced loudly. 'They ain't got no future.'